THE TEAR COLLECTOR

SHAWN BURGESS

The Tear Collector

Shawn Burgess

RhetAskew Publishing

United States of America

Cover Illustration
& Interior Design

ISBN-13: 978-1-949-39827-4

CHAPTER 1
Reprisal

The summer heat pelts the woods, the stagnant air sticky as candy glaze, but Brady Palmer and his friends aren't fazed. Special Forces Commandos don't surrender to the elements; they tame them. The boys sprint through the woods, BB guns raised in an intense, imaginary battle, following that all too familiar path to Copperhead Creek. They fire off wild shots into the trees, the ricochets causing birds and squirrels to scatter, before cocking their BB guns for more action.

As the boys file into Grief Hollow, they pause for a breather. High atop the fork in the oak tree near Copperhead Creek, their beloved tree fort nestles between two sturdy branches.

Ryan glimpses a few tent caterpillar nests in the surrounding trees and points to the high limbs. "Thought they took care of those in the roundup."

Jimmy gives a bunched-lip shake of his head. "Nah, only in town. Didn't touch no woods."

Brady counts nine silky nests in the trees surrounding the fort. The warnings from the news chime in his mind. *Largest outbreak in history. Extensive defoliation and the death of many trees if something isn't done.* But the town responded to the threat, organizing roundup parties of volunteers armed with long poles to pull down the nests.

Ryan's round eyes linger on the tree fort in the oak. "You reckon they gonna kill our tree?"

"Better not. That's our fort," Jimmy replies, even though it really isn't. Some older kids built it, but all the kids play there.

Brady wanders near Copperhead Creek. Something draws his attention. He locks in, his keen ears tuned to something that drowns out the conversation of the other boys. Brady smiles and nods, but there's no one around.

"What you think, Brady?"

Brady blinks his eyes several times as Ryan's question registers.

"Huh?"

"So, what ya think, man? Them caterpillars gonna get our tree fort, or what?"

"No. No, they're not. I know what to do now. I'll be back." Brady hurries out of the hollow. Ryan and Jimmy exchange a lifted-lid glance before they resume playing.

When Brady returns to Grief Hollow, he's carrying a long pole, a metal pail, and a can of gasoline. Jimmy and Ryan chase each other through the hollow, oblivious, as Brady begins his meticulous work. Brady removes nest after sticky nest from the surrounding trees. As he lowers each one, he deposits them in the large metal pail. Eventually he clears the trees of tent caterpillar nests, and the pail brims with tangles of squirming caterpillars.

"Watch this, guys." Brady pours the gasoline in the pail. The sopping caterpillars writhe in the acrid fuel bath.

The other boys stop playing and focus their attention on Brady's unusual undertaking. Brady places the bottom of the pail onto the surface of slow-moving Copperhead Creek, careful to keep it upright. He pulls a matchbox from his pocket, strikes a match, and tosses it into the pail. A whoosh of air startles the boys as the bucket ignites into a tall flame.

"Whoa." Ryan retreats a step.

"Now they won't ruin our fort." Brady wears a gratified smile.

The floating bucket spins in a slow twirl. Black smoke billows from its top as the fire rages. The flaming pail rafts Copperhead Creek, accelerating as the creek narrows. The top of the pail jars as the base lodges against a submerged rock, stopping it there for a moment. Creek water piles on the bucket, climbing its sides, until the force becomes too great, and the bucket topples. In an instant, fire darts across the surface of the creek in different directions, setting it ablaze.

"Oh shit!" Jimmy backpedals away from the creek.

The fire roars, its tendrils spreading to the vegetation on the bank of the creek. The bone-dry brush by the tree fort ignites into flames like a sparking wick; the fire from the brush spreads to the oak tree that houses the fort.

"Jesus!" Ryan staggers a step as a wave of heat from the burgeoning fire hits his cheeks.

The peaceful hollow transforms into a war zone. Slicks of burning gasoline flow downstream, small fires litter the banks of the creek, and one large fire swells, building in intensity. Within seconds, its flames climb the oak tree and lick the bottom of the tree fort. The blaze engulfs the entire structure. A girl's high-pitched shriek rises above the crackles of burning wood.

"Oh no." Brady draws a gasped inhale. His eyes swell and his lips quiver, a tear darting his cheek as the terrible shrieks emanate from behind a wall of ravenous flame and a thick curtain of smothering smoke. *Oh my God. What have I done?* The incessant shrieking from the tree fort siphons the air from the boys' lungs and collapses their stomachs.

Brady runs to retrieve the burning pail from the creek. He screams in pain as he clasps the searing metal handle. The bucket jostles, splashing flaming gasoline and molten caterpillar ooze onto his arms. With arms ablaze, he fills the bucket with water from the creek and rushes to the oak tree. He tosses the water onto the base of the tree, but there's little effect. The stench of burning hair and roasting flesh permeates the hollow. Tears gush from Ryan and Jimmy's eyes.

The agonized screaming coming from the tree fort reaches a deafening pitch. Jimmy turns and runs from the hollow. After taking several retreating steps, Ryan turns and runs too.

Brady continues to refill the pail with water and toss it onto the flames. The flames on his arms extinguish, leaving behind horrible burns that cover the majority of his charred skin. The screaming subsides, replaced by an occasional pop from the dry wood above in the tree fort as it burns. He collapses by the bank of the creek, singed arms splayed out, sobbing and waiting for help to arrive.

CHAPTER 2
6 Years Later - Initiation

Pain knifes through my foot.

"Ow!" I dance on the other foot.

I try to navigate the darkness of the basement, my arms outstretched before me. I tiptoe so the Lego pieces don't puncture my feet. *I can't believe I'm doing this. But joining the Markland X Crew... so worth it. A dream come true.*

"Come on, guys?" I navigate the Lego minefield. I hope they'll spare me, but the snickering suggests they won't. An entire bucket of Legos strewn across the basement floor awaits my bare feet. Robby showed me his handiwork before cutting off the lights.

Tee snickers through the darkness. "Brook, you want in, or what?"

"Brooks, my name is Brooks!"

It makes me mad when people call me Brook. Sammy calls me Brook all the time.

"Well?" Robby draws the word out, and there's a smile buried in his voice.

I roll my eyes and shrug my shoulders before lumbering forward. This isn't what I envisioned. Sure, I want to join the Markland X Crew. Why wouldn't I? Tee and Robby make friends with ease, and their popularity rivals some of the hottest girls in our school.

"OUCH!" Another jagged plastic Lego jabs my foot.

A chorus of belly laughter cuts through the pitch. I push through the pain of the occasional sharp plastic Lego assailing the soles of my feet. I reach the far wall and let out a sigh of relief. *This is really happening.* I can't wait to tell everyone after summer break that I'm officially Markland X Crew.

The first year of Markland Middle School surprised me with its unforeseen brutality, making it the toughest year of my life. My first couple of days there, I attracted the attention of a bully, Sammy Needles, who I would later come to discover reigned as the grand colossus of them all. I spent sixth grade ducking behind lockers and running for my life between classes and after school, enduring whatever torment Sammy could dish out before he tired of me.

But today marks my new beginning. I'm joining the Markland X Crew, an action I hope scribes Sammy Needles into the annals of ancient history, along with the swirlie treatments I've become so accustomed to receiving.

"So that's it, huh?" I let my shoulders relax, the tension leaving my body.

Tee turns on the lights, blinding me for a moment.

Robby unleashes a roar of suppressed laughter "Are you kidding? We just needed to make sure you're serious."

Tee grins. "Yeah, that's just the beginning. Now, we can see if you really want to be in the Markland X Crew."

My heart sinks. More torture. The soles of my feet sting like I slalomed barefoot.

"Really?"

"Really!" Tee and Robby chime in unison.

Robby smiles. "Just meet us at ten tomorrow morning at Jennings Bridge."

"And bring your swimsuit." Tee snickers out the words.

I flash frazzled eyes. "Okay, yeah. For sure. I'll be there."

I dash out the door for home. It's getting late and near dinner time even though it's still light outside. Days seem to stretch into forever this time of summer, but the dwindling sunlight tells me dinner, and an upset mother if I don't make it home in a few minutes, awaits. I hop on my bicycle and pedal furiously. I cover the two-mile distance in record time, wiping the sweat from my brow as I rush inside.

CHAPTER 3
Sammy Needles

I wake early, intending to meet Robby and Tee at Jennings Bridge at ten. I shudder, thinking about what they have planned for me, but that doesn't suppress my appetite. I devour two bowls of cereal before heading for the door.

My mom intercepts me. "Brooks, where are you off to? Going to play with Mark?"

"No, not today mom. I'm going to go play with some friends." A big smile stretches across my face.

My mom draws her head back, and her eyes grow wide; but after a moment, her face lights up in a big smile too. She isn't accustomed to me running off to play with friends, as in more than one. I can tell she's pleased. With each passing day, I find less in common with my friend Mark Crudleman, an awkward neighborhood boy who I play with on occasion. I like Mark, but he's a fourth-grader, and he always wants to play dorky little kid games.

"Okay, be home before dark."

Be home before dark. Are you serious? Mom never says that. Dark isn't until around eight o'clock. It's always 'get home before dinner,' and that's always at seven.

I check my watch, nine-fifteen. It's about a thirty minute bike ride to Jennings Bridge and that's if I make good time. I grab my bike, pull out of my driveway, and turn onto Slippery Hill—nicknamed as such for its superb winter sledding. Racing down the hill, the wind shuffles through my hair and buffets against my face making my eyes water. I blink several times to clear my blurry vision. Two kids on bikes await at the bottom of the hill. As I approach, I recognize one of them. *Oh God, Sammy Needles!*

Sammy and his friend Myron reposition their bikes to block the road. I swerve but can't get around them. I slam on my brakes to avoid crashing into them. As I skid to a stop, Sammy hops off his bike and hustles to me. My heart's racing.

"Brook, didn't know you'd be joining us today. Nice of you to stop by."

Sammy wraps an arm around my neck and pulls me off my bike.

Myron piles on after he moves their bikes off the road. "Yeah, Brook, what you doing out here? Selling Girl Scout cookies? Where are the cookies, Brook?"

Myron grabs my backpack and rifles through it. He pulls out my Star Wars-themed swim trunks and tosses them off the road.

Sammy compresses my neck between his strong forearm and bicep, using his height advantage and pudgy frame to subdue me. Sunlight glints off his short, spiky red hair, and his pasty, freckled skin glistens with sweat. My proximity to his armpit wafts his sour summer odor into my nostrils. Uniformed in his normal attire, a ratty No Fear T-shirt two sizes too small, the bottom of his belly hangs over his waistband, protruding even further with his arm raised over my shoulder. He tightens his headlock, and a jolt of pain travels my spine.

"Let me go, Sammy!" I squirm to free myself.

"Or what, huh? What you gonna do, Brook? Run home and tell your mommy? You ain't gonna do nothin', no how."

I muster all my strength and break free from Sammy's grip. My momentum carries me in a backward stagger. Oblivious, Myron continues plundering my backpack. My bike and its promise of freedom beckon from a few feet away, but Sammy takes several steps to block my escape route. My eyes grow as big as silver dollars, and my heart pumps at a blistering pace.

"Alright, turd muffin. Now you're going to get it." Sammy flashes a menacing smile as he steps forward.

Without hesitation, I rear back my leg and swing it forward as hard as I can. In an instant, my foot connects squarely with Sammy's nuts. His legs crumble beneath him, and he hits the pavement with a thud where he writhes in agony, his hands clutching his privates.

I dart to my bike, hop on, and peddle as fast as I can. Myron turns from rummaging through my backpack to find Sammy rolling around on the ground, moaning and coughing. After a few moments, Sammy struggles to his feet, but I'm already putting as much distance as I can between us.

"Don't just stand there, get him!" Sammy roars, his cheeks firing bright red.

Oh, Jesus! Oh, Jesus! They're going to beat the crap out of me.

Sammy lets out a furious yell as he and Myron jump onto their bikes to give chase.

"You're so dead, punk! After I'm through with you, they're going to have to peel you off the pavement." Sammy's scream sends my heart into another frantic sprint as he pedals like a boy possessed.

I hang a hard right on Chambers Road, nearly smashing into a stopped mail truck. I whiz by it, my legs firing like pistons in a redlining engine. Before Sammy and Myron can turn onto Chambers Road, I turn on Parson Street. I race to the bottom of the hill, jump off my bike, and run it into the safety of the woods.

I peer out through the leaves and branches to the top of Parson Street as beads of sweat roll down my cheeks and forehead. Sammy and Myron circle on their bikes at the top of the street.

Oh my God, what have I done? Sammy's going to kill me for sure. It happened so fast. Not like I even made a decision to kick him in the nuts. My instincts kicked in. A grin lands on my lips, a small chuckle at the ironic thought. Perhaps it's because I'm so close to becoming part of the Markland X Crew. I won't let Sammy stop me from meeting Robby and Tee.

There's no way to use main roads anymore. Sammy and Myron will undoubtedly be searching for me. No backtracking either. I can't risk Sammy finding me. I look at my watch, 9:31. *No choice now.* As much as that place creeps me out, taking a shortcut through Grief Hollow offers me my only chance to get to Jennings Bridge by ten.

CHAPTER 4
Encounter with Margo

I gather fallen tree limbs and underbrush and camouflage my bike with them. *It'll still be here. Myron and Sammy won't see it from the road.* I begin the long trudge through the woods. It's about a mile to Grief Hollow, and about a mile and a half farther to Jennings Bridge, but I'm determined to get there.

Twigs and macerated leaves crackle as I walk underneath the tall trees. Sunlight shines through the openings in the canopy, hitting the forest floor like small spotlights. The absolute silence of the woods rattles me, an eerie feeling collecting in my bones. Gnarled tree trunks spiral skyward, sunlight blotted out by an awning of leaves, casting looming shadows that slither through the timbers.

Tiny hairs, as if pulled by static electricity, rise on my neck. *Someone's watching me.* The pressing weight of unseen eyes sends a shiver to my spine. I cease walking.

There's a huge rustle of leaves and a brown flash launches from behind a cluster of trees. I let out a stifled scream, spin my head around, and stumble backward. I trip on a root and fall. The hind legs of a deer bound away from me, its white tail a flash of cotton against a juniper collage of forest. My heart rumbles in my chest, threatening to pry itself loose from its fittings. *Holy crap! Calm down. Calm down. Breathe.*

I take a deep breath and lift myself off the forest floor, brushing the leaves from my shorts and shirt. Large twigs snap behind me. *Sammy's found me!* I wheel around to face my attacker. But it isn't Sammy, it's Margo. She's in a dirty white night gown, with no shoes, and she's covered in mud to her ankles. My mouth lolls. I tilt my head and squint my eyes at Margo. She's bobbing her head like she always does. She's *very* different from the other kids, even goes to a different part of the school that Tee calls *School for the Specials*. But she's smart too, figures things out— puzzles, riddles, complicated things. *What in the world is she doing out here in the woods by herself? Never seen her without an adult outside of school.*

Her head stops rocking; she lifts it, and her eyes lock with mine.

"Margo, are you los—"

"It's coming."

My eyes widen. Margo rarely speaks. Her focused eyes tunnel through me in the direction of Grief Hollow.

"Coming? What's coming, Margo?"

"The Collector. The Collector is coming. And Grief Hollow will be its home."

"Grief Hollow? What? Wait, collector? What is the Collector?"

"It's coming." Margo raises her arm and points behind me in the direction of Grief Hollow.

I blink my eyes several times, and my face contorts. I turn and scan the forest. *What in the world is she talking about?* There's nothing there, only forest.

"Margo, maybe I can help you get back—"

She's gone. Vanished into thin air. I swivel my head in every direction, but there's no sign of her. There's only silence once again.

"Margo?" My voice trembles.

There's no response.

"Margo, this isn't funny."

Still there's nothing. No sound. No movement. *Nothing.*

CHAPTER 5
Grief Hollow

A rolling tremor descends my body. *What's Margo doing in the woods? Who's the Collector? How'd she vanish like that without me hearing her retreating footsteps?* So many questions, and I'm starved for answers. My stomach is as hollow as a conservatory teeming with butterflies.

I take a gulping swallow. *Crap. I don't want to go to Grief Hollow. Now, especially. I hate that place.* I work to settle my trembling hands. *Calm down. You can do this. You're meeting Robby and Tee.* I hoist a fabricated air of confidence and push forward. As I come to the top of a hill, I find a small stream that winds through a maze of trenched earth. Gnarled roots jut from its steep banks. I recognize this stream; it leads to Grief Hollow and Copperhead Creek. I mince down the hill using the dry streambed like a guide wire.

The ground begins to flatten beneath my feet as I near the hollow. My parents warned me to stay out of Grief Hollow. *This is different though. What choice do I have with Sammy and Myron after me?* The terrible thing that happened here imprinted itself on the landscape. The blackened burn scars on the trees remind me of the stories: the fire, Misty Owens dying, Brady sent to juvie. A chill races the length of my spine.

Inside the hollow, the thick tree canopy covers everything in a film of shadow. Quiet reigns, the normal animal chatter noticeably absent: no squirrels, no birds, no katydids, nothing. The charred remains of the tree fort stake claim to my eyes.

The tree managed to survive the fire and serves as a horrible reminder of what happened that day.

Enough lingering. Time to get out of here. Just follow Copperhead Creek to Jennings Bridge already.

A sudden wind bursts into the hollow, a rustle of leaves drawing my attention to the tree canopy, the quiet forest opening its eyes with life. The branches and limbs stoop above me as if straining to hold the weight of something. A shower of green leaves somersaults through the air, swaying to the forest floor.

A large stick snaps on the forest floor behind me followed by another. I spin around, but the footsteps stop. There's nothing behind me. I feel eyes bearing into me through the trees, cutting away at my nerve.

"I've got a knife!" My voice echoes through the trees. True, I have a knife. It's a Swiss army knife, but it's very small. It's not much protection from anything. I'm just hoping to scare whomever or whatever is in the forest with me.

Is that children's voices? Faint whispers straddle the wind. I concentrate hard to try to understand them. The voices grow gargled and distorted. *Just kids playing in the forest? Calm down.* The wind dies and the voices stop.

I can't believe I did this. Why did I come here? So stupid. So what if Sammy beat the shit out of me? It's better than this. I can't control the trembling of my hands. My legs malfunction, failing to detect desperate signals from my flustered mind.

The wind starts again, slow at first. But it begins to howl, blowing even harder than before. The voices return as well. This time they're much louder.

"You've come home, Brooks. You're home." The ominous voice trails off into a groan.

This isn't happening! I freeze.

"Who's doing that?" The forest swallows my scream. My heart races, thumps against my palm clenched tight to my chest.

Wind gusts come in even harder, and the branches above me clash in a violent sway. A thick black mist coalesces near the fork of the oak tree where the tree fort once stood. I stagger back a step as the opaque mist renders itself with definite reptilian scales. It coils like a large black snake around one of the giant branches on the oak tree. Without warning, the branch snaps with a huge *pop*. I scream and dive for the creek, landing at the edge of the water with my hands buried into the sandy bank. The heavy branch shakes the ground as it crashes to the forest floor, inches from my face. I leap to my feet and take off running alongside Copperhead Creek. The black mist descends the tree and dissipates once it reaches the bottom.

I let out a terrified scream as I run. Footsteps trail me, crackling fallen tree limbs with every stride. I yank my head around as I sprint, and large indentations form like footprints into the muddy bank of Copperhead Creek. They progress into the creek sending large splashes of displaced water hurtling into the air with each step.

I dig deep, excavating a bounty of adrenaline that fuels my retreat. Several minutes seem to pass in an instant. My legs motor, and I'm nearly out of Grief Hollow. I don't stop running until I burst out of the woods by Jennings Bridge.

CHAPTER 6
Jennings Bridge

I collapse on the edge of the gravel twenty yards downriver from Jennings Bridge, panting from my sprint through the woods. My knees dig into the dirt as I gasp for air. *What the hell was that? The voices. Oh, Jesus! The mist thing. I don't jump at that second and I'm dead. That branch would've flattened me.*

I lift my head, and Jennings Bridge climbs to the foreground of my peripheral vision, the gray, oxidized wood showing the effect of the perpetual advance and retreat of the seasons. A tall pine forest rises behind it, planted after a logging operation stripped it of its hardwoods. I pant for air, glimmers of light floating through my field of vision. Tee and Robby's approaching chatter rises above a continuous roar of the Waupecony River's charging current. *Thank God. They're here.* They work their way across the abandoned railroad bridge, taking careful steps to avoid any rotten boards. Tall weeds springing between the rails and rotting railroad ties slap their shins on their accelerating approach.

Robby's the first to arrive. "Dude, we thought you chickened out."

"Yeah, it's ten-fifteen. What gives, Brooks?"

My chest heaves for air, my lungs a stinging inferno. My stomach muscles clench tight, and I vomit into the gravel, the chunky splatter settling in between the rocks. From my hands and knees, I pant for air, the sweltering heat of summer spilling into my burning lungs. I settle onto my butt and drape my elbows over my folded knees.

"Nasty!" Robby curls one side of his lip, eyes squinting.

"Whoa. Are you okay, man?"

Tee's eyes grow wide as he inventories my disheveled appearance, lingering on my sweat-soaked shirt that's covered in dirt, the sand and dirt caked on my hands, my ripped shorts, and my bug eyes. They saw me come tearing out of the woods like a mad man.

"Give him some water, Robby."

Robby opens his canteen. He hands it to me, but his eyes still possess it, standing guard over the last gift his father gave him before the accident. I grab it by the olive-green canvas cover. The compass built into its face glints sunlight as I take a large gulp of the lukewarm water. My rapid breathing slows. I draw a couple of deep breaths before trying to speak.

"Thank you."

I hand the canteen to Robby. Tee sweeps a clump of dirt off my shoulder as he examines me.

"What happened to you? Did Sammy get you?"

"No, well yes, well sort of..."

What do I tell them? The truth? They'll think I'm crazy. Might not let me in the Markland X Crew. But what else can I tell them? Nothing's going to explain this. But the truth? Risky. And I really need the extra protection now. Sammy's going to kill me. But lie to them? I can't. I wouldn't even know what to say. The truth it is. Here goes...

Robby and Tee listen as I recount my near miss with Sammy and Myron.

"I broke free and was going for my bike. Sammy jumped in front of me. I screwed up, guys."

Tee lifts a brow at me. "Screwed up how?"

"I'm not sure how it happened. It didn't even feel like me doing it." I pause, expelling a deep breath. "I kicked Sammy in the nuts. *Hard.*"

Robby and Tee erupt into a thunderous roar of laughter. Robby pumps his fist once as he grins at me. "Oh my god, I can't believe you kicked him in the nuts."

"Brooks the Nut Cracker! That's your new name."

Robby chuckles. "Man, I wish I'd been there to see that. Ole Sammy Needles, kicked in the nuts."

"Yeah, so long Sammy," Tee says.

"Serves that piece of shit right, Brooks. Ain't no wonder he ain't got no friends."

"Yeah, none 'cept Myron and Bo. And they might be even bigger pieces of shit."

Robby nods agreement with Tee and gives me a pat on the back. "I guess we'll let it slide that you're late."

"That explains why you look like crap."

"Well, no, not really." I swallow hard. Wide grins overtake Robby and Tee's faces, but the rest of the story isn't as funny.

I tell them why I decided to go through Grief Hollow, which brings pause to their grins. No one plays in Grief Hollow. Not since the fire.

"So, on my way to Grief Hollow, I got a weird feeling. You guys ever get the feelin' someone's watching you?" Both boys nod. "So, I stopped walking to just kind of listen. A deer jumped out from behind some trees and scared me half to death. And I fell down."

The chorus of laughter rises once more. Tee collects himself first. "Oh my god, Brooks, we gotta hang out more."

"You must've taken a hard spill to do all that."

"No guys, listen. I get up, and there's Margo standing right next to me."

"Margo? Margo Combs?" Robby purses his lips, and his eyes meet mine. "I know you're not talking about Mysterious Margo, right?"

"Yeah, Mysterious Margo."

Robby narrows his eyes. *He doesn't believe me.*

"*In the woods*?"

"Yes, in the woods."

"Oh man, now I know you're lying. And you really had me going too. Next thing you're going to tell us is she was doing them weird drawings she does."

"No, I'm serious, Tee. *Seriously.* She was there in her night gown with no shoes, just bobbing her head up and down." Both boys' postures perk. "You know like she does?"

The boys both nod, and their smiles go slack. Robby digs his eyes into mine.

"So Mysterious Margo did this to you?"

"No, she didn't, but she spoke to me."

"What, *she spoke*?" Tee's eyes grow wider. "What did she say?"

"She kept saying something weird like 'the Collector is coming'. And then she said, 'and Grief Hollow will be its home.'"

Tee shoots a crinkle-faced glance to Robby. *They're sizing me up. Trying to decide if I'm full of crap.* After a moment, Robby turns to me.

"What the hell does that even mean?"

"Yeah, what's the Collector? That's weird, man."

"I know, *right*? I don't know. I have no idea. She pointed past me in the direction of Grief Hollow, so I turned to look."

"Then, what'd she say?" Tee's brows furrow in the wake of his crumbled smile.

"Nothing. When I turned back around, she was gone. I called out her name a few times, but nothing. Weirdest thing was that I never heard her walk away."

"Dude, you had one hell of a day. And it's only eleven." Robby manufactures a half-smile, but his lighthearted words fail to lighten the mood.

"Wait, then how'd your shorts get ripped? And how'd you get so dirty?"

"Grief Hollow." My voice cracks, and I clear my throat. "Something happened in Grief Hollow. Something that I can't explain."

Both boys' eyes grow wide as I begin telling the story. Robby rubs his thumb and finger together, and a fidget slips into Tee's foot.

"At first, I thought I heard whispering, thought it might be children playing. Then, the wind died and so did the voices."

Robby's stomach emits an audible grumble. "What did the voices say?"

"I couldn't make it out at first, but then the wind started blowing again, *viciously*. The trees were shaking. I was right by the old oak tree with the burned-out tree fort. Then, I heard the voice say, 'You've come home, Brooks. You've come home.'"

Tee grins. "Somebody's *messin'* with you, *man*."

"*Right*, that's what I thought. Okay, so this part's going to sound crazy, but there was some type of black cloud thing that began forming on the oak tree. It kept growing larger until it started to look almost like a snake. It wrapped itself around one of the giant branches on that oak tree. The branch snapped and came crashing down. I dove out of the way. It almost killed me, guys!"

"Whoa, that's jacked up." A deep-set frown settles on Robby's face in the wake of his words.

"What'd you do?" Tee shifts his weight from foot to foot.

"I ran. I ran as fast as I could. When I looked back, I saw something following me. I mean, I didn't see it. I saw the footprints it was making as it chased me and the splashes in the water as it moved into the creek."

The blood funnels out of Robby's face. His legs wobble, and he eases himself to the ground. Tee's shaking his head and scrunching his lips.

"For real, man?" Tee continues shaking his head.

I nod.

"Maybe, it was like lightning or something."

"There's not a cloud in the sky, Tee." Robby crosses his arms and shakes his head.

Tee looks at the sky and frowns. Both boys appear troubled by my story. I let out a slow exhale. *Thank God. They believe me. Don't think I'm crazy.* I'd risked my future in the Markland X Crew by telling them what happened, but I already feel closer to them.

Tee kicks up a cloud of dust, still trying to register everything. "That's messed up, man. So messed up."

CHAPTER 7

The Pact

Robby and Tee try to shake off the story I shared with them. We take seats on the old bridge, feet dangling above the swift current. Tee grabs a can of Force Energy Drink out of his backpack.

"Stole this from my sister."

Tee's older sister, Angela, graduated high school in May. She's the same age as Brady, who lives on my street. She visited his house from time to time when I was younger. But the fire changed all of that. Brady went to juvie, and Angela didn't come around anymore.

After taking a sip, Tee hands the can to me. I recognize the can, but my parents vowed never to buy any of the stuff after what happened with Tommy Tanner. All the parents called him Tommy Tantrum because he used to pitch the biggest fits. *Abhorrent, social-circle changing fits.*

"Guys, remember Tommy Tanner's Force incident at the pool?"

"Remember it?" Tee grins wide. "No way to forget that, Brooks." Tee wiggles his index finger by his crotch and snickers.

"Oh man, I heard that was a show. Can't believe I missed that. I heard his whole family had to move to Knoxville because of it. I'm telling you, I would've easily traded Space Mountain to see that."

"That's one warped dude. You shoulda seen it, Robby. He drank a can of Force, disappeared. Then, he shows back up, and Shirley Morris screams. And the crowd by the bathroom parts like a school of minnows racin' away from a bass." Tee brings his palms together and flings them apart. Robby snickers.

"Basically, the whole town was there, Robby. It bein' Labor Day and all."

"Come on, Brooks. This is my story." Tee manufactures stern eyes but can't suppress his budding grin. "So, where was I? Oh yeah. So, he was butt-ass naked. Stripped all his clothes off."

Robby shakes his head. "What in the hell?"

"I know, man. It was crazy. He starts twirlin' down the pool deck." Tee hops to his feet and begins twirling, hand atop his head like a ballerina, giving a faithful reenactment. Robby and I giggle. "The parents are gaspin', just freakin' out, man. But nobody does nothin', just mouths hangin' open. He starts singin', *'I'm a pretty girl, such a pretty, pretty girl.'*"

Robby bursts out laughing. "What in the hell is wrong with that kid?"

"Got me. So, he's doing these ridiculous hops." Tee leaps mid-twirl and the bridge creaks as he lands.

"Careful, Tee." I flash my open palms, wearing a wide grin.

"So, his chubby, red cheeks are bouncing, and you can guess what else. I couldn't hold it in no more. I was cracking up. Couldn't believe what was happening. And his dad sees, right? Comes running up with a towel. But you know Tommy Tantrum's crazy ass wasn't goin' out that easy." Tee jumps into a karate pose and starts waving his arms. "Tommy screams, 'Naked ninja attack,' as his dad lunges at him." Tee makes an exaggerated jump to the side. "And he sidesteps his dad. He starts doing karate jabs, *hi-yah, hi-yah*."

I nudge Robby's shoulder. "This is the best part."

"What'd I say, Brooks? This is my story."

"So, his dad misses him again. Ends up behind him. And Tommy screams, 'Naked ninja fury kick,' and kicks him in the butt, *hard*. He went headfirst into the pool in his clothes. Man, after all the parents gasped, the whole place erupted with kids laughin'. It was the craziest thing I've ever seen. And Tommy takes a naked bow to the crowd. Lifeguard's screamin' at him. Drags him out of the pool while he's doin' the shake and screamin', 'Watch my wiener dance. You know you can't resist my wiener dance.'"

We all chuckle as Tee returns and takes a seat with us on the bridge. As soon as one of us stops laughing, a simple grin initiates another cycle. I manage to compose myself enough to speak.

"He got banned from the pool after that."

Tee nods. "For life, bro."

Robby shakes his head and chuckles. "What a dumbass."

I grip the can as both boys' eyes gather on me. After the whole incident with Tommy, my mom didn't allow me to try a Force. It headlined the gossip of the town for weeks, moms on the phone with other moms, telling and retelling the story. By week two, there wasn't a person in Harper Pass who hadn't heard the pool story of Tommy Tantrum. Some concerned moms made such a stink about the whole thing they banned Force from all the schools.

I'm pretty sure I won't end up like Tommy, so I take a big gulp. It's warm and tastes terrible. It's bitter and foreign going down, a chemical swirl. I squint my eyes and clench my face tight like I bit into the sour pulp of a lemon.

"Eww, that's awful." I pass the can to Robby.

Tee laughs. "It's an acquired taste."

"Why in the world would anyone drink that?"

"Gives you energy, man." Robby grins and takes a swig.

"So, what you think, Robby? Should we let him in the crew?"

"Well, we were going to give you some hell today. But since you've already been through twice as much as we were even planning on dishing out, yeah—I think so."

A huge smile blooms on my lips. This feels like the most perfect moment in my entire life. I can tell things are going to be different for me now—*better*. Tee pats me on the back.

"Welcome to the Markland X Crew. Brother from another mother."

"So that's it?"

"Well yeah, 'cept the rule." Robby pauses and locks his eyes to mine. "You never leave a member of the crew behind. *Never.*"

"And you have to take a dare. If another member of the crew dares you to do something, you have to do it."

"And what if I don't?"

"You have to." Robby's stern eyes bore into mine.

"I got it!" Tee raises both of his index fingers to the sky. "In honor of Tommy Tantrum, you refuse a dare, then you go bare."

"Yes, that's perfect." Robby snickers and we all nod to seal the accord.

As we swallow our laughter, we move into a semi-circle. We all make fists and put them together to signify the agreement. *The pact is made.*

We share our Force Energy Drink and swap stories all afternoon on Jennings Bridge. It feels like we've known each other all our lives. I've never felt so connected before. It's effortless, a natural chemistry we share together. And before we leave Jennings Bridge, I know two things for sure.

I've found two friends I will keep forever, and I've never felt happier in all my life.

CHAPTER 8
Missing Margo

The sun rests its head on the horizon, the day growing dim. Robby and Tee pack their things as we get ready to head home.

"Can I catch a tow with ya, Tee?"

"Come on, man." Tee motions me to his bike.

Tee lives a few short blocks from my house. I hop on the BMX pegs on his bike and grab hold of his shoulders. We set off on our bikes on the dirt road that leads to Jennings Pike, a hazy cloud of dust roiling in our wake. The sun setting behind the trees casts long shadows on the roadways, and a warm orange glow percolates on the horizon, washing through the treetops.

Robby turns onto his street. "Later fellas." He jumps a curb and lands on the sidewalk before bunny hopping and pedaling out of sight.

Tee pedals hard for a half mile before hanging a left on Chambers Road. A police patrol car zooms up on us from behind. As the police car prepares to pass us, it slows to match our pace. Pulling alongside Tee's bike, the older officer in the passenger seat studies us. The officer says two words to the driver before the car accelerates and zips past us. Even though the siren isn't on, it looks like they're trying to get somewhere in a hurry. Tee turns on Parson Street, and we coast to the cul-de-sac at the bottom of the hill where I hop off.

"Thanks for the tow, Tee."

"You got it, man."

"So, what you guys doin' tomorrow?"

"You mean, what are *we* doing? You're in the crew now. *Brothers*."

Tee smiles and gives me a fist bump. Relief tugs at the corners of my lips, drawing them upward. I don't need to worry about my future in the Markland X Crew anymore.

"I'll come by your house tomorrow morning, and we can go meet up with Robby."

I flash a smile. "Cool. Later, man."

"Try not to run into Sammy, *Nutcracker Brooks!*"

Tee grins and rides away. I walk into the edge of the woods and retrieve my bike as the sun sneaks below the horizon, the moon already beaming full in the clear sky overhead. I jump on my bike and pedal home. The street lights begin flickering on as I pull into the driveway, the last remnant of daylight a faint orange glow on the tree line.

My mom lifts a warm smile as I amble through the door. "Brooks, how was your day?"

My face and eyes brighten. "Amazing." My mom's smile grows larger, her squinty eyes sparkling. "Mom, you care if I go and play with Tee and Robby again tomorrow?"

"Sure. When do I get to meet your new friends? I know of Tee, Sandra Mitchell's son. But I don't think I've met the other boy. Robby, you said?"

"Yes ma'am, Robby, and I'm sure you'll meet them soon. I think you'll really like 'em."

"I'm sure I will, sweetie. You boys must've played hard. *Look at you.* You're a filthy mess. Why don't you go get washed up for dinner? We had dinner earlier, but I saved you a plate. Your favorite, spaghetti and meatballs."

"Thanks, mom."

After cleaning up for dinner, I join my mother at the kitchen table. She's reading a detective novel. My mother loves reading. For as long as I can remember, she's surrounded herself with books.

Over the past year, my mom developed a particular obsession with true crime novels. She reads them day and night. Several weeks into her crime book reading binge, she started insisting everyone lock all the doors. We all kind of laughed at her. Dad said, "Really Susan, *it's Harper Pass.* You've been reading too many of those damn books."

A supervisor at the power plant, dad works most nights. He goes in around seven-thirty in the evening and doesn't get home until the middle of the night. But mom's always here, though.

I take a seat at the kitchen table and join my mom. She's reading her book and half-listening to the local news on TV. My hollow stomach growls. During my tussle with Sammy, I lost my lunch when Myron took my backpack. The crazy events of the day suppressed my appetite, made me forget I hadn't eaten. But presented with my favorite meal, I'm shoveling food into my mouth like a rescued shipwreck survivor. My mom looks up from her book before setting it on the table. She hoists the corners of her lips.

"Hungry, are we?"

With a mouthful of food, I nod through my chewing and voice an *uh-huh* through my nose. I twirl my fork through my spaghetti collecting another heaping portion of saucy spaghetti noodles. A car commercial ends on the television and a loud newscaster comes on.

"We have breaking news. I'm going to take you now to our reporter, Kasey Norton, who is live on scene, and we are going to hear from a family who is desperate for the community's help tonight. Kasey, are you there?"

"I'm here, Tom." The young reporter flashes a beaming smile. She's standing by a small, one-story house. The camera pans to a man and a woman. In the light of the camera, the petite woman's body quivers. Frizzy gray hairs jut out from the sides of her disheveled dark brown hair. Her hands tremble, and her mascara runs in faint black lines underneath her eyes, tattling her tears. Fat beads of sweat rappel the large man's forehead. His thick white eyebrows furrow at his shaking wife—concern stitched across his face. Patches of wispy gray hair, strategically combed to one side, dot the top of his head, but he's nearly bald. Two large areas of sweat, shaped like sideways crescent moons, dampen patches of his light blue t-shirt below the flab of his chest.

"I'm standing here with Jim and Linda Combs. Tonight, they have a desperate plea to the community. Their little girl, Margo, has gone missing, and they are asking for the community's help." A picture of Mysterious Margo flashes onto the screen. I drop my fork to my plate with a loud clank.

"Brooks, are you okay? Brooks. Honey. Are you okay?"

My parted lips won't make words. The reporter places the microphone near the woman's mouth.

"Please, please, my baby girl's gone missing. She's been missing since yesterday. She can't be all alone. She, she..." The woman breaks into tears and sobs. The man puts his arm around her before speaking.

"Our little girl has autism. Please, if you see her, please call the Harper Pass Police." He wipes away tears from his cheeks. The reporter brushes her blonde hair away from her eyes.

"Tom, can you flash that picture on the screen again?"

"It's on screen now, Kasey."

"Folks, this is Margo, and this family really needs your help. Margo was last seen when her parents put her to bed Tuesday night. She was wearing a white, floral-patterned nightgown at the time. Please call the Harper Pass Police Office immediately if you have any information so that we can reunite this special needs child with her parents."

My stomach free falls. I saw Margo hours earlier in the woods near Grief Hollow, no idea at the time she was missing. The number for the police office flashes on the screen below Margo's picture. A million disjointed thoughts swirl around in my mind. A dizzying rush of air deluges my head, overcoming me with a sensation of traveling outside of my body.

"Back to you, Tom."

"Great reporting, Kasey. Really sad story. We'll stay on this story for you with any new developments. Let's hope it has a happy ending. And now we'll send it to Kevin for your Tri-County weather report."

"Brooks!" My mom's shout leaks into my mind. Her hands are gripping my shoulders tight. She's shaking me. As I come out of my trance, I realize she's been shaking me for a while. I blink my eyes several times as a quick tremor passes through my body. I lock eyes with her. She's trembling, and her light green eyes glisten with concern. *But a mother's concern is intuitive.*

"Brooks, do you know something about that missing girl?"

I nod.

CHAPTER 9
The Questioning

"**B**etter bring him in." I overhear the man's gravelly voice on the telephone.

I'm still sitting at the kitchen table, but I've lost my appetite. I sit there in silence, my blank eyes cast straight ahead, listening to my mother's phone call and thinking about Margo.

"We'll be there in ten minutes."

My mom grabs her purse off the kitchen counter and kneels in front of me. She clasps both my hands and looks into my eyes.

"I don't want you to be scared, Brooks. But we're going to go to the police station now. It's very important that you tell them everything you just told me. I want you to tell them the truth, tell them everything you know. Do you understand?"

"Yes ma'am." My words fall out as a timid whisper.

A couple of minutes before, I told my mother the story of how I ran into Margo in the woods. I told her how Margo spoke to me and how she disappeared. My mother didn't ask why I went into the woods, and I didn't tell her about Sammy and Myron. Nor did I mention Grief Hollow.

My mother leads me out to the car.

"Buckle your seat belt." She gives me an affectionate pat on my knee. "Try not to be nervous. It's all going to be okay."

We pull out of the driveway and onto the road. We pass strands of ticky-tacky houses, each cut from the same mold as if originality dawned as an afterthought, never truly realized, its only expression coming in the form of different shades of paint. We drive in silent contemplation to the police station.

A faint mist hovers in the air of the black night, the streetlamps casting miniature rainbow halos. My stomach grumbles, a cauldron of nervous bubbles. *Have I done something wrong?* I replay the events from earlier in my mind. *I was just about to help Margo get back home when she disappeared. Given a chance, I would've done the right thing. But she disappeared. Just vanished.*

The brakes squeak as the car rocks to a stop. Our headlights illuminate the lettering on the small, one-story building. Mounted on the faded red brick, large tarnished brass letters spell out *Harper Pass Police Station*. We park between two late-model police cruisers, balding tires hinting to a small-town budget.

"Remember what I told you, Brooks?" It's more of a reminder than a question.

"Yes ma'am."

"Well, let's go then. That poor girl's family needs your help."

I scoot across the seat and follow my mom out her door. We walk the ramp together to the door of the police station. My mom places a delicate hand on the nape of my neck as we walk inside.

"Hi, I'm Susan Raker. I called about my son, Brooks Raker." She places her hand on my back presenting me.

"Have a seat over there, please. Detective Holt will be with you in just a moment." The desk officer flashes me a warm smile.

The desk officer's name badge reads *Marcy Peterman*. Her curly, brown, shoulder-length hair accentuates her chubby cheeks, and her swollen belly tugs against the buttons on her shirt, giving her a comic-strip appearance of disproportion. Pausing from her paperwork, Marcy grabs the telephone as we take a seat on a wooden pew in the lobby.

"Detective Holt, Susan is here with her son."

Upon ending the call, Marcy flashes a smile at me before returning to writing on her papers. My mom lays her purse on the bench and drapes an arm around me.

I squint in the glare of the lobby, the steady hum of the fluorescent lights a monotone soundtrack. Scanning the walls, I spot a fire safety poster filled with information about forest fire prevention and a ridiculous caricature of a bear, wearing a ranger hat and wagging a stern finger. A familiar visage draws my eyes. I crimp my lips at the missing persons poster tacked to the bulletin board, a picture of Margo on it. The upheaval in my stomach is audible, as bile churns a queasy stew.

My mom rises from the pew and greets a man in a suit.

"Tripp, how are you?" She gives him a hug, her voice warm and genuine.

"I'm good. Kirsten's good. We're good. Thanks for calling. Is this your son?"

"Brooks, this is Mr. Holt. I mean Detective Holt."

"Well, it's nice to meet you, son. You know, me and your mother have known each other for a long time. Any son of your mom's is a friend of mine."

Detective Holt extends his palm for a handshake. His massive hand swallows my own, burying it beneath a cluster of fingers and knuckles. The detective applies firm pressure to his grip, trace perspiration in the creases of his palm dampening my hand. His red neck tie hangs crooked and loose, the knot dangling away from his neck a couple of inches.

"What grade are you in, Brooks?" He twiddles the end of his thick mustache.

"Sixth grade, sir. Well, seventh grade, when we start back next year that is."

I begin to fidget.

"Over at Markland Middle?"

"Yes sir."

"Very good. Brooks, I have some questions that I need to ask you. Is it okay if I ask you some questions, son?" He studies me with discerning eyes.

I nod.

"Susan, if it's okay with you, I'd like to take Brooks to the back of the station."

"Okay. Yeah, sure. Let me grab my purse."

The detective's voice lassos my mom on her way to the pew. "I'd like to speak with him alone if that'd be alright, Susan."

"Oh. *Ohhh*. Okay. I guess that would be okay." She looks at me and at the detective.

"You know, just protocol really. Missing persons investigation and all." He slathers his words in an air of nonchalance.

My mother's tensed face relaxes. "Well, I guess that makes sense. Brooks, please go with Detective Holt. Remember what I told you. I want you to answer all of his questions. I'll be right here waiting for you." My mom pats the top of my head.

"Thanks, Susan. Okay, son, we best get moving. Just follow me."

My mom sits on the pew as I follow Detective Holt past the desk officer. My mother mouths *I love you* as I'm led away. We walk through a narrow passage between two rows of desks. Each of the desks displays a name plate, but the desks are all empty at this late hour.

Detective Holt opens a door and we enter a dark hallway. The fluorescent lights above flicker and hum to life. They light a long, windowless hallway, its empty walls painted drab gray. There's an underlying odor of sour mop water permeating the air. The faint buzz of an old-fashioned soda vending machine greets us as we pass. We walk through its cherry glow to the end of the hall, the clacking echo of the detective's shiny shoes announcing our advance, before we come to an abrupt stop at one of the doors. Detective Holt fumbles with his keys before placing one of them into the large metal door and opening it.

He clicks on the light and leads me inside the square, windowless room. One large metal desk in the center with two chairs occupies most of the room. There's a tan folder, a notepad, and a pen ordered on one side with a glass pitcher of ice water and two empty glasses beside it on the other. A nineties-era box video camera in the top corner of the room, positioned to face the table, stands alert as a dutiful scribe, a silent witness. A little red light near the camera lens blinks every other second.

"Go ahead and have a seat." Detective Holt pulls a chair out for me.

I sit. The vent above me rattles as icy air blows into the room. I shiver before crossing my arms and clutching my elbows to stay warm.

"So, I know you know why you're here, and I appreciate you comin' down to the station tonight. You're not in any trouble, so I don't want you to feel nervous in any way." Detective Holt fetches the pen and opens the notepad. "It's *very* important that you tell me the truth. This is a *very* important case, and you know it's against the law to lie to the police, right?" Detective Holt leans forward on the table.

"Yes sir."

"Good stuff. So, your mom told me that you saw Margo Combs this morning, is that correct?"

"Yes sir, I did."

"Where did you see her, son?"

"She was in the woods, sir. Behind the end of Parson Street."

Detective Holt jots something down on his notepad before continuing. "Can you be a little more specific?"

"Well, she surprised me. She was wearing her nightgown. I was walking in the woods. On my way to Grief Hollow."

Detective Holt lifts his eyes from his notepad.

"Why were you in the woods? And why were you going to Grief Hollow? I know your mom wouldn't approve of that."

"It's a shortcut, you know, to Jennings Bridge."

"Not really. Sounds more like a long cut." Detective Holt cocks his head, and his eyes narrow on me. "Why wouldn't you just take Chambers Road to Jennings Pike?"

He's right. Not a shortcut. Much quicker to take the roads. But he doesn't know about Sammy and Myron. It was a shortcut for me at the time. Crap! My story doesn't make sense. He's suspicious. I'm frozen.

"Brooks, I'm going to ask you again, *why* were you in the woods?"

"Umm..." My brain flusters. *Sammy'll come after me even harder if he thinks I snitched on him. And to the police! Sammy always says snitches end up with stitches.*

"Kid, *come on.* I'm a police officer. I can tell when you're not telling me the truth, so I'm going to ask you again. Why were you in the woods?" His abrupt tone sends my heart into a sprint. His face splotches crimson and his jawline tenses. *I have to tell the truth.* I blurt it before I think better of it.

"Sammy Needles and Myron were chasing me, sir."

"And why were they chasing you, son?"

Oh no. The question I was dreading. Can I go to jail for what I did to Sammy Needles? Will he arrest me for kicking him in the privates?

"Look kid, there's a little girl's life that hangs in the balance here. So you'd better start talking." His eyes tunnel into mine as he taps the tip of his shoe on the polished white tile.

"They were picking on me, sir. Umm... I... umm, I kicked Sammy Needles in his privates and got away on my bike. I was hiding from them in the woods."

I'm prepared for the worst, ready for Detective Holt to remove the shiny handcuffs from his belt and latch them around my wrists. Instead, he lets out a small chuckle underneath his breath and grins. A wave of relief washes over me, and I melt into my chair as I exhale the breath I've been holding. Detective Holt reaches for the water pitcher and pours a glass. He slides it across the table to me. He shakes his head.

"I swear that Sammy Needles kid is going to end up in my jail sooner than later."

I take a sip of my water and release a deep breath through my nose. The icy water cools my thermal insides.

"Do you know Myron's last name, son?"

"I don't, sir."

"Did they follow you into the woods?"

"I don't think so, but I'm not sure."

"Have you ever seen Sammy pick on Margo before?"

"Umm, yes sir. I've seen him call her a freak before and trip her."

Detective Holt pauses for a moment, glances up and to his left as if he's chasing a thought, before writing something on his notepad.

"Do you think Sammy Needles would have any reason to hurt Margo?"

"I don't think so, sir." My voice wavers as I consider the question. *Would he hurt her? Maybe he would.*

"So when you ran into Margo, did she say anything to you?"

"Umm, yes. But it was *very* strange. She said that the Collector is coming and that Grief Hollow would be its home."

Detective Holt's face crinkles. "What in the Sam Hell does that mean? Is that some kind of Pokémon thing?"

"I'm not really sure."

"Did she say anything else?"

"No sir. That was it."

"What happened next?"

"Well, she pointed in the direction of Grief Hollow, so I turned to look. When I turned back around, she was gone."

"What do you mean, *gone*? Like she was running away from you?"

"No sir, she was just gone. Disappeared."

Detective Holt scratches his temple and squints his eyes at me. "You know that doesn't make a whole lot of sense, right?"

"Yes sir. I do know that, sir. But that's what happened."

"Okay, well, did you hear her footsteps? Maybe what direction she went in?"

"No sir, I didn't. I called out her name a few times. I was going to try to help her get back home. She didn't answer and I couldn't find her. Then, I got kinda creeped out and decided to leave."

"And you're *sure* you didn't hear which way she went? Like the rustling of leaves or something." Detective Holt raises hopeful eyelids.

"No sir. I really didn't."

"And what time did this happen?"

"I think it was around nine forty-five this morning."

Detective Holt draws in a breath and releases a long exhale through his nose as he lifts his head. He scrunches his lips and narrows his eyes on me. He closes his eyelids tight for a moment and rubs his temple.

"So, you mentioned you were going to Jennings Bridge. Why were you going there?"

"To meet up with my friends, Robby and Tee, sir."

"And were Robby or Tee with you when you ran into Margo?"

"No sir. I was alone."

"Do you think there's anyone who can verify your story?"

"Well, I told Tee and Robby about it when I got to Jennings Bridge."

Detective Holt's eyes brighten. He pulls out his walkie-talkie from inside his jacket, turns the dial at the top and presses the button.

"Marcy, can you get Sandra Mitchell, Tee Mitchell's mom, on the phone for me? I need to have Sandra ask Tee a quick question. Over." Detective Holt studies my face for any change of expression.

Static crackles before the line goes quiet, and a woman's voice comes on.

"On it, Holt. Give me a sec. Over."

Detective Holt looks me over again, studying me with discerning eyes.

"Got her on the line, Holt. What did you want me to have her ask Tee? Over."

"Have her ask Tee if his friend Brooks told him about running into one of their classmates in the woods today, and if so, who was it? Over."

The ear-scratching static lasts for a few moments before Marcy's voice returns.

"Holt. Tee just told Sandra that Brooks *did* tell him and Robby that he ran into Margo Combs in the woods this morning. You want me to have her bring him into the station? Over."

"No, that won't be necessary, Marcy. But go ahead and send a patrol car over to the end of Parson Street, and have them take a look there in the woods for Margo. Over."

"Will do, Holt. Over."

Detective Holt turns off his radio and puts it away inside his jacket. He's tapping his fingers on the desk, glancing at me sideways and scrunching his lips. He moves forward, grabs the tan folder on the table and opens it. He spreads out a few drawings.

"Do these drawings mean anything to you, son?"

I inspect the strange drawings. In the first one, some type of clawed hand holds a boy high in the air. The drawing contains considerable detail. The creature's defined legs and elongated claws appear in the foreground, but it really doesn't mean anything to me. The sketch of the boy's body ends with his neck straddling the top edge of the page, the omission of his face preventing any further clues.

The second drawing appears mostly black and features a circular whirlpool thing by a gnarled tree, but it really makes no sense to me.

The third drawing looks familiar, but I can't place it. I flip it around and my mouth drops. It's clearly a sketch of Copperhead Creek in Grief Hollow. There's the burned-out tree fort. And my eyes bulge as they follow the detail to the snake thing that I saw form from the mist earlier. There's a large tree branch on the ground, and to my horror, even the footprints appear in the bank of the creek that I saw form earlier that morning. My heart bounds in my chest.

I lift my wide eyes to meet Detective Holt's, my mouth still ajar. "Where did you get these?"

"Margo's house. Why? Does that picture mean something to you?"

"Yes. Yes, it does. That's Grief Hollow." My voice quakes.

Detective Holt takes the drawing and inspects it.

"Sure is, isn't it?"

Detective Holt thanks me for answering his questions and leads me to my awaiting mother. I give her a tight hug.

Detective Holt smiles. "You've got a great boy there, Susan. We're all done here. Brooks was great. You guys can go on home. Thank you for calling and coming in."

"Of course. And thank you, Tripp." She shakes his hand.

"Oh, and Susan. If we don't find Margo tonight, I might need to come by in the morning and have Brooks take us to the spot in the woods where he saw Margo. Would that be okay?"

"Of course, Tripp. Whatever we can do to help out. Tell Kirsten we're thinking about her." My mother puts her arm around me and leads me outside to the car to go home.

CHAPTER 10

The Find

The doorbell rings at 8:34 a.m. I jump up from my perch by the TV, leaving my bowl of cereal and cartoons playing in the background. I hustle to the door, an extra bounce in my step. Tee's supposed to meet me before heading to Robby's house. As I open the door, my big smile dissipates.

Detective Holt's standing there, his police cruiser idling behind him in our driveway.

"Good morning, Brooks. Is your mom home?"

"*Mom*." I never break eye contact with him. He flashes a forced half-smile, his eyes like sinking sunsets.

My mom comes to the door. "Hey, Tripp. What's going on?"

"Well, I hate to do this, Susan, but we didn't find Margo last night. She's been missing for three days. We really don't have any leads. I was hoping I could take Brooks with me real quick to show me the spot in the woods where he last saw Margo."

"Yeah, sure, whatever you need. Brooks, go and put on your shoes please."

"What's all the racket?" My father grumbles as he emerges from the bedroom, squinty-eyed.

"Hey, Travis." Detective Holt gives my dad a wave. My dad wears his late-night hours at the power plant on his face.

"Well, go on and get your shoes, Brooks. Travis, Brooks is going to take Tripp to the place in the woods where he saw that missing girl. To help with their investigation."

I walk to the kitchen to grab my shoes, tying them as I listen.

"Hey, Tripp. Real shame about that missing girl. Susan told me about it when I got home last night. Let us know if we can help." My father shakes Detective Holt's hand.

"I might just do that. Thanks, Travis."

"I'm so sorry about the baby. How's Kirsten holding up?"

"*Travis!*" My mom smacks my father on the shoulder.

My dad flips his palms over and crinkles his lips. "What?"

"It's okay, Susan. Really. Kirsten... she's doing okay. Just taking it day by day."

"Give her our love." My mom gives Detective Holt a warm smile before cutting razor eyes at my dad.

"We'd better get going, Brooks. I promise I won't have him gone that long." Detective Holt is already moving to the door.

"No problem, Tripp. Buddy, do your best to help Detective Holt, and make sure you listen to what he tells you. Love you, son. Good to see you, Tripp." My dad retreats to the bedroom.

My mom kisses me on the top of the head, and I follow Detective Holt to his police cruiser. He opens the passenger door for me, and I get in. A metal platform juts out from the dashboard, holding a laptop computer, and several interesting buttons that I haven't seen before in any car protrude from the dash. I buckle my seatbelt as Detective Holt gets into the car.

"Ever been in a police car before?" Detective Holt eases out of our driveway.

"No sir. It's pretty cool." I point to one of the buttons. "What's that do?"

"Oh, that? That's for the sirens. Probably a little bit early for that. Don't want to wake up the whole neighborhood just yet." He grins at me. "Tell you what. Since we're on official police business of sorts, you want to turn on the lights?"

My eyes grow big and I nod.

"Hit this switch right here."

I hit the switch and the lights come on. I smile out my window as the flashes of blue and red lights dance on the passing mailboxes and houses. We turn on Parson Street and coast to the end of the hill. There's a police patrol car already parked at the end of the street, and we park behind it. Detective Holt cuts off the emergency lights, and we get out of the car.

Two police officers, dressed in navy blue uniforms, step out of the other patrol car. I recognize the older officer as the one I saw the day before when Tee was towing me on his bike.

"Brooks, this is Officer Morrow and Officer Clancy. They're going to help us. All right, gentlemen, let's get moving. Brooks, can you lead the way?"

I retrace my steps. I find the place where I stashed my bike the day before. We continue walking and I start to recognize some of the trees. We walk several hundred more yards before I stop.

"Here. I was standing here. I tripped on this root yesterday. Margo was right over there." I point to a flat spot by a small pine tree.

"Okay, good work, Brooks. Guys, go ahead and spread out and see what you can find." The men fan out.

Detective Holt walks to the spot I pointed out and kneels. He begins sifting through the damp leaves on the ground with the tip of an ink pen.

He moves a clump of leaves revealing a small child's footprint in the soggy earth. "Well, I'll be damned."

I walk closer as he brushes away more of the leaves with his hands and uncovers more small footprints. He begins sifting through more of the leaves, following the path of the footprints for a couple of feet.

Kneeling, Detective Holt draws in his lips in contemplation, eyes scanning the surrounding forest floor. He gives a squinty-eyed shake of his head at the abrupt end to the path of footprints, before he clears an even larger area of leaves. Still, no additional footprints. Unsatisfied, he clears an area of about ten feet by ten feet, but there's nothing. The footprints are contained in a small five-foot radius with no indication of how that person got there or left. He touches a few spots on the ground and determines that the moisture content of the soil seems similar.

"Got something, Holt."

"Stay with me, Brooks." I follow Detective Holt as we hustle in the direction of Officer Morrow's voice.

We weave through trees and thick brush before coming into a clearing. Officer Morrow's standing by what looks like my backpack.

"I found this Holt, but I didn't want to open it."

"I think that's my backpack."

Detective Holt cocks his head at me. "Did you leave it out here yesterday?"

"No sir. When I ran into Sammy and Myron yesterday, Myron took it from me."

"Open it up, Charles."

Officer Morrow fiddles with the backpack trying to find the zipper.

"Holt, it's got some kind of black... well, I don't know what it is. Slime or something."

"Put these on." Detective Holt pulls a pair of blue nitrile gloves from his pocket and hands them to Officer Morrow.

"Now go ahead and open it up." Detective Holt moves in closer.

Officer Morrow reaches into the backpack and pulls out an Uncrustables peanut butter and jelly sandwich. *My lunch from yesterday.*

"Detective Holt, that's my backpack. I had an Uncrustables in it yesterday!"

There's a rustle of leaves behind us, before Officer Clancy walks out into the clearing. "Didn't find anything, Holt. What'd you guys get?"

"Here, give me a hand, guys. Let's clear some of these leaves and see if we can get a shoe print."

The three men kneel above the forest floor and brush piles of leaves away near my backpack.

"Got something here. I think... I think it's blood. *Oh wow*, and there's a lot of it." Officer Clancy's stoic voice cracks as he clears away more leaves.

"Okay, back up, guys. We may be dealing with a crime scene here." Detective Holt pulls a little glass vial from inside his jacket pocket.

He uncorks the top of the vial, inverts it and grabs the wooden end of a cotton swab. He dips it into the thick liquid, and the tip of the white cotton swab turns crimson as it absorbs the gelatinous liquid. He pulls out a resealable plastic bag from his pocket and deposits the cotton swab inside before sealing it.

"I want you to go back to the station and spray this with luminol. If it hits, get some labs run ASAP." Detective Holt hands the bag to Officer Clancy who turns and hurries through the woods to the patrol cars.

Detective Holt pulls out his walkie-talkie.

"Marcy, are you there? Over."

"I'm here. Over."

"We're going to need to bring Sammy Needles into the station. Can you send Officer Ivansek to his house? Over."

"Dispatching now, Holt. Over."

"Also, find out anything you can on Sammy Needles' friend, Myron. And reach out to all the churches, any community groups really. Tell them we need volunteers. *Lots of them.* I want to organize a search party for this afternoon. Everything just got a lot more urgent. I want everyone to meet at the end of Parson Street at noon. Over."

"Will do, Holt. Over."

"Brooks, I'm going to need to get you home now. Officer Morrow, please stay here with the backpack until I get back. Grab a sample of that black substance on it. Don't let anyone get near this area. Matter of fact, tape off this area as best you can. I don't want someone from the search party trampling all over my crime scene. Let's go, Brooks." Detective Holt leads me through the woods to the patrol car.

We drive home in silence. I retreat to my thoughts. *Is Sammy a killer? Has he done something to poor Margo? Will anyone ever see her again?* My chest tightens as I wonder how her parents must feel and the overwhelming fear Margo must've felt if something terrible happened to her.

Detective Holt pulls into my driveway and puts the car in park. His eyes meet mine.

"Thank you for your help, Brooks. I need you not to talk about what you saw back there. It's very important for the investigation that you do not tell anyone what you've seen. Do you think that you can do that for me?"

"Yes sir." Another wave of heaviness pours into my chest.

"Okay then. Go back inside." He reaches across my body and opens my car door.

I get out of the car, and Detective Holt backs out of the driveway and speeds off.

CHAPTER 11
The Interrogation of Sammy Needles

Detective Holt walks into the interrogation room and closes the door behind him. He's carrying a folder, notepad, and pen. He pulls out a chair and lays his things on the table. Sammy Needles sits sideways in the other chair. He crinkles his nose and crosses his arms.

"Well, no need for introductions really. I think you probably remember me, Detective Holt." He opens his notepad.

"Yeah, I remember you, *cop*." Sammy breathes an agitated sigh.

"*Good*. Sammy, I have a few questions to ask you. I'm going to record our conversation today." Detective Holt presses a button on the mini recorder on the desk.

"Good for you."

"Sammy, do you know why we brought you in here today?" Detective Holt trains his eyes on Sammy with razor focus.

"This is Brooks' doing, ain't it? I'm gonna kill that twerp!" A shot of color speckles Sammy's cheeks as he clenches his pudgy fists.

"And why would you think that Brooks had something to do with you being here? Is there a reason that Brooks would want to get you in trouble, Sammy?"

"Well, no. I mean, I just don't trust him. You know, he kicked me in the nuts yesterday."

"That's funny, he—"

"How's that funny? *Ha, Ha*. Well, ain't you gonna do something about it? Like go arrest him? I just told you he kicked me in the nuts."

"If you'd let me finish, what I was going to say is that he doesn't strike me as the violent type. I'm a pretty good judge of character being that it's my job and all." Detective Holt cracks his neck.

"Well, maybe you just suck at your job."

"Or maybe *you* did something to him before he kicked you."

"No man, me and Myron was just minding our own business. And he just comes up and kicks me in the nuts for no good reason. I mean, he's the one you should be talkin' to, not me. That little weirdo's probably got something to do with this whole thing."

"What whole thing? What do you mean?" Detective Holt studies Sammy's facial expressions.

"Me gettin' brought down here and all, that's all." Sammy shifts in his chair.

"This Myron friend of yours, does he have a last name?"

"What kind of stupid question is that? Of course he's got a last name." Sammy pushes back in his chair and grins.

"Well, what is it?"

Sammy crosses his arms. "Why do you want to know, anyway?"

"Let's see if he can back up your story, and maybe I'll consider going to arrest Brooks."

A thin grin emerges on Sammy's face, and a vengeful twinkle flits through the rims of his eyes. "Finally gonna do your job, huh? Thompson. His last name's Thompson. Now, why don't you let me out of here and go arrest Brooks?"

"And do you know where I might find this Myron Thompson friend of yours?"

"How the hell should I know? What do I look like, his keeper? Probably at his house. What? I gotta do your job for you?"

Splotches of red appear on Detective Holt's face. Sammy's grin spreads wider. Holt's nostrils flare, and he leans into the table, delivering his words like blunt force trauma. "What do you know about a brown backpack?"

"I got no idea what you're talking about."

Sammy squirms a little in his chair. His eyes swim around the room like skittish fish while Detective Holt studies him. Detective Holt opens the tan folder and pulls out a picture.

"You and your friend Myron *didn't* have a brown backpack yesterday? Something that may have looked like this?" Detective Holt slides the photograph across the table to Sammy. Sammy sneaks a glance at the picture of Brooks' backpack. He takes a deep breath and a big gulping swallow. He clenches his jaw tight as he comes to the furious realization that Brooks must've gone to the cops on him.

"Man, I don't know nothing about no brown backpack." He pushes the photo across the table, crossing his arms in defiance.

"Sammy, you remember when you got in that bit of trouble last year for breaking into those cars?"

"So what? Judge said just community service. And I done cleaned all them nasty bathrooms at Rife Park, twice."

"Yeah, but do you remember what we did when we brought you in that day?"

"Yeah, you fed me some nasty bologna sandwich."

"We fingerprinted you, Sammy. You know we *keep* all those fingerprints, right?"

"So?"

"And guess where we found your fingerprints? On a brown backpack that you 'don't know nothing about.' So, I'm going to ask you this again, where'd you get the backpack, Sammy?"

A ripple flits through Detective Holt's facial muscles, before they harden.

A faint grin buds on the corners of Detective Holt's lips as Sammy digests his lie about the fingerprints. Sammy's eye twitches as he squirms in his skin. Detective Holt cements his rigid glare. Sammy shuffles in his chair. Detective Holt bores his eyes into Sammy until his posture wilts.

"Me and Myron found it." Sammy's words gush like a broken fire hydrant. "On Chambers Road. But I don't see what business that is of yours."

"It's my business because one of my deputies found that backpack in the woods near a whole mess of blood. Do you want to tell me what happened in the woods, Sammy?" Detective Holt leans into the table.

"I wasn't in no woods. It must've been Myron. He's the one who had the backpack anyway," Sammy blurts out. His eyes pulse wide, a subtle tremble settling on his lips.

"When's the last time you saw Myron?"

"Yesterday."

"What time yesterday?"

"I don't know, man, around one. I went to go get some lunch, and he didn't come. That's the last I seen him."

Sammy's legs fidget, and he rubs his hands over his fat knees, eyes drifting to the ceiling.

"Do you know Margo Combs?"

"No. Who the hell is that?"

"I think the kids call her Mysterious Margo. Do you know her?"

"That freak. Oh man. Yeah, I know of her. Why?" A smirk slithers onto Sammy's face.

"Have you ever bullied Margo?"

"Man, I don't bully no one, no how. Just mind my own business."

"So, you never called her a freak or tripped her?"

"What's with all the stupid questions? I done told you I ain't bullied no one." Sammy's pitch climbs a ladder of denial, amplified at each contentious rung.

"Margo Combs is missing. There's a bunch of blood next to a backpack with your fingerprints on it, right near where Margo was last seen. So, cut the shit and tell me what happened in the woods." Detective Holt slams his hand on the metal table.

The sudden slap startles Sammy, and he jumps in his chair. Even though the room's frigid, a torrent of sweat seeps from his pores, dampening his shorts underneath him.

"I told you I whatn't in no woods. That's the truth." Sammy's eyes glisten.

"There's a backpack with your fingerprints on it that says otherwise."

"I already told you, Myron had the backpack." His voice stops a couple of decibels short of a yell.

"Well, that blood's being tested right now, and if it turns out that's Margo's blood, you're in a whole heap of trouble, son."

Detective Holt's eyes inventory Sammy, studying all facets of his body language.

"I didn't do nothin'. I didn't do nothin' to nobody, no how."

"Where did you go yesterday after you left Myron?"

"I already said, I went home to eat lunch."

Sammy's face grows flush. The judge warned him about additional offenses. If he got into more trouble, the judge warned, he'd spend some time at Longfellow Juvenile Detention Center.

"And where else did you go after lunch yesterday?"

"Nowhere, man. I was at my house."

"Is there anyone who can verify that?"

"*Yeah cop*, my mom and my sister!"

"You're a real wise ass, ain't you, son? We're going to go pick up your little friend Myron and ask him some questions. If I find out you're lying, lying about anything, I'm going to march your ass right back down to the station. And if you so much as lay a finger on Brooks or any of his friends, I'll have your ass hauled in here so fast in handcuffs that your head will spin. Got it?" Detective Holt's nostrils flare again, his cheeks turning fiery red.

"Yeah, whatever, man. I ain't done nothing. You can't hold me, no ways."

Detective Holt jumps from his chair and erupts. "Get the hell out of my station! You can find your own way out." He flings the door into the wall.

Once Sammy leaves the room, he grabs his walkie-talkie.

"Marcy, you there? Over." A hint of anger straddles his words.

"Here, Holt. Over."

"That Sammy Needles is a real piece of work. Can you please find out where Sammy's friend Myron Thompson lives and dispatch a unit there? We're going to need to bring him in for questioning. Over."

"I'll call the school principal and see if we can get his address. Over."

"10-4." Detective Holt straightens his tie and collects his things from the table.

CHAPTER 12
Search Party

The doorbell rings again. I exhale a deep breath before going to answer it, a drag in my step. Tee's standing at my doorway with Robby, their bikes parked in my driveway. At the sight of me, a big smile climbs Tee's face and Robby grins. Robby gives me a fist bump.

"Ole Brooksie Boy, what you got cooking?"

Tee grins wide. "Yeah man, what you been getting into? I swear we can't leave you alone for a few hours."

I smile big at the welcome arrival of my friends. "What's up, guys?"

"Oh, not too much, just a phone call to my mom from the police last night." Tee lifts his eyelids in a playful gesture. "What's that all about?"

Oh, man. They don't know. "You mean, you didn't hear? Margo's missing."

Robby's jaw goes slack. "No way! But you just saw her."

"Oh man. But they don't think you had anything to do with it, do they?"

"No. I don't think so. Come on in, guys."

Tee's wearing a blue basketball tank top and gym shorts. Even though he's quite a bit shorter than most kids in our grade, Tee's a great basketball player, good enough to beat out an eighth-grader to take the starting point guard position for our basketball team.

Robby's also a basketball player. He hit a growth spurt much earlier than most of the other kids in our grade. He's one of the tallest kids in our school. He's long, lean, and lanky but not nearly as coordinated as Tee. He made the basketball team too but doesn't play much.

"Let's go down to the basement. I gotta tell you guys something, anyways."

My mom rounds the corner, laundry basket in hand, overflowing with clean clothes awaiting folding. "Ahh, so these must be your new friends."

Tee smiles at my mom. "Hi, Mrs. Raker."

"Hello Tee. And you must be Robby?"

"Yes ma'am."

"Well, it's a pleasure to meet you boys. Brooks tells me—"

"We're going to head down to the basement if that's okay, Mom?"

Please, please don't embarrass me in front of my friends. I'm not sure what she's getting ready to say, but my red face pleads for mercy.

"You boys have fun. There's some Gatorades and Cokes in the fridge downstairs if you get thirsty. It was nice meeting you boys." My mom smiles at us as she carries the laundry basket to the couch.

"Thanks, Mom!"

Robby returns her smile. "Nice meeting you too, Mrs. Raker." We storm the staircase to the basement. Robby turns to me with laughter in his eyes. "Dude, your mom's kinda hot!"

"Not cool."

Both boys chuckle.

"I'm just messing with ya."

"No, but seriously, she's kinda hot. Maybe not as hot as Alyssa, but pretty hot!" Tee laughs out the words before giving Robby a fist bump.

"Dude. Gross!"

Alyssa Everly's one of the prettiest girls in our school, earning her the nickname, Heavenly Everly, a name coined by a tenth-grader who shared the same bus route. She looks angelic with her silky blonde hair, big, light blue eyes and a smile that buckles boys at the knees. Like the rest of the boys in our school, I'm infatuated with her. To make matters worse, she stepped into womanhood at the end of the seventh grade, and her budding chest harnesses gazes. She caught me gawking at her in the hallway a couple of times. To my astonishment, she returned a smile of her own at me as she walked by, but I never found the courage to talk to her. News of her breakup traveled the hallways on fleeting whispers. Boys bragged, promised to woo her, but no one did.

Robby drops like a falling timber onto the couch. "So, what's the story?"

"Yeah, why'd they have you at the police station?"

"Guys, I was the last one to see Margo, so I had to tell them where I last saw her. They say she'd already been missing for a couple of days when I ran into her."

"No way. That's crazy!" Robby straightens up in his seat.

"But that wasn't the craziest thing! The detective asked me to look at some drawings. They were really weird. He'd gotten them from Margo's house. Two didn't really make any sense to me, but they were really creepy. But the third one..." My brows furrow.

Tee leans in. "What? What about the third one?"

"When I flipped the third one around, I almost threw up."

Robby's eyes slowly widen. "What was it?"

"Guys, it was Grief Hollow."

"Aw man. You had me freaked out for a second. So, she drew a picture of Grief Hollow. That's not that big of a deal."

"No, Tee, it was what was in the picture. The black snake thing was wrapped around the tree. The large branch that almost killed me was on the ground. And the footprints of the thing that chased me were drawn into the bank of Copperhead Creek."

"Whoa!" A sudden chill wriggles through Tee's shoulders.

Robby scrunches his face for a moment. "Wait, how's that possible?"

"Yeah, you said she's been missing for a couple of days. How could she have drawn that picture?"

"I don't know."

Tee pushes a blast of air through his nose. "That's super freaky, man!"

"So'd they find her?"

"No. I heard the detective say that they're organizing a search party today at noon. They're calling all the churches and everything for volunteers. Supposed to meet at the end of Parson Street."

Robby springs from the couch. "That's like right around the corner!"

"Markland X Crew's gonna solve this one. Oh yeah. Legendary status." Tee does a couple of dance moves, ending in a celebratory dab.

"Wait. No." I raise my hands in protest.

"Why not, man? Tee's right. We can help."

"You know it."

"I mean, I guess so. But..." I waver and Robby jumps in to fill the void.

"No guesses, no buts. Let's do it."

A few moments of silence pass, before Robby extends his fist to me and Tee. Tee smiles and extends his fist into the circle as well. "In."

A big smile climbs Robby's lips. "In."

Tee and Robby narrow their eyes on me. *Oh no. Not those woods again. They're not going to let me say no. At least I won't be alone.* After a deep exhale, I relent. I make a fist and put it in the circle joining theirs.

"In. Okay, let's do it."

"Aww yeah! Oh, oh, aww yeah! Oh, oh, aww yeah!" Tee sings, his eyes aflame, as he resurrects a poor imitation of some Michael Jackson dance moves. He looks ridiculous.

Robby and I burst out laughing.

Robby looks at his watch. "It's eleven forty-five. We gotta go!"

Tee catapults an arm forward. "This way to glory, boys!" Our rapid-fire steps strike the staircase like an ascending herd of frenzied buffalo.

"Mom, we're heading out to play."

"Have fun, boys."

Tee and Robby hop on their bikes. I grab my bike from the garage and roll it into the driveway. We grin at each other, bright-eyed for our first adventure together as Robby leads us off the driveway. We follow him by instinct, a de facto leader, wisdom beyond his years. We coast to the end of Slippery Hill, side by side, like a pack of outlaws.

We make the turn onto Chambers Road before turning on Parson Street. A large crowd of at least fifty people congregates at the bottom of the hill. Parked at the end of the road, two police cruisers sit stationary. We come to a stop by the main gathering and lug our bikes off the road. Tee points into the crowd.

"Heavenly Everly."

Alyssa stands there with her parents. We snake through the crowd of people. There's a large pickup truck pulled into the grass near the woods with two police officers beside it, one holding a bullhorn. Detective Holt climbs into the bed of the truck to face the crowd, another officer passing him the bullhorn.

"Heyyy, Alyssa." Tee lofts his flirty voice in her direction as we're walking past.

She smiles, her eyes moving like the second hand of an antique clock, a momentary pause on each of us.

"Hey, Tee, hey, Robby, hey, Brooks. It's nice of you guys to come help look for my cousin."

She knows my name! I try to keep a straight face, but I feel it contorting into a goofy grin. A rush of heat pulses into my cheeks. *She's gorgeous. Stop staring.*

Robby's brows lift. "Oh wow, Margo's your cousin?"

"Distant cousin. But yes." She smiles at me, her bright blue eyes sparkling like alluring diamonds in the sunlight.

Detective Holt raises the bullhorn and switches it on emitting a high-pitched shriek, which causes some grumbling in the crowd.

"Now listen up. I want to thank all of you for coming out here on such short notice. I know that Margo's parents, Jim and Linda, are very grateful for each and every one of you being here today. We're here to help this family find their missing daughter. Now, Margo was last seen in these woods yesterday. Each one of you has been given a flyer with her picture on it. If you see her, try your best to calmly get her to come to you. Thankfully, there's a lot of us out here today, but that could also frighten her. The last thing we want to do is scare her away. When we go out into these here woods, I want you to spread out ten feet apart. We're going to walk slowly, *as a group*. And let's keep this orderly. If you find something, you are to blow the whistle that we've given you to wear around your neck. Under no circumstances should you touch anything you find. You wait for a police deputy or myself to come to the sound of your whistle. Does everyone understand?"

There's a grumbling of *yeses* from the crowd.

Robby's eyes grow wide and he points. "Holy crap! Is that Brady Palmer?"

Audible gasps rise from the crowd as Brady walks toward a large cluster of volunteers. Ray Owens, the father of Misty Owens, knifes through the crowd and moves to block Brady's path.

"No. *No!* No one wants you here!" Ray's cheeks ignite in a blaze of fiery hues while he waves his hands in crisscrossing patterns trying to ward off Brady's advance.

Brady flashes his open palms as leering eyes cut into him. "I just want to help."

"*Haven't you already done just about enough? You killed my girl! You killed my Misty!*"

Ray's body shakes, eyes misting, blotches of red spreading from his face to his neck.

"It was an accident." Brady's meek voice trails off.

"Accident? Lighting gasoline up ain't no accident. They never should've let you out."

Ray's nostrils flare as his eyes drill into Brady. A sobbing Pamela Owens wraps trembling arms around her husband's waist, but he slices through her fragile grip. Detective Holt hops off the pickup truck and comes rushing through the crowd. He jumps between Ray Owens and Brady Palmer.

"Now Ray, you got to calm down." Detective Holt places a firm outstretched palm onto Ray's chest.

"Calm down? He killed my girl, Tripp. You know he killed my girl."

"I just want to help find Margo."

"Tripp, he probably had something to do with this. Maybe you should take him in, question him. He's probably done somethin' to that poor girl. Just like he did to my Misty."

"Enough!" Detective Holt's shout halts Ray's advance. "We're here to help find this girl, and quite frankly, the more help that we can get the better. If Brady wants to help, then by God, we're going to let him help. Ray, you and Pam get on over there to the left flank. And Brady, you get on the right flank way over there."

"But Tripp—"

"But nothing, Ray. Please get over on that left flank where I asked you to."

Ray Owens' nonplussed expression sours, and he casts a contemptuous frown at Detective Holt. He shakes his head as his wife collects his hand and leads him to the left flank of the search party. He mutters to himself all the way there. Brady Palmer lowers his head and makes his way to the opposite flank.

Detective Holt's sullen eyes linger on Brady as if he's revisiting some distant memory, a hint of heavy shadow flitting through the rims of his eyes. Onlookers leer at Brady. Their sharpened stares tear through the air all around us like a murderous frenzy of vengeful daggers. I wince at the palpable scorn before turning away. Tee, Robby, and I grab whistles from a milk crate and hang them around our necks. We pass a stack of flyers with Margo's picture, but we don't grab one.

Officer Morrow approaches Detective Holt and leans in close.

"We tried to pick up that Myron Thompson kid. The sister said he never came home last night. The father's out of the picture, and I got the impression that the mom's not around too much. The sister said that Myron doesn't come home from time to time. We'll try to pick him up again tomorrow."

"Can't worry about that now. Why don't you go ahead and take the left flank? And keep Ray in line if you can."

"I'll do my best." Officer Morrow hurries to intersect Ray Owens.

"We've wasted enough time already. Now, let's get moving." Detective Holt waves his arm in the direction of the woods, his shout prompting a mass forward advance.

CHAPTER 13
The Awakening

We file in near the right flank as the search party begins a forward creep. Several men in hunting fatigues encircle a group of about twenty bloodhounds. They put some of Margo's dirty clothes to the dogs' noses. The dogs crinkle their snouts, drawing her scent deep into their olfactory. Once all the dogs get a turn, the men release them. The dogs, moving slow at first, sniff the ground around them, and walk into the woods before beginning to trot. As her scent gets stronger, they dash deeper into the woods, their loud barks rising above the whispered conversations in the crowd.

The search party enters the woods. The barks of the dogs ahead echo through the trees as we trudge forward, spaced ten feet or so apart. The other boys and I stay a little closer together, within a few feet of each other.

Dark clouds gather, the treetops set to a light sway in the headwinds of an approaching thunderstorm. The foreboding sky threatens, greenish-tinged black clouds swirling overhead. *Don't storm. Don't storm and we can still find Margo.* All around us, the forest crackles, crunching leaves and snapping twigs as the search party descends deeper into the forest.

Clouds obscure the sun, and heavy shadows fall onto the forest floor. As we move deeper into the woods, the spacing between each person widens. A couple of volunteers on the flanks move ahead of the rest of the search party while the dogs' barks grow more distant.

Oh my God, is that... it is. It's Mr. Wadlow. What in the world's he doing here? Kids in our town often dare each other to ring his doorbell and run. Like running through a graveyard at night, the unsubstantiated rumors and legends of a small town, grown ripe with time. Stories of repetition, a piece added with each retelling. Ever-changing. Wadlow, a mad scientist, a killer. His house haunted by his victims. Bodies buried in his basement. All the kids fear him.

Mr. Wadlow collects something from the ground and inspects it, his body positioned to guard from prying eyes. He surveys the people marching forward on his flanks, gauging their level of attention to him, before slipping it into his pocket. He stops moving forward, falling behind the group. He slithers sideways behind the search party line to the edge of the right flank. He walks with brisk determination, putting more distance between himself and the search party with each labored step, clutching at his knee as he moves. He surveys any eyes cast in his direction one last time before he takes off in a hobbled run in the opposite direction of the search party, disappearing into the trees.

"Did you see that?"

Tee nods his head at me with wide eyes. "Yep, that dude's up to something for sure."

"What happened?"

Tee points Robby to the trees where Mr. Wadlow disappeared. "Mr. Wadlow picked something up off the ground and ran."

"What's he doing out here?"

Muted screaming in the distance stops us in our tracks, and most of the search party stops with us. The wind intensifies, rustling through the trees as storm clouds threaten. A couple volunteers on the left flank of the search party trudge too far ahead, and we lose sight of them in the trees.

"Boys."

Tee, Robby, and I jump. We all spin around. It's Brady Palmer. My wide eyes trail the length of the hideous burn scars on his arms, the skin disfigured, twisted all up on itself in grotesque knots of scar tissue and pinkish patches of grafted skin.

"Sorry to scare you. Something's going on in Grief Hollow. You need to stay out of there. It can do things. It can change. It can be whatever it wants to be, make you see things that aren't there." His eyes swell big and scour the surrounding tree line.

The wind begins howling again, and the branches in the trees above us scrape each other as they shake. More faint screams riding the wind pull everyone's attention in the direction of Grief Hollow as the roiling sky growls. John Watson breaks ranks with the search party line and charges forward.

"John, wait!"

John ignores Officer Morrow's call and accelerates. He carries his rifle high with both hands as he runs like a soldier storming an enemy location until he disappears behind the ridgeline and out of sight. A moment later the faint screams resound much louder and clearer. *Those aren't screams. It's dogs' yelping. Not screams at all.* The yelps crescendo before coming to an abrupt stop. An eerie silence blankets the forest. My heart hammers, pounding against the walls of my chest. I turn to Brady, but he's gone.

Everyone's frozen in their spots. There's an oncoming rustle of leaves beneath the heavy brush, interspersed in a hundred-yard area. A small sapling about thirty yards ahead of us jerks forward as if something speeding in our direction collided with it. The rustle of leaves quickly closes in on the search party line, but whatever's making the commotion remains hidden. I jump as a dog runs past me at full speed in the opposite direction we've been walking. And another. And two more. With their tails tucked, the dogs make a furious sprint out of the woods, barks quieted by something that's frightened them.

Quiet returns for a moment. We all start to move forward again, before someone's whistle blows far ahead on the left flank. We stop again to listen. It's a whistle blow every other second at first. Detective Holt and the other police officers break ranks with the search party line and race in the direction of the whistling. A moment later, the whistling becomes more rapid, and the pattern irregular. A gunshot rings out from the distance, followed by a momentary pause, before two more gunshots ring out in rapid succession, echoing through the forest. Another short whistle blast, followed by a scream, shatters the quiet. *That's not a dog's yelp. That was a human scream, a man's!* Tee and I take a retreating step. Robby's frozen.

A thousand simultaneous droplets tap on the leaves of the trees above, before big drops of rain begin to fall into the woods and land on our bodies. A roar of thunder crashes ahead and the rain intensifies to a deluge.

"Let's get out of here!"

Tee's sharp scream acts as a starter's pistol. We race through the woods, chilly rainwater soaking our bodies. Moments later, the search party breaks apart, everyone heading to Parson Street. We're the first ones to come sprinting out of the woods into a torrential rainfall. As we leave the shelter of the tree canopy and move into the clearing, angry raindrops pelt our faces. Roaring rivers of rainwater flow into the storm drain at the end of Parson Street.

"What the hell was that?" Tee screams at me through the clamor of the storm as we jump on our bikes.

"I don't know!" Water drips from my face, my shivering scream barely audible in the fury of the storm.

Face blanched, Robby stands there trembling, rain water cascading his face before rolling off his nose. I grab him by the shoulder and shake him.

"Robby, come on!"

A close flash of lightning zips to the ground, unleashing an ear-shattering boom, and the thunderous rumble shakes the ground beneath our feet. Robby snaps out of his trance and jumps onto his bike. We pedal as fast as we can, furious lightning bolts dropping from the sky all around us. We pull into my driveway as the sky continues licking the earth with its slender, brilliant, white tongues. After rolling dismounts, we sling our bikes into a haphazard pile on the lawn and rush inside to escape the storm's fury.

CHAPTER 14
Paradox

Officer Clancy stoops and winces. "I think it's John Watson."

The rain begins to subside, but loud roars of thunder crackle in the distance. Detective Holt stands above what remains of John Watson. *What in God's name? Dammit. This is on me. I called for this search party.* Detective Holt and Officer Clancy arrived at the scene less than two minutes after the first whistle blew. None of this makes any sense to Holt. *How can something do all this damage in such a short period and not still be here?*

Officer Morrow comes running to the area. His jaw drops. "Jesus."

Though positioned closest to John Watson in the search party line, Detective Holt and Officer Clancy passed the much older Officer Morrow with ease. Flirting with his sixties, their youthful speed outmatched him, proving too fast for him to keep pace.

Officer Morrow surveys the immense damage. It looks like something ripped John Watson to pieces, his left leg severed at the thigh, his shredded camouflage pants draping gore and his right arm severed an inch above the elbow. A few yards away from his body lies his missing arm still clutching the whistle. The whistle string snapped, ripped from his neck with violent force. He's missing a big chunk of flesh from his left side, exposing torn muscle and portions of his rib cage. Large puddles of blood and chunks of flesh litter the ground around his body. His fresh wounds still ooze thick arterial blood. His pale, lifeless face rests sideways on the saturated soil, wide-open eyes stuck in a forever gaze and his mouth agape mid-scream.

Officer Morrow breaks the silence. "Did you check for a pulse?"

"Are you kidding me? There's hardly enough of him left to check for anything." Officer Clancy gulps and shakes his head. A moment of digestible silence ensues. "You reckon a bear got him, Holt?"

A bear hadn't attacked anyone in eleven years in Harper Pass. Even when attacks did happen, they typically didn't result in death. Fatal bear attacks tended to transpire over an extended period of time. This happened in a couple of minutes. Detective Holt grimaces. *What kind of bear could do this much carnage in less than two minutes*?

Officer Morrow frowns, shaking his head. "That had to be a huge bear."

Detective Holt nods and motions his eyes to the creek.

"I'd say the same thing that got John is what got those dogs, too."

"Maybe John came up on a mama bear and her cubs. They can get pretty vicious," Officer Clancy offers.

Officer Morrow approaches the body and stoops, tilting his head as he surveys the wounds.

"It doesn't look like any bear attack I've ever seen, I'll tell you that. I mean, have you ever seen a black bear do something like this? Maybe a grizzly bear, *and I do mean maybe*. But there aren't any grizzlies in these parts."

"Yeah, I mean, it looks like he's been torn limb from limb." Officer Clancy swallows hard as his stomach turns on itself.

"Anybody see this happen? You were with them on the left flank. Anybody say they saw anything as you were running up?"

"No, John ran so far ahead of everyone when he heard his dogs in trouble."

"Those dogs didn't fare much better either." Clancy surveys the heap of canines. It's hard to tell for sure because of the mangled mess, but it looks like seven dead dogs lie there in Grief Hollow. They're torn apart. The various grave injuries range from one missing its head to several missing multiple legs. Clancy gulps as he eyes a disemboweled dog several yards from the others, its body lying on the edge of Copperhead Creek, blood still flowing from its wounds. Canine blood and mountain water mix, tinting the creek water a light shade of vermilion.

A faint whimper underneath the tangle of dead dogs and severed limbs cuts through the silence. Officer Clancy lifts away one of the dog carcasses to find another dog beneath, mortally wounded and bleeding profusely but clinging to life. Several gaping holes in its body give gruesome glimpses of its organs, no chance it will survive.

The wounded dog lifts pitiful eyes to Officer Clancy, mustering only a soft whimper, death climbing its trembling body, tightening its embrace. Officer Clancy kneels and pets the suffering dog's head.

"Shhhh, shhhh, it's okay, girl."

A tear rolls down Officer Clancy's cheek as he unsheathes his service weapon and takes aim. A loud bang breaks the silence and echoes through the forest.

The light rain ceases, but small droplets of water fall from the leaves above to the forest floor. The men, soaked through by the sudden thunderstorm, trudge around in their heavy uniforms, carrying on with their work without complaint.

Detective Holt scans the surrounding woods, hairs lifting on the nape of his neck. His eyes flit to the trees to his left, his hand finding his holstered pistol as his eyes work through the rest of the tree line in Grief Hollow. Nothing out of the ordinary that he can place, but a chill travels through him. Holt flinches at Morrow's voice.

"Let's see if we can find some bear tracks."

The men kneel, sifting through the debris on the forest floor. They work with swift determination, uncovering large patches of the ground to the damp earth. Officer Clancy shifts a large pile of leaves with his fingertips and hits something solid.

"Got something here, Holt. It looks like John Watson's rifle, but it's all twisted up." Officer Clancy lifts the rifle from the earth.

The steel barrel of the rifle is twisted like a child's curly straw. Three spent shell casings line the ground near the spot where Officer Clancy found the rifle.

"Looks like the rifle jammed. Holt, there's some kind of oily black stuff on the stock." Officer Clancy changes his grip to hold the twisted barrel instead.

"Let's see that."

Detective Holt examines the rifle, his eyes still making momentary stabs at the tree line. Officer Clancy brushes his hand and fingertips on his pant leg, cleaning off the black smudges while Detective Holt studies the rifle. The black goo looks similar to the substance they found on the brown backpack. *But how can this be Sammy and Myron's work? Sammy's a degenerate, sure, but his eyes— He was telling the truth at the station. He wasn't in the woods with that backpack. Got to be connected though. Myron? Maybe so.* Detective Holt shakes his head. *Can't see how he would've done all this though.*

Detective Holt lifts the stock of the rifle near his nose and sniffs the black oily substance. No discernable odor, but its tackiness clings to his fingers. He pulls a glass vial from his jacket pocket and retrieves the wooden cotton swab from inside. After collecting a small glob of the oily substance, he puts the cotton swab inside the vial and closes it.

Officer Morrow nods in the direction of the rifle. "Whatcha make of that? I've never seen anything like it."

Officer Clancy shrugs his shoulders. "Maybe the bear got it twisted up against the tree or something and bent it all up."

"Maybe." Detective Holt draws in his lips. "But there's not a scratch on it."

"Strange," Officer Morrow replies.

Detective Holt squints at several bare patches of earth and surveys the surrounding forest floor.

"You guys see any bear tracks when you moved those leaves?"

Officer Clancy shakes his head, lips tucked in a frown. "No. Not a one."

"Me neither."

"Let's see if we can't find some." Detective Holt lays the rifle on the ground and begins clearing the leaves from more areas. *Something seems wrong. Bear tracks. Got to be bear tracks.*

The other men join and sift through the leaves. As Officer Morrow steps closer to Copperhead Creek, he scoops his arm across the ground and sends a pile of leaves plummeting from the steep bank.

"Well, that's odd."

"What's that?" Detective Holt continues sifting through leaves, never lifting his head, still chasing an explanation.

"There's some big animal tracks here, but they're not bear tracks. Not sure what to make of it. If I didn't know any better, I'd say they look like the tracks of a chicken. Like a giant, four-hundred-pound chicken."

Officer Clancy's eyes perk. "Hey, not that this matters, but isn't John Watson a chicken farmer?"

"Yeah, he is. Let me see that." Detective Holt joins Officer Morrow to inspect the tracks. Several large indentations, patterned like the innards of a peace symbol, appear compacted into the soggy earth. Gouges at the tips of the toes extend several inches deep. *Claw marks?* Holt rubs his temple and frowns. "Clancy, I want you to make sure we get a cast of this."

"You got it, Holt."

"Marcy, you there? Over."

"Yes, I'm here, Holt. What you need?"

"Can you send for Mr. Latrell? Over."

"Mr. Latrell? You mean *the coroner*?"

"Yes, have Mr. Latrell meet us down here in Grief Hollow. Over."

"*Oh no*. Did you guys find that poor girl?"

"No, not Margo. It's John Watson. We may have had some kind of animal attack. It's hard to say. I'm not really sure. Can you also call someone from the State Fish and Wildlife

Service in? We're going to need to have them examine the body. Over."

"I'll call them both now. Over."

The three men stand there for a few minutes, studying the gruesome scene, trying to piece something together. But the pieces aren't coming together, they're falling away, fragmented and misaligned. None of it makes any sense. Officer Morrow's a thirty-year veteran officer, but he's never seen anything similar. His stomach grows queasy. The walkie-talkie breaks the silence.

"Holt, Mr. Latrell is on his way. The State said they can have someone out here by tomorrow. Over."

"Thanks, Marcy. Over."

CHAPTER 15

The Dare

My mom delivers a tray of hot chocolates. "Here you go, boys."

"Thanks, mom." I grab a mug.

Tee and Robby respond in unison. "Thanks, Mrs. Raker."

My mom smiles and walks away. I snicker at the clothes I loaned Tee and Robby to wear after my mom threw our drenched clothing in the dryer. I'm not sure who looks funnier. My T-shirt swallows Tee like a gown. The shorts extend a few inches past his knees like some kind of hybrid between pants and shorts.

Robby can barely fit into my clothing. The shirt doesn't even reach his waistband, creating a gap of several inches that exposes his stomach. I grin. The shorts pay homage to old basketball movies, ending above his mid-thigh.

I motion to the basement door with my eyes and keep my voice to a whisper. "Downstairs."

We file out of the room as silent as a funeral procession, descending the staircase to the basement, making our way to a round poker table where we all take a seat. Tee breaks the silence.

"Somebody wanna tell me what happened back there?"

The memory of what transpired replays in my mind. "I don't know. I heard four gunshots, I think."

Robby shakes his head. "Three. There were three gunshots."

"Who in the world was shooting? And who... or what were they shooting at?" Tee shakes his head slowly. "I mean, I thought we were supposed to be looking for Margo, not shooting at her."

Robby gets up from his chair and paces. "I don't think it was the police. I could still see all of them when we heard the shots."

"What about Mr. Wadlow? *That was weird.* He ran off in the middle of the search party."

"Definitely strange. He picked something up and put it in his pocket before he took off running. You saw it too, Tee. But those shots came from Grief Hollow. That's not the direction he ran in."

"Could've changed direction after we lost sight of him. But I don't know how he could've gotten so far ahead of us. Then again, he *was* running."

Robby wears the carpet thin, traveling in the same six-foot path. "Did you guys see what he picked up?"

Tee gives a subtle shake of his head. "Couldn't really tell. Looked like something small and white, but the end was black, I think."

"It was skinny. But I didn't get a good look at it either."

Robby pivots, reversing his walking direction. "The question's why would he pick something up in the woods in the middle of a search party and then run off?"

"Maybe he's got something to do with Margo being missing." Tee rolls his hands over to his open palms. "Maybe it was like evidence or something."

"I don't know. But whatever it was, he didn't want anyone else to see. Did you see how he looked all around to see if anyone was watching him?"

"Yeah, then he put that thing in his pocket and ran. That guy's up to something for sure."

Robby comes to an abrupt stop. "We should follow him."

My startled eyes meet Robby's.

"Follow him? That guy's creepy. Bad idea!"

"You said yourself, he was acting strange. And I'd say suspicious. He might lead us to Mysterious Margo."

"Or lead us to our death." I cut eyes to Robby. His facial expression remains unchanged. *He's serious.* "Robby, that's the police's job."

"Relax, Brooks. We're just going to follow him. You know, *from a safe distance.* He won't see us. Let's just find out what he's up to."

"Yeah, Brooks. Let's figure this thing out. Gonna be heroes. Then, I'm gonna ask out Heavenly Everly. And she's going to say yes." Tee raises both of his arms like a referee signaling a touchdown in a football game.

Robby snickers at Tee. "Not dressed like that, she's not."

"You'll see." Tee grins, standing up. He grabs the ends of the shirt, billows it out like a skirt and twirls. We all snicker.

"You're so stupid, Tee." Robby wears a persistent grin. A few moments of silence pass before he lifts his head. "What about Brady Palmer?"

Tee draws the corner of his lip. "What about 'em? Kid's a weirdo. I think juvie may've messed his head up good. I mean, what was he talking about?"

"Yeah. But that was weird. All that talk about Grief Hollow." I check both boys' eyes but find Tee's dismissive.

Robby shakes his head, expelling a deep breath. "'It can be what it wants to be.' What's that even mean?"

"Means the kid spent too many years in juvie. I'm telling you, man. The guy's got issues." Tee circles his index finger around his ear.

"Yeah, but something's up with Grief Hollow. The snake thing I saw. Now today. Maybe he knows something."

"That big can of crazy? Dude's nuts! Bet he doesn't even know what he's talking about."

Robby frowns at Tee. "Well, what's up with people disappearing? First, Margo does it on you yesterday. Where'd Brady go?"

I shake my head twice. "Looked away when I heard the dogs yelping. That's the last time I saw him."

Robby nods. "Yeah, me too."

"Okay, so he's crazy, *and quick*. Doesn't mean anything. So what if he's the fastest nut in the nuthouse." Tee's joke elicits a snicker from me and Robby.

Robby pauses from his pacing. "Speaking of quick, one of those dogs almost knocked me over."

"Me too!"

Tee's eyes widen. "Now that was weird."

"My dad used to take me deer hunting. I've never seen trained hunting dogs do anything like that."

I nod at Robby. "Those dogs were scared. Did you see how they all had their tails tucked? I mean, they would've run through a tree if it was in front of them."

"I still think the answer to all of this has got something to do with Mr. Wadlow." Robby checks our eyes for agreement.

"It's a start."

"Maybe. What he did back there doesn't make any sense. But what are we supposed to do? I mean, really." I swivel out both of my palms. "Not like we can just go up to him and say, 'Hey, Mr. Wadlow, what'd you do with Mysterious Margo?'"

"No man, it's like Robby said. We follow him. See what he does."

"Sounds risky. What if he *did* do something to her?" I take a deliberative pause. "What if he does the same thing to *us*?"

"This is covert ops. Like Cloak of Assassins. He's not even going to know we're there." Robby mimics operating a controller, his grinning eyes landing on me.

"Dude, that's a video game. This is real life. *Our life!*"

"Chillax man. It's going to be fine." Robby's grin deepens as I shift in my chair.

"Yeah, man. Plus, we got the N.C.B. with us."

I shake my head. "What's the N.C.B.?"

"Nut Cracker Brooks!" Tee and Robby crack up laughing.

"Funny, but I'm serious."

"I'm serious, too. If Mr. Wadlow messes with us, we'll have the N.C.B. take care of him. Crush his nards." Robby chuckles at Tee's joke, grinning at him.

I flash big eyes and frown. "I don't think it's a good idea."

"We're doing it," Robby blurts out in an overbearing tone.

"No. I'm not."

"Oh yes you are." There's no hesitation in Robby's delivery.

"Yeah, I dare you to, Brooks."

"What do you even mean? That's a stupid dare. This could be dangerous." I shift in my seat, eyes volleying between Robby and Tee.

Robby clears his throat. "Remember the rules. If another member of the Markland X Crew dares you to do something, you have to do it."

"But I can't. My mom's going to kill me."

"Your mom's not even going to know."

"But it's a stupid idea. And a dumb dare."

"Didn't say it wouldn't be a dumb dare, and you agreed to the rules, Brooks." Robby lifts his brows at me as if testing my loyalty to the Markland X Crew.

A windup grin forms on Tee's face. "Yeah. Refuse a dare and you go bare!"

"Guys, we're not going to find anything out."

"I say we make him go bare in front of Heavenly Everly, Robby."

My face becomes a furnace at the mention of Alyssa Everly and me going nude, heat pouring into my cheeks. My recurring dream bobs to the surface of my consciousness, its scenes assaulting my mind: standing in the school hallway unaware of my own nudity, approaching her at her locker, regurgitating my memorized lines asking her to the dance. The change of her expression, the uncontrollable laughter, the terrible pointing, the humiliation. It's too much. I wince. Robby grins at the terror in my eyes. They *own* me and he knows it. *I'm screwed.*

"So, it's settled then." Robby slaps his palm on the table.

"Yeah, let's find out what that Wadlow creep is up to. He lives right there on High Street."

I take a deep breath and accept that I've lost. "Okay, so what's the plan?"

CHAPTER 16
New Neighbor

My mom greets us as we emerge from the basement. "Oh, there you are boys."

She's standing near a pretty woman with jet-black hair and a boy who looks to be around our age. The woman smiles at Tee, Robby and I. Cherry-red headphones dangle from the boy's neck. He seems foreign to me with his tan skin juxtaposed against my alabaster complexion. And no way he escaped Culver's Barber Shop with that long bleach blonde hairdo intact. Several wavy strands dip past his eyes to the tops of his cheeks, and the longer hair in the back collects on his shoulders—not the style in Harper Pass. Though slender, his arm and leg muscles show definition, the kind of body tone that eludes most boys our age.

"Boys, I want you to meet the Trask's. This is Mrs. Trask and her son, Devin." My mom gestures for us to come forward.

Devin gives a quick head nod and a little half-smile as he surveys the funny fitting clothes that Robby and Tee are wearing. Devin's wearing some dark blue board shorts and a white Volcom T-shirt, a strange ensemble for Harper Pass.

"Boys, Devin just moved in next-door in the old Ellis place. They're from San Diego, California. Brooks, Mrs. Trask tells me Devin's going to be in seventh grade next year, too."

"Cool. Hey, Devin." I give him a small wave before trying to get to the business at hand. "Mom, we're going to go back out to play. Okay?"

"Oh, that's great. Tee and Robby's clothes just finished drying." *Guess she hasn't heard about what happened at the search party yet.* My mom turns to Mrs. Trask. "The boys got caught in a rainstorm earlier. You boys can show Devin around the neighborhood."

My mom always does this. Going out of her way to welcome new neighbors. She did this with Mark Crudleman and his mom when they moved onto the street. Her eyes fix on mine. This isn't debatable. The other boys sense it, too. *At least now we won't have to follow Mr. Wadlow. No telling what he's done. Or might do. And this kid looks okay. Strange, but okay. This worked out perfect.* I smile.

"Here you go boys." My mom hands them their dry clothes. "Why don't you boys go ahead and get changed? One of you can use the half bath there, and the other can get changed in Brooks' room." She directs Tee and Robby in opposite directions.

My mom continues making small talk with Mrs. Trask. Devin flashes me a momentary smile, shifting his weight from foot to foot. *Looks nervous. Probably should try to talk to him. Bet he feels weird with mom inserting him into our group.*

"Hey, man, I'm Brooks." I extend my hand for a shake.

Devin swings his hand, hitting my hand on the palm with his palm, following through before reversing his swing in the opposite direction, tapping my hand a second time. *That's a weird shake.*

"S'up, man? I'm Devin. But my friends call me Dev."

"Cool. Nice to meet you, Dev." Silence ensues. *Awkward. Not really sure what else to say.*

"Hey, brah, really sorry about moms. Didn't know she was going to bring me over here. I feel bad about crashing your guys' deal."

"It's okay, man. Really. We're probably just going to go play or something. You can come along."

"So what's to do in this town? No waves, I know that."

"We ride our bikes and stuff. Tee and Robby play on the school basketball team."

"That's cool. Like to shred that hill outside, that's for sure."

Tee descends the staircase, and Robby makes his way out of the bathroom. They exchange a glance followed by a grin. My mom walks to the door.

"Now why don't you boys go have some fun. Show Devin around." She ushers us out the door.

"Guys, this is Dev. He's from California."

"Yeah dumbbell, we heard your mom." Tee slathers his words in sarcasm.

Robby grins and gives Devin a fist bump greeting. "So, what's up, man? You ready for an adventure?"

"Sounds sweet. I'm in."

I lift my brows at the suddenness of his answer, not a moment of hesitation.

"Like you already, Dev. You're much more agreeable than Brooks." Tee gives me a playful punch on the shoulder.

"Wait, you guys can't be serious. You still want to go through with this?"

Robby grins wide. "A dare's a dare."

"But what about Dev?"

"You just heard him. He's in." Robby gives two thumbs up with a grin, his chestnut eyes shimmering in the sunlight.

"I'm up for whatever, brah."

"Quit trying to back out of the dare, Brooks." Tee nudges me, sporting a grin.

"What's the dare?"

"Follow me." Robby leads us to the end of the driveway. He tells Devin about Mysterious Margo and what transpired at the search party earlier that morning. Devin listens as Robby recounts how Mr. Wadlow acted suspicious and about the unusual things Brady Palmer told us. Tee tells him about the dogs yelping and freaking out. I can't help but jump in the mix.

"And then there were three gunshots!"

"Yeah, it was like *pow*." Tee mimes the recoil of a pistol. "And then, *pow*, *pow*!"

"And I thought this town was going to be boring."

"That's not the half of it. Brooks saw Mysterious Margo in the woods yesterday. She was saying some weird crap to him, and then something chased him in Grief Hollow." Tee puts ominous emphasis on Grief Hollow leaving Devin with questioning eyes.

"So that's it, man. We think Mr. Wadlow might have something to do with the disappearance of Mysterious Margo, so we're going to go do some recon. Cloak of Assassins style." A reckless luster brews in Robby's eyes like a gathering storm.

"Love that freakin' game, brah. And hell yeah. I'm in."

"Alright Dev, my man!" Tee gives him a celebratory fist bump.

"So, where's your bike?" Robby surveys the driveway. "Mr. Wadlow lives on High Street. We figured we'd roll over there and check it out."

"No bike, but I got this." Devin walks to the stoop by the brick stairs. He reaches into the bushes and pulls out a skateboard. It's covered in dings and scratches, the bottom emblazoned with a crazy skull with vampire fangs. Tee sniggers.

"How you gonna keep up with us on that thing? You gotta be kidding?"

"Watch!" Devin tosses the skateboard onto the driveway and jumps onto the deck. Giving the ground two quick pumps with his foot, he accelerates, racing to the end of the driveway. In an athletic crouch, he maneuvers the skateboard like an extension of his body, commands it as he would one of his own limbs, making it respond to every subtle movement he makes. He hops the curb and launches into the air, grabbing the board as he sails. The wheels strike the street with a thud. With expert precision, he shifts his weight to his back foot, lifting the front of the skateboard into the air. The back of the skateboard grinds into the pavement as he skids to a stop. He looks at us, wearing a huge grin. He taps his foot on the end of the skateboard popping it into his awaiting hand before strutting the length of the driveway to us.

Tee's lower jaw lunges. "Holy crap! That was awesome!"

"Okay. *Impressed.*" I can't muster anything else.

Robby shakes his head with a grin. "Where'd you learn how to do that?"

"Memorial Skatepark. Back in San Diego. I can teach you guys if you want."

"Dev, I'm definitely going to take you up on that. But not right now... Right now, we have a mission."

"Let's do it." Devin flips his hair from his face with a quick head whip.

"Now that's what I'm talkin' 'bout." Tee's eyes are aflame.

It's clear that we're feeding off Devin's energy. We all instantly love him.

CHAPTER 17

Mr. Wadlow

"Let's do this." Robby hops on his bike and rolls into the street.

"Yeah, buddy," Tee chimes, following close behind.

I grab my bike as Devin jumps onto his skateboard, veering out of the driveway and onto the street. We coast together down Slippery Hill. Devin carves a meandering descent, riding a wave of asphalt, leaning in like he's attacking the apex of a cresting wave before making a swift weight adjustment, sending him charging to us. Robby and Tee exchange grins, a giddy acknowledgment of our flawed assumptions. Devin finds no issues keeping pace with us on his skateboard.

Robby jumps the curb at the corner of Slippery Hill and Chambers Road, landing on Chambers without missing a beat. Tee and I stay in the roadway and hang a hard right. As if responding to an unspoken challenge from Robby, Devin jumps the corner of the curb as well and gets massive air before landing on Chambers Road and righting the direction of his skateboard. After a few quick leg kicks, he catches Tee and I. Robby grins as he leads the group on Chambers Road.

Curiosity commandeers my gaze, casting it down Parson Street. Robby points to the spot where the search party began, providing context to the story we told Devin. The two squad cars remain parked at the end of the street. The pickup truck is gone, but there's a new vehicle in its place, a shiny, black station wagon.

Tee's eyes grow wide. "Whoa! Did you see that?"

I swivel my head around for another look. "Yeah, what was that thing?"

"That's a hearse, bro." Devin's words spill out nonchalant as he glides on his skateboard.

My stomach tumbles. "Like for picking up bodies?"

Robby frowns, crimping his lips. "Yeah, wonder who they found?"

"Hope it's not Margo."

Robby shakes his head. "No way, Tee. We'd've already heard about it."

My stomach turns on itself. *This is a really bad idea.* "Maybe we should go back and try to figure out what's goin' on."

Robby looks at me and grins. "Nice try, Brooks. That's what the news is for. We're going to Wadlow's house."

Robby starts pedaling faster. I can tell what he's doing, trying to set the pace of the group so fast that it stifles any further debate. Tee raises his eyebrows, eyes wide, a hint of a frown on his lips, but he's pedaling hard to match Robby's pace. Devin's grinning ear to ear and pumping his leg to gain speed.

This isn't an argument I'm going to win. I stand on my bike pedals to gain more power and leverage. I pedal hard until I catch the group as we make the turn onto High Street.

My smile crumbles as we coast onto the cracked pavement of Mr. Wadlow's street. My pulse quickens as the reality of what we're doing here begins settling in, plucking my nerve endings like guitar strings. Robby hops off his bike while it's still moving and hustles it over the curb, rolling it into a vacant lot. Tee, Devin and I follow, stashing our bikes and

Devin's skateboard between some trees and thick brush. We huddle there in a circle. Robby points to a one-story house.

"Mr. Wadlow's house is that yellow one over there."

"So, what do we do now? Just watch?" A crackle in my voice betrays me.

Devin grins. "I think we should go over there for a closer look."

How the hell is he smiling?

Tee cuts skittish eyes to Devin. "Dude's car is parked out front. He'll spot us for sure."

Finally! Another person with some common sense. I can tell Tee's comfort level with what we're doing is wavering. Sure, he talks a big game, but Tee resembles me more than Robby, our daring not our most effervescent personality trait.

"Chill out, Tee. Dev's right. We can't see anything from here."

"We can just walk down the road. Nothing should look unusual about that. Kids walk down the road in this town all the time, right?" Devin checks our faces for agreement and settles on mine as if waiting for an answer.

"I mean, I guess so. But what are we supposed to do when we get down there? Just stand in front of his house and stare?"

"No, we walk past the house. You see that hedgerow over there between Wadlow's house and the next house?"

"Yep, and then we go down the hedgerow to the side of the house for a closer look." Robby hoists a big smile. He's already beginning to complete Devin's thoughts.

"Exactly!" Devin fist bumps Robby.

"He's gonna see us for sure if we do that." Tee's voice crackles like distant thunder.

"Yeah, what are we supposed to say if we get caught?"

"We won't get caught."

"Dev's right. Look. You see the side of the house, right?" Robby points to the side of the house closest to us. "This side doesn't have any windows. I bet the other side's exactly the same."

My stomach churns and I frown. "I've got a bad feeling about this."

"Yeah. I don't know about this, guys." Tee's eyes swim around the group. "Why don't we just watch from here?"

"Well, I got good vibes, man." Devin grins, bright eyes sparkling. He bounces his shoulders playfully. "Lighten up, guys. It's going to be fun."

"Or dangerous," I reply with wide eyes.

"Tee, we can't see anything from here. And Brooks, it's going to be fine. Trust me."

"I guess." My voice wavers at Robby's assurance. Tee shoots wary eyes in my direction.

"Don't forget about Heavenly Everly," Robby reminds with a smile.

"Who's Heavenly Everly?"

"The hottest girl at our school. Alyssa Everly. Tee thinks she's going to go out with him after this."

"Not think, I *know* she is, Brooks."

"Not if she finds out you puss'd out!"

Tee shakes his head at Robby. "Okay, okay. I'm in." His voice is a begrudging grumble.

Everyone turns to me; I shrug my shoulders and mentally prepare for the worst. Robby reads my body language and grins.

"Glad to see you have your winning attitude back, Brooks."

I take a deep breath trying to settle my nerves. Robby and Devin lead the way with Tee and I following. Devin and Robby both sport an extra bounce in their step. *They're excited about this? Really? This is so dumb. We're going to get into so much trouble.* But from somewhere unknown, a faint smile finds my lips, and a tingle blooms in my chest. *Seriously, Brooks? You too? Excited? Don't be an idiot. Listen to your fear. So what if Harper Pass is boring? Better bored than dead!*

As we walk past Mr. Wadlow's house, Robby and Devin act nonchalant, mimicking enthralling conversation. They avoid making eye contact with the house.

Tee and I don't exhibit as much discipline. We both turn our heads to sneak a peek.

Everything looks quiet. Three large, overgrown rose bushes in the yard reflect the overall neglect of the property. Though unkempt, beautiful blooms of red and white spiral out from their branches, and their sweetness perfumes the air. An older silver sedan sits parked on the curb. Dingy, yellow siding clings to the house like a deteriorating exoskeleton, the blinds drawn, and curtains shut. There's no sign of Mr. Wadlow. *How's this even going to help us find Margo? We're never going to know if Mr. Wadlow had anything to do with her disappearance.*

As Devin and Robby approach the hedgerow, they change direction in unison as if choreographed and beeline down the hedgerow in Mr. Wadlow's yard. Tee and I follow. Once Robby and Devin descend far enough into Mr. Wadlow's yard that they can avoid detection from the street, they dart across his driveway to a cluster of bushes by the house. They're crouching behind the bushes as Tee and I rush in behind them.

My heart thumps in my chest. "This is crazy, guys. We can't even see anything over here."

"Yeah, we could get into a lot of trouble." Tee's eyes frantically scan our periphery.

"Relax, guys." Robby motions open palms to the ground. Robby and Devin rise and grab a quick view of the house before crouching with us. "Guys, there's a window." There's hushed excitement in Robby's voice.

"I didn't see any windows."

"That's because it's right by the ground, Brooks. It's like a half window."

"I think it's to the basement." Robby motions to the house with his thumb like a hitchhiker and whispers, "We need to get over there and take a look inside."

"*For what*?" Tee's voice jumps several decibels.

Devin and Robby both turn to Tee and latch their pointer fingers to their lips.

Tee lowers his volume. "For what?"

Robby tilts his head and flashes big eyes at Tee. "So we can see if he has Mysterious Margo."

Devin nods at Robby. "Basement's a good place to hide someone."

"We're gonna get busted." Tee's words collide together like a freeway pileup.

"We're not going to get busted, Tee. If you'd just keep your voice down." Robby narrows cutting eyes on Tee.

"Follow me." Devin gets low to the ground, crawling, weaving through the bushes to the window.

"*Love this guy.*" Robby grins at Tee and I before he trails behind Devin.

"Come on, Tee." I follow them to the window.

Upon reaching the window, we lie flat on our bellies in the dirt. The window sits about two feet off the ground and rises about twelve inches tall by three feet wide. It's covered in grime and pollen dust, obscuring the view inside. Robby rubs the window with his palm, careful not to make any noise, and the dirty haze begins to clear away. Devin joins in on the glass, and they work their way to the middle. I get a foggy view of the ceiling inside. A shining lightbulb with no fixture protrudes from a wooden ceiling joist. From my vantage point a couple of feet away from the window, my view of the room cuts off about three feet below the ceiling.

There isn't space for all of us by the window. Robby and Devin secure the best view for themselves. They press their faces close to the glass, shielding their eyes with their hands to eliminate the glare of sunlight.

"What do you guys see?" I whisper.

"A guy." Devin presses his face closer to the glass. "He's looking through a microscope or something."

"Is it Mr. Wadlow?"

"Yeah." Robby's voice is no more than an exhale. "Yeah, I think so."

"You see Mysterious Margo anywhere?" Tee asks.

Robby turns his head to us. "No. I don't see her."

"What *is* that?" Devin sinks his head deeper into the shadow of his shielding hands. "Looks like he's cutting something."

"Let me take a look." Robby places his face to the glass.

"Can't tell. It's small. It looks white," Devin says.

"The part he's cutting. I think it's black."

"Sounds like what me and Tee saw him pick up in the woods."

"Dev, let's back up so Brooks and Tee can get a look."

Devin and Robby ease down from the window, crab crawling away to make some room. Tee and I crawl on all fours, taking their place at the base of the window. We raise our heads and peer inside.

Mr. Wadlow stands by a workbench, positioned against the wall, in the dimly lit basement. Stacks of old dusty books and newspapers tower high on a wire shelf in the middle of the room. Mr. Wadlow lifts something small from the workbench between his thumb and forefinger. As he shifts his weight, it glints in my direction. *Metal... A razor blade*?

My heart's thundering in my chest; it's beating so loud that—irrational as it seems—I'm worried that Mr. Wadlow might actually hear it. Even though we're outside, less than twenty feet separate us. He moves aside offering a glimpse.

"That's it, Tee. That's the thing he picked up in the woods." But I can't make out what it is with certainty through the hazy window.

"I think so too." Tee's voice trails into a soft trickle.

It appears he's making a precision cut. He takes the sliver, puts it on a glass slide and slides it under his microscope. As he stoops to place his eye on the lens of the microscope, we get a much more inviting view, but I still can't make an identification through the dirty glass. Tee jockeys for a closer position but loses his footing. He extends his hand to break his fall, and it hits the glass with a bang. Wadlow shoots his head in our direction.

"Down!" I grab Tee's shirt and yank him to the ground with me.

"Oh crap, I think he saw us!"

"What do we do?" My heart gallops, pumping hot blasts of blood.

"Take another look," Robby urges.

My eyes bulge. "*What*?"

"See if he saw you guys."

"We gotta run." Tee flashes high-beam eyes at me.

"Just look!"

I pant for air, frazzled nerves nudging my need for more oxygen, sweat tumbling from my open pores. My body shaking, I ease my eyes a couple of inches above the window ledge at the same moment Mr. Wadlow's legs disappear up the stairs leading out of the basement.

"Oh shit! He saw us. He's running up the stairs."

Tee spins his eyes around our surroundings. "We're trapped!"

My eyes career in all directions. *Nowhere to run*. A tall fence in the backyard and a thick, impassible, high hedgerow on the side box us in. Our lone option to flee requires us to run up the driveway to the street. And that isn't an option because Mr. Wadlow will catch us for sure.

"Spread out in the bushes and hide!" Devin jumps to his feet, runs a ways and dives between two hedges.

Tee and I scurry on all fours and hide in a cluster of bushes, both curled into the fetal position, trying to shrink our bodies as much as possible and dissolve into the cover of shrubbery.

Robby runs across the driveway and finds a small opening in the hedgerow. He forces himself inside it and slinks into the bush.

The loud thuds of footsteps round the corner of the house. Tee's rapid breathing steams my face, his eyes swelling with the intensity of the moment.

An older man's voice booms out. "Who's there?"

I peer around the corner through the bushes. It's Mr. Wadlow. He looks agitated and out of breath, his roaming eyes focused lasers. He inspects the bushes near the basement window. He looks around for a minute. *What will he do to us if he finds us? He'll kill us, surely.*

Tee's cheek hugs the dirt, facing me, arms tucked into his chest with his elbows together, his lips trembling. His eyes scream *please help me*. His hands quake, perpetual aftershocks rocking them. I shake my head at him, my eyes frozen wide. *Don't do it, Tee. Don't you dare make a noise!* I reach out my hand and take hold of his shaking hands, gripping them tight.

"*Damn kids!*" Mr. Wadlow fumes, followed by his retreating footsteps ascending the driveway.

A car engine sputters to a start on the street, tires briefly squealing. Robby peers out before running across the driveway. Devin rises from his hiding spot between two bushes.

Devin flashes big eyes at Robby. "Holy shit. That was close."

"Thought he had you for sure, Dev. He was right next to you."

Tee and I vacate our spot and run to Robby and Devin. Instead of moving away from the house, Robby ventures to the basement window. Once Robby catches the scent of something, it's difficult to pull him off.

"What are you doing?" Tee throws his hands in the air at Robby. "We gotta get the hell out of here!"

"No. This is our chance."

"*It's our chance to get away*!" My voice quavers, adrenaline still rocketing through me.

"Wadlow's gone. We're golden." Devin's eyes sparkle with mischief.

"He could be back any minute." I cut a glance to the street. "People go to jail for this stuff."

"This is what we came here for. To find out what happened to Mysterious Margo. I'm not going anywhere." A stubborn rigidity settles into Robby's tensed jawline.

"Yeah. And if anyone's going to jail, it's that Wadlow creep." Devin moves to the window with Robby.

Tee and I stand in the driveway with our mouths slung open. Robby drops to his knees by the basement window. He fiddles with it for a moment and the window comes open.

Robby casts eyes in our direction. "Who's going in?"

"What? *Are you crazy*?" My words fly out like a siloed missile, coordinates locked in on Robby.

Devin steps forward. "I'll go." Robby holds the window for him.

Devin crouches and slides a leg inside. He tries to work his body inside the window but can't fit in the small opening.

"Damn. I'm too big."

Robby's eyes lift suddenly. "Tee. Tee can get inside."

"*No way, man*!"

"Keep your voice down, bro." Devin pushes his palms at the ground.

"Come on, Tee. You're the only one who can fit."

"Yeah man. Don't you want to save your friend Margo?"

Tee throws eye daggers at Devin. "She's not my friend. You guys are my friends, *but you're not acting like it.*"

Devin taps his wrist with his forefinger. "We're wasting time."

Robby levels his eyes at Tee. "Do it, Tee."

This is crazy. "Guys come on. This is—"

"Fine. I'll do it. But you guys better not leave me." Tee hurries to the window.

"No way, man. You know that," Robby replies.

"Tee, you don't have to do this."

Tee looks at me and frowns.

Tee lifts one leg inside the window followed by the other. Robby and Devin each hold one of his arms, lowering him inside. A moment later his head disappears inside the basement. Robby and Devin both fall backward, and Tee's shoes smack on the basement floor. I surge to the window to secure a better view.

Robby scrambles to his knees and calls out. "Go see what that thing from the woods is."

Tee weaves past the wire rack with the dusty books and newspapers. A shaft of sunlight pours into the basement from behind me, collecting on a wall-mounted shelf that's lined with large glass jars, containing different animal specimens embalmed in fluid. Tee lingers by it, his eyes wandering the row. I crane my neck for a better view. In the jar closest to the window, a fetal pig's snout presses up against the glass lifting its mouth at the gumline, exposing its canines and sharp needle teeth. Another contains some type of strange, fan-finned sea creature.

"There's some weird shit down here, guys."

Tee steps closer to examine one of the jars. He tilts his head sideways, squinting his eyes at it before reaching for the jar. He screams and my head flinches as a cat jumps out from behind the empty jar of amber embalming fluid. It flies past Tee's head, lands on its feet, slides sideways, and scurries away. My heart hammers in my chest, growing more frantic with each ticking second that passes.

"What was that?" Devin calls out.

"A cat just jumped out at me!"

"Quit wasting time! Go see what's on that workbench." Robby barks the order with a quick headshake.

Tee scampers to the workbench. He stalls by the microscope and shuffles around the desk.

"I can't find it."

"Keep looking. It's got to be there." Robby draws in a deep breath through his nose and expels it through his mouth, his eyes fastened to Tee's every movement.

This is bad. He needs to get out of there. "Maybe he took it with him." Robby's lips tuck into a momentary frown as my words stumble out, but he doesn't reply or alter his gaze. I scooch in for a closer view, my forehead breaching the opening of the window.

Tee picks up a white cloth from the table, examining it closely. As he inspects the cloth, a visible tremor passes through his body, and it dangles from his shaky fingers. "Oh shit! Blood." His head rifles around the basement before returning to the cloth. "I gotta get outta here." His muttered words ride the coattails of his frantic exhale. As Tee goes to return the cloth to the spot where he found it, he abruptly recoils. His pallor grows ashen, and his eyes inflate like balloons on helium nozzles. The scarlet speckled cloth falls, fluttering from his fingertips. He takes a tentative step forward before anchoring his legs in place. He slowly cranes his head forward, squinting at something on the surface of the workbench. His head jerks back and his eyes burst wide.

"Oh Jesus!" He stumbles backward.

His back slams into the wire rack shelf, and it begins to tip. A car comes to a stop on the street, the squeak of its brakes alerting us to its arrival. Tee scrambles to hold onto the heavy wire rack to keep it from toppling, his fingers blanching white as he strains against its accumulating weight, his sliding feet surrendering ground.

Robby cuts big eyes to Devin. "Dev, go check that out."

Devin skirts the side of the house, running to the corner and peers around the rosebush at the street. "Wadlow's back! Get him out of there!"

The accumulating weight of the wire rack overpowers Tee. He loses his grip and jumps out of the way as it goes crashing to the basement floor, making a huge clamor. I cringe and stagger back a few steps into the grass. I gasp a breath before my whole body flash-freezes, becoming inanimate granite as Wadlow moves through my peripheral vision. But he doesn't see me. He's fumbling with his keys while hustling for his door. *Shit! He heard it!* I race back to the window. The boards on the front porch creak, marking Wadlow's steady advance.

"Get him out now!" Devin yells as he runs to us at the window, his voice a hushed torrent emanating from his throat.

Tee shakes his head, trying to clear the daze. He brushes off several old newspapers strewn on his body.

"Come on, Tee! Come on!" I twirl my hands in frantic circles, motioning him to the window.

Robby leans into the opening of the window and yells. "Tee, get out of there! Wadlow's back!"

The front door groans on its hinges. I crowd the basement window with Robby. Swift, thudding footsteps move through the house above, and corresponding sprinkles of dust rain from the unfinished ceiling as Wadlow makes his rapid advance. Tee sprints to the basement window, his gaping eyes glistening. Devin surges in from behind us, the force of the incidental collision knocking me aside. Robby and Devin reach their arms inside the window but can't reach Tee's raised arms. Tee's jumping, trying to grab their outstretched hands, but he isn't quite tall enough. The footsteps above close in on the basement door at the top of the staircase. My heart stampedes.

"We gotta go!"

Robby flashes cutting eyes in my direction. *"Never leave another member behind!"*

Tee's eyes ricochet around the room. He runs to a box in the corner of the room and sleds it to the window. The basement door squeals, and a widening sliver of light illuminates the basement staircase. *Wadlow's going to catch him for sure. He's dead!*

Tee makes one last jump from atop the box as the racing footsteps descend the staircase. Robby and Devin catch Tee's hands by his fingertips and work fast to secure their grip on his wrists. They tug him out of the window as Mr. Wadlow storms into the basement. Tee falls onto Robby and Devin in a jumbled pile.

"Let's go!"

My shrill shout springs all three boys to their feet. We break into a sprint on the driveway. Tee and Devin flash their speed, building a lead on Robby and me. Our arms pump with the ferocity of pistons in a redlining engine as we barrel down High Street to the vacant lot, adrenaline surging.

In a flash we grab our bikes and Devin grabs his skateboard. Running them out onto High Street, we mount our moving bikes and Devin jumps onto his board. We scream up High Street, a whirling blur of pedaling. Devin's leg churns, giving him more and more speed. After a quick turn onto Chambers Road, we continue our furious pace. We don't slow our speed until we reach the base of Slippery Hill.

We stop on the corner of Chambers Road and Slippery Hill. The speed of our escape prevented Mr. Wadlow from following us. Tee collapses in the grass, grasping for air to fuel his lungs. I'm doubled over desperate to pull more oxygen into my fiery lungs and calm my pounding heart. Robby hunches with his hands on his sides, his breathing devolving into loud, slobbery pants. Devin takes a seat on the deck of his skateboard. He pretzels his body, arms wrapped around his folded knees as he tries to quell his frantic breathing.

CHAPTER 18
Undercurrent

We're still catching our breath from our desperate escape from Mr. Wadlow's house. Tee lands shrieking eyes on me, his body caught in a perpetual cycle of tremors. Robby works to compose himself, managing words between heavy breaths.

"What... did you see? Did you... see Margo?"

"No, a finger."

Devin's head recoils. "What do you mean a finger?"

"A finger, *a human finger!*"

"Oh my god." My words crackle like a windswept flag. *Did Wadlow see us? Maybe. Oh God, he's going to kill us!*

Devin's burgeoning eyes settle on Tee. "Seriously?"

In the huddle of blood-drained faces, my thoughts race. *That was SO STUPID! What did we expect? It felt like a game. But oh Jesus. A finger... He's got a finger! He's a killer. We're so dead. We gotta tell someone.*

"We gotta go to the cops."

"What are we gonna tell 'em, Brooks? That we broke into Mr. Wadlow's house?"

"I'm not going to jail, man."

"Nobody's going to jail, Tee." Devin places a steadying hand on Tee's shoulder.

"But he's a killer!"

"We don't know that for sure, Brooks."

"What are you talkin' about, Robby? I'd say having a human finger in his basement's a pretty good sign. It's probably poor Margo's finger. He's probably got the rest of her body in his house somewhere, too."

Robby's eyes pulse wide, and he lifts his head. "Wait, didn't you say the finger was the thing you guys saw him pick up in the woods?"

"Yeah, so?"

Devin scrunches his lips. "But if he's a killer, why would he pick up a finger and bring it back to his house?"

Robby nods at Devin. "Yeah, why wouldn't he just get rid of it?"

"He's probably just covering up for his crime. Dude's a psycho. You should've seen all the creepy stuff in his basement."

"Or maybe it's like a trophy. My mom reads these books, *crime books*. She says sometimes killers take trophies."

Robby turns to Tee. "Well, did it look like Margo's finger?"

"*I don't know.* How am I supposed to know that?"

"Where'd you find it?"

"On his workbench. Under a cloth. Looked like he'd been taking slivers out of it. There was a razor blade by it." An animated shiver roars through Tee's body. "It was cut to the bone. I could see the bone!"

Robby shakes his head. "Why would he *do that*?"

"When me and Tee were at the window, I think I saw him put something he had cut on a glass slide and put it under the microscope."

Devin paces beside us. "That still doesn't make sense. I can't see why he'd do that."

Tee scowls. "Why? 'Cause he's a sicko! That's why."

"There's got to be another reason."

"No there doesn't, Robby. And why don't *you* think he's a killer?"

"I'm not saying he's not, Tee, but it just doesn't make sense is all."

I flash wide eyes at Robby. "Neither does picking up a finger in the woods and running off."

"True. That's why we need to keep an eye on him." The glimmer in Devin's eyes accompanying his words troubles me.

"Let the police do that. They can arrest him."

"We can't go to the police, Brooks. They'll know I was in his house."

"So, we make an anonymous phone call. Like a tip."

Devin shakes his head. "They can trace those calls back now. We'll get busted for sure."

"I say we just keep an eye on him." Robby pauses and surveys the group. "We don't know that he did anything yet."

"We know he took a finger!" My words explode like a cannon shot.

Tee shakes his head at Robby. "You can keep an eye on him, but I'm not getting anywhere near him or his house again."

"Dudes, even if we went to the police, Mr. Wadlow knows someone was in his house now. He knows someone was in the basement. There's no way he doesn't get rid of that finger. The police aren't going to find anything. And then, Mr. Wadlow's going to find out who was in his house."

Robby nods. "Good point, Dev."

A deep frown forms on Tee's face. "No way I want that creeper to know who I am."

I gulp hard at Devin's proclamation. *We're screwed! Can't go to the police. Can't go to our parents. Not like we can leave town. We're sitting ducks.*

"I say we find out whatever we can on him."

"I'm not going back there, Robby. Dare or no dare."

"No. That's not what I mean, Brooks. We can't go back there now, anyway."

"You wanna like ask around about him?"

Devin stops pacing. "That's a bad idea, Tee. Somebody might tell him we've been asking about him. He'd put two and two together."

Tee's eyes brighten. "We should search the internet. See what we can find on him."

Devin and Tee turn in my direction. I shake my head. "We can't do it at my house. My mom will know something's up for sure. Especially since school's out."

"Our stuff's not even unpacked yet."

"We can go to my house. Use my laptop."

"Sounds like a plan. But what about your mom and dad?"

A frown fissures Robby's face at Devin's mention of his dad. He lowers his eyes, scraping ground with his gaze, his hand drawn by instinct to the canteen on his belt. A solitary tear streaks Robby's cheek.

"What's wrong, man?"

"Robby's dad." I glance at Robby before wincing out more detail. "He was in an accident... A drunk driver."

"Bro, I'm so sorry. I didn't know."

"It's okay, Dev. You didn't... It's just... it just still..." Robby sputters before he can no longer choke back the tears.

Robby's eyes cloud with darkness. Tears stream his cheeks. He pulls his trembling arms tight around his quivering chest. His stomach tightens, growing concave, pulling into the turmoil beneath his skin. It's as if I can see the darkness moving through him, overtaking him. His posture slumps, his body curling in on itself like a wilting daisy. His tear ducts open like a faucet. He takes in abbreviated, rapid breaths through his nose—sobbing. Tee puts his arm around his shoulder, and I place my hand on his back.

Tee firms his hug. "It's gonna be okay, man. You got us. We're here. We're always gonna be here for you."

"I just miss him so much." Another powerful wave rocks Robby's body, whipping him toward the emotional jetty. His sobbing grows louder.

"Go ahead and let it out. Let it out, Robby. It's okay to let it out." A tear escapes Tee's eye with his words.

"You guys are the best friends I've ever had. I'll always be here for you. No matter what. *Brothers*." My voice fractures, the tortured grimace on Robby's face leaving my stomach as hollow as an empty grave. *It's not fair. Man... It's just not fair.* I deliver several soft pats on Robby's back, moisture gathering in my eyes.

Devin's face collapses into a deep-set frown. "Robby, I am so, so sorry. I feel terrible." Devin's eyes glisten and he places a hand on Robby's shoulder.

I've never seen Robby this way—vulnerable. He's always full of life and ready to tackle the next big challenge. He looks defeated.

As Devin's face flounders, I feel the weight of everything unsaid pressing upon me, the sharp divide separating Devin from the truth of Robby. The boy in pain behind that carefully constructed mask. The boy who lost his dad but also his mother to the long work hours and two jobs she had to get to support them. How the church turned its back on Robby and his mother after his grandparents paid for a Disney trip following his dad's death. How small-town grumblings, a secret stash of money, the family better off than they're pretending to be, became rumor that's accepted as fact. And how those rumors spread quick as wildfire in a small town like Harper Pass until the spigot of compassion runs dry. But it's not my place to tell.

Robby lifts his head and wipes away the tears from his weepy eyes. He takes in several deep breaths as he collects himself.

"Dev, it's fine. I'm fine." Robby sniffles as he wipes away the last of his tears.

"It's not fine. I know it's hard. My dad left me and my mom. Left us for another woman. That's why we're here. It's not like you, but I know how bad it hurts. He hasn't been to see me in over a year." Devin frowns and drops his head. "He didn't even call on my birthday."

I lift soft eyes to him. "Dev, that's terrible. Sorry, man."

"Yeah, that's awful." Tee shakes his head.

Robby regains his composure and lifts his hand away from the canteen. "Guess we have to rise above it. Be better because of it."

"That's right. I'm going to show *that bastard* just who he left behind. And you. *You, Robby. Your dad would be proud of you.*

He'll see the person you become. You keep him here... always." Devin taps his palm a couple of times over his heart.

Tee places his hand on Robby's shoulder and ropes his attention with tender eyes. "I believe that too, Robby. He sees you."

Robby's glistening eyes drift skyward to where the heavens meet the murky unknown. He lingers there, questions lifting from his longing eyes, rising silent as sky lanterns. After a moment, he draws a deep breath and sighs.

"Look man, I'm sorry I got so worked up. And I'm sorry to hear about your dad, Dev. My mom's at work. She's pretty much always at work. We can use the computer at my house. No one's gonna bother us."

"No worries, man. I totally get it. And I'm sorry too, about your dad."

After a moment of silence, Robby hardens his jaw. "Let's see what we can find out about Wadlow."

Tee points to the apex of the hill. "Hey, is that Seth and Shane?" Two kids emerge, pedaling their bikes at full speed.

I nod. "I think so."

Robby squints his eyes to the hill. "Wait. Who's that behind them?"

Tee shapes his hands against his forehead like the bent bill of a ball cap. "Looks like Cam Givers."

Robby's head whips around to us. "Dudes, not a word about Mr. Wadlow. Okay?"

"No way," Devin utters under his breath as the trio approaches.

Tee and I nod as the three boys come to a rolling stop on the corner. Hair disheveled and clothes torn, Cam continually checks to make sure no one is following them. Tee and Robby are friends with Seth and Shane, twin brothers in our same grade. I know Seth a little better because we shared a math class.

I wince at the sight of Seth's top lip, which is fat, busted, and oozing blood. My mind works through the possibilities, settling on the most likely, as I gaze at the thin stream of blood trickling out of Shane's nostril and the large goose egg rising like a dinner roll on his forehead. The number 5 scrawled on Cam's forehead in dark black ink confirms my suspicion. Robby, Tee and I meet each other's eyes and share a silent recognition of what that means. *Sammy Needles.*

"Watch out guys! Sammy and Bo are out there. Sammy's looking for you, Brooks! Look what he did to my head." Cam pulls out his asthma inhaler and takes a quick puff.

"Why'd he write that on your head?"

Cam, Shane, and Seth glance at Devin. The three of them study him for a moment, gauging the threat level he poses, if at all.

"Guys, this is Dev. He just moved in next-door to me."

Cam gives a small wave to Devin, his slight frame trembling, before taking another puff off his inhaler. He stashes the inhaler in his pocket. "Because he's a jerk. Always calling me 5-head."

Sammy Needles torments Cam Givers, an easy target for Sammy's wrath. Sammy coined the term *5-head* because of Cam's large, pronounced forehead, wielding it like a sledgehammer for relentless torture. And much to Cam's dismay, the name stuck.

Devin draws his lips up, sucking a puff of audible air through his clenched teeth. "Oh, sorry man. Sounds like a real scumbag."

Shane nods. "He is. Biggest bully in the Tri-County area."

"His dad's a mean drunk. *Beats him.* How's the saying go? The apple doesn't fall far from the tree," Robby explains for Devin's benefit.

Tee studies their various wounds and addresses Seth. "What happened?"

"Yeah, him and Bo was holdin' Cam down. Sammy wrote that 5 on his head with a marker. They was twistin' his arm real good. Wanted to know where you was, Brooks. Me and Shane tried to stop 'em."

"God, I hate those guys!" Tee's eyes seem to spark aflame.

"They was waiting in the woods on the side of Jennings Pike. Ambushed us." Shane's voice creaks like a rickety bridge.

Seth swivels toward me. "What'd you do, Brooks? He's out to kill you."

Robby grins. "Ole Brooksie Boy kicked him in the nuts yesterday."

Cam gasps.

"Nut Cracker Brooks!" Tee snickers.

"Are you crazy?" Seth blurts out, impulse conscripting his tongue. His eyes enlarge to the size of golf balls.

"I didn't mean to. It just happened." I draw in a deep breath. *Shit. I'm in big trouble.*

Shane shakes his head at me. "You're going to have to move or something. He wants to kill you now."

"That's not going to happen." Devin delivers the steely words with force.

Robby nods and hoists a subtle grin. "Yeah, Brooks is Markland X Crew now."

Devin shoots a glance to Robby. We haven't told him about the Markland X Crew. He searches Robby's eyes for meaning. I exhale a deep breath as a wave of tingling warmth inundates my chest. *Thank god. They're planning to stick up for me.*

"You guys better watch out." Cam's eyes linger on me like an undertaker measuring me for my coffin.

"We'll be careful." I swallow past the lump in my throat. *We'd better be.*

Tee flicks his chin at the trio. "Thanks for the heads up."

"Did you guys hear about what happened in the search party for Margo?" Shane's voice carries an ominous undertone.

"Hear about it?" Tee grins wide. "Hell, *we were there*."

"Did you see the bear?" Seth's wide eyes land on Robby.

"What bear? *You mean the dogs*?"

Shane's eyebrows draw close, skin contorting around his goose egg. "*No*...the bear. The one that killed John Watson and his dogs."

"*Whaaat*?" My response hangs in the air like a suspended kite.

Cam nods. "Yep, got him right there in Grief Hollow's what I heard."

Robby narrows his eyes on Cam. "Are you sure? That can't be right."

"Right as rain. Heard it from my cousin. His friend's dad's a deputy with the force, you know."

Devin shakes his head. "That's crazy sauce."

Seth dabs a bit of blood from his lip and shifts his eyes to Robby. "We're going to Cam's to lie low for a bit. You guys wanna come?"

"Thanks for the invite, but we're going to my house for some lunch."

Shane winces as he touches the swelling lump on his forehead. "You better go to Brooks' house. They'll catch you guys for sure if you go to your house."

"Well, there's four of us."

Cam lifts a brow at Devin. "I guess *you* haven't seen Sammy and Bo before, huh?"

"Nope."

"Well they're big, *real big*. And mean." Seth slides a finger across his bloody lip.

"We gotta go, guys." Cam's voice trembles. He continues casting glances at the apex of the hill where they emerged.

Tee gives a small wave. "Catch you guys later."

"*Good luck.*" Shane embeds his doubt for our fate in his inflection as the three boys start to pedal away.

We wait until they're a considerable distance away and can no longer hear our voices. *Grief Hollow, again. What's going on? Too much coincidence. Feels connected. Margo's disappearance, Mr. Wadlow, John Watson's death.*

"A bear attack? And in Grief Hollow? I'm telling you guys, something's going on in Grief Hollow."

"Maybe we should go check it out."

We all whip our heads in Devin's direction.

"*We can't go there*! You heard him. John Watson just got killed. Brooks almost got killed there." Tee shakes his head at Devin with eyes wide enough to ward off the devil.

Robby nods. "Yeah, plus the cops will be there. They're not going to let us anywhere near there."

"I guess you're right, but we should think about going there sometime. Maybe after this dies down. Might help us figure this thing out."

Tee cocks his head and delivers a sideways glance to Devin. I'm not sure what to make of Devin. In the few hours I've known him, I've already determined he's one of the bravest kids I've ever met. But I wonder what's behind that bravery. *Crazy or just curious*? *Maybe curious. We talked about it a lot. And he's never been. Probably just doesn't know any better.*

"Let's stick to the plan. Find out what we can about Mr. Wadlow," Robby overrules.

"I agree," Tee seconds.

I curl and unfurl my fingers several times. "We need to watch out for Sammy and Bo."

Robby hops on his bike. "Stay close together, guys. If Sammy or Bo try to do anything, we can hightail it away from them."

"They ain't catching me!" Tee flashes a grin as he hops onto his bike.

We cluster together on Chambers Road like a herd of antelope ready to evade a predator. Or in this case, *two predators*.

CHAPTER 19
Missing Pieces

Marcy Peterman pauses from her paperwork when Holt walks into the police station. "Holt, that TV reporter, Kasey Norton, keeps calling. I think she got wind of what happened to John Watson."

"Can't fart in the wind in this town without everyone knowing about it."

"She wants to talk to you for comment. What should I tell her?"

"Tell her *no comment.*"

Detective Holt walks past Marcy and through the row of cubicles. Officer Clancy sits hunched at his computer screen, studying something, toggling between two documents. Detective Holt hovers and fiddles with his mustache.

"What you got, Lance?"

"Labs are back on the blood we found by the backpack in the woods. It's human blood all right, but it isn't Margo Combs."

"How do you know?"

Lance enlarges the lab report on the screen and points at a line on the document. "Says here the blood we found was type AB+." Officer Clancy opens another document, a medical record. The top corner reads, *Combs, Margo.* Officer Clancy points on the screen to the middle of the document. "We subpoenaed Margo's medical records. Says right here she's O+. So, unless she changed blood types, that's not her blood we found."

"Well, if it's not Margo's blood, who the hell's blood is it?"

"I don't know. But whose ever blood that is, I'd say there were at least several pints there. Hard to believe they just up and walked away."

"We got any new missing persons reports?"

"No, nothing new. Still just Margo."

"Has Officer Morrow picked up that Myron Thompson kid yet?"

"No, not yet. Went by there again, but he still wasn't home."

"I need to talk to that kid. Have him keep trying."

Officer Clancy nods. "Hell of a week, ain't it? A missing girl and now John Watson..."

Detective Holt frowns and nods his head. "We got anything back from Mr. Latrell?"

"Just some prelims. I asked him for a rush like you said. Here you go." Officer Clancy hands Detective Holt a manila folder.

Detective Holt opens the folder and begins reading the preliminary autopsy report.

"You know, I just can't get over a bear attack. I mean, *here*? *In Harper Pass*? I can't remember..." Officer Clancy's voice sinks into the recesses of Holt's mind, droning on as Holt continues to peruse the report, which reads:

Probable animal attack. Severity of the wounds are consistent with a large Black Bear attack, but the wounds and lacerations themselves do not match the expected patterns consistent with Black Bear teeth or claws. An unidentified substance has been found inside several of the deeper lacerations. The substance is an oily black color and appears to have mucilaginous properties. Further chemical analysis for identification is recommended.

"So, what you think? *Weird, right*?"

Detective Holt lifts his eyes from the report. "Huh? What's that?"

"That we get a fatal bear attack and a missing persons investigation all in the same week."

"Yeah. Sure. It's unusual."

Marcy calls out from the reception area. "Detective Holt, line one. It's Jim Combs."

"*Shhhhit*," Detective Holt exhales. He walks to his desk and grabs the phone handset. He clicks the button on the phone for line one.

"Jim, we—" The agitated voice on the other end of the phone silences Detective Holt. His nerves draw his index finger and middle finger to his lips, a phantom gesture. A smoker for many years, he quit three years prior at the urging of his wife, *her prerequisite to them having children*. They started trying less than a week later. Holt suspected she made the ultimatum as more of a test of his commitment to her rather than how it concerned the baby, but he complied after a few grumblings of protest.

In nervous situations and without conscious thought, he finds himself pulling his fingers to his lips as if he's about to take a draw from a cigarette, similar to an amputee scratching at a phantom limb, an impulse triggered by years of conditioning. Cigarettes provided a coping mechanism for the more stressful moments in his chosen field.

"I understand. And I assure you, we're doing everything we can to find Margo."

Officer Clancy monitors the call in his peripheral vision and tries to disguise his eavesdropping. Detective Holt's rigid jawline suggests the phone call isn't going all that well.

"Yes, we have everyone working on this. We're not going to stop loo—"

"Find my daughter!" Officer Clancy overhears the frantic voice through the phone before the line goes dead.

Detective Holt takes a deep breath and rubs his palms over his cheeks and eyes, then runs them through his hair. His hands meet at the back of his head, instinct interlocking his fingers, elbows out as he draws a couple of deep breaths.

Detective Holt loves his job. He loves the fact that he's able to help people in a way most people will never get an opportunity to help. But with the job also comes the people you can't help. He's always hopeful initially when assigned a new investigation. But as time passes the likelihood of a happy outcome becomes far less certain, especially in cases like this. The loved ones of those affected become much more frantic and desperate. As the urgency of solving the case crescendos, so does the pressure that comes along with the job. He's reached that moment for this investigation, and all he can think about is how badly he wants a cigarette. Line one on his desk flashes again and he answers it.

"Jim, let me explain what we're—"

"No, this is Kasey Norton with Channel 4 news. *Do you mean Jim Combs*?"

"How'd you get this number?"

"I'd like to interview you."

"No, *out of the question*."

"But I have questions. *Our viewers have questions. The Combs family has questions*."

Dammit! Did Jim Combs give this damn reporter my number?

"Look, lady, I understand you have a job to do, but I'm in the middle of a missing persons investigation. I doubt that the Combs family would appreciate me stopping to do interviews instead of trying to find their daughter."

"Is it true that you've diverted resources from the Margo Combs missing persons investigation to the fatal bear attack today?"

"No, that's not true. Who told you that?" His pitch jumps a few decibels.

"So, it's true there *was* a fatal bear attack then?" *Shit! She didn't know, and I just substantiated the story.*

"No, we don't know what it was."

"So, you *are* using resources to investigate the death of John Watson?"

Detective Holt clenches his jaw. "I assure you we're using all the resources at our disposal to find Margo Combs."

"So, you don't have enough resources to handle both investigations. Can you confirm that the Harper Pass Police Office budget was cut by twenty percent earlier this year? And that you let two seasoned officers go?"

"Lady, *I'm just a detective*. That's a question for the Chief. And we have all the resources we need." Letting the lie leave his lips cuts like a katana.

The department does need more resources. The town cut the Police Office's budget to fund a revitalization project of the town square. It's the mayor's pet project, so Detective Holt doesn't dare wade into the politics of the matter. They actually let three veteran officers go from the police force. Officer Clancy benefited from this move, as a couple of months later, he got hired, but at half the salary of the men who got let go.

"Can I speak to Chief Barton then?"

Detective Holt expels a deep breath in the receiver. "You could if he wasn't on vacation with his wife in Hawaii."

"I want an exclusive," the reporter blurts out.

"And I want a cigarette. But I assure you, *both* aren't going to happen!"

"What were the circumstances surrounding John Watson's..."

"*Enough*! This phone call is over. *Goodbye.*"

Detective Holt bangs the phone on the receiver. Pools of hot blood puddle below the skin in Detective Holt's face; his pulse is racing, his heart a stamp press, imprinting anger, pumping it into his bloodstream with each successive beat. He's accustomed to doing the interrogating. His blood steams like saltwater meeting lava flow.

"Marccccy!" Detective Holt's voice booms out.

"Yeah, Holt?"

"I need that Myron Thompson kid ASAP!"

"I'll get some people on it, Holt."

A goofy grin spreads on Officer Clancy's face. "Was that Kasey Norton?"

"Yeah, damn reporters!"

"Oh man, she's hot."

"*Keep it in your pants, Officer Clancy*. Let's keep our mind on the task at hand."

"Yeah, you're right. Sorry."

"It's fine. But I need you to stay focused. I want you to authorize that chemical analysis Mr. Latrell recommended. Also, I want you to send the blood we found to Lexington or Knoxville, *whichever's going to be faster.* Get a rush DNA test on it. And check with Morrow. I think he's got some connections."

"No problem. I can do both."

Detective Holt rubs his temple for a moment. "What do you make of Latravious Wadlow?"

"Oh man, I haven't heard that name in years." A sliver of a smile slides onto Officer Clancy's face.

"So, what do you make of him?"

"Oh wow. *You're serious.*"

"Yes. Yes, I am." Detective Holt's face hardens. Officer Clancy takes a moment to gather himself.

"Sorry. I thought you were joking. The guy's a total shut-in. Never leaves that house. I mean, I grew up on High Street. My parents knew his parents, but he was long gone by then. You know, local boy makes good. Became a hotshot Ivy League professor or something. Supposedly brilliant, that is until he went crazy. Lost his job. Ended up back here. He moved into his parents' house on High Street. They'd passed a few years earlier. He's been a recluse ever since. Wait, why are we talking about him, anyway?"

"Why do you suppose a recluse would show up to a search party for a little girl with dozens of people around?"

Officer Clancy's lips separate. "What? Are you sure? *You mean you saw him today?*"

"I'm positive. When Sammy Needles was breaking into those cars a while back, we had a call for one on High Street. I went to all the neighbors' houses to see if anyone had seen anything. Latravious Wadlow's house was one of them."

"You got him to answer his door?"

"Yeah. Well, yeah. After I rang his doorbell about twenty times and kept banging on the door."

"You think he's got something to do with Margo's disappearance?"

"I don't know. But that's what I intend to find out."

Officer Clancy shakes his head. "Could this week get any weirder?"

"Just get me that analysis and that DNA test. I think I'm going to need to have a discussion with Latravious Wadlow."

CHAPTER 20
Search Engine

Robby hunches over the laptop keyboard. "How do you spell it?"

"I think it's just like it sounds, Wad-low. W-A-D-L-O-W." I draw out the letters slowly.

Robby types the name into the search engine. We huddle around the laptop at the small kitchen table in Robby's house. As soon as he punches enter, a flurry of results come rushing to the screen.

Devin peers over Robby's shoulder. "Is it Robert Wadlow?"

"*Ha!* I don't think so. Says this guy's 8'11". Also known as the Giant of Illinois." A grin sneaks across Robby's lips. "Like your cousin or something, Tee."

"Ha, ha. Very funny, dick."

Devin narrows his eyes on the results. "Yeah, there's like over a million results. You have to narrow it down, guys."

"I think his first name starts with L." *Does it? I don't know. Seems right for some reason.*

Robby types *L Wadlow* and presses enter. Robby shakes his head.

"Still over a half million results."

Tee jockeys for position. "Try Wadlow. High Street."

Robby types it in and presses enter. Tee pushes a blast of air through his lips.

"*Damn*. Still this Robert Wadlow guy. What's with this dude?"

I tap Robby's shoulder. "Try Wadlow, Harper Pass."

Robby types it in, and we all wait for the screen to refresh. Tee rolls his eyes.

"Are you kidding me? This guy's everywhere!"

"Wait." Devin points to the screen. "There's a lot less results. Scroll down."

"James Wadlow, High Street." Robby's eyes light up. "I bet that's it."

"Click on it." Tee rises on his toes. Devin cranes his neck.

"It's an obituary. For James Wadlow."

Tee continues shifting, searching for a better angle at the screen. He huffs in frustration. "Read it."

Robby clicks on the read more button and reads aloud.

"'JAMES HERBERT WADLOW OF HARPER PASS PASSED AWAY PEACEFULLY ON FRIDAY, FEBRUARY 7TH, 1997, IN THE COMPANY OF LOVING FAMILY AND FRIENDS. HE WAS BORN TO ERDIS AND KERMIT WADLOW ON JANUARY 18, 1928. HE WAS A LONGTIME VOLUNTEER AND PARISHIONER AT CHRIST UNITED METHODIST CHURCH. JIMMY, AS HE WAS KNOWN TO HIS FRIENDS AND FAMILY, WILL BE SORELY MISSED. HE WAS ALWAYS KNOWN FOR HAVING A BIG SMILE ON HIS FACE AND GROWING THE MOST BEAUTIFUL ROSE BUSHES IN HARPER PASS. HE'S SURVIVED BY HIS LOVING WIFE, AGATHA WADLOW, AND THEIR SON LATRAVIOUS WADLOW.'"

"That's it! That's his name. *Latravious*."

Devin sniggers. "That's a weird name."

Tee nods. "A weird name for an even weirder dude."

"Put in Latravious Wadlow."

"Yeah, I'm on it, Dev."

This time the computer returns four results, and all of them appear related to the Latravious Wadlow we're searching for. The first result mentions Princeton in the header. Tee bounces behind us, pointing.

"Click on that one."

"*Seriously, Tee*?" Robby clicks on the link and shakes his head. "Relax, man."

The newspaper article features a picture of a much younger version of Mr. Wadlow. The headline reads,

RENOWNED PRINCETON MOLECULAR BIOLOGIST AND PROFESSOR, LATRAVIOUS WADLOW, DISCOVERS PROMISING BREAK THROUGH.

"Holy crap! This guy was a professor."

Devin gives Tee a wide-eyed nod. "Yeah, and at Princeton."

"What's molecular biology?" I ask.

Tee nudges Robby's shoulder. "Look it up, man."

Robby opens another internet window and searches molecular biology.

"Says it's the study of biology that deals with the structure and function of macromolecules."

"What's that mean?"

"I think it means like DNA. Like genetic code or something," Devin replies to Tee.

I point to the screen. "Go back to the article."

"Says here he was being cited for groundbreaking research on transient properties in DNA.

'PROFESSOR LATRAVIOUS WADLOW IS A PIONEER IN THE FIELD OF DNA RESEARCH AND HAS UNCOVERED THAT THERE CAN BE NATURALLY OCCURRING TRANSIENT STRUCTURAL DISTORTIONS IN DNA.'"

Tee's face goes blank. "What in the hell does that mean?"

I shake my head. "You got me."

"Keep reading." Devin leans in closer to Robby's chair.

"'PROFESSOR WADLOW HYPOTHESIZES THAT THESE OCCURRENCES COULD THEORETICALLY CAUSE MUTATIONS IN AN ORGANISM AND THAT THESE MUTATIONS MIGHT BE REPEATED AND HONED IN FUTURE OFFSPRING TO THE BENEFIT OF THE ORGANISM IN ITS ENVIRONMENT. BECAUSE OF HIS LEADING-EDGE FINDINGS, PROFESSOR WADLOW HAS BEEN GIVEN A $500,000 FEDERAL GRANT TO CONTINUE THIS RESEARCH.'"

"*Wow.*" Devin's head springs upright. "This guy's crazy smart."

"Or just plain crazy," Tee quips.

Devin's squinty-eyes scroll the screen. "What's the date on that article?"

"September 4, 1996. Less than a year before his father died."

My eyes meet Robby's. "What you think, Robby?"

"I think we need to check out these other articles."

"Hey, you don't think he could like do the DNA on me and find out I was in his house, do ya?"

Devin grins as Tee bites his bottom lip. "No, not without knowing who you are. They have to have two samples to match DNA."

Tee lets out a big exhale as Robby readies another article.

"Look at this one. It says,

'CONTROVERSIAL STUDY MARGINALIZES PROMISING PROFESSOR. ONCE LAUDED AS A LEADING MIND IN HIS FIELD OF RESEARCH, THE SCIENTIFIC COMMUNITY SEEMS TO BE IN NEARLY UNANIMOUS AGREEMENT ON PROFESSOR WADLOW'S LATEST WORK. PEERS IN THE SCIENTIFIC COMMUNITY HAVE BEEN VOCAL ABOUT DISCREDITING PROFESSOR LATRAVIOUS WADLOW'S LATEST RESEARCH. SOME ARE GOING AS FAR AS TO CALL IT JUNK SCIENCE. PROFESSOR WADLOW INSISTS THE RESEARCH IS VALID AND CONTENDS THAT IT'S POSSIBLE FOR CERTAIN SPECIES TO CONSCIOUSLY MODULATE THEIR DNA STRUCTURE, THEREBY MODIFYING THE CHARACTERISTICS OF THE ORGANISM OR EVEN ITS OWN SPECIES ENTIRELY. PROFESSOR WADLOW CONTENDS THAT NOT ONLY MAY AN ORGANISM MIMIC THE DNA STRUCTURE OF ANOTHER ORGANISM THAT ALREADY EXISTS IN NATURE, BUT HE GOES FURTHER TO SUGGEST THAT THE ORGANISM MIGHT EVEN GO SO FAR AS TO CREATE SOMETHING ENTIRELY NEW AND DO SO INTELLIGENTLY. SCIENTIFIC PEERS HAVEN'T BEEN ABLE TO REPLICATE OR VERIFY HIS FINDINGS. DUE TO THE FIRESTORM OF CRITICISM SURROUNDING THIS STUDY, LATRAVIOUS WADLOW'S FEDERAL GRANT FOR HIS RESEARCH HAS BEEN REVOKED. ADDITIONALLY, PROFESSOR WADLOW HAS BEEN SUMMONED TO APPEAR BEFORE THE PRINCETON BOARD OF TRUSTEES.'"

"*Whoa.*" The word slips out of my mouth on an exhaled breath. "That's crazy."

Devin leans over Robby's shoulder. "What was the date on that one?"

"December 10th, 1997."

"Sounds like he was already going nutty." Tee's jovial tone departs. "What's that next one?"

"Looks like another obituary. It's for his mom, Agatha Wadlow. Looks like she passed away in March of 1998."

"I kinda feel sorry for him."

Tee whips his head to Devin.

"Seriously, Dev? And I was just beginning to like you."

"It just looks like he had to deal with so much with his dad dying and his job going south. And then his mom dies. *It's a lot.*"

I nod at Devin. "Yeah, no wonder he lost his marbles."

"What's that last one?"

Robby obliges Tee and clicks on the last link.

"It says,

'PROFESSOR LATRAVIOUS WADLOW FORCED TO RESIGN IN DISGRACE. PRINCETON PROVOST CHARLES LANGLEY ANNOUNCES THE RESIGNATION OF LATRAVIOUS WADLOW FOLLOWING A LENGTHY REVIEW OF WADLOW'S CONTROVERSIAL RESEARCH. THE PROVOST WAS QUOTED AS SAYING, 'PRINCETON UNIVERSITY PRIDES ITSELF ON EXEMPLIFYING THE HIGHEST ACADEMIC STANDARDS, BOTH IN THE CLASSROOM FROM OUR STUDENTS AND FROM OUR RESEARCH PERSONNEL AND FROM OUR FULLY TENURED FACULTY. THIS TRADITION OF EXCELLENCE WILL NOT BE COMPROMISED BY THE ACTIONS OF ANY INDIVIDUAL. AFTER A THOROUGH EXAMINATION OF PROFESSOR LATRAVIOUS WADLOW'S RESEARCH BY THE BOARD OF TRUSTEES, A JUST DECISION WAS REACHED TO ASK FOR LATRAVIOUS WADLOW'S IMMEDIATE AND FULL RESIGNATION. PROFESSOR LATRAVIOUS WADLOW HAS TENDERED HIS RESIGNATION EFFECTIVE IMMEDIATELY.'"

Devin breaks the heavy silence. "Holy crap. They really stuck it to him."

Tee nods agreement with Devin. "Yeah, man. That's harsh! Even for this crazy."

"What's the date on that?" I ask.

"January 7th, 1999."

A car pulls into the driveway.

"Somebody's here." Tee hurries over to the blinds, cracks them and peeks through. "It's your mom, Robby."

"Crap! I didn't realize it got so late. Bet she's here to get changed for her night job at Frogg's." Robby shuts the laptop.

I back away from the table. "I gotta get home, anyway."

Tee directs his wide eyes to Robby. "What are we gonna do?"

"Let's meet up in the morning and make a plan."

Tee nods. "I'm in." He looks to me.

"Me too."

"If you guys want me to come, I can—"

"Shut up, Dev." Robby grins at him. "*You're in, man.*"

"Cool, man. Yeah. Sounds awesome. I'm in, then." Devin flashes a big smile.

"I'll catch you guys tomorrow. Let's meet up at Brooks' house at nine." Robby fist bumps each of us.

Robby's mom rushes through the door. She's wearing a faded red blouse and a wrinkled black skirt that's endured too many wash cycles. Large, dark bags sag the skin beneath her eyes and her hair looks disheveled. She rushes through the kitchen, oblivious to our presence, and disappears into one of the bedrooms.

"So, we'll see you tomorrow, Robby?"

"Yeah, your house. Nine o'clock."

CHAPTER 21
Close Call

Tee, Devin, and I gather in Robby's yard. Fallen into a state of disrepair, the house seems to lean on its footings. Tall weeds stand like stanchions, the grass long dead, replaced by large areas of bare dirt and clusters of clover patches. The dull, yellow paint on the house is flaking off in large chunks revealing the bare, wood siding beneath. The once black shingles on the roof show the effects of the seasons, faded to porpoise gray, several clusters of shingles having fallen away, accumulating in the corners of the gutters. Two tall, bright green weeds sprout from the gutter like tiny spruce trees.

The humid air coats our skin in salty slime, like the sticky residue of saliva-emulsified cotton candy. Less than a minute outside and my forehead trickles with beads of perspiration. The sun hangs low on the horizon, the storm clouds from earlier in the day having pushed through the area, revealing a sky painted in orange pastels.

"I can't believe Mr. Wadlow's a professor."

Tee cuts eyes in my direction. "*Was* a professor."

"Yeah, well the guy's smart," Devin says.

I nod. "That's what worries me."

Tee paces the yard. "He did something to Mysterious Margo. I know it."

Devin exhales as his eyes meet Tee's. "Does seem like too much of a coincidence with the way you guys said he was acting earlier. First, he takes a finger and runs off. And now we know he was already crazy."

"*Certifiably*! If they were handing out crazy awards, he'd be the first guy in line. They'd be like, 'and here you are good sir, here's your crazy certificate.'" Tee's overplayed British accent ignites me and Devin into a giggling frenzy.

As the laughing dies, I grab my bike. "We best get headed home."

"Yeah, moms probably thinks I ran away or something. But I had fun, guys. Truly, I had fun. Thanks." A warm smile gathers on Devin's lips.

"Me too, Dev." I give him a fist bump.

"*Oh, you know it's true.*" Tee's eyes sparkle.

Tee and I hop on our bikes. Devin grabs his skateboard and jumps aboard. We pull out of Robby's driveway and make our way to Jennings Pike.

Robby lives on the outskirts of town. The sparse population on this stretch of Jennings Pike means there's rarely any traffic. Other than a couple of streets like Robby's with a few houses, it's nothing but thick woods on Jennings Pike between Robby's road and Chambers Road. Tall oak trees line the roadways, casting black shadows onto the asphalt. The woods here grow thick, the canopy from the trees above so complete that this late in the day scant sunlight filters through the leaves to the forest floor below. From the road, you can only see a few feet into the woods before shadow overtakes form and structure, surrendering the beyond to your imagination. It always gives me an eerie feeling, my mind creating monsters who lurk on the edge of the darkness, waiting for an opportunity to pounce. A shiver scales my spine as I peer into the woods, half-expecting some horrid creature's eyes to meet my own.

I've fallen behind Devin and Tee. Devin jumps something laced across the roadway with his skateboard, and Tee rides over it. Tee's voice echoes from ahead.

"Sweet jump, Dev."

As I get closer, the definition of the rope comes into view. It stretches perpendicular to the street and feeds into the woods on both sides. Without warning, the rope rises off the ground and snaps tight. I scream as it collides with my chest and flings me backwards from my bicycle. I fly through the air before crashing to the pavement. My scalp hits the asphalt with a thud, and my vision goes blurry. Waves of pain ripple through me. My body seizes with uncontrollable coughing, the force of the rope colliding with my chest ripping the air from my lungs, leaving me wheezing in agony. My scalp pulsates with a warm sting of blood. And my elbows burn from grinding to a halt on the asphalt, leaving me with large scrapes from the massive impact.

"I got you now you son of a bitch!" Sammy Needles emerges from the darkness of the woods.

"You're a dead man, Raker." I roll my head in the other direction as Bo Swindle tears out of the woods on the opposite side of the road.

Tee circles on his bike and shouts. "Brooks! Run!"

Survival instinct kicks in, and I drive my palms into the pavement, pushing myself up through the pain with every bit of strength I can muster. I stagger to my feet as Sammy and Bo converge on me from opposing sides of the road. A menacing smile snakes across Bo's lips, and he hulks his muscles, accentuating his 5'11" height and his imposing muscular frame. *Oh god! I'm dead!* My body tenses like a wounded gazelle surrounded by a pride of hungry lions. *Bo's a dropout. What's he got to lose? Probably a killer like his moonshining daddy.*

As I get my bearings, I realize there's no place to run. Sammy's fat cheeks bounce with every determined stride, his eyes ablaze with anger. A wicked smile slithers across his lips, cementing itself to his face. Dirt and sweat cover my tormentors' shirts. It's clear they laid waiting in the woods for quite some time for this moment.

Sammy climbs onto the road, eyes gleaming like roaring bonfires. "Thought you could just go to the police on me, did ya? Snitches get stitches!"

"Sammy, I didn't tell the police anything." I raise my hands in surrender as if that can somehow magically resolve the situation.

"Kick his little bitch ass, Sammy."

Bo moves behind me to cut off any escape route. I turn my body sideways as my foes begin tightening their circle around me like a noose. I swivel my head looking for an opening as they approach. I dart for a gap, but Sammy jumps in front of me and shoves me to the middle of the road. I stagger backward until a set of powerful arms wrap around me. Bo wrenches my arms behind my back and laces his arms through my elbows. He interlocks his strong fingers on the back of my head like a vise. The more I struggle, the more the pain shoots through my arms and shoulders as he constricts me with his large forearms.

Bo leans into my ear to whisper. "You little bitch. Now you're dead." A spatter of saliva hits my ear. There's pure enjoyment in his voice.

Bo's hot breath, reeking of decay, glances the nape of my neck. Sammy takes a hopping step and swings his fist forward in an uppercut, plunging it deep into my stomach. I gasp as all the air leaves my lungs, and the immense pain from the impact radiates across my solar plexus.

Tee comes running up and screams. "Leave him alone!"

"What you gonna do about it, Tee?" Sammy spins around and pushes Tee to the pavement.

"You tell the cops I did something to Margo? *Huh, Brook*?" Sammy jabs his pudgy pointer finger into my chest several times.

"Nothing. I told them nothing." I garble the words between gulps for air.

"Don't lie to me! You're going to tell me everything you told the cops. *About the backpack.*"

Tee's body trembles as he screams, "Leave him alone!"

Bo whips his head to Tee and snarls, "We don't give a damn about no Markland X Crew, Tee. So shut it!"

Sammy's eyes swell. "What the hell?"

Devin races behind Bo with his skateboard. He flips the skateboard sideways, grips it in both hands, and swings it hard. It makes a loud crack as the top deck of the skateboard strikes Bo in the back of the head and neck. Bo lets out a large groan as his legs crumble underneath him. His tight grip on me releases, and his limp body slides away from mine, hitting the road with a loud thud. In a flash Devin jumps between Sammy and me. Bo lies motionless on the asphalt other than the rise and fall of his chest, knocked unconscious by the blow. Sammy's head quivers, and he blinks his eyes a few times. No one ever stands up to him or Bo this way.

"Hell yeah, Dev!" Tee jumps to his feet and pumps his fist.

Sammy's face grows bright red and his lips curl. "You're dead!" Sammy growls as he lowers his head and shoulders and charges Devin, his arms outstretched, fingers curled like claws. His eyes swell and fill with darkness as he launches himself at Devin, who sidesteps him, nimble as a bullfighter evading a charging bull. He swings his skateboard as Sammy passes by him. The skateboard connects with Sammy's forearm with a huge slap, followed by an audible, sickening snap. Sammy falls to his knees and clutches his forearm, veins in his neck protruding. He lets out a couple of horrible, high-pitched screams.

Tee's face alarms. "Oh shit! I think you broke his arm!"

"You little assholes! You're all dead!" Tears stream Sammy's bright red face.

"*Let's go.*" My voice wails like a burglar alarm. I skirt past Bo's still body.

I grab my bike and run it away from the scene. Devin hops on his skateboard and lingers for a moment, admiring the carnage that lies in our wake. Sammy's nose crinkles as he glares at him from the road with dagger eyes.

"What are you looking at? I'm gonna kill you! All of you!" Sammy hunches, hobbling on his knees, his good arm shielding the broken one.

"Nope, don't think you are." There's an even measure to Devin's intonation.

Sammy tries to push himself up from the pavement. He lets out a cry of agony and grabs his forearm to brace it. He clenches his teeth tight, his lips blanching from the immense force. *Sammy will never be able to let this go.*

"We'll find out who ya are. We'll be coming for you. And the whole Markland X Crew, too!"

Devin grins and flips his hair from his eyes as he gives the ground a few quick leg pumps, veering his skateboard between Sammy and Bo.

This changes everything. Sammy, Myron, and Bo will come for us. Revenge. A hurricane of pain. Nothing like the child's play we've endured in the past. A shoulder-shaking shiver rumbles through me. Devin joins us on his skateboard, and we all retreat from the scene on Jennings Pike.

"Thanks, man. For saving me back there."

"You got it, man. Are you okay?"

"I'm good. Little sore, but good."

"That was freakin' bad ass! They got handled by my man, Dev." Tee's eyes gleam as we all turn onto Chambers Road.

"What's wrong with those guys, anyway?"

"Serious case of inbreeding." Tee snickers to himself.

Devin chuckles. "They *are* kind of like mutants."

I nod at Devin. "They got the big, dumb, and ugly part covered. That's for sure."

"Why'd the strawberry-faced one ask if you told the cops he did something to Margo?"

A wide grin overtakes Tee's face. "Ha! You mean Sammy."

"Yeah, Sammy. Why'd he ask that?"

I'm not really sure how to answer the question. Tee levels his eyes on me, narrowing his on mine. *Oh shit. He can tell. He knows I know why. But the detective. Dammit!* Tee sharpens his eyes on me.

"Brooks, seriously, man. *Why*?"

"Umm...I guess maybe because the detective asked me if I had ever seen Sammy pick on Margo." My voice wavers.

"And what'd you say?" Tee imprisons me in his stare.

"I said I'd seen him call her a freak and stuff like that."

Devin tilts his head, scrunching his lips. "Why was he asking about a backpack?"

My stomach plummets. *I'm going to get in a shitload of trouble. I can't tell. This sucks.* I pause for a few moments and lower my head. "I'm not really sure."

Tee slows his bicycle and comes to a stop. Devin follows Tee's lead and stops his skateboard as well. I come to a stop. I lock my shame-ridden gaze to the road. *This sucks. I hate lying. To my friends, no less.* My eyes meet Tee's. His eyes core into mine.

"Cut the crap, Brooks. Tell us the real reason. You're part of the Crew. You know that being part of the Markland X Crew means that we tell each other everything."

"I'm really not supposed to say."

"Are you part of the crew or—"

"It was my backpack, okay!"

"What do you mean your backpack?"

"The cops. They found it in the woods. Near where I saw Margo."

"What does that have to do with Sammy?" Devin asks.

"Myron took it from me when he and Sammy got me yesterday. And they found it in the woods by a bunch of blood. The detective told me not to tell anyone."

Tee's head flinches. "Whoa."

"You guys can't tell anyone I told you. I could get in big trouble."

"Secret's safe bro." Devin lays his finger across his lips.

"Yeah, man. What's said in the Markland X Crew stays in the Markland X Crew."

"They're going to come after us for sure. You heard him. The whole Markland X Crew and Devin too. He thinks I ratted him to the police."

"So, what's the Markland X Crew?"

"Robby and I started it about a year ago. Brooks is in it too."

"So what is it?"

"We just hang and stuff. You know, look out for each other's back. That type of stuff."

"Oh, that's cool," Devin says, grinning. "Can I get in?"

Tee nods. "Far as I'm concerned, Dev, you're already in. But that's not my decision alone to make."

"I say he's in. Dev just saved us back there."

"Yeah, me too. We'll talk to Robby. Has to be unanimous."

"Sweet. Thanks." A smile rises on Devin's lips.

"What are we going to do about Sammy, Bo, and Myron?"

Devin grins at me, mischief in his tone. "I think I have a plan."

"What's that?" I ask.

"Do either of you have a fishing pole?"

"Yeah, I have one. But how's that gonna help?"

"Good. Bring it to Brooks' house tomorrow. After we all meet up there, let's go over to my house. I want to show you guys something."

Devin flashes a big smile before we make the journey to our houses.

CHAPTER 22
Strange Exchange

High Street is quiet. Detective Holt turns off his headlights as he eases his unmarked vehicle to a stop on the curb by the vacant lot.

He checks his rearview; he cranes his neck around until the familiar beige sedan accelerates from its creep and leaves. Sitting there in silence, he studies Latravious Wadlow's house. A meticulous nature, honed by his years of detective work, Holt surveys the scene. The porch light is on, but there's no movement on the property. A solitary, four-door sedan parked on the street by Latravious Wadlow's property sits idle. *One way in, one way out.*

A young man emerges from the door into the light, but the poor angle shields everything except the profile of his face. He's wearing dark clothing and engaging in conversation with someone inside the darkness of the doorway. Detective Holt leans forward, but he's too far away to clearly make out the face in the dark. The young man's movements appear animated, flaring arm gestures denoting the intensity of the conversation.

An arm emerges from the darkness of the doorway and hands the young man something. The young man takes it and makes an abrupt turn away from the door. The door closes behind him, and the porch light shuts off.

Detective Holt pulls away from the windshield and sinks in his seat. He lowers his body so that only his eyes remain above the window as the young man leaves Latravious

Wadlow's sidewalk and turns onto High Street, moving in Detective Holt's direction with his head hung low. It appears he's still muttering to himself, chewing on the remnants of an argument he's taken with him. He's holding the indiscernible object in his hand. And as he walks into the glow of a streetlamp, a flash of recognition strikes Detective Holt like a thunderbolt. *It's Brady Palmer.*

A flurry of thoughts race through Detective Holt's mind. *Stop Brady Palmer and question him? Of all people, why would Brady Palmer be inside a recluse's house?*

Despite having grown into a young man, Detective Holt can't help but picture Brady as the young child he first knew. The conversation with Brady in the hospital after the fire always bothered him, and he carried it with him through the years. His gut told him at the time that the tragic fire lacked any malicious intent. The boy's suffering apparent, he omitted one of Brady's answers from his police report; he just couldn't bring himself to include it. It carried little meaning to the investigation, but the prosecution would've surely pounced upon it to acquire a harsher punishment. The oddity of the words he spoke at the time still stick with Detective Holt. *'If they burn, they won't return'. What the hell did that even mean?* But Holt attributed it to a distraught boy not making any sense. In the end, it didn't matter. Brady still received the maximum sentence.

Detective Holt fights off his urge to stop Brady. Not alerting Latravious Wadlow to his presence takes precedence. Brady walks past the unmarked car, unaware he's moving through Detective Holt's ocular crosshairs. He clutches a small glass vial with some type of green liquid in it. He stashes the item in his pocket and turns on Chambers Road before dissolving into the black night.

Detective Holt gets out of the car and walks to Latravious Wadlow's home. The house looks dark inside, all the window blinds drawn. He steps onto the wooden porch. The old boards beneath him whine, announcing his arrival. He gives a firm knock on the door and listens for corresponding movement, but quiet persists inside the home. After a few more moments of silence, he bangs on the door three more times, the heavy hand of a seasoned officer grown impatient. A burst of light filters through the cracks in the blinds and illuminates the darkened peep hole, which now glows a warm, white. Thudding footsteps close on the door. The porch light comes on and the peep hole darkens once more.

Detective Holt pulls his badge from his jacket pocket and raises it to the peep hole.

"Harper Pass Police."

"Just a moment, Detective," an older man's voice calls out from behind the door.

The unlatching of several deadbolt locks click in quick succession before the door creaks open, coming to a stop as the chain that's still fastened to the door frame reaches its full length. Professor Latravious Wadlow peers through the opening, his curly gray hair flaring out at the sides. Black and white hairs dart out in all different directions from his long, scraggly beard. Latravious Wadlow eyes Detective Holt through the circular lenses of the glasses he's wearing, which have fallen from the bridge of his nose.

"I'm Detective Holt."

"Yes, I remember you, Detective."

"Would it be alright if I come in?"

"And what is it I can help you with, Detective?" Latravious Wadlow examines Detective Holt.

"I have some questions. May I come in?"

"I'm not accustomed to receiving guests, but I suppose you may." Latravious Wadlow closes the door enough to slide the chain free.

The door opens revealing the foyer and a stack of unopened mail piled nearly two feet high on the table against the wall behind Latravious Wadlow. Holt's eyes shift left to an empty sitting room and right to a room that looks like a den, but there's no TV. The room looks like it's rarely used, the furniture draped in clear plastic.

"Follow me." Latravious Wadlow motions Detective Holt inside the door and closes it behind him.

Detective Holt trails Latravious Wadlow past the plastic wrapped furniture, his shoes shuffling on the dingy, threadbare carpet that looks like a relic from the 1970s. Seven tall stacks of yellowing newspapers rest against the far wall in the den. *Hoarder?* Several yellow rings of various sizes stain the white, popcorn ceiling where rainwater has worked its way inside the house. The two men move through the dimly lit house to the kitchen where Latravious Wadlow pulls out one of the chairs for Detective Holt.

"Thank you." Detective Holt takes a seat at the round kitchen table.

"Coffee?" Latravious Wadlow gestures to the kitchen.

The sink overflows with dirty dishes, a constant *tink, tink* of dripping water from the faucet, striking an overturned pot entangled in the filthy mess. A collection of several weeks' worth of dirty pots, pans, and glasses, idling in dishwasher purgatory, hide the surrounding countertops. The top of the coffee maker peeks out from behind the jumbled mess, but it looks like Latravious hasn't used it in years.

"No, I'm fine. Thank you. The wife can't stand when I have coffee in the evening. I toss and turn too much."

"Best to keep the lady of the house happy." Latravious Wadlow places a hand on the kitchen table and begins to ease himself into a kitchen chair.

Detective Holt lifts a brow. "You ever think about getting someone to help you around here? You know, tidy up the place a bit."

"Don't particularly like visitors." Latravious Wadlow hoists a forced smile, bone cracking on bone in his knee joint as he sits.

Lines of age mark Latravious Wadlow's face, accented by distinct frown lines—a canvas recording years of disappointment and tragedy. Now, in his sum total, he appears nothing more than a feeble and broken old man. He's aged well beyond his years, and whatever vigor of youth he once possessed had extinguished long ago.

"I suppose this is not a house call. So, what can I do you for, Detective Holt?" Latravious Wadlow's dark brown eyes set in an intense gaze upon Detective Holt.

"I noticed you came to the search party for Margo Combs this morning. Any particular reason?"

Latravious Wadlow frowns. "*Missing girl*. There was a call for volunteers."

"That's just it. You seem like an unlikely volunteer. Everyone knows you're a shut-in. It's a bit odd for an agoraphobe to show up to a crowd of people. I'm curious. How'd you hear about the search party?"

"I think I got a flyer on my door."

"Can I see the flyer?"

Latravious Wadlow reaches into his pants pocket, pulls out a folded piece of paper, and passes it to Detective Holt. Detective Holt unfolds it. It's a flyer with Margo's picture on it like the ones they handed out that morning.

Detective Holt latches his eyes to Latravious Wadlow's. "And you say someone put this on your door?"

"Yes."

"See, funny thing about that, Mr. Wadlow, is we didn't pass out these flyers until this morning at the end of Parson Street. Right before the search party started." Detective Holt's eyes cut like lasers into Latravious Wadlow.

"Someone must've brought one by before."

"Not possible. I picked these up from the printer myself just thirty minutes before that search party started. They never left my car until we got ready to hand them out. You want to tell me how you really found out about the search party?"

"Detective Holt, I am just an old man. My memory is not really what it used to be. Perhaps I heard about it from a neighbor. I can't recall."

"You don't strike me as the forgetful type. You remembered me from over a year ago."

"*Faces.* Faces, Detective Holt. I remembered your face. But time is a cruel mistress. You're still a young man, but you will come to understand what I mean. Some of the more trivial things escape me." Latravious Wadlow lifts a small grin.

"A missing girl is hardly trivial."

"When you get to my age, most everything's trivial. Breakfast, lunch, the death of an old friend. A missing girl. Trivial."

"That's a rather dark view." *He's too calm.*

149

"Indeed. A dark view for a dark world. You'll come to discover it, as well. *I'm certain of that.*"

"Is that some kind of threat?" Detective Holt makes a subtle movement with his hand to his holstered weapon underneath the table.

"No, not at all. Do I look like a person capable of making good on threats?" Latravious Wadlow chuckles.

"Well, that's a very odd thing to say."

"That's the problem, isn't it? Everyone feels that the world is perfectly ordered. You expect to elicit a certain reaction or response with a question. That things should naturally fall into some artificial construct we've all created. That everything to figure out has already been figured. As if all that's left for us to do is to glide through this world while some master puppeteer is pulling all the strings from above. But, alas, this is not the true order of things. The true order of things is constant change and adaptation." His eyes blaze with intensity.

"Mr. Wadlow, I didn't come for one of your lectures."

"But why have you come? What yarn are you unraveling?" Latravious Wadlow lifts a brow at Detective Holt. "You should be careful how far you follow it. Often curious what you find at the end."

"Let's stop talking in riddles. Do you know something about the disappearance of Margo Combs?"

"No, I do not know the girl."

"Then why come to a search party for her?"

"Sometimes the answers for what we seek are entangled, caught together—*in the clutches of circumstance.*" Latravious Wadlow's eyes resonate with some deeper, hidden meaning.

"Goddammit! What did I just say? Enough with the fucking riddles!"

"Life is a riddle. One beautiful, terrible mystery. Is it not?" Latravious Wadlow gazes off into the dark corner of the room.

"What the hell does that even mean? You've been off the grid too long."

"Precisely the opposite. I'm inside the grid. You're inside the grid. This whole town's inside the grid." Latravious Wadlow brings his hands a few inches apart like he's holding a ball. "There's no escaping it, really. What's been unleashed."

"So, when's the last time you had a visitor here?"

"You said yourself, I'm a shut-in. *A recluse.*"

"That's not what I asked," Detective Holt barks as he pulls on the side of his mustache with his thumb and index finger.

"I have visitors from time to time."

"Like Brady Palmer?"

"He's been here before, yes. Is there something wrong with that?"

"Other than it's really strange that a recluse somehow knows a boy who's been in juvenile detention for almost half his life. Yeah, nothing other than that." Detective Holt tilts his head and bores his eyes into Latravious Wadlow.

"Paths sometimes collide unexpectedly."

"Cut the shit. How do you know Brady Palmer?"

"I visited him a couple of times at the juvenile detention center."

"Why?"

"He seemed like a troubled young man."

"Did you know him before?"

"No. I read about him in the papers."

"So, he was a troubled young man. There are a lot of troubled young men. Did you visit anyone else at the juvenile detention center?"

"I think it's getting late, Detective Holt." Latravious Wadlow plants a firm hand on the table to push himself up.

"Are you asking me to leave?"

"I think it would be best." Latravious Wadlow's face remains devoid of emotion.

"Best for what? I've got a missing girl. Why don't you just answer my questions? What did you give to Brady Palmer tonight?"

"You will not find the answers you seek here, Detective Holt. Let me show you to the door." Latravious eases his body from the kitchen chair.

"Fine. That's fine. But don't make any plans to leave town."

"Detective Holt, again, you said it yourself. I'm a shut-in. Where would I go?" Latravious Wadlow smiles, and Detective Holt clenches his jaw as blotches of crimson bloom on his cheeks.

"Didn't look like a shut-in this morning."

Latravious Wadlow begins walking to the door, and a begrudging Detective Holt follows him. Latravious Wadlow opens the door and motions Detective Holt outside with his arm.

"Good evening, Detective Holt."

"This conversation's not over. I meant what I said. Don't leave town."

"Good night, Detective." Latravious Wadlow closes the door.

A rapid succession of locks and deadbolts close on the other side of the door, and the porch light cuts off leaving Detective Holt in darkness. He makes his way to his vehicle, still pondering his odd exchange with Latravious Wadlow. It hadn't turned out anything like what he anticipated.

CHAPTER 23
Visit

"I'm fine, mom. I told you. I wrecked my bicycle, but I'm fine."

My mom points to my various injuries. "But your elbows. They're so torn up and the back of your head. Ooh, it's been bleeding."

"Mom, I told you. When I wrecked on my bike, my head hit the concrete."

"But maybe we should take you to the hospital. Just to be safe. You might have a concussion."

"Mom, I'm fine. I promise."

"Okay, but promise you'll tell me if you start to not feel right."

"I promise."

"It's late. Why don't you go and get cleaned up for bed?"

"Okay, mom."

"I love you, Brooks. Just let me know if you need anything. Okay, honey?" She squeezes my cheek and kisses the top of my head.

"I love you too, mom."

I climb the staircase. I walk into my bathroom, click on the lights, and close the door. I shed my clothing in an instant and start the shower. I study myself in the mirror. I wince as I touch the small abrasion on my cheek bone. A line of rope burn stretches across the entirety of my chest, the skin pinkish and tender. *Glad I didn't have to explain this one. Mom'd go on the warpath.* Raising my elbows, I examine the extent of my injuries. The skin is abraded, but the wounds appear to be mostly superficial. I'm gathering my courage to face the sting of the shower.

I turn on the sink faucet and put my hands underneath the cool running water. I close my eyes and douse my face several times. I reach for the hand towel, and a small hand wraps around mine.

"Mom, I said I was fine."

The hand releases mine and I open my eyes. There's no one there. A chill races through my spine. I rip open the door and fling my eyes down the staircase, but it's empty. *That was a hand. I felt it. How's that possible? Is Mom right? Do I have a concussion, and it's playing tricks on my mind?* My body trembles, my eyes surveilling my surroundings. I hum a song to myself, trying to settle my nerves as I get into the shower.

I wince as the warm water rushes over my raw elbows sending tendrils of pain shooting the length of my arms. I clench my teeth together before the sting levels off, and I return to my humming. The water sheeting off me into the white tub collects the filth of the day from my body, turning it brown and murky. Moving forward, I let the water douse my hair. I take a deep breath, exhaling through my nose, the stress of the day leaving my body as the warm water cascades my skin. My heart rate drops. I reach for the shampoo and lather my hair. Closing my eyes to rinse it, I can no longer contain myself to humming.

I belt-out my favorite song. *"A love lost-and-found box - is a place where no tears drop. It's a place where you can settle - those old bad memories. And with a love lost-and-found box, you can turn back the clock—"*

"And you can change - your past history." A young girl's whisper finishes the lyric.

My terrified eyes shoot open. I listen, *frozen*, to the patter of the shower water hitting the tub and the gurgle of the water passing through the drain. Through the translucent shower curtain, I spot the outline of my bathroom vanity and the toilet, but I can't make out any shapes that resemble the outline of a person. My heart's thundering in my chest, and my muscles set like hardening plaster.

I turn off the faucet, my gaze still fixated on the bathroom, hands shaking. I stand there, listening. The last bit of water in the tub gurgles through the drain followed by the haunting still of silence. Beads of water lurch like inchworms, descending my trembling body, a bit of a chill ushering in goosebumps.

I ease my hands to the edge of the shower curtain, gripping it with both hands. Courage building. *One... Two... Three.* I yank the shower curtain. A billow of steam rolls out of the tub, but there's no one there. I grab a towel from the rack and begin drying myself, careful not to lose eye contact with the rest of the bathroom.

I wrap the towel around my waist and step out of the tub. *What just happened? There's no explanation for it.* My eyes dart around, a pulley of nerves stringing them across the room. *Maybe I do have a concussion. Should I go downstairs and have mom take me to the hospital? Maybe a little more time. It's possible I imagined the voice. That's the next lyric in the song after all. If something else strange happens, I'll tell mom something might be wrong with me and that we should go to the hospital.*

I take a couple of deep breaths and turn on the sink faucet. Condensation covers the mirror from the hot shower, so I rub it with my forearm revealing my reflection. I grab my toothbrush, stripe it with toothpaste, and begin brushing my teeth. The monotony of my normal routine levels off my tremble. That was a hard fall. But I feel okay. I finish brushing my teeth and wash my mouth out. I spit the sudsy water into the sink and raise my head.

"*Jesus!*"

Mysterious Margo's reflection looms behind me in my mirror with her head cast to the floor. I whip my head around, but she isn't standing behind me.

"Come home, Brooks. She has made a place for you."

I shoot my head around. Margo glares at me through the mirror, but she looks different, a faint blue glow in her eyes and an unsettling grin on her face. I grab the door latch and yank, but it doesn't move. I turn my body to the door, frantic hands trying to open it, but it won't budge. My heart races and my hands convulse.

"Let her take away your tears," Margo offers in a wicked voice.

"Leave me alone!" I scream as I make another desperate attempt on the door while tears stream my face.

"Come home, Brooks. Come to Grief Hollow." Her horrid voice grows more and more distorted with each word.

"Mom! Help! Help me!" I scream at the top of my lungs as I pull on the door handle with all my strength.

"Why do you fight?" My eyes jump at the proximity of her voice.

I spin around. Margo stands behind me in my bathroom with her pale lips curled in an evil grin. My whole body is shaking. A gush of air swarms my head, tingles descending through my body, my vision flecking with glimmers of light.

Scream! Just scream! Nothing comes. She plods forward, her wicked smile growing wider with each methodical step. I plaster myself to the bathroom door, all my weight thrust against it. My frantic hands rip at the doorknob. A blue glow swirls through her eyes and disappears. *Oh Jesus!* Other than the terrible grin, she looks identical to Margo.

As she closes in on me, she reaches out her arm. I turn around to the door, trying to escape. Her cold, bony fingers wrap around the soft flesh above my collar bone. I scream as her icy fingers burn my skin where they make contact. I'm hyperventilating and trying to burrow my body through the door to escape. The door swings in. I go tumbling onto the carpet and roll into the banister railing, my mother standing over me.

"Brooks! Brooks! Are you okay? What's going on? Why are you screaming?" My mother grabs my arm, her eyes wide.

I heave my body into an animalistic stance and shoot my head sideways into the bathroom. It's empty. There's no sign of Margo. She's gone.

I jump to my feet and embrace my mother, sobbing and shaking uncontrollably.

CHAPTER 24

Reunion

Angela Mitchell is sitting on her bed surfing the internet for places in Knoxville and listening to music on her iPhone. She starts college in the fall, and she bounces her head to the beat as she views more pictures of the college. Her acceptance letter created quite the stir when she ran into the house screaming. Startled at first, her parents joined in the celebration once they realized the reason for the uproar. Angela promises to become the first person in the Mitchell family to go to college, so the whole family celebrated her achievement.

Tee said, "Aw man, I thought we won the lottery."

Angela gave him a big hug as she waved the letter in the air with a beaming smile on her face and said, "This is better than the lottery, Tee!"

The approaching reality of living on her own for the first time kindles a flame of possibility in her mind, and her eyes meld with the images on the screen until the grinning girls in the photos become projections of herself. Knoxville seems like such a big town compared to Harper Pass. *So much to do. Sorority life, football games, restaurants, parties, shopping, and of course school. Ha! Oh, and the boys. There will be lots of boys! Not like the boys in Harper Pass. Sophisticated boys. Ones capable of having real conversations. Oh my God! I can't wait!*

A small tap on her bedroom window startles her. She lifts her head from her laptop computer. Beneath the glare, the black of night presses against the glass, but nothing stirs.

She returns to exploring on the internet. But a few moments later, three louder taps strike her window. *Deliberate and measured.*

The glare of her lights transforms her window into a mirror, another version of herself casting frightened eyes back at her. A swirling tingle flits through the nape of her neck, but she gathers her courage and rises from her bed. She's careful to keep her steps quiet as she creeps to the corner of the window and puts her face close to the glass. Out of the corner of her eye, a dark figure emerges.

"Jesus!" Angela staggers backward.

"Angela." The muffled voice from behind the glass rings familiar.

As Brady Palmer steps into view, he puts his index finger to his lips. Angela returns to the window and unlatches it. She eases it up, careful not to wake her parents.

"What the hell are you doing here, Brady? I haven't seen you in almost seven years, and you show up to my window at midnight? You scared the shit out of me!"

"I know, I know. I'm sorry. But I had to see you."

"It couldn't have waited until the morning?"

"Can I come in?"

"What? *Nooo*! You're going to get me in trouble."

Brady locks eyes with Angela. "It's important."

"So is me not getting in trouble."

"Angela, *please*."

"Fine, but make it quick. My parents are going to kill me if they catch you in here. Actually, my dad will probably kill you first."

Brady climbs in through the window. He's grown into a man, standing at 6'1", but still carries the pudge in his cheeks that he did as a child. Flashes of their time together as childhood best friends besiege her mind. She tries to expel the flood of painful memories, Brady convicted and sent to juvie—the end of their friendship. Accompanied with the memories, the sight of him conjures a flood of emotions that she's kept locked up, compartmentalized. A sense of dread engulfs her, familiar but unplaceable.

Angela lifts her doe eyes, a heaviness spilling into them. "Why are you here, Brady?" Her voice trails off into a whimper.

"You're in danger." She draws her head back at his abrupt delivery.

"What? What do you mean I'm in danger? You're kinda freakin' me out, Brady."

"Not just you. We're all in danger." Brady's eyes grow wide and wild. "The whole town, really. It can take any of us any time it wants."

"Brady, did you take something?" Angela's eyes run to his, studying them.

"No, *wait*. What? What do you mean?"

"*Are you on drugs*? You come to my house at midnight and knock on my window. Then, you tell me I'm in danger. That the whole town's in danger. I think you'd better go."

"I'm not on drugs and I'm not crazy, Angela. This is serious."

"And I'm serious, too. I think you need to leave." Angela motions her agitated eyes to the open window.

Brady flashes his palms. "Just hear me out. Then, I promise I'll go."

"I don't know. This is weird." Angela crosses her arms high on her chest and wraps her hands around her shoulders.

His pleading eyes meet hers, lingering like a caged mutt. "Angela, we were best friends once. Come on. *You know me.*"

She shakes her head and sighs through her nose. "Okay. Fine. But make it quick."

"So, this is going to sound crazy—"

"You're not off to a good start."

"Just listen. I've been meeting with Latravious Wadlow."

"*The crazy professor*?"

"Yeah, but he's not crazy. I know that's what everyone thinks, but the guy's not crazy. Actually, he's really smart. He might be the only one who can save us."

"Save us from what?"

"The thing that killed John Watson."

"A bear? Save us from a bear?" She huffs through her nose. "You've got to be kidding me."

"It wasn't a bear that killed John Watson." Brady's wide eyes darken like train tunnels.

"Yes, it was, Brady. It's been all over the news tonight. My parents told me not to go in the woods."

Brady clenches his lips and shakes his head. "It wasn't a bear. It was something else."

"How do you know?"

"Me and the professor have been tracking it. Trying to figure out a way to stop it."

"This is crazy, Brady. You sound really crazy right now."

"I know what it sounds like. I do. But I needed to warn you. This thing can change. Change what it looks like. Change what it is. Your parents are right about one thing. Stay out of the woods, especially Grief Hollow."

"You're scaring me, Brady."

"You should be scared. This thing's smart and it's not going to stop." Angela bites her bottom lip and her brows furrow.

"That's not what I mean. *You* are scaring me. I think something's wrong with you. I think you need to see a doctor." Her heart races, her eyes mapping a path to her bedroom door.

Brady's eyelids droop and his shoulders slump. "Angela, I'm not crazy. We're best friends. I needed to warn you."

"Brady, the only reason I let you in here is because we *were* best friends. But that was over six years ago. I moved on. *I had to move on.*" Angela's voice crackles as it wilts, resigned acceptance in her tone.

Brady drops his head and his face droops into a frown. "You don't believe me."

"I mean, *come on*? Who would believe that story?"

"But it's true, Angela. There was a finger with this black stuff on it. Professor Wadlow looked—"

"*Get out.*"

"What?"

"Get out of my room. Get out of my house."

"But Angela, this thing is coming and—"

"Brady, I hope you get the help you need, I really do. But I can't help you with this. You need to go now."

"Angela, I don't need help. It's going to happen—"

"Get out now! Get out now or I'm going to scream." Her body trembles like a cornered animal.

"Angela, I just want to help." Brady outstretches an arm to her shoulder.

Angela recoils from his hand and takes a few steps backward. Her body shakes, but remains poised, ready to burst into a running retreat at any second. A dejected frown overtakes Brady's face. His wilting eyes meet hers. Her lips quiver. His frown deepens and his eyes glisten as he registers what's written in her eyes. Their friendship is over.

"Okay. I'm going. Just stay out of the woods."

"Don't come back, Brady."

Brady climbs out the window. "Don't worry. I won't bother you again." His wounded words hang in the air as he disappears into the night.

Angela rushes to the window and slams it shut, tears streaming from her eyes. She locks the latch and pulls her curtains. She retreats to her bed where she wraps herself in her comforter, still shaking from the encounter.

CHAPTER 25
Excavation

Detective Holt takes a big swig of his black coffee as he pulls into the station. He's still tired, his eyes painted red from the lack of sleep. Troubling cases like this fracture his sleep, breaking it apart with intermittent bouts of restless stirring. The sun climbs to the first rung of the horizon as he exits his car. He lets out a groggy yawn, his body unaccustomed to arriving at work at this early hour, but a sense of obligation to work as many hours as possible on the Margo Combs disappearance prods him. And work does provide him an escape from dealing with his own life, the cruel reality of losing a first child. Kirsten's recent sleeping patterns mimic his own, her fresh wounds festering and her pain palpable. It grows in every cold corner of their home.

As he walks into the police station, an old Tucker Jacobs song peppers the air with Mississippi Delta twang and Officer Morrow sings, "*I did it all for you, baby... till you said we was through, baby, ain't that the truth, baby.*"

Officer Clancy's at his desk as well, not unexpected as Holt asked both men to work overtime.

Holt walks into the row of cubicles. "Can you turn that down?"

"Yeah. No problem, Holt." Morrow presses pause on his CD player.

Clancy grins. "Thank you! That crap's killing me."

"Lance, you wouldn't know good music if it slapped you in the face."

"Pretty sure that ain't it. Holt, that Myron Thompson kid. His mom just called the station 'bout fifteen minutes ago in somewhat of a panic. Said that Myron hasn't been home, and they haven't heard from him in days. Said they want to report him missing."

"Dammit! Got to be kidding me. The press is going to kill us for sure. Chief picked a hell of a week to take a vacation."

Morrow nods. "Ain't that the truth."

"Did you tell 'em to come into the station?"

"She sounded pretty drunk. Guessing not in any shape to drive. I told her we'd be out in a bit."

"Okay, good."

Clancy turns in his chair to Holt, a smile creeping into the corners of his lips. "So, did you talk to Latravious Wadlow?"

"Yeah, but it was a bizarre conversation. Not sure he's playing with a full deck."

"Oh yeah? What happened?" Clancy rubs his hands together like he's warming them over a fire.

"First off, you wanna guess who was leaving his house when I got there?"

"Kasey Norton with Channel 4 News." The words spill out of Clancy like an impulse flung from his tongue.

"No." Holt draws his head back and his face crinkles. "Why would you guess that? What is it with you and that reporter, Lance?"

"I don't know." Clancy blushes. "I just thought if Latravious is involved with Margo's disappearance, maybe the reporter figured it out."

"Well, it wasn't Kasey Norton with Channel 4 News... It was Brady Palmer."

Morrow lifts his eyes from his paperwork. "Well, if that ain't the most unlikely pair."

"Seriously? What was he doing over there?"

"I'm not sure, but Latravious handed him something in the doorway. A glass vial, I think."

Clancy tilts his head. "You don't suppose they're mixed up in some kinda drug ring, do ya?"

Morrow laughs. *"A drug ring? Moving product in a vial?"*

"You got a better explanation, Charles?" Color floods Clancy's cheeks.

"Could be anything, 'specially based on Latravious' background. How do they even know each other, Holt?"

"Said he visited Brady a couple of times at Longfellow Juvenile Detention Center. Said he read about him in the papers and took an interest in the boy. But what I can't figure is why a recluse feels compelled to visit a stranger at juvenile hall."

Clancy scrunches his lips. "Why'd he say he visited him?"

"Gave some vague and convoluted answer about paths being intertwined or something like that."

"Sounds like he's hiding something."

"Charles, I'm telling you, this guy's answers were all over the place. Can't tell if he's lying, hiding something, crazy, or what. I want you to call over to Longfellow, Lance.

Request a copy of the visitation log for Brady Palmer. Let's see if his story checks out."

"No problem, Holt. I'll get right on it." Clancy gets the phone number from his computer, grabs his phone and dials.

"Charles, can you get over to Myron Thompson's house? Go ahead and take a statement from the mom and sister. I'd like to keep this one under wraps for a few more hours if possible."

"I'll do my best. The mom's kind of a loose cannon. Might go to the press."

"Just do what you can."

"Will do, Holt." Morrow grabs his coffee and walks to the door.

Clancy hunches forward in his chair and presses the telephone receiver to his ear. "So, you do see his name on the log. Well, how many times did he visit?"

Holt sits at his desk and starts his computer. He takes another big swig of his coffee, fighting off a yawn.

"Wait, did you say three or forty-three? *Realllly...*" Clancy cups the bottom of the phone with his palm and swivels in his chair to face Holt. "Holt, Longfellow Detention Center says that Wadlow visited Brady forty-three times."

"Well, I'll be damned. That's a hell of a lot more than a couple. Have 'em send over a copy of that log, Lance."

The phone rings on Detective Holt's desk, and he answers it.

"Hello, Detective Holt here."

Detective Holt waits for a response, but no one replies. There's a crackling of static, before a little girl lets out a muted giggle.

"Hello? *Who is this*?"

Again, there's silence, but it's soon replaced with the hum of static. The static levels off, and the little girl's giggling begins again.

"This is a police line. You can get in a lot of trouble for this! You hear me?"

The giggling returns even louder.

"What do you want?"

"*You*," the little girl whispers before she begins giggling again.

"This isn't funny! Stop laughing! I'm warning you..."

The intensity of the giggling ratchets up and distorts, morphing into a deeper, raspier voice.

Holt cups the receiver on his phone. "Lance, get a trace on line one."

Holt places his mouth back to the receiver. "What the hell is so funny?"

The voice hisses a whisper. "If they burn, they won't return."

"*What did you just say*?"

There's more static before the voice replies louder. "If they burn, they won't return."

Holt's stomach plummets and his face blanches. His eyes grow wide, his hand trembles and his mind races.

"Holt, there's no one on line one. Are you sure you got the line, right?"

Even though the phone slides away from his ear, the uncontrollable giggling coming through the receiver remains audible. Line one flashes on his phone. Detective Holt slams the phone down to end the call.

"Holt, who was that? Holt? What's wrong?"

Detective Holt's mouth hangs ajar, but no words come. He hasn't heard those words in over six years. He heard those words once, and he never repeated them. A flood of memories crash into him like powerful waves. His mind plays images of the past. A severely burned and traumatized eleven-year-old boy says that a voice told him, *if they burn, they won't return.* Brady claimed that's why he did it, set off that chain of events that forever changed the course of his life and ended Misty's.

Detective Holt knew killers, and Brady Palmer was no killer. At the time, Detective Holt omitted Brady's peculiar statement from his police report for fear of stacking the deck against a boy he presumed innocent of anything malicious. But given this phone call, Detective Holt wonders. *Did Brady share those words with someone else? Perhaps, Brady told Latravious Wadlow, and Latravious orchestrated the call.*

"Holt, are you all right?"

"Yeah." His voice travels on a big exhale of breath, a nonplussed expression shrink-wrapped to his chalky-white face. Holt swallows hard.

"Who was that?"

"Prank caller." Holt's utterance perishes in the air, his eyes dimming like dying stars.

"There was nobody on the line. I checked it on Stingray. All the lines were dormant."

"Must be a glitch in the software."

Clancy shakes his head. "Weird. What did they say?"

"They didn't say anything. Just laughing."

"But it sounded like you were talking to someone."

"Thought they may have said something, but it was just laughing."

"Holt, you don't look so good. Maybe you should take a day off. Me and Charles can handle this."

Holt's jaw goes rigid and he huffs. "Lance, I'm fine, okay?"

"Okay, okay. Just worried about you is all. I know you and Kirsten are going through a lot right now."

"We're fine. I'm fine. Can we just drop it?"

"Yeah. No problem, Holt."

The phone starts ringing again, drawing Detective Holt's eyes. Line one flashes, taunting him. The phone continues ringing. His stomach plummets.

"You want me to grab that?"

"No. I'll get it." Detective Holt picks up the phone and slowly raises it to his ear. "Harper Pass Police Office, Detective Holt here." There's nothing but silence on the other end of the phone. Holt pulls the receiver close to his mouth. "I don't know who you are, but I've had about enough of your damn gam—"

"Detective Holt. Just the man I wanted to talk to. Sorry, accidentally muted the phone. This is Frank Gibbs with the State Fish and Wildlife Service. Sounds like you're having a day."

"Hey, Frank. Sorry. Just some kids prank calling the station."

"So, I hear you had a bear attack yesterday."

"Yes. Well, maybe. We're not really sure. That's why we wanted you to come out."

"Isn't really much else it could be based on what I've already seen from the photos, but I'll take a look. Listen, I'm about twenty minutes out. There some place I can grab a quick bite before headin' over? I'm starving."

"Uh, yeah. I guess. The Cracked Egg. It's on Main and 5th."

"'Preciate that, Detective. Shouldn't be more than about forty-five minutes. So, the body. You got that at your place?"

"No. The body's at Jenson Funeral Home."

"On ice I hope?" Frank's question widens Holt's eyes.

"Yeees." Holt's drawn-out inflection unveils his thoughts on the oddity of the question.

"*Whew*. Three weeks ago, I had a real stinker. Over in Calhoun. Some ole boy out huntin' fell into a moccasin pit. Must've got snake bit fifty times. They didn't find him for four days. And man alive, the smell was enough to sicken a skunk."

"Okay."

"Well okay then, Detective. I'll see you at your place soon."

"We'll be here. See you soon then."

CHAPTER 26

Intersections

"So, what'd you need me to bring a fishin' pole for?" Tee holds the Cast Master 5000 his father purchased for him from TV. I'd seen the very same infomercial promising it as *the most important piece of fishing equipment you'll ever own.*

Devin gives a subtle grin. "I got an idea. But let's wait for Robby."

We're all standing out in my driveway. I yawn, still tired from the long night. The details of my evening claw at my insides, yearning for release. *But what do I say? Margo was in my bathroom last night... but wasn't. They'll think I'm crazy.*

Tee cocks his head at me. "What's with you, Brooks? You're like a zombie this morning."

"It was a long night."

"What's that on your arm?" Devin's brows rise as he points to my wrist. "Is that a hospital bracelet?"

I lift my arm like I'm checking a watch. I'm still wearing the band around my wrist from my hospital admission the night before.

"Dude! You go to the hospital last night?" Tee's words erupt, his eyes wide with anticipation.

"My mom was worried I might have a concussion."

Devin narrows his eyes on me.

"Why's that? I thought you were fine."

I avert my eyes from Devin's and glimpse Robby pedaling the hill on his bike. "There's Robby."

Tee flashes a grin. "'Bout time you showed, Robby."

"Cool it, dork. I don't live right around the corner like you." Robby wipes away the sweat from his brow.

"S'up, Robby?" Devin gives him a fist bump before Robby turns to us.

"What's up with you, guys? You ready to get to the bottom of this Wadlow thing?"

A wide grin spreads on Tee's face. "Aww man, do we got a story to tell you."

Robby looks me over. "What the hell happened to you, Brooks?"

"Your boy went to the hospital last night!" Tee blurts out.

"What? Why?"

Devin tips his chin into the air. "Run in with Sammy and Bo on the way back from your place yesterday."

"Dev knocked Bo out, and I think he broke Sammy's arm." Tee throws a couple of spirited air jabs.

"Whaaat? What happened?"

"Sammy and Bo were hiding in the woods. They had a rope stretched across the road. They pulled it tight right before I was about to cross over it."

Tee sweeps his arm through the air. "Knocked him clean off his bike!"

"Yeah, check it out." I lift my shirt to reveal the rope burn across my chest.

"Ooh, *damn*." Robby surveys my wound.

"That's not all. Look at his elbows, bro." Devin motions his eyes to me.

"That's jacked up. I hate those guys. Seriously." Robby shakes his head and grits his teeth.

"Dev got 'em good though," Tee adds with a grin.

"Bo had me locked up and Dev came running up."

"Knocked the crap out of him with his skateboard!" Tee takes an exaggerated step and swings an imaginary skateboard through the air.

Devin chuckles. "That Bo kid fell like a ton of bricks."

"Whoa."

"Then Sammy charges Dev." Tee puffs out his cheeks and belly, adding imaginary weight to his scrawny frame. He synchronizes thudding sound effects with his plodding steps.

"Yeah. And Dev hit him in the arm with his skateboard!" I slap my hands together making a loud clap.

A wide grin overtakes Tee's face. "Man, you should've seen Sammy Needles crying."

"Dev saved me."

"Guess I wasn't quick enough, Brooks. Seeing as how you had to go to the hospital."

"That's not really why my mom took me. Something else happened. Later that night."

"What?" Tee's wide eyes land on mine. Devin turns to me.

"What happened, man?"

"I saw Margo."

"Shut the front door." Devin's eyes grow wide.

"I don't even know how to explain this. It was like a dream. I was taking a shower. I started singing."

Tee snickers. "You're such a dork. Singing in the shower."

"No. Wait, listen. Then I heard a girl sing the next line in the song. Freaked me out so bad. But there was no one there. I thought I was losing it." The other boys' eyes seem to inflate with my own. "Then I get out of the shower. I'm thinking I imagined it, right? I brush my teeth, spit out the toothpaste, and there's Margo, in my mirror. But she's not really there. Because she's not standing behind me."

"What the hell?" Robby's words escape on an exhaled breath.

"But I turn back around and she's still there! In the mirror!" Tee's eyes inflate like balloons, a fidget falling to his foot. "She said to come home. To Grief Hollow. That *she* had made a place for me there. I was trying to get out the door, but I was locked inside the bathroom. Next thing I know, she's standing in the bathroom behind me."

Robby shakes his head. "That can't be."

"But it happened. I was screaming and trying to get out. She grabbed me, and then my mom opened the door. I rolled out, looked back and she was gone. My mom was so worried about me; she took me to the hospital."

Tee shakes his head with wide eyes. "But how can we have the same dream? That's not possible."

"Because it wasn't a dream, Tee! It really happened." I stretch my shirt by my collar, exposing the blistered imprint of four fingers on my skin.

"*What the fuck!*" Devin's eyes bulge, the physical evidence adding somber punctuation to my story.

"It's where she grabbed me. You saw her, too?"

A rolling tremor passes through Tee. "I'm so not cool with this. What the hell's going on? This doesn't make any sense."

"I don't know, but I'm pretty sure it wasn't Margo. It looked like Margo, but it didn't."

Robby tilts his head at me. "What do you mean?"

"Did she have a blue swirl in her eyes?" Tee's voice trembles.

"*Yes*! Oh my god, you really did see it too!"

"But I was asleep. It was a dream. I woke up screaming. I sweated through my sheets."

Devin shakes his head. "This is like 'nother level freaky!"

Robby's eyes meet mine. "What was it that Brady said the other day?"

"Stay out of Grief Hollow."

Robby shakes his head. "No, the other thing."

"Said it can be what it wants to be." Tee's words come out slow and measured.

"That's right! He said it can make you see things." *What the hell's going on?*

"Guys, what do you suppose that *IT is*?" Devin's voice quavers.

I give a slow head shake. "I don't know. But whatever it is, it's not friendly."

Robby bites his lip for a moment. "Thought Brady was crazy. Maybe he's not."

Devin nods. "And maybe he does know something."

Robby turns to Tee. "Angela was best friends with Brady, right?"

"No. Absolutely not."

"Tee, it might be the only way to figure out what's going on."

"Figure out what's going on? Do you hear yourself? There's no way to figure out what's going on. There's no explanation for this stuff."

"But if you could talk to Angela, maybe—"

"I said no, man!"

"Tee, Robby's right. Just ask her if she's talked to him." Tee scowls at my urging.

"This ain't the Hardy Boys. This shit's getting real weird, real fast."

"Dude, she's your sister. What's the big deal?" Robby argues, narrowing his eyes on Tee.

"It *is* a big deal. *Brady* was a big deal. It about killed her when he went to juvie. He was her best friend. I can't bring that up again."

"It's been like seven years."

"I know, but you don't know how bad it was."

"Come on, Tee. How bad could it have been?"

"She tried to kill herself, *alright man!*"

"Oh my god!" The utterance sails from my mouth, and it remains hanging open.

"After he went to juvie, my dad wouldn't let her see him. She got in a really dark place. After a couple of months, she took a bunch of pills and tried to kill herself."

Robby's posture wilts. "Tee, I'm sorry. You know—I didn't know, man."

"Nobody knows. And it better damn well stay that way."

"Of course, man."

"Not a word." Devin presses his thumb and forefinger together and runs them over his lips like a zipper.

I shake my head as Tee's eyes meet mine. "Never, man."

"And since we're sharing secrets." Tee continues to hold me in his gaze. "Tell Robby what you told us yesterday."

"What's that?"

"About the backpack."

"This goes without saying, Robby, but you can't repeat this. I could get into a lot of trouble."

"No way, man."

"So, when Myron and Sammy got me the other day, Myron took my backpack. The police detective wanted me to show him where I last saw Margo. They found my backpack near a bunch of blood. Said it might be a crime scene."

"That's nuts. Why didn't you just tell us?"

"The detective warned me not to tell anyone. Said I could get in a bunch of trouble if I did."

"Do they think it was Margo's blood?"

"They weren't sure. They were going to have it tested."

"So that's why Seth, Shane, and Cam were saying that Sammy was so pissed at you?"

Tee nods. "Yeah, he thinks Brooks ratted him to the police."

"But I didn't. They just asked me if I'd ever seen Sammy pick on Margo. But we've all seen that." Tee and Robby nod. Robby's eyes connect with mine.

"Bet they think he killed her."

"They're not going to stop. They're going to be coming even harder for us, now."

A small grin appears on Devin's face. "The best way to stop bullies is to beat them at their own game."

"What do you mean, Dev?" Tee asks.

"We make it so there are consequences, real consequences, for them coming after us. Then, they'll move on."

"I don't want to get into any trouble."

"I'm not talking about trouble, Tee. I'm talking about outsmarting them."

"So, what's your plan?" I ask.

"Come with me fellas, I've got something to show you." A mischievous grin slips onto Devin's lips.

CHAPTER 27
Examination

"You're late." Frank Gibbs lifts a brow at Detective Holt's barbed wire tone.

"Well, hey to you too, Detective Holt."

Holt's eyes cut into Frank Gibbs as he adjusts his waistband on his girthy midsection. "I left the station almost an hour ago when you called and said you were leaving The Cracked Egg."

"Sorry. Got tangled up with a slice of pecan pie back there." A goofy smile spreads across Frank's pudgy face. "Hey, you didn't tell me they had such good desserts there."

"It's nine in the morning."

"Never too early for a good dessert. Spice of life, I tell ya."

Holt surveys Frank's untidy appearance, noting his half-untucked shirt and his gelatinous belly that hangs over the waistband of his faded blue jeans, collecting in his shirt above his belt. *Christ. Looks like he's never missed a meal. Hard to imagine his expertise extends beyond competitive eating.* Holt grumbles and shakes his head.

"Follow me." Holt leads Frank into the funeral home, a band of tension pulling tighter with each of Frank's plodding steps.

"You get the body out?" The trailing voice grates him as the two men descend the stairs to the basement. Holt stops in his tracks and buries his eyes into Frank's.

"Yeah, we got the body out, *thirty minutes ago*. Mr. Latrell's waiting. I've been waiting."

Frank tosses his hands.

"He's already dead, Detective. What's the big hurry?"

Holt's face splotches red, and his words spew sharp as frostbite from his icy tongue. "I've got two active missing persons investigations. Not like I have a bunch of free time."

"Okay, okay. I get it. Sorry."

The men file into a basement room.

"Just tell me what happened to John Watson."

The remains of John Watson lie out on a stainless steel embalming table in the center of the room. One of the fluorescent lights above loops a continuous flicker, but the fixture affords enough light for the examination. A row of refrigerated slide-out lockers lines the wall behind the embalming table. One of the locker doors protrudes into the room, its steel rollaway table extended. Mr. Latrell, an older man wearing coke-bottle eye glasses, lifts his head. Wearing a mask and apron, he stands by the body.

Frank walks forward and extends his hand. "I'm Frank Gibbs, State Fish and Wildlife."

Mr. Latrell raises his blue gloved hands. "Mr. Gibbs, probably not the most sanitary to shake your hand as I've been prepping the body."

"True, true. *Wow*. He really did get quite the vicious attack." Frank's eyes glimmer as he surveys the remains.

"Here's some gloves and an apron." Mr. Latrell passes them to Frank.

"Thanks. How long did you say this attack lasted for?"

"Two minutes, tops. We ran there as fast as we could after we heard the shots."

Frank slips on the apron and the gloves. "Did you see the bear?"

"No, and we couldn't find any bear tracks either. Just some large tracks, almost like a chicken but much bigger." Holt shows Frank the cast of the track they found. Frank's eyes linger on it for a second before he disregards it as nothing more than random indentations they found in the earth. No animal makes a track resembling the cast.

"I got to tell you, these wounds don't look like what we typically see in bear attacks. Nope, not at all." Frank slides his gloved fingers over the perimeter of a wound on John Watson's chest. Holt cocks his head.

"What do you mean?"

"It's very unusual to see limbs severed like this from a bear attack."

"Well, you think it could be something else then?"

"Not really anything in this part of the state, or the whole state really, that can do this kind of damage that quickly."

"Some of the wounds to his back are also very deep. Wide, as well." Frank's head perks and his eyes meet Mr. Latrell's. "I measured several, the deepest of which was 173mm."

"That's interesting. That'd also be very uncharacteristic for a bear. You know if anyone who lives around here might have any kind of exotic pets?"

"Exotic pets?" Detective Holt tilts his head slowly at Frank. "What do you mean?"

"Lions. Tigers. Panthers. Anything like that?"

"Mostly simple folk here, really. Most everyone couldn't afford something like that even if they wanted one."

Mr. Latrell nods. "Even if someone did get something like that, hard to imagine they'd be able to keep that secret in this town."

Frank slides his hands under John Watson's shoulders. "Can we turn him over?"

"Yes. Can you give us a hand, Holt? There are some gloves right there." Mr. Latrell points to a glove dispenser on the wall.

"Did you uncover anything on the body that might indicate foul play?"

"Not conclusively, no." Holt struggles to slide his damp hands into the gloves, the ends of the fingers resembling reservoir tips. He gives each a gentle pull from the wrist.

"The deep wounds in the back. They're odd. I'm no bear expert, but they seem to be more like the depth of a knife than a bear's claws or teeth. But they're also not consistent with a knife."

Frank lifts a brow. "What do you mean?"

"Let me show you. All right. So, what we're gonna need to do is roll the body up on its side. I will take the head and shoulders. Frank, you can get his legs."

"You mean leg," Frank quips with a grin.

"Show a little decorum for God's sake."

Frank frowns, averting his eyes from Holt's cutting glare.

"And Holt? Holt, if you can push on his torso when we get the body on its side."

Holt recoils his hand from the body. "He's stiff as a board."

"Yeah. The rigor mortis has set in pretty good. All right, let's do this."

The men gather around the embalming table. Mr. Latrell grips John Watson's shoulders and Frank Gibbs grips John Watson's right leg and left thigh. The two hoist the body onto its side, and Detective Holt pushes the body until it settles face down on the table.

"This is what I was talking about." Mr. Latrell points to the wounds on John Watson's back.

"Damn! You weren't kidding. Looks like somebody hit him over and over with a mace."

Mr. Latrell shakes his head. "Doesn't make any sense. You ever seen anything like this?"

"Nope. Never anything like this. Wasn't a bear, I can tell you that much."

Holt whips his head to Frank Gibbs. "How do you know?"

"The shape of these wounds isn't consistent at all. Like I said, looks like he was hit by a mace repeatedly. The wounds are deep, wide and triangular in shape. I'd expect to see narrow slashes and flesh possibly torn away. But these wounds are clean."

"What about more than one bear?"

"Still would have the hallmarks of a bear attack even if it was more than one. Look at the contusions around the surrounding tissue of the wounds. Whatever hit this man, hit him with tremendous force."

"So, if it's not a bear, then what kind of animal could do this?"

Frank levels his eyes on Holt. "I don't think it's an animal at all. I think you have a murderer on your hands."

CHAPTER 28
Unpacking

We move through the towers of moving boxes in Devin's room, each of us focusing on a different stack, tearing away packaging tape.

Devin lets out a deep sigh through his nose. "Dammit! This isn't it either. I can't remember which box." He opens another moving box as I survey the daunting task.

"They all look the same."

Tee plunders through packing paper inside of one of the boxes. "What are we looking for, anyway?"

"Yeah man, seriously." Robby lifts his eyes to Devin. "It might help if we knew what we were looking for."

"Just keep opening them up." Devin runs the blade of a pair of scissors through the taped seam of another box.

"Dude, just more movies here." Tee's fingers lock onto one of the DVDs in the box. "Ah sweet! Transformers. That movie's kick ass."

Devin's eyes light up. "Found them."

His hands disappear inside the moving box, a big grin on his face. He lifts two assault rifles out of the box. Tee's eyes bulge.

"Holy shit man! You've lost it. I ain't killin' nobody."

I narrow my eyes on him. "Dev, you should put those away."

"Chillax dudes. They're paintball guns."

"Those are freakin' awesome!" Robby yanks his hands free of his box and skitters to Devin.

"Oh wait. There's more." Devin's eyes gleam as he pulls out two more assault-rifle style paintball guns and two paintball pistols. He lays them on the carpet.

Tee chuckles. "Damn, Dev. Looks like you're ready for World War III."

Devin winks at Tee. "Precisely."

I survey the armament on the floor. "Why do you even have all of these?"

"Used to play paintball back in San Diego. At the Park. We'd have all-out wars, man. It's a blast, but they hurt like a mother when they hit your skin." A mischievous grin slips onto his lips.

Tee twists his closed lips to one side and tilts his head in the opposite direction. "So, what does this have to do with a fishing pole?"

Devin chuckles out his response. "I'm so glad you asked."

My eyelids jar wide, and I inhale a deep breath through my nose. "Dude, you're not thinking we're going to shoot up Sammy, Bo and Myron, are you?"

"Bullies don't stop until they've met their match. We're going to show them they can't mess with us."

Robby grabs one of the paintball rifles and funnels a squinty eye through the sights. "So, what's the plan?"

"So, the way I figure it, we set up somewhere we know they're going to come through. We hide on the edge of the woods. Like the Neanderthals did to us yesterday." Devin pulls out a twenty-dollar bill from his pocket. Tee locks eyes with it.

"What's that for?"

"Bait."

"Oh yeah!" Robby's eyes gleam above his wide grin.

"We put it on the end of the fishing line. When they go to pick up the money, we reel it back in towards the woods."

"Then we spring the trap!" Robby mimics a recoiling gun as he moves his aim across the room, spraying it with imaginary bullets.

"Exactly!" Devin bounces his eyelids. "We come out of the woods guns-a-blazin'."

"Dude, it's just paintballs. They're going to kick our asses."

"Just paintballs. You ever been hit by a paintball, Tee?" The question lingers in the air, a smirking gleam in Devin's eyes.

"Well, no, but it seems like we'd have to be really close to them to pull this off."

My wide eyes seek out Tee's and come back to Devin's. The gleam in his eyes doesn't waver. "Yeah, we might make this worse than it already is."

"Trust me, they're going to be running in the opposite direction once the paintballs start flying. And Brooks, do you want to have to look over your shoulder the rest of your life?"

Tee shakes his head as his eyes scrape the ground, and his voice wavers. "I don't know."

"I'm so in!" Robby takes aim with his rifle and acts out shooting it.

"We take 'em by surprise." Devin's grin widens. "They'll never know what hit 'em!"

"This is a bad idea." My voice crackles.

"Are you kidding? It's the best idea!" Robby wears a grin as he fist bumps Devin.

Tee tips his chin forward. "Dev, let me see one of those."

Devin tosses one of the rifles to Tee. Tee grips the rifle. One of his hands slides down the stock, and the other comes to a rest on the trigger instinctively. A wide grin comes across Tee's face as he looks through the scope.

"Awesome, right?" Robby's eyes sparkle.

"Pretty bad ass."

"Guys, if we do this, there's no turning back."

"We already passed the point of turning back when they knocked you off your bike yesterday, Brooks."

"Dev's got a point, Brooks. They're just going to keep coming."

Damn. Tee, too?

"You're both right. They're not going to quit. That's why this ends today. Ends now." Robby's jaw clenches with his decree. He seems emboldened by the sense of power he gleans from the paintball rifle in his hands.

Devin grins at me. "So, what you say, Brooks?"

"Yeah. Yeah, okay. Let's do it."

CHAPTER 29
Escalation

The sizzling sun scorches, and waves of heat radiate from the black pavement. Bo follows Sammy on his bike, scanning the roadways. The hours of unsuccessful searching for Brooks whittle away at Bo's patience. But Sammy's unwavering eyes remain fastened to the roadways, a robotic churn of his legs powering him forward.

A fresh cast covers Sammy's forearm, the words, Markland X Killer, scrawled on it in black Sharpie, a prominent display of his anger. Beads of sweat cascade Sammy's chubby cheeks as he pedals through the summer heat. The events of the day before roll through Sammy's mind like chunks of freeze frame. His cheeks fire like a kiln, furious heat gushing through them at the sharp memory of Devin's grin taunting him, pressing him forward to reestablish the normal order of things.

"We can probably sneak some shine from my dad." Bo lifts a hopeful brow.

"No. We're going to get Brooks and that new kid. They're going to pay for what they done!" Hate dwells in his chiseled expression.

"Sammy, we done rode around half the town. They's probably just hiding out somewheres."

"They can't hide from me, no how!" Sammy pulls a switchblade knife from his jeans pocket.

"What you gonna do, Sammy? I ain't goin' back to juvie, man."

"Look what they did to my arm." Sammy lifts his casted arm, putting it on display, his sharp yell echoing through the trees.

"I know, man. That new kid suckered me upside the head, too."

"You think that's okay? Those shits is gonna pay." Sammy grits his teeth and presses his full body weight into his pedals.

"Let's kick their asses. But ain't no need to be stabbin' 'em."

"Quit being such a damn pussy!"

"Who's that?" Bo points to three kids on bikes at the bottom of the hill.

"Looks like that turd, 5-head. And Seth and Shane. Those little shits will know where Brooks and that new kid are. Come on." Sammy slides the knife into his pocket and pedals faster, fueled by his lust for revenge. Bo follows, pumping his legs on his pedals to keep pace.

As Sammy and Bo close in on their location, Shane points frantically. Without hesitation, all three boys send their bikes rolling into the gully and sprint into the woods.

The front tire of Cam's bicycle juts into the air sideways, still locked in a decelerating spin as Sammy and Bo come to a stop.

"Hey! Come back here you little shits!" Sammy's scream chases them through the woods. He jumps off his bike and scans the edge of the tree line, blood engorging his cheeks.

A frantic rustling of leaves ascends the hillside in the woods adjacent to the road. Sammy paces, stooping and craning his neck in different directions while facing the thick foliage.

"Sammy, look. Dumbasses ran off so fast they dropped their money." Bo reaches to pick up the twenty-dollar bill.

"*Dammit.*" Sammy's head remains locked on the hillside.

"*What the hell*?" The twenty-dollar bill scurries away from Bo. It flutters across the road.

"Quit screwing around."

"Dude, it's a twenty-dollar bill. I ain't screwin' around." Bo walks toward the bill that's come to rest on the side of the road.

"Let me see that." Sammy marches forward.

As Bo approaches the twenty-dollar bill again, it flutters, moving off the road and toward the woods. Sammy joins Bo, both walking off the roadway.

"Damn wind." Bo shakes his head as the twenty-dollar bill skitters to the tree line.

"Owwee!" Bo screams, his face contorting into a grimace as he grabs at his chest. His eyes swell at the scarlet spatter on his t-shirt.

"What's wrong with you?"

"Something bit me! Something just fucking bit me!"

"What bit you?"

"I don't know! I'm bleeding. Damn! It stings." Bo clasps his chest.

Leaves rustle as we move in the tree line, but we remain cloaked by the foliage. Here, definition dissolves into black shadow a few feet into the woods. Sammy snaps his head in our direction.

"Who's there? That your punk ass, Cam?"

"Now!" Robby shouts from our hiding spot in the woods.

A paintball whizzes by Sammy's head. Sammy and Bo exchange a wide-eyed glance before a torrent of our paintballs rain down on them, striking multiple spots on their bodies. They cover their faces with their arms, enduring the storm. As the rapid succession of paintballs strike their bodies and arms, their clothes transform into a patchwork of blue, red, orange, and green.

Devin's the first to clear the tree line, all the while walking forward with slow, methodical deliberation, firing round after round at Sammy and Bo.

Robby follows steps behind, alternating shots between Sammy and Bo.

Tee's screaming, "Markland X Crew gonna get ya, oh yeah," as he fires off shots with wild abandon.

I focus all my fire on Sammy. A steady flow of my green pellets spatter across his body, giving him no quarter. He lifts his cast to protect his face, the once white plaster a kaleidoscope of color.

"Cam set us up!" Bo screams, retreating to his bike as paintballs continue pelting him.

"He's dead! Seth and Shane are dead!" Sammy screams as he runs in retreat to the road.

Sammy grabs his bike as paintballs hiss by his head.

Bo starts pedaling. "Let's get out of here."

Sammy turns, defiant to the danger. "You're all so dead! We're going to kill you!"

"Don't mess with the Markland X Crew." Robby's voice is unwavering as he marches forward and takes aim.

Robby pulls the trigger and a paintball sizzles out of his rifle. In an instant, there's an explosion of blue paint on

Sammy's cheek. Sammy screams in pain and doubles over, grabbing his face where the paintball struck. His eyes rain fat, ugly tears. Crying hysterically, he jumps on his bike and furiously pedals away while clutching his face.

"Yesss!" Tee shouts, lifting his rifle into the air.

I blink several times. "Dude, you shot him in the face."

Robby's jaw hardens. "Now he'll know better than to mess with the Markland X Crew."

CHAPTER 30
It Goes Without Saying

S ammy and Bo pedal off. Climbing the hill on their bikes, they dissolve into the distance, and the air of invincibility that once seemed to surround Sammy disappears with them, punctuated by his hasty retreat.

Tee's strutting around with his paintball rifle held snug against his chest in a quasi-march, his high steps ridiculously exaggerated and a goofy grin plastered across his face. Devin and Robby celebrate our victory, high-fiving and chest bumping. I stand there still trying to process what happened. While our ambush might give Sammy and Bo some pause from approaching us, they'll be more hell-bent than ever to exact revenge.

"Dev, that was the best idea ever!" A triumphant gleam glows like growing fires in Robby's eyes.

"Evvveer!" Tee raises his rifle into the air. "Did you see Sammy's face? That little pudge ball was crying like a little baby."

Devin puffs out his chest. "They'll think twice about messing with us."

"Yeah, you're probably right." I pause, my lips wilting into a frown. "But they won't give up so easy. They'll try to catch us with our guard down."

"Or your pants down!" Tee grins.

"Brooks is right." The playful joking departs Devin's voice. "They'll try to find one of us separated from the group."

"So we stay together then." Tee's face tightens. "Markland X Crew protects its own."

"About that."

"Yeah, Robby, what you think? Markland X Crew material, right?" Tee frames his hands around Devin's face.

"You know how I feel. I think it goes without sayin', but I vote Dev's in," I weigh in without hesitation, directing my words to Robby.

Robby grins and fist bumps Devin. "Brother from anotha motha."

"So, that's it then?"

"Oh, hell no!" There's laughter in Robby's voice. Tee snickers.

"What you got in mind? Lego minefield?"

"I think we can do better than that, Brooks." Robby wears a plastered grin.

"Dudes, whatever it is, I'm game."

Tee nudges Devin on the shoulder. "I wouldn't be so sure of yourself."

Poor Devin. Been there. Done that. "So, what is it, Robby?"

"Shiners' Gorge." Robby's eyes gleam.

"Whoa." The word leaves my lips as involuntary as an exhaled breath.

Tee's smile evaporates in an instant. His round eyes connect with Robby's, but Robby's expression remains unchanged. Tee gives a frowning shake of his head. Devin looks around at the group with questioning eyes. *He's got no idea what Shiners' Gorge even means.*

"Robby, you know it's shine season right now." Tee's words rattle out like clanking metal.

"I know. This is supposed to be a test. It's not supposed to be easy. It's a commitment."

"Hey, man, I'm committed. I really am. Let's do what we need to do."

"Dev, you don't understand." My eyes meet his. "Summer's when they cook the shine."

"Come on, man. I'm good." Devin strikes a triumphant pose with his paintball rifle. *He just doesn't know any better.* I shift my attention to Robby.

"Robby, they got that whole area booby trapped."

"Remember what happened to Jacob Russman?"

"Nobody knows what happened to Jacob Russman, Tee. He disappeared. That's just what parents tell their kids to scare them away from Shiners' Gorge."

"Automatic weapons. Machine guns, man!" My words fall out in a hasty spill.

"So we'll be careful."

"Or dead." I shake my head as I deliver the words.

Devin bounces around in his black and white checkered shoes. "Guys, I'm good. Let's go."

"Yeah, listen to Dev. Quit being such a pack of pussies."

"This ain't cool, man. It's dangerous out there." Tee makes a sweeping motion to the woods. "You're going to put us all in danger, Robby."

"Cam Givers just ran up into them woods just a few minutes ago. And Seth and Shane. Heard any shots?"

"Yeah but—"

"Yeah, but nothing, Brooks. No shots. It's fine. We're fine. This is supposed to be just a little dangerous."

Tee shakes his head, wearing a frown. "It's more than a little dangerous."

"Look guys, we just faced off with Bo and Sammy." Devin's rally cry eyes circulate through the group. "I think we can handle this."

Tee scrunches his lips for a couple of moments. "Fine, but it's a bad idea."

"A terrible one." There's not a moment of hesitation in my reply.

"Follow me." Robby walks to the edge of the tree line. He straps his paintball rifle across his shoulder and trudges into the woods. Devin follows close behind. Tee and I hesitate a moment before making our way behind him. Sunlight sprinkles through the rustling leaves above. The shifting light hits the forest floor, mingling with shadow. The wavering bands of light cast an illusion like rippling water reflecting on a seabed in the shallows.

The ground beneath us crackles as we march up the ridge in a silent procession. *What the hell are we doing? Shiners' Gorge? This is a mistake!* Tee's eyes cloud like an impending storm. Devin exudes extra bounce in his step. He catches Robby and they climb the hill together, both boys wearing mischievous grins on their faces. As we venture deeper into the woods, dark tendrils of shadow creep between the trees, the thick canopy beginning to blot out the sun. Only flecks of ashen sky peek between the patchwork of interwoven hardwood limbs, and with each step we take, we slip deeper into the darkness.

Robby and Devin reach the top of the ridge and stop. Robby pulls his canteen from his belt and takes a gulp. He takes small steps, rotating his forward-facing position a few degrees, studying his bearings.

Tee tosses his chin at Robby as we reach the ridge line. "Let me get a sip of that."

Tall hardwood trees, flush with summer growth, limit the view into the valley below. Though at a high vantage point, there's no sign of Cam, Shane, and Seth, and the valley below us is portrait-still.

"Guys, that's north." Robby points off to the distance. "We're going due west. The way I figure it, we need to go north-northwest, and we'll run right into Shiners' Gorge."

Tee hands Robby the canteen and shakes his head. "Still say it's a stupid idea. Shiners being so active and all."

"Hey, how come they're so active now?"

Robby chuckles. "What, Dev, you ain't got shiners in California?"

"Uh, no."

"They cook in the summer 'cause the helicopters can't see 'em through the trees." I point to the thick canopy of leaves above us.

"That makes sense."

"What doesn't make sense is what we're doing."

"Tee, are you more of a chicken shit than Cam Givers? I mean, seriously."

"Dudes, we still got our paintball rifles, you know. In case something does go down."

"They got real rifles, Dev." I meet his eyes with mine.

Robby rolls his eyes at me and shakes his head before turning to Devin. "How much ammo you got left?"

"I still got this whole container." Devin pulls a plastic canister from his cargo shorts pocket. "It's enough to fill us all back up and then some."

"Lock and load gentlemen." Robby opens the reservoir for paintballs on his rifle and pours in more ammo.

Devin follows his lead and reloads. Tee and I circle around Robby and reload our rifles as well. Once loaded we sling the guns on our backs and wrap the straps across our chests.

CHAPTER 31
Ghosts from the Past

"We gotta go in that direction." Robby points in the direction of a thicket of hardwoods.

"Surprised we didn't run into Cam, Seth, and Shane." Tee lands wide eyes on me.

I shrug. "They're out here somewhere. They left their bikes back there."

"Let's go gentlemen!" Devin starts hustling down the hill.

"Wait up, Dev." Robby trudges through the underbrush after him.

Tee looks at me with wavering eyes and shrugs his shoulders before following behind Devin and Robby. Our pace slows as we descend the ridge, each step growing steeper beneath our feet. Robby and Devin ease their way around a jagged rock outcropping that springs out from the hill before dropping out of sight behind the giant rock. I clasp the sun-warmed boulder, following Tee's lead while steadying my footing as we inch our way around it.

"Shit!" Tee's feet slide.

"Tee!"

Tee's fingertips brush my outstretched hand as he falls. He lands on his butt with a thud, bounces once, and begins sliding. I scurry around the boulder, my fingers gripping the rock tight, clinging to the patches of bright green furry moss that cover it. Tee comes to a stop in a patch of ferns at the bottom of the hill. Robby runs over.

"Tee! You okay, man?"

I stay low to the ground, scampering down the hill.

"Told you this was a bad idea!" Tee's tone is scalding.

Devin helps him to his feet. Tee sweeps his hands across his shirt and pants, brushing away decaying leaf debris, dirt and underbrush.

My eyes meet his. "You okay, man?"

Tee inspects the fresh scrapes on his elbows and palms. He dips his head and shakes it while letting out a simmering sigh through his nose.

"Yeah, I'm alright."

"Dudes, not far from here, I think." Robby points to the steep embankment that lies before us. "Over that ridge."

I narrow my eyes on Robby. "We don't have to do this. Tee could've really been hurt."

"We stick closer together. Be more careful."

"I *was* bein' careful, Dev."

"Sorry, Tee. I didn't mean it like that. I just meant we can just help each other. Stay close together's all."

"Quit the bickering, Sally's. And let's get a move on."

Tee eyes the embankment. "You sure that's the right way?"

"Should be going north-northwest the way I figure it. Which should be that way."

I draw the corner of my lips. "Should be? Or *is* that way?" My tone reflects my growing frustration with our endeavor.

"I don't know, man. I mean, I think so."

Tee flashes a big grin and grabs the canteen off Robby's hip. "Okay dum-dum, let's see what your compass says."

Robby gives Tee a playful shoulder shove. Tee holds the canteen, and we all gather around as the fluttering compass needle begins to settle on due north.

"Told you guys!" Robby trumpets as the needle verifies his proposed direction. Devin points to the compass.

"Dude, look at it. That thing's broken."

The compass needle resumes its movement, a slow spin at first, moving like the second hand of a timepiece. Tee hits the canteen as if to reset it, but the spinning needle accelerates. The needle begins moving so fast that it becomes a whirring blur. Robby shakes his head.

"What the hell?"

I lift my widening eyes to Robby's. "You ever seen it do this?"

"Never."

Tee frowns as the needle whirls like a propeller. "Thing's broke, man."

A rustling of leaves near the top of the steep embankment grabs our attention. We hoist our heads like a group of startled deer. Cam Givers scampers the hill, his complexion ghastly white. He descends the steep hill with far too much speed, his rapid steps turning into momentary slides before regaining his footing. In a flash, he goes from upright to a treacherous tumble. We start running to intersect him. I wince at his uncontrolled fall, his limbs flailing as he spins. Cam yelps as parts of his body thud on the hard earth. He nearly collides with a large oak tree, but he tumbles past it before his momentum finally stalls.

Cam's pitiful sobs echo through the quiet forest. He clutches his body in the fetal position, clothes torn and bloodied. A trickle of blood drips from his nostril, and a swollen knot high on his cheekbone suggests he struck a rock during his fall.

"Cam, are you all right?" It's as if my words are razor-tipped arrows slicing into the ground around him.

He rolls sideways onto his knees, and his head and eyes shoot up. As if by instinct, his hands grab some earth in an animalistic stance, ready to thrust his body into action and resume his retreat.

Tee's wide eyes settle on his trembling body. "Cam, you almost killed yourself."

Robby offers his hand. "You okay, man?"

"Myron's here! Oh my God! He's got Seth and Shane!" The words explode from his lips.

Chiming alarm bells fill my head. My last encounter with Myron wasn't one I'd soon like to repeat.

A shivering twitch passes through Tee. "Did you see Sammy and Bo?"

"No, Myron. It's just Myron. But something's wrong with him!" The pitch of Cam's voice rises, his hands frantic in expression.

Tee smirks. "No shit something's wrong with him. Kid's a mutant."

"No. Something's wrong! Really wrong!" Cam flashes fear-bulged eyes.

I tilt my head at him. "What do you mean?"

"We gotta get out of here. We can't stay here. He'll kill us all!" The shrill alarm in Cam's voice sends a parade of tingles to my spine.

Tee levels his eyes on Cam's. "Where is he? Where's Shane and Seth?"

"There. Over the ridge, on the next hill."

Devin's eyes follow the direction of Cam's shaky pointing finger. "Can you show us?"

"No, you don't understand. We can't stay here. I've got to get out of here. You need to get out of here. I think he killed Seth, and he was going after Shane. I ran as fast as I could." Cam's nearly hyperventilating as he spews his frantic words. He pulls out his asthma inhaler and takes a few quick puffs.

Robby places a steadying hand on Cam's trembling shoulder. "You mean he punched Seth or something?"

"No, I think he killed him. He picked him up by his throat and smashed the back of his head over and over into a tree. There was so much blood! Oh my God! So much blood." Tears stream from Cam's eyes.

Devin shakes his head. "That can't be right. How big is this kid?"

"He's pretty big." My voice cracks.

"He ain't that big. Not to do that. Cam, *you sure* about what you saw?" Robby locks eyes with Cam. "I mean, you said you were running away. Maybe you didn't see it right."

"Honest, I seen it all. He picked Seth up by the throat with one hand, lifted him into the air and started smashing his head into the tree."

"What'd you do?" Devin asks.

"I screamed. He turned his head all the way around and glared at me. And he kept smashing Seth's head into the tree while he stared at me and grinned. And I ran. I ran as fast as I could."

Robby's facial muscles tense, and the skin around his nose crinkles. "We gotta go help Seth and Shane."

"Didn't you listen to me? He killed them! He'll kill you too! Something's wrong with him." Cam's voice trembles, a wailing alarm.

"You bastard!" A scream echoes through the trees from the adjacent ridgeline.

Tee's eyes bounce wide. "That's Shane!"

"Let's go!" Robby takes off in a sprint.

Devin falls in pursuit behind Robby and, as if adjoined to the other boys by an invisible rope, Tee swivels around in a fluid, running-start movement, joining the chase. Tears stream Cam's face, his eyes bursting wide. I hesitate for a moment. Cam shakes his head as if to tell me, *don't do it.*

"Go get the cops, Cam."

I turn around and chase after the other boys. Shane's scream echoes through the trees as we storm the ridge. We're moving at full speed, leaping fallen logs and semi-exposed boulders like Olympic hurdlers. My adrenaline surges as we charge ahead to save our friends.

Robby reaches the top of the ridge first and bounds it, descending into the valley below. Devin, on a different route than Robby, swivels his body over a partially fallen tree in one fluid movement, his feet striking the forest floor midstride.

Tee and I give chase behind, our legs locking into occasional decaying leaf-matter slides as we charge ever forward.

"No, nooooooo!" Shane's desperate voice breaks through the trees.

We race through the trees, approximating the origin of his scream. The forest falls quiet, except for the stamping of our own feet. As we reach the ridgetop, we unwind our sprints and come to a stop where the ground plateaus. But there's no sign of Shane, Seth, or Myron.

"Look." Tee's voice trails off. He points to a large oak tree.

An oblong, thick patch of dark liquid sheen six feet high on the tree trunk draws our eyes. *Is that blood? Is Cam right? Did Myron really kill Seth?* I take a couple of slow steps forward, examining it. The dark red fluid flows with the consistency of honey, trickling between the valleys in the bark like small streams on divergent paths meandering to the ocean. My eyes trace a rivulet of the fluid to the forest floor where a small amount rolls over the top of a gnarled root and pools on a fallen maple leaf. My heart skips at the discernible scarlet hue. And my vagrant eyes wander my surroundings, never staying in one spot long.

"Shane," Robby bellows out, his voice echoing through the trees and hills.

"We need to get the cops." My voice passes right through Devin. He stands there, slack-jawed, eyes at five-alarm.

"Seth!" Tee's frantic shout ricochets off the trees.

A sudden crackle of sticks yanks our heads as if tethered together. Myron trudges by a thicket of trees, oblivious to us. Tee's mouth falls open, and I retreat a step, a chill settling deep into my bones. Myron's shoulders hunch and his gaze scrapes the ground. Robby pulls his paintball rifle off his shoulder into a ready position.

"Myron!" The intensity of Robby's yell carries an implicit warning.

Myron freezes in his tracks a couple of steps away from the thicket of hardwood trees. He rotates his head, his face devoid of expression, eyes lost in some perpetual vacuum of time and space.

"What did you do to Seth and Shane?" Robby raises his rifle and points it at Myron.

A glimmer of life pulses into Myron's face. He glares at us from underneath his raised brows. His thin lips curl into a menacing grin.

"Something's wrong with him," Tee frets.

Devin pulls his paintball rifle off his shoulder and takes aim. Tee retreats a step and positions his body for a quick escape. I'm frozen, locked on Myron's eyes. He starts walking again, and I catch a glimpse of that familiar blue swirl flash in his eyes. *Oh shit!* The momentary flicker steals the breath from my lungs and sends a cold chill charging my spine. It's the same as I saw in Mysterious Margo's eyes in my bathroom.

"*Jesus.*" Tee's body erupts in a cringing shiver.

"Stop!" Robby yells in Myron's direction.

My heart thuds in my chest as Myron disappears behind the thicket of trees. "Did you just see that? The swirl! It's the blue swirl."

Devin's mouth hangs ajar. "What the hell was that?" The words fall from his mouth. His eyes balloon and his body trembles.

Oh shit. Oh shit—oh shit—oh shit. If he's scared, we should be really scared. A rolling tremor roars through my body. I expel the ascending tingles, shivering them out of my neck and head.

A steady whirring noise draws my eyes. The compass needle on Robby's canteen hums with ferocity, the needle vanishing like the spinning prop of an airplane. *What the hell's going on?*

Tee's eyes dart around. "What's he doing?"

I shake my head. "I don't know. *This is not good.*"

"I think he's hiding. Hiding behind those trees." Devin's voice quavers.

"Come out, Myron!" Robby's yell bounds through the trees but goes unanswered. "What'd you do with Seth and Shane?"

We stand yards from the thicket of trees, huddled close together, each one of us too unnerved to investigate. Tee shifts his weight from one foot to the other, eyes sprinting about. Devin's rolling his bottom lip inside his mouth and biting it with his teeth. Robby grinds his, clenching his jaw.

A rustle of leaves behind the thicket of trees breaks the silence. Robby and Devin hoist their rifles to their shoulders and take aim. A tall figure emerges from behind the trees.

"Robby." The voice rings familiar.

Robby's mouth drops. His hands fall away, the rifle sliding to a rest on its shoulder strap. His eyes glisten.

"Dad?" A tear traverses his cheek.

"Son, I've missed you so much." The man lifts his face, a warm smile emerging on his lips.

"Holy shit!" Tee's eyes pop wide.

There's no mistaking the man. It's Robby's dad. He looks just like I remember him. *Not possible!* I cringe. Tee's lower jaw lunges.

"But how are you...How could you...You..."

"I don't know, son, but I love you. I've missed you so much. You and your mom."

"I miss you too, Dad." Robby takes a couple of steps forward.

"That's not your dad, Robby." Tee launches the words at Robby.

"Tee, thanks so much for looking after Robby." The man's eyes land on Tee. Tee's shoulders jump for his neck, and he averts his eyes from the man's gaze. The man smiles at Robby. "Come and give your dad a big hug, Robby."

Robby takes a few more steps forward.

"*Your dad's dead, Robby*. It's not him! Stop!" Tee's shout grinds Robby to a stop like a failing gear.

"I'm not, Tee." The man crosses his arms and pats his shoulders as if to say, *here I am, right here in the flesh*.

"Come and give your old man a hug, and we can go home together." The man outstretches awaiting arms.

Devin trains his paintball rifle on the man and screams. "Don't do it, Robby!"

"Don't shoot him, Dev." There's an underpinning of emphatic urgency in Robby's voice.

I shake my head at Robby, my eyes glistening. "Robby, it's not your dad. It's something else. He just came from where Myron disappeared."

"It's me, son. I love you." The man takes a couple of measured steps forward. Moving closer. Ever closer.

Devin's eyes grow wider. "We need to go, *now*!"

"Robby!" Tee's scream halts Robby's progress for a moment.

"Guys, it's my dad. Look at him. I don't know how, but it's him." Tears wobble from Robby's eyes and his body trembles.

"Come home, Robby. Let's go home." The man kneels and opens his arms wide to receive a hug.

Robby runs forward and embraces his father in a tight hug. Tears stream from his eyes, and his body trembles in the power of the moment. Robby's lips climb into a cathartic smile as he drowns in his father's long-absent embrace. The two meld, Robby's chest heaving with raw emotion. I shake my head as my body trembles. *This isn't possible! Everything about this... everything... it's not right!*

Robby's dad pats his back with tenderness as they hug in a warm embrace. He closes his eyes, a soft smile on his face. But a moment later, the patting turns into sequential finger strumming on Robby's back. The man's eyes shoot open. *Something's wrong!* His lips thin as they curl into an odious grin. A flicker of blue swivels around his irises.

Devin takes two steps forward, drops to his knee, raises his paintball rifle and pulls the trigger. The rifle hisses, and the paintball strikes the man in the shoulder. The man recoils, releasing his grasp on Robby and lets out a furious, animalistic growl.

"You will all come home!" the man booms as he rises to his feet. He whips his arm forward, and his fingertips rake across Robby's arm. Hot blood wells from the broken skin.

Robby staggers backward. The man's warm, soft face transforms into a rigid glare in an instant. His lips snarl, exposing a top row of jagged teeth. The fleshy color of his pallor retreats, leaving the dullish-gray hue of death in its wake. His puffy cheeks shrivel into his face, creating cavernous valleys that sharpen the outlines of his facial bones. His smooth skin crinkles before pulling taut against the underlying bones. His eyes sink into his skull and halo with dark rings. His bony fingers elongate, his dirty fingernails growing thicker and pointed, resembling claws.

"RUN!" Tee screams as he bursts into a sprint on the steep decline.

My legs carry me away before I even understand what's happening. Paralyzed in shock, Robby stares at the thing, which moments before mimicked the appearance of his late father. With blank eyes, his brows furrow, renewed tears streaming his cheeks. As it continues making its hideous transformation, Devin runs and grabs Robby, shaking him for a moment until he comes to.

"Let's go! Run, Robby, run!" Devin screams as the creature rises even taller.

"You're all coming home!" It hisses, a forked, serpentine tongue spilling out of its mouth as it speaks.

Branches and underbrush slice at our shins as Tee and I make a sprinting escape. We're racing down the steep ridge as Robby and Devin come surging over the top of the hill kicking up showers of dirt, eyes glazed with terror. The creature follows behind them, moving on all fours, snarling as it gives chase.

"Runnnn! Run faster!" I scream as blasts of terror-induced adrenaline course through my veins.

Tee lets out half screams with each retreating step. Fear pumps shots of hot blood through my body like a fuel injector, powering my retreat. I catch Tee, something I've never done. The menacing creature trounces on all fours behind Robby and Devin. Their legs motor beneath them, feet kicking high into the air with every stride. Even though we're racing at full speed, the creature's closing on us. It's still accelerating its forward speed, its movements more akin to a charging bear than a human. The creature closes the gap on Robby and Devin. *This is going to be bad! Real bad!*

Devin trips and tumbles to the ground. He comes rolling to a stop. The creature slows from full speed, the protruding bones of its shoulder joints projecting upward and pushing against its creased skin as it lurches forward.

Robby screams. "Dev! Get up! Run! Run!"

It's too late. The creature stands over him, snarling, its breath lashing Devin's face, strands of his wavy hair feathering with each of its exhales, the air all around us ripe with the stench of rotting flesh. Thick saliva rolls off its fangs as its bony leg presses on Devin's shoulder, anchoring his body to earth. Devin's frozen, his eyes screaming. The creature lowers its head, its mouth and razor-sharp fangs inches away from his face, ready to devour him at any moment. Devin whimpers, tears trickling on his cheeks. The creature sniffs his face and hair, drawing in rapid, shallow breaths through its bristle-haired snout, before its long tongue uncoils from its mouth. Devin closes his eyes, unable to watch his own undoing. Devin winces as the beast's serpentine tongue traces his cheek. He curls his limbs toward his stomach like a dying spider, all the fight having abandoned him. I shake my head, my lips quivering and eyes glistening. *Get up, Devin! Try to get up!* But he's bracing himself for the unbelievable pain that's sure to follow, accepting his inevitable fate.

The creature's tongue coils back into its mouth and its head springboards. It takes a deep breath in through its nose in the direction of Robby and rises, releasing Devin from the grip of its powerful paw.

Before any of us can process what's happening, it's moving again. And it's zeroed in on Robby. Devin lies in the fetal position in the creature's wake, trembling, tears saturating his cheeks. Robby takes off in a full sprint, but his delayed reaction costs him valuable time and distance. The creature's already at full speed and closing fast.

From the corner of my eye, I catch a glimpse of something dart out from a tangle of trees. I let out a stifled scream before realizing it's Brady Palmer. He's running in the opposite direction as us, into the oncoming danger. Robby screams as the wiry-haired creature readies to pounce. It launches itself airborne, claws outstretched, ready to deliver him a death blow. Brady sends a glass vial hurtling through the air. It shatters on the menacing creature's face, splattering its green liquid contents. It lets out a horrible groan, like a dying elk, as it tumbles to the earth. Robby ducks and the creature's body grazes his before plummeting to the earth and tumbling forward, carried by its own powerful momentum.

The creature rolls to a stop ten yards past Robby, groaning in pain. Its skin pulsates like the top of a bubbling cauldron, bits of its elastic hide rising from the surface. Brady rushes to Robby and pulls him from the ground. Robby inspects himself, his eyelids tacked wide, but he lacks any gaping wounds. Devin's impulse for flight activates. He jumps to his feet and runs to us.

The creature lifts on its haunches and begins to drag itself to a cluster of trees several yards away. Its body undulates, getting smaller. I'm frozen, slack-jawed. As it reaches the tree line, it gives us a blood-thirsty glare before dragging itself behind the cover of the trees.

"What the fuck is that thing?" Devin's frantic scream breaks the stunned silence.

"It worked! I can't believe it works!" Brady pumps a fist.

Tee circles back but roots himself about a hundred yards away, his legs trembling. As my mind thaws from a deep freeze, I start to take steps backward, putting more distance between myself and the trees the hideous creature retreated behind.

"What works? What the hell was that thing?" Robby's eyes scream for answers.

A squirrel scurries the trunk of a tree, orbiting the tree on its ascent. It moves onto a branch, stopping. It rises on its hind legs, its eyes locking onto us. It begins barking. *Its eyes! Oh my God! Its eyes!* A similar flash of blue moves through its eyes like twin indigo hurricanes rotating. Its chest heaves unnaturally with great determination.

Brady turns to us. "Let's go. We can't stay here. It's not safe here. We need to go now!"

No one questions Brady's command. We're all racing through the woods to the road. I struggle to keep up with the blistering pace as the endorphins that worked to mask the pain of my fatiguing muscles begin to fade.

CHAPTER 32

Redirection

As we move out into the clearing of the road, wailing police sirens approach from the distance. *Thank God! The Police.* Seth and Shane's bikes lay strewn in the gully by the road, but Cam's bike is gone. *Cam must've gotten to the police.*

Brady's eyes follow the road into the direction of the sirens. "We have to get out of here."

"We need to tell the cops what happened."

Tee jerks his head to me. "Did you see that thing? Cops can't do nothing about whatever that thing is."

"Yeah, but they'll know we were here."

"What are we going to tell them, huh?" Robby throws his hands into the air as the words leave his mouth. "Myron turned into my dad, then turned into a monster. And then turned into a squirrel?"

"Yeah, Robby's right." Devin's wide eyes lock on mine. "They'll lock us all up in the nut bin for sure."

"We can't stay here. That thing'll be back. It's changing. Gathering its strength."

How the hell does he know these things? And where'd he even come from?

"We're not debating this here." Tee scans the tree line. "I ain't about to wait for that thing to come back. Know that time when you're screaming at the TV in a horror movie, telling them all to run? That's *now.*"

I swallow a shallow breath through my mouth. "So where? Where should we go?"

"Far away from here as possible." Tee's words spill out, overlapping my own.

"Follow me." Brady takes off running to the opposite tree line.

We stay huddled in the middle of the road. None of us really know Brady Palmer, other than the stories we've heard. None of them good. The police sirens continue growing louder, dwindling the seconds before the squad cars roll over the hill and spot us. *The point of no return.*

"Come on!" Brady screams as he emphatically motions for us to come.

"Dammit." Robby turns and sprints to the hill.

It's a decision of necessity, not choice. None of us want to, nor could we explain what happened in Shiners' Gorge. Nor do we want to get tangled with Brady Palmer, but that course charted itself for us. We all start running and work into the tree line at the same moment the patrol cars breach the hill, and by the slimmest of margins, we make it into the woods undetected.

Our procession moves with haste through the woods in silence. Brady leads the way in an unwavering push forward.

Where's he taking us? A predetermined location? I study him. He takes purposeful steps, a silent rudder steering at the stern of our fate. Replayed images of the horrible happenings in Shiner's Gorge trample my internal questions, squashing them underfoot a wave of waking nightmares. I wince as I succumb to the onslaught of fresh memory. Haunting screams. Blood. The creature.

The other boys' eyes glaze, becoming uninhabited, as if they're abandoning this world and slipping into their own minds. My mind swims, treading rough seas, head making occasional surface breaches for a breath of conscious thought before all that churning uncertainty pulls me beneath the dark waves. There's little clarity, mostly turbulence. Synapses misfire, little connection possible in the murkiness of my mind. Everything's disjointed.

The events we've just experienced imprint me with an indelible mark, calling into question everything I thought I understood about this world. I imagine the Aztecs we learned about in our history class experienced the same, when the conquistadors first strode ashore in their silvery armor—my dominion is reduced to a paltry shadow of my former understanding of the way of things.

CHAPTER 33
The Disappearance of the Rogers Twins

Two patrol cars come to a screeching halt on Timberline Road. Trees overhang the roadway, the bony branches splintering sunlight. Clancy's stomach gurgles, a silent acknowledgment of the dangers imminent in this location on the outskirts of town. The desolate, rutted road lies on the way to nowhere. Originally cut through the forest as a firebreak line, and later paved with federal DEA grant money, the police occasionally patrol here for illegal activities emanating from Shiners' Gorge, but this only marks Officer Clancy's third time here.

They turn the sirens off in quick succession but leave the lights on both cars flashing. Streaks of red and blue trail across the trees as Officer Clancy steps out of the lead squad car. Clancy stares in mild surprise at the two bicycles. When Cam Givers ran into the police station telling a fantastical story about Myron Thompson attacking and killing his friends with superhuman strength, Clancy harbored serious doubts. Another boy who read too many comic books with an overactive imagination gone wild. But the bicycles corroborate a bit of Cam's story and make Clancy wonder if some of his story might prove true. While claims of Myron's superhuman strength strike Clancy as ludicrous, it's possible to attribute this to a scrawny, sixty-five pound boy's honest perception of a much larger boy attacking his friends. It still seems strange that a missing boy would turn up in the woods to attack some classmates. Although, by all accounts,

Myron's a total degenerate piece of shit. Clancy turns his walkie-talkie on.

"Marcy. Over." Clancy surveys the edge of the woods.

"Go, Officer Clancy."

"So, there's two bikes out here on Timberline Road. This part of Cam Givers' story checks out. Think me and Officer Ivansek will have Cam lead us to where he says his friends were attacked by Myron Thompson and have a look around. Over."

Clancy waves at Officer Ivansek, trying to get his attention. He's taking a bite of his beef jerky, shuffling in his seat. A beat cop as well, and also the beneficiary of the veteran layoffs in the department, Officer Clancy asked him to come along, not because he put much credence into Cam Givers' story, but because of the dangers inherent to Shiners' Gorge. Officer Ivansek fails to notice Clancy waving his hand.

"You want me to phone Holt? Over."

"No. *DON'T phone Holt*. He's in a session. Over."

Because of the terrain in Harper Pass, Detective Holt swears by the shortwave radios. Spotty cell phone signals make service intermittent at best. He never carries his radio into session but always carries his cell phone.

"Are you sure?"

"Marcy, they're going through a lot right now." Clancy looks into his backseat at the awkward, little, bottle-nerved boy staring out the window. "This still might be just a boy's imagination. Let's leave Holt alone. They've got some issues to work through. Over."

Officer Clancy motions again for Officer Ivansek to get out of his patrol car. Ivansek hoists his large frame out of the vehicle. The police cruiser rocks on its axles as if taking a big sigh of relief. Ivansek's an oafish man, clumsy in appearance and in his police work. *Not the worst guy to bring to Shiners' Gorge. May not be smart, but he's a big sonna bitch!*

"So, what's the story, cap'?"

"Dude, I'm not *your* captain. Or *a* captain. I started like three weeks before you did."

"Yeah, yeah." Officer Ivansek hoists his belt to his protruding belly. "So, what's the sitch?"

"Look, we need to have Cam Givers show us where he says his friends were attacked by that Myron kid. This whole story smells like bullshit, but sure as shit, there's those Rogers brothers' bikes."

"Yeah. Sounds good, cap'."

"Dammit! What did I just tell you?"

"Oh yeah. Right. Sorry, Clancy. Just habit."

"All right, man. Well, just cut it out. It's unprofessional."

"You got it ca… I mean, Clancy. Sorry."

Clancy shoots him eyes that scream, *are you serious*?

Clancy opens the back door of the cruiser and Cam Givers scurries away. He sandwiches himself between the other door and the steel mesh divider that protects the front of the vehicle from its run-of-the-mill criminal passengers.

"Cam, come on. I need you to show me where you and your friends were."

Cam Givers wedges himself in tight and shakes his head no. His eyes drip with fear at the prospect of reentering the woods.

"Kid, come on. *We're* here now. Nothing's going to happen." Officer Clancy taps the firearm on his hip.

"I...I can't."

"Sure you can. Just get out of the car. Take us to where you were with your friends. You can do that, right?"

Tears well in Cam's eyes, and he gives a vehement shake of his head. Cam's body shivers as if he's cold, but it's summer and pushing ninety-five degrees.

"Listen, Cam, me and Officer Ivansek will protect you. Isn't that right, Officer Ivansek?"

Officer Ivansek's finger worms around deep inside his nostril. With the weight of two sets of eyes resting upon him, he wriggles it out of his nose, pulling a stringy booger out with it. Officer Clancy frowns in disgust as Ivansek brushes his hands across his pants, discarding the evidence.

"That's right. We're right here with ya, kid. Aunt Melissa gonna keep ya safe for sure." Officer Ivansek hoists a goofy smile as he places his hand on his holstered service weapon.

Clancy shoots Ivansek a sideways glance, intended to say, *you're not helping, not at all.* Ivansek gets the message, shrugs his shoulders and retreats to his patrol car. Officer Clancy leans into the patrol car.

"Look, Cam. Officer Ivansek. He ain't the brightest bulb on the tree. But he's just the kind of person you want with us. I mean, look at him. The guy's a giant, right?"

Tears stream down Cam Givers' cheeks, and he doesn't surrender an inch of ground. Clancy lets a deep exhale escape his lungs. *Shit. This kid ain't going nowhere. I'd have to drag him out.*

"Okay, how 'bout this? You just get out of the car, *just* for a second. Point us in the direction of where you last saw those boys, and you can stay here in the car. Can you do that for me, son?"

"Uh…yes sir." Cam's meek voice crackles. He makes a tentative exit out of the vehicle.

"We was over there. About three ridgelines away." Cam points into the woods. "Top of the third ridge is where Myron was. Where he attacked us, sir. I mean, where he attacked Seth and Shane."

"That sounds real near Shiners' Gorge. What were you kids doing playing there?"

"We wasn't playing. We was hiding. Hiding from Sammy and Bo. They were after us."

"Did you see Sammy and Bo with that Myron fella'?"

"No. It was just Myron."

"Okay. Me and Officer Ivansek are going to go check this out. You'll be safe here. We'll leave the car on for ya." Officer Clancy's words leech the color from Cam's face. "Don't worry. There's no way to unlock the back from outside the car. This is reinforced glass, too." Clancy taps the glass with his Mag Light.

"Okay." Cam's voice wavers.

"You're going to be fine. Just stay in the car. Play a game or something. We'll be back before you know it."

A wide-eyed Cam climbs into the backseat, and Clancy closes the door behind him before putting the air conditioning on full blast. He closes and locks the door behind him. He motions to Ivansek and points to the woods.

Clancy narrows his eyes on Ivansek as the two men ascend the hill. "What the hell was that back there?"

"What?"

"Aunt Melissa? Are you serious? What does that even mean?"

"Oh. *Ohhh*." A shot of color rushes into Ivansek's cheeks. "Man, I tell ya. I had this mean ole aunt growing up, Aunt Melissa. She didn't take any guff."

Clancy rolls his eyes. "So you named your service weapon after her?"

"Well, yeah. I mean, seemed appropriate. She was one tough cookie, and so is this little beaut'." Ivansek rubs his hand on the black leather holster.

The two officers reach the top of the first ridge and scan the valley below. Their eyes traverse narrow passageways between the girthy trunks of hardwood trees. Nothing stirs, and the eerie silence of the forest scales Clancy's spine. The men descend the ridge, careful attention paid to their periphery. As they approach the valley at the bottom of the ridge, a sudden flash of movement snags their attention. Clancy unsnaps the button on his holster, readying his weapon. The men pause, focused eyes funneling through thick summer foliage. They wait, but nothing stirs. Clancy's shifty eyes land on Officer Ivansek.

"Let's go, but make sure you watch our six. And be careful. This whole area could be booby trapped. Trip wires and such."

The real danger of an ambush by nefarious criminals near Shiners' Gorge concerns Officer Clancy far more than Myron Thompson. As they move through the valley and begin their ascent of the second ridge, Clancy scans his periphery, his eyes flitting through the tree line.

Ivansek's pores seep summer sweat, saturating spots in the fabric of his uniform. His heavy mouth breathing sounds their advance. The damp patches materializing on his uniform swell in size with each new step he takes. *How in the hell'd he pass his fitness exam?* Clancy gives a subtle shake of his head and mutters.

"You need to lay off the snack cakes."

"Whatever, pretty boy. That's Stroman's Light, not snack cakes." Ivansek rubs his beer belly, proud as an expectant mother.

Nothing wrong with his hearing.

Clancy scans the ridgeline above. A persistent still smothers it with silence. He points to the top of the hill.

"All right. That's it right there. The top of that ridge. That's where Cam Givers said everything went down."

"Let's go get this kid."

"Not convinced there is one. But stay alert, we're damn close to Shiners' Gorge." Clancy's words float out as a hushed whisper.

The men climb to the top of the hill. Clancy motions for Ivansek to check their flank while he investigates. There's no indication of anyone in the area. Ivansek waddles to an area of disturbed earth, inspecting the ground, noticing the subtle difference. Two patches of bare earth contrast against the surrounding areas of uniform detritus covering the ground. Ivansek follows the areas of disturbed earth to the base of a large oak tree. He stands beneath the canopy, inspecting them. The imprints bear a strong resemblance to shoe prints. Clancy spots Ivansek lingering and joins him.

"Clancy, what do you make of this? Looks like two shoe prints, right?"

But Clancy's eyes fixate on the tree trunk. He shuffles around Ivansek for a closer inspection, hoping it's sap, but his instincts scream otherwise. The tree appears spattered in blood stains, soaked deep into the soggy bark. Ivansek rises and follows the direction of Clancy's gaze. Ivansek flinches and his eyes bulge.

"Jesus!"

Clancy pulls an ink pen from his pocket and runs it across one of the thick rivers of semi-gelatinous fluid between the bark. The silver housing near the tip of the pen coats with a dark red residue. Clancy's heart primes, a racehorse in a starting gate. It's blood beginning to coagulate and a lot of it.

Officer Clancy pulls his service weapon from his hip holster, raises it into a firing position, and orbits the tree. His eyes dart in all directions, but there's no sign of anyone, only distant katydids singing a chorus in the summer heat.

He fumbles over his belt, never lowering his eyes. He collects his radio and raises it to his lips. "Marcy? Over."

"You think that boy's telling the truth?" Ivansek unsheathes his firearm.

"Don't know. Maybe his perception of what happened. Marcy! Over!"

There's no answer on the other end of the radio, only the hum of static. Clancy pulls his cell phone from his pocket and clenches his jaw at zero bars on the display. Despite that, he enters the station number and presses dial. It doesn't work.

"Dammit!"

Ivansek lifts a brow at Clancy. "What should we do?"

"We need to secure this scene as best we can. Don't think it's a good idea to leave just one of us behind so close to Shiners'

Gorge. Let's tape this area off and then head back to the cars to call for backup."

The two officers work in concert to seal off the area as best they can.

CHAPTER 34
Brady Palmer

We follow Brady through the woods in silence, not one of us so much as raising a question. My fears and uncertainty worked to suppress some of my intrinsic skepticism. But with a healthy amount of distance separating us from the creature that tried to kill us in Shiners' Gorge, my faculties begin to resurface. So do my doubts about where Brady Palmer is leading us.

As Robby follows close behind, he narrows his eyes on Brady's swift progress. Robby's voice sprints to catch Brady. "Can you just stop for a second?"

"Almost there." Brady doesn't slow his advance.

"Almost where?" Tee asks.

We arrive at a clearing. Most of the hike through the woods I spent preoccupied, so lost in my own mind that I didn't realize where Brady was leading us. As we clear the tree cover, it's obvious. We've emerged from the woods into the cul-de-sac on High Street. Mr. Wadlow's house and the vacant lot where we stashed our bikes the day before, lie ahead. *Had we escaped one terrible fate only to be dealt another*?

Tee stops in his tracks. "What are we doing?"

"We're going to Professor Wadlow's house."

"Like hell we are. I'm not going near that place."

"Relax. He *knows* it was you in his house yesterday."

"What! And that's supposed to make it better?"

"Calm down. He's not mad. We're on the same team here. Besides, we have bigger fish to fry."

Devin tilts his head at Brady. "What do you mean? On the same team?"

"This thing, whatever it is, we've been tracking it. Professor Wadlow's trying to figure out how to kill it."

Robby squeezes Brady in a vise glare. "You *knew* about this? Why didn't you warn anyone?"

"Warn 'em about what? That there's a monster stalking and killing people it's marked?"

"What do you mean marked?" My words rattle off my lips as a hollow tremble.

"This thing'll kill anything in its way. It literally exists to cause pain. But from what we can tell, it's after certain people."

"That's crazy. *Marked*?" Tee shakes his head. "This is bullshit."

"Is it? It could've easily killed him." Brady motions his eyes to Devin. "And do any of you actually doubt it would've killed Robby?"

"But *marked*. That doesn't make sense. Why would this thing want to kill specific people?"

"I don't know, but that's what we intend to find out."

Tee's lips tuck into a slow frown, his eyes growing wide as an owl's at dusk. "Wait. So how do we know if we're marked?"

"Have any strange dreams lately? Something happen to you beyond comprehension?"

Tee takes a huge swallow. A dreadful image of Margo flashes in my mind from her surprise visit to my bathroom and of my encounter in Grief Hollow. *Shit! I'm marked. Tee, too.*

Devin gives a smirking headshake. "You mean beyond our comprehension more than what just happened back there?"

"No. That's not what I mean. You're not marked. You'd be dead right now if you were. I already know Robby's marked by how that thing came after him."

Robby's brows furrow before his jawline hardens. "Well, that's easy for you to say, coming from a guy who's not marked."

"I've been marked for over six years. And if you want to survive as I have, you'd better come with me." Brady's words linger in the air, somber as a funeral director.

CHAPTER 35
A Rising Tide

Cam stares out from the squad car. A quiver scales his spine.

The branches in the tree line begin to sway in an invigorated breeze. *Myron got them. Oh God, I know it! It's been too long. He got them! He'll kill me, too! Like Seth. Gotta get out of here.*

Cam jumps as he detects movement in the woods. He peers through the window into the edge of the tree line, but the shadows swallow everything a few feet inside the woods. He reaches for the door handle, readying a path for his escape, but realizes there isn't one in the backseat. He's trapped.

He starts fiddling with the steel mesh divider that separates the backseat from the front of the squad car. But the steel mesh divider lacks any vulnerability, no alternate means of escape. *If I can't get out...Myron can't get in?* He takes a deep breath trying to settle his nerves, but his body continues to tremble.

His frazzled eyes return to the spot he last detected movement, but he finds nothing unusual. A cringe- inducing scratch on the glass behind him yanks his head around. He lets out a startled scream at Myron's face in the window and launches himself across the backseat. He pins himself against the door. Myron flashes a wicked grin at him before curling his lips and exposing a row of jagged teeth.

"You're coming home," Myron growls before he disappears below the window.

Cam gasps for air, his heart fluttering as he surveys the area trying to locate Myron. "Jesus!" The top of Myron's head emerges above the hood of the car. Myron rises, his body like a giant centipede with a waxy, burnt umber exoskeleton banded black at the edges of its body segments. Dozens of spiny legs screech over the steel bumper, shimmying forward in unison. The long, dagger-like legs that taper to fine needlepoints at the tips slice through the clear coat on the hood of the car. Cam's breathing devolves into unmeasured, frantic panting. His heart jackhammers in his chest at the grotesque sight of its glossy, alabaster underbelly passing over the windshield, his ears in a state of revulsion as its lance-like legs chisel out chunks of glass as it ascends. The roof creaks before groaning under the weight of the creature, the squeal of scraping metal serrating Cam's eardrums as it pulls the last of his hideous body over the windshield.

Cam dives for the floorboard and curls into a trembling ball. He shrieks as Myron's face appears in the rear windshield. Myron's mouth opens, and a pair of razor-sharp digits emerge like the leading edge of a carnivorous insect leaving its burrow. As they slide farther from his mouth, the waxy appendages unfurl on crispy joints. In one rippling motion of its body segments, the venomous fangs spring forward and impale the glass like swords. The creature's lower legs work to brace itself against the car, and it heaves its powerful body, causing the window to let out a hideous creak. It gives way, the tempered glass separating from its housing in one shattered piece. With a quick head shirk, it sends the glass airborne, hurtling it into the grass.

A sudden jolt of adrenaline charges Cam's muscles. He leaps on the seat to make a dive out of the car. But the creature whips its head around and plunges its venomous fangs deep into Cam's chest.

Cam's eyes shoot open and he screams. He's hyperventilating, his lungs closing. A frantic scan of the car finds it undamaged. The terrible nightmare trembles his small body like an earthquake. His sweat-saturated clothes cling to his skin. The engine purrs against a backdrop of silence, the cold air blowing out of the vents glacial across the surface of his dewy skin. He scavenges his pockets until he locates his asthma inhaler and takes a long draw, trying to control his breathing.

As he steadies the rhythm of his breathing, Cam looks to the place where the two officers entered the woods, but there's still no sign of them.

"Time to come home." The raspy female voice jolts his eyelids.

Cam whips his head around. A skeletal female stands outside his window, her deep-set eyes burrowing into him. Her long, black stringy hair falls around her decomposing face, the corners of her corroded lips curled in a wicked smile. In one violent motion, she rips the door off the car frame, unleashing screams of tearing steel and pops of snapping bolts. Cam whimpers as the full vision of the grotesque creature assails his eyes. His lips tremble at its terrifying visage, patches of its skin rotting away from its body revealing the putrid sinew and grayish bones underneath.

"No! No, please!" Cam screams and lifts his arms to defend himself.

"They'll bear no fruit!" it growls as it rockets into the backseat.

Cam screams as its sharp, bony claws tear into his skin and dig deep between the spaces of his rib cage. It curls its claws inside him, latching onto his bones. He coughs up a thick spurt of scarlet. Its gray, putrid tongue traces the tears rolling from his eyes. It pauses for a second. A gratified smile crosses its hideous face before it leaps from the patrol car and drags Cam's body like a rag doll into the woods.

CHAPTER 36
Wadlow's House

Once inside Wadlow's house, we pass through a sitting room. Brady leads us through a door to the basement below. An unwelcoming odor of old books and damp earth permeates the musty air. Latravious Wadlow stoops at his microscope.

"Professor Wadlow, this is Tee, Robby, Brooks and..."

"Devin. I go by Dev."

"Right. And Dev."

Professor Wadlow glances at us through his thick glasses and frowns. Tee fidgets, averting his eyes from Professor Wadlow's gaze to the remnants of the mess he created the day prior.

"Why did you bring them here?" Latravious Wadlow's voice is flat. He returns his attention to his work and lowers his head to his microscope on his workbench.

"The compound. It works! Well, sort of."

Professor Wadlow raises his head from his microscope at Brady's declaration. He scans us again, eyes shimmering with renewed vibrance.

"You saw it? Where?"

"Near Shiners' Gorge. It was trying to take Robby."

Professor Wadlow's jaw tenses, a subtle frown accumulating on his lips. He rises from his workbench and snags a green thumbtack. He approaches a map of Harper Pass and the surrounding area that's attached to the wall. His hand comes to a rest on Shiners' Gorge, and he pushes in the pin. I notice the many other pins in a variety of colors already pushed into the map, many of them located near Copperhead Creek and Grief Hollow.

Devin points to the map. "What's that for?"

"I've been tracking it for years. Trying to establish its territory."

"What do the colors mean?"

"Astute question, young man." Professor Wadlow lands grinning eyes on me. "Each color represents a different year. We're green this year. Six years ago, we were black." I notice a black pin, among others, on Grief Hollow. Tee shakes his head.

"Wait. So, you're saying this thing has been around for six years?"

"Oh no. Probably quite a bit longer than that. That's how long I've been tracking it." Professor Wadlow releases a deep sigh through his parted lips.

"*How long*?" Robby's voice quavers.

"Hard to say. Six years. Ten years. Fifty years. One—two hundred years."

"That's impossible." The declaration explodes from Tee's lips.

"Impossible? Or improbable?"

"Impossible, man. Ain't no way that thing's two hundred years old."

"And why would you say a silly thing like that?" Professor Wadlow's inquisitive eyes lock onto Tee.

Tee shrugs his shoulders. "I don't know, man. Nothing lives to two hundred years old."

"Kids." Professor Wadlow shakes his head with a frown. "There's a world of knowledge at your fingertips. And yet, you still insist on relying on faulty logic rather than science."

"Not logic, just common sense. Nothing lives to two hundred."

"Indeed, some things do and beyond. Certain species of whales live two hundred years or more. There's even a species of clam that can live to be five hundred years old."

"But that thing wasn't a clam. It was human. Well, kinda... it... it looked like my dad. Before it changed."

"Precisely. It changed. Modified its own DNA, making it possible to live indefinitely."

"*What*?" The response falls from Devin's lips.

Professor Wadlow adjusts his glasses. "Think about it. What are some of the biggest causes of death?"

I lift my head. "Car crash."

"Yes, but what are some of the more natural causes?"

"Cancer."

"Exactly." Professor Wadlow nods at Robby. "And if it can continually modify its DNA, it gets a fresh start. Like a renewed lease on life."

I tent my brows, considering the supposition. "But how would no one know something like this exists? It doesn't make sense."

"But they *have* known. We've known for a long time. The stories were always there. It's largely been dismissed, categorized as folklore and legend today. The Navajo call them skin-walkers.

The French call them loup-garou. Nearly every culture and civilization throughout time has a name for them and these stories go back hundreds and even thousands of years. They've been here all along."

I take a big swallow. *Can this really be real?* Tee shuffles his weight from foot to foot. Robby bites his lip, his eyes cloud and his face contorts like he's revisiting some troubling thought. His somber eyes seek out Brady, and Robby gives a slow, subdued shake of his head as if he's coming to terms with something.

Devin frowns and locks eyes with Professor Wadlow. "What does it want?"

"Depends. Depends on who it is."

Robby flinches his head back at Professor Wadlow's words. "You mean *what* it is."

"No, I mean *who* it is. The Navajos spoke of the skin-walker being a man that can transform into animals and other people. They attributed this ability to supernatural power, whereas I attribute it to science. But in the end, the result is the same. They leave a trail of death and devastation in their wake."

Devin inhales a deep breath and straightens his posture. "So how do we kill it?"

"If we can identify who it is, then we might be able to identify its purpose. If we identify its purpose, we can better predict its movements."

"Professor's been working on a formula. The one I threw at the creature."

"I've isolated a gene. I call it the Polymorphic Infinity Gene. This gene is what's allowing it to take different forms at will. Normally, as is the case with ants, a typical polymorphic gene allows for the same gene to produce different versions of the same species or for it to take different adult forms. In this case, those changes happen in seconds. And they aren't restrictive to the same species. The formula I'm developing intends to disable that special gene, thereby stripping the skin-walker of its ability to transform. Here, let me show you." Professor Wadlow walks to his microscope.

Professor Wadlow applies a thin layer of black goo from a petri dish onto a glass slide. He positions the slide and gives the dial on the microscope a gradual quarter turn, bringing an image into sharp focus.

"Come here, boys." Professor Wadlow motions us to the workbench. Robby's the first to look through the lens. "Do you see all of the changes happening? Like the substance is in a state of flux?"

Robby nods his head, and we all take turns peeking through the microscope lens at the mysterious substance underneath. The material lacks a discernable pattern. The particulates undergo rapid shifts of shape and size.

"What you are looking at are cells that lack their host. Without their host, the cells are in a state of flux because the underlying Infinity Gene cannot be controlled."

Tee's eyes widen and he takes a subtle step back. "You're saying that this is part of that *thing*?"

"Yes, organic residues left behind from the transformation. But without the host, the cells are wildly mutating from one type of cell to another. Prior forms it has taken no doubt."

I land round eyes on Professor Wadlow. "Is it dangerous?"

"No, not in this form. But let me show you what happens when we introduce a few milliliters of this formula." Professor Wadlow grabs a dropper bottle. He unscrews the lid and draws some green fluid into the dropper from the bottle. He positions the dropper above the slide and gives it a light squeeze. "Now take a look."

The cells undergoing rapid changes begin to spasm. Within a few moments, they become uniform and the movement ceases.

"Whoa." I lift my head from the microscope.

The other boys take turns at the microscope. *Wow. He's brilliant! Could cure diseases...cancer even. Lucky he's here. Bad for the world, I guess. But glad he's here.*

"When I said earlier *who* it is versus *what* it is, it was for this very reason. Once the formula is applied, the cells default back to their pre-transformative state, human cells." Professor Wadlow smiles.

Devin shakes his head. "I can't believe you figured all of this out."

"I didn't. I still don't know who it is or what it wants."

"How can we find out?" Robby asks.

Professor Wadlow sighs. "I don't know."

"The map!" I point to it. "You said that this thing is human, right? That this thing could be really old?"

Professor Wadlow nods. "I did."

"So what if we use the map? Research the places it's appeared most. See who lives there or lived there."

"Actually, that's a brilliant idea. A bit of a long shot, but a brilliant idea." He narrows his eyes on me, a faint grin tugging on the corners of his lips. "What did you say your name was again?"

"Brooks, sir." My lips stretch into a wide smile.

"Well, Mr. Brooks, that's a fine idea. And here, Brady, I thought you brought me just a bunch of frightened kids. Ah, but this one's clever." Professor Wadlow taps me on the shoulder wearing a playful smile.

We study the pins clustered on the map. Pins cluster near Shiners' Gorge, Davis Quarry, and a large group congregate near Copperhead Creek and Grief Hollow. I also notice pins spread sporadically throughout the Harper Pass area. Robby breaks the contemplative silence.

"Seems like Grief Hollow and Copperhead Creek have the most pins."

I nod. "That's where I first saw it."

Tee lifts his brows at Robby and me. "Yeah, but so does Davis Quarry."

Devin points on the map. "And Shiners' Gorge."

"Look over here. That's Mason Avenue." Brady runs his finger on a street on the map. "There's a few pins, right? And if you look behind that, that's Chandler Trace. There's even more pins there, too. When you add those together, that's even more than Grief Hollow or Davis Quarry."

Tee lifts his head with a sudden jolt. "Wait, doesn't Sammy Needles live on Chandler Trace?"

Robby nods. "Yeah. He does."

"And Margo lives on Mason Avenue." I point to the street behind Sammy's.

"The missing girl. *Interesting*," Professor Wadlow remarks, but he's talking to himself more than to us.

Robby turns to us with a gleam in his eyes. "We should follow Sammy."

"Dude, you sure about that?" An underlying reticence resonates in Tee's voice.

"Yeah, let's see what he's up to. Only one way to find out," Devin suggests.

"We should go to the library. See if we can find anything on Grief Hollow, Shiners' Gorge and Davis Quarry." I check Robby and Devin for agreement but don't find it in their faces. *Crap. Getting close to Sammy is a mistake.*

Robby gives a wobbly-headed nod. "Good idea. But first, we follow Sammy."

Tee gives a subtle eye roll to Robby and shakes his head. "Fine."

"How much of the formula is left?" Brady's question pulls Professor Wadlow from thought. He opens a cabinet above his workbench. There's one tray holding three glass vials filled with green liquid. "Professor, the formula forced it to change. Almost killed it, I think."

"This is good, good news. How did you introduce the formula?"

"I threw the vial at it. It shattered on its face. It forced it to change forms. It was struggling."

"Limiting it to control its changes no doubt."

Brady furrows his brows. "But maybe the formula needs to be tweaked. Needs to be stronger."

"I suspect it needs to be injected."

"*Whoa.*" Tee raises his hands. "Injected? I'm not getting that close to that thing."

"Maybe we won't have to." Devin taps his paintball gun.

"Inject the paintballs!" Robby's excited voice echoes in the confines of the basement.

"It's the right idea boys, but it will need to be introduced below the skin."

Professor Wadlow opens a drawer and pulls out six bullets. He sets them on the workbench. The tips of the bullets are hollowed out.

"I'm going to put a few milliliters of the formula inside of these bullets. Solder off some metal caps and voilà."

"Skin-walker killing bullets!" My face beams.

"Yeah, but what about now? We're not safe. No one's safe." Tee's wide eyes roam the group.

"We know the formula can slow it down." Brady extends his hand. "Let me see your paintball gun."

Tee hands Brady his paintball rifle. Brady opens the ammunition cap, turns the gun sideways and the remaining paintballs spill out onto the workbench. Brady inspects the spherical paintballs.

"Professor. Can we spare a vial?"

"Yes. I can synthesize more this evening. Should be ready by tomorrow."

Brady grabs a syringe from the workbench and eases the needle inside one of the paintballs. He draws on the piston, pulling the paint into the syringe. He empties the paint into a petri dish. He draws the green fluid from one of the vials and injects it into the paintball. With the remaining formula, he's able to fill seven more paintballs.

"Get rid of all the paintballs you have left in your guns," Brady instructs. "This will give you two shots a piece. *Make 'em count.*"

We all empty our ammo into the waste basket and take two paintballs each. We load our guns.

"Listen. We all meet back here tomorrow. Noon." Brady's tone lands stern as a commanding general.

"Be very careful boys. This thing is highly intelligent. Even if you're not marked, it will kill anything that stands in its way. So stay together and stay alert."

Brady's eyes meet ours. "And don't go back into the woods."

CHAPTER 37
Aftermath

Officer Clancy and Officer Ivansek break free from the woods about one hundred yards from the previous spot they entered. As his eyes locate the patrol cars, Clancy's brisk walk turns into a sprint. Ivansek struggles to match his pace, his fat rolls jiggling with every stride.

"Jesus Christ!" Clancy comes to an abrupt stop and surveys the battered patrol car.

Ivansek shakes his head as he joins Clancy. "What the hell happened?"

"Get on the horn. Get Holt! Get everyone!" Clancy assesses the situation.

"Holy shit! Is that the door?" Clancy follows Ivansek's eye line to a heap of twisted metal loosely resembling the cruiser's door in the tall grass by the road. "My God. It's like it's been ripped right off the frame."

"Just get on the damn radio!" Clancy's voice blares alarm.

The words that Officer Clancy spoke to Cam, *you'll be safe here*, haunt his guilt-ridden mind. *The kid? Oh Jesus! Is that?* A substantial amount of blood pools, canals of it collected in the grooves of the leather seats. Blood spatter streaks the windows and drips from the steel mesh grate. All of it's fresh, hasn't even begun to coagulate.

Ivansek clacks into his radio. "Marcy! Over!"

He waits for a response as Clancy notices the blood trail that leads from his patrol car into the street. Clancy pulls his service weapon from his holster and begins following the crimson spatter.

"Marcy! Over!"

"Jiminy crickets, can't you give me just a second?" Marcy's voice crackles through the radio.

"Get everyone out here. *Now*! Get Holt! Get everyone!"

"Why? What's wrong?"

"Everything! It's a blood bath! That Myron Thompson kid ain't missing. He's done killed a bunch of kids." Ivansek's voice arcs like an electric current.

"Oh! Oh no. Dispatching now. But shouldn't we send Cam Givers home? Over."

Ivansek takes a deep breath and winces into a frown. "Cam Givers is one of them."

"Dear God."

"Put out an APB on Myron Thompson. Suspect he's armed and dangerous. Over."

Clancy proceeds with caution. The blood trail leads him across the street and into the tall grass adjacent to the roadway. A visible path of matted grass triggers a frightening supposition. *Cam was dragged over this area.* Clancy's stomach somersaults, bile rising into his throat. As the senior responding officer, he carries full responsibility for the well-being of that little boy, and in all likelihood, that little boy is dead. *I should've given the boy's story more credibility.* The palpable fear in Cam's eyes alone provided a reason to believe him, but Clancy hadn't. He discounted Cam's story from the get-go, a rookie mistake. He alone made the judgment call to leave Cam Givers locked in his patrol car while he and Officer Ivansek investigated in the woods. *So stupid! Why? Why'd I leave him? Jesus, what was I thinking? They'll fire me. Probably should.* The same cavalier audacity that propelled the upward ascent of his career threatens to end it.

Clancy swallows hard as the blood trail thickens and leads him to a steep embankment. He's no blood spatter expert, but even a novice can recognize a shift in the spatter pattern from occasional splatter to heavy spurts like that from a deep arterial wound. Every couple of feet, clumps of tall fescue soak in blood. As he makes a wary trudge into the woods, Officer Ivansek files in behind him.

"Oh Jesus." Ivansek's stomach turns on itself.

Clancy doubles over and vomits. Beneath some low-lying brush, a human leg, severed at the knee, lies in a ruddy sludge of gelatinous blood. The child's sneaker, still attached to the foot, bears the signs of the grotesque trauma, the canvas spattered and the laces stained with blood. The shoe sets Officer Clancy's world to a wobble underfoot. It matches the blue tennis shoes Cam Givers came running into the station wearing.

"Is it him?" Ivansek's voice crackles.

Clancy musters a somber nod and bends on one knee. "I'm so sorry, kid." Tears streak Clancy's cheeks as his heart caves in on itself.

CHAPTER 38
Divergent Truths

Officer Morrow arrives first on scene, but Detective Holt follows at less than a car's length. Clancy's sitting in the back seat of Officer Ivansek's patrol car with the door ajar. His chin hovers near his chest, his complexion stonewash. As Morrow comes to a stop alongside Officer Ivansek's patrol car and shuts off his siren, Clancy doesn't stir.

Detective Holt exits his cruiser and snags a quick glance at the empty roadway behind him. *No beige sedan today*. He turns and takes determined strides to Ivansek's patrol car. Officer Morrow drafts behind him. Holt scans the scene, notices the damaged cruiser and the blood on the roadway. With a prolonged silence for a greeting, Detective Holt looks at both men with disapproval.

"Somebody better start talking."

Ivansek glances at Clancy, but he doesn't even lift his head to acknowledge Holt.

"*Well*?"

"Holt, that Myron Thompson kid's done gone nuts. We think he attacked, maybe even killed, Cam Giver's friends, Seth and Shane Rogers. That's what Cam said. Swore he killed them. Me and Lance went to investigate it. You know, where Cam said it happened. We found a whole heap of blood on one of the trees out there." Morrow's eyes grow wide.

"Where?"

Ivansek points to the woods. "Shiners' Gorge, 'bout three ridge lines that way. We was trying to get Cam to show us where. But the kid was scared. Wouldn't get out of the cruiser. Ain't that right, Clancy?" Ivansek's voice quavers as he eyes Clancy for backup.

Officer Clancy raises his head with a blank expression, musters a slight nod, frowns, and resumes his empty gaze at the floorboard. Holt's eyes flood with disbelief.

"And you *left* him in the car all by himself?"

"We left the car running. Thought he'd be okay. Didn't want to go into Shiners' Gorge with just one of us." Ivansek casts his head at the roadway.

"Why in God's name didn't you call me or Officer Morrow?"

Ivansek lifts pitiful eyes and frowns. "It was a bad call."

"You're damn right it was. Clancy...*Clancy*! Snap out of it. Where's Cam Givers?" Holt levels a rigid glare at him.

Without raising his head, Clancy lifts his hand and points. Ivansek motions to Morrow and Holt and leads them along the blood trail to the remains.

"Sweet Jesus." Morrow gulps.

Detective Holt surveys the severed leg, the tibia and fibula bones splintered and exposed above the lacerated flesh. He inspects the black substance around the perimeter of the wound. *Same as on John Watson's wounds. Same killer. Hell, killers. Who knows? Why in the hell didn't Clancy just call me? Dammit! I taught him everything. Ivansek, sure, but Clancy? He ought to know better. Chief'll probably fire him. Hell, he might fire me. Shit... shit, shit, shit!*

"Wonder what makes a boy go crazy like this. Go on a killin' spree and all," Ivansek wonders aloud.

"It wasn't Myron Thompson."

Officer Ivansek cocks his head, taken aback. It wasn't just the words that struck him, but the confidence with which Holt delivered them. And those words flew in the face of everything Officer Ivansek already accepted as concrete truth about this incident.

"Well, you do know Cam Givers told us that he witnessed Myron Thompson kill them other boys, right? Says he smashed one of those boy's head into a tree over and over. We found all the blo—"

"It wasn't Myron Thompson."

Officer Ivansek squints his eyes and tilts his head at Holt. "But I don't understand. How can you be so sure?"

"'Cause we got the DNA tests back from Lexington on all that blood near that backpack. We got a hit. It's Myron's blood."

"Noo...I mean. Are you sure? Cam Givers was adamant."

"Only a one in three-hundred million chance it's not his blood."

"Pulled a huge favor from an old friend to get it expedited," Officer Morrow boasts. "And it doesn't get much more definitive than that."

"Maybe it was his blood. But maybe he walks away from that. There wasn't a body after all."

Detective Holt shakes his head at Officer Ivansek.

"There must've been five or six pints of blood there. Only eight in the body. No way he walks away from that."

"I'm telling you though, Cam Givers swore it was Myron Thompson. Said something was seriously wrong with him. So, if that *was* Myron's blood, maybe somebody helped him or something."

"Kid would've needed several transfusions. That's assuming he could even survive that much blood loss," Morrow interjects.

"Just doesn't add up. That kid was scared. Real scared. Said that Myron boy had been bullying him for years. You'd think he wouldn't mistake a person that's terrorized him. And it kinda makes sense, right? He seizes the opportunity to finish what he started in the woods. Being that the kid was a witness and all."

Morrow crosses his arms. "You can't argue with science based on a kid's idea of what happened."

But Detective Holt still lingers on Ivansek's words. *Damn. That's the most sensible thing he's ever said. He's right. What the hell's going on? This doesn't make any sense. None of it. Something's really wrong here.* Holt's eyes meet Ivansek's.

"You find any bodies in Shiners' Gorge?"

"No. Just a bunch of blood on a tree. Checked out with Cam's story. Oh, and when we were wrapping up, footprints. At least five sets."

Holt twiddles the corner of his mustache. *Five sets. Cam, his friends... that's three. Latravious Wadlow... four. And Brady Palmer... five. Possible. What are they up to? Something weird going on there. Brady at Wadlow's house last night. And Wadlow's hiding something. No way he's not. But a killer? Don't know about that. Possible, I guess.*

"I want you to make a cast of those footprints. Get a sample of the blood. Morrow, you go with Ivansek."

"You got it, Holt." Officer Morrow tips his head to Holt.

"It'll be dark soon." Detective Holt checks his watch. "You got about an hour and twenty. Don't want to be in Shiners' Gorge after nightfall. You guys better hump it."

"Hear that, cap'."

"I'll secure the scene here. Going to try to knock some damn sense into Clancy." Holt shakes his head. "He looks catatonic."

Ivansek follows Morrow to his car. They pop the trunk, grab some casting supplies, and disappear into the tree line.

Ivansek's car idles, the whir of the engine a soft purr against a backdrop of silence. Clancy droops forward, hunched in the backseat. As Holt approaches, Clancy lifts his head, face devoid of expression. *Damn, why'd you do this, Clancy? Just a mistake though. A costly one, but a mistake.* He places his hand on Clancy's shoulder.

"Holt, I screwed up. I screwed up so bad. That little boy's dead because of me. What are we going to tell his parents?" Tears resume streaming on Clancy's face.

"I don't know, Clancy, but the best thing we can do for that family now is to find out who did this to their boy."

"It just doesn't make sense." Clancy slowly shakes his head. "I mean, have you ever seen anything like it? That door was pried right off the frame."

"No. Not till this week. Lot of things don't make any sense this week."

"Am I fired?"

"It's not my call, Lance. That's up to the chief. But right now... right now... I need you to get yourself together. We've got a job to do. You think you can manage?"

A basset hound-eyed Officer Clancy looks up and nods. He wipes the tears away from his cheeks and gets out of the police cruiser.

He's basically me. A decade ago me, at least. I made mistakes, too. Not this bad. But mistakes. Gonna be hard to recover from this one though. But hell, even I couldn't have foreseen this happening. Kid was basically in a prison, reinforced glass, steel frame. No way in. No way out. Somebody had to pull that door off with a vehicle and a tow hitch. SUV or Truck maybe? Or they used a shitload of elbow grease and a crow bar. But either way, they wanted that boy. Damn determined to get him, too. Why would killing this little boy be so important to someone? Was this in response to what he'd seen?

"So, tell me exactly what happened."

"Cam wouldn't get out of the car. He swore up and down that Myron Thompson killed his friends, Seth and Shane. I tried to tell him, look, you'll be safe with me and Ivansek. The kid was terrified. Wouldn't budge. I didn't know what to do. Knew me or Ivansek shouldn't go into Shiners' Gorge alone. I didn't want to pull you out of your session."

"I wish you had."

"Me too. *Dammit.* That was so stupid."

"What's done is done. No way to change that now. So, then what happened?"

"I finally get Cam Givers to get out of the patrol car. I had to concede that I wasn't going to force him to come along just to get that far. He points us in the direction where he says his friends were attacked. And then I locked him up in the backseat of the car with the air on full blast. That's what I was worried about, you know. Him being too hot in the car. And then we left him. Oh God, I *left* him."

"Did Cam Givers say anything about two other people being there? Like Latravious Wadlow or Brady Palmer?"

"No. He said it was just Myron...Wait. He did say that the reason they ran into Shiners' Gorge in the first place was because they were hiding from Sammy and Bo."

This reminds Holt of his premonition a couple of days prior of Sammy Needles soon finding his way into his crosshairs. *Has Sammy Needles finally gone and done it, crossed the line that'll put him away? Not much of a stretch to imagine Sammy capable of something like this. Kid's a violent sociopath.*

"Really? But Cam said that they *weren't* there in the woods?"

"That's what he said, but the kid was all shook up."

A glimmer flashes in Clancy's eyes as he retreats to his racing thoughts. *Be the break! Please, God, let it be. We can arrest Sammy. Bo, too. Easier conversation with Cam's parents. Still awful, but easier. And the media loves a killer. They'd obsess over it. No questions on the finer points. How it happened under our care. But no killer. Lots of questions about the circumstances leading up to the murder.*

"We'll bring Sammy back in, but first, let's secure this scene. It's getting late. I want to collect any evidence we can before nightfall. Why don't you jump on the horn and get Mr. Latrell out here?"

"Yes sir." Clancy grabs his radio from his belt.

A white van breaches the hill and comes into view on Timberline Road, speeding in the direction of the four police cars. As it approaches, Detective Holt's stomach drops.

"Marcy over." Clancy walks to the edge of the road.

"Shit! It's that damn reporter. Put down that radio, Clancy! Use your cell."

"What?"

"Clancy. Go. Over."

"Put it down! Put the radio down!" Detective Holt yells as he runs to Clancy, waving his arms and pointing to the oncoming van. "It's Channel Four News. They must be monitoring our radio channel."

"Clancy? You there, Clancy? Over."

"Call Marcy on your cell. And do it discreetly. From one of the cars. And not a damn word to that reporter!"

"Yes sir." Clancy retreats to Officer Ivansek's squad car.

Detective Holt grimaces at the approaching news van, a nightmare scenario. *Dammit! What's she already know? A lot if she's been monitoring our radio channel. And how else would she know to be here? Shit! And I don't have any answers. Suspicions, leads maybe. Nothing definitive. Hell, I can't even give legitimate confirmation of the deaths without bodies. No next of kin notifications. The parents don't even know something's wrong. I'm screwed!* He takes a deep breath and prepares himself for the impending onslaught.

CHAPTER 39
Horse Trading

Before the van even comes to a complete stop, Kasey Norton is airborne, leaping from the sliding door. She lands with graceful precision on the pavement in her high heels. Her black skirt, plucked from the discount racks of Ann Taylor, flutters as she hits. She clutches a microphone, determination in her eyes and an air of confidence in her stride. She brushes her blonde locks from her eyes and closes in on Detective Holt. She can smell it, taste it, feel it. This story is going to grab the Cincinnati Network's attention, her station's parent affiliate. She's always dreamed of working in the big city. *Big City—Big Stories*. Her big career break stands a few yards away with his arms crossed and a temperment matching scowl on his face.

Once the van comes to a stop, her cameraman emerges from the opening and takes a twisting step onto the roadway, tweaking his ankle. He regains his footing and hobbles after Kasey, lifting the camera lens to his eye, ready to follow his young reporter into the fray.

She doesn't wait for an invitation from Detective Holt. Without saying a word to him, she positions herself at his side. She motions to her cameraman, directing him into position for the shot she wants.

"Right there's perfect, Norman."

"Perfect for what?"

"For our exclusive." Kasey's reply comes without hesitation.

"Whoa, whoa, whoa. Wait just a damn minute." Detective Holt raises his arms in protest and takes a few retreating steps.

"Detective Holt, the way I see it, you've got two choices. Give me my exclusive. Tell me what your department's doing to protect the public. Where you're at in your investigations—"

"These are official investigations. They're open. Notifications haven..." Detective Holt stops for a moment and clears his throat. "*If* there were a need for that type of thing, *notifications*, they wouldn't have even gone out yet."

Kasey takes a few steps forward and leans near Detective Holt's ear. "I'm going on air *with* or *without you*. I'd rather it be with you. Wouldn't want this to be a *speculative* story. We heard the radio transmissions on our scanner about the killings, or *bloodbath*, wasn't it?"

Detective Holt takes an assertive step forward. "You're compromising our investigation. This is official police business. We're going to need you both to leave. Now!"

Kasey, undeterred, motions to her cameraman and twirls her pointer finger in small circles.

"Don't you dare turn that damn camera on!" Detective Holt delivers an icy glare to the cameraman. He lowers the camera.

"Roll it, Norman." Kasey's defiant words push a shot of color into Detective Holt's cheeks. Norman raises the camera to his eye.

"You want to go to jail for interfering in police business, son?"

Norman's face contorts.

"No sir."

"Norman, roll it. You can't go to jail for setting up for an interview and Detective Holt knows it. He's just trying to scare you."

As Norman begins to raise the camera, Detective Holt pulls his handcuffs from his leather pouch, a proven tactic he uses to deescalate dicey domestic disputes. Success hinges on the authenticity of his deadpan stare instilling fear of imminent arrest. His own unwavering eyes bore into Norman. In Holt's experience, people confronted with the perceived reality of jail staring them in the face tend to acquiesce. He senses Norman's susceptibility to his ruse, detects a semblance of surrender in his wilting posture, and determines him as the weak link. If he breaks, Detective Holt can avoid giving this interview under such precarious circumstances. *No cameraman, no story.*

He begins lowering the camera.

"Norman... Norman!"

"Kasey, I can't go to jail. My divorce."

A rush of relief washes over Detective Holt, and a hint of a smile creeps into the corners of his lips. Norman's breaking. Holt takes pride in the subtler nuances of police work, whether sculpting an outcome into reality through manipulation or breaking a suspect in the interrogation room. It's gratifying. There's a certain primal pleasure that's derived from it each and every time.

"He's bluffing."

"You know how that's going to look. Maggie's blood sucking attorney's going to use it like a sledgehammer. Try to make sure I don't have any shared custody rights. I can't lose—"

"Norman, I feel for you. I really do. But I need you to do your job. You're not going to jail. Detective Holt's bluffing."

"I'm not bluffing, Norman." Detective Holt opens the cuffs and conjures a grave expression. "What's more important? This interview or seeing your kids?"

"How dare you!" Kasey storms forward. "Bringing his kids into this. *Really*? And Norman, what do you think J.T. is going to do when I tell him what happened? Tell him why we didn't get the story. It's going to look worse to a judge if you don't have a job."

"*What*?" Norman's word wobbles out on an exhale. "Kasey, please don't do this."

"I'll call him right now if I need to." Kasey pulls out her cell phone and flips to the keypad screen. "I can get Joe out here if need be. But you know that probably doesn't bode well for your career."

A rush of anxiety pours back into Detective Holt's gut. Kasey is quite adept at this game. Each latched on to one of Norman's jugulars, a tug-of-war ensues. They're both playing bad cop, destroying the old paradigm. The resulting gridlock paralyzes Norman. *Dammit! She's going to win. She's got the benefit of the relationship. Ah, shit. He's breaking. Time to change the tact.*

"Look, I know you have a job to do. So do I." Detective Holt softens his posture and employs a more compromising tone. "Right now, my job is to protect the integrity of this crime scene."

"So, it *is* a crime scene then? You know I have a responsibility to Channel Four's viewers as well."

Detective Holt nods. "Yes, I know that too." *Oh bullshit. Other than traffic, weather, and sensationalizing news, what real responsibility does your station feel toward Harper Pass?*

Detective Holt holds a pleasant smile. *You and your station serve one responsibility and one responsibility only—ratings.*

"Detective Holt, I need an exclusive. Channel Four should be the one to break this."

Detective Holt moves in closer trying to get out of earshot of the cameraman. "Okay. Look. Off the record?"

"You know I can't do that."

"Just hear me out. I'm going to tell you what's going on, what we know is going on, but you've got to give me an assurance that it's off the record. Could jeopardize our investigation."

"And what do I get?"

"You get the on-the-record exclusive on the Margo Combs missing persons investigation."

"That's not enough. We're talking about murder here." Kasey narrows her eyes on Detective Holt. "That *is* what we're talking about, right?"

Detective Holt takes a deep breath, mulling his limited options. *Just one bargaining chip left. Matter of time before the details get out, anyway. Loose lips in Harper Pass. Deputies, coroner and shit, Frank Gibbs from Fish and Wildlife. Hell, he's probably telling the story in some neighboring jurisdiction right now.*

"And I'll give you the exclusive on the John Watson murder."

Kasey's eyes ignite. "*Murder*? I thought it was a bear attack?"

"We did too. But now we're not so sure. Things aren't right."

Kasey bites her bottom lip. If Detective Holt's telling her the truth, this promises to become a huge story, one with the capacity to launch a career. But if it's subterfuge, she could miss out on one of the biggest stories to ever happen in Harper Pass. The deliberation doesn't last long.

"If you're lying to me, misleading me in any way, you're going to look just as bad as me. And I can assure you, by the time I'm done, you'll look a hell of a lot worse than—"

"I'm telling the truth...So, do we have a deal?"

"Promise I get to break the story on this too?" Kasey bites her lip.

"You were the first to get wind of it. Only seems fair that you'd get to break this story too, but *only* when it's ready to be broken."

"And you won't leak this to Channel 3 first?"

"You have my word." Detective Holt extends a hand. "Do we have a deal?"

Kasey pauses for a moment before extending her hand. She clasps Detective Holt's worn hand, which wraps around her own.

"Deal." The two shake hands.

CHAPTER 40
Exclusive

Angela Mitchell sits on the living room couch playing with Snapchat on her cell phone. She contorts her body and pushes her chest out into an unnatural pose. With phone in hand outstretched, she makes an awkward attempt to capture the right angle. She radiates her best smile, puckers her lips a smidgen, and it's a simple click, but she's far from done. She tries applying different filters while attempting to capture the perfect selfie, a process that takes ten minutes or longer on occasion. The television show in the background fills the empty house with white noise but fails to capture much of her attention. She clicked it on merely out of habit and didn't bother to change the channel. She's somewhat pleased that it's only an animated sitcom playing in the background, one she has already seen.

Her mom, Sandra, somewhat of a local news junkie, tends to keep the television tuned as such for all the latest tidbits of gossip and scandal. And she feeds her addiction with her favorite fix, Channel 4 News. They rarely disappoint.

Angela kicks her feet up onto the couch, something she would never do with her parents at home. But they went out to dinner and assigned Angela to watch Tee under the guise of her learning some responsibility and self-reliance before she heads off to college. *Responsibility, bah! More like date night on the cheap.*

The first rosy hues of sunset creep through the blinds and spill onto the carpet. The gradual retreat of light and deepening shadows suggest Tee should make an appearance soon. *Better make dinner. What'll it be tonight? Chicken nuggets, a frozen pizza, or frozen dinners? Frozen Pizza, no hassle.* After starting everything, she plants herself on the couch and pours her attention into her smartphone.

The tail end of a teaser for the evening news pulls her out of her trance. Something they said struck a chord deep in the recesses of her subconscious, but with her attention split, she can't decipher what, only that it carries the feeling of importance. The buzzer in the kitchen alarms indicating the preheated oven, and she leaves her perch.

After getting the pizza in the oven, she returns to the couch. Images of a reporter at the scene of a three-car pile-up flash on screen. *Boring.* She opens her Instagram. *Why's the news even on? This is prime time. Where's...* After a quick transition, a singing competition comes on the television. *That's more like it!*

She lets her phone hand drop but never relinquishes her clutch on it as she switches her full attention to the show. It's one of her favorites, and the tall country singer judging it is one of the biggest reasons why. She's enthralled by him, by boys in general, really. After one of the contestants gives a rousing performance, the judges give their feedback. As the camera pans to the country star, the image on the television switches to the news anchor desk.

"Oh... my... God." She throws her hands up. "Come on."

"We break from our regularly scheduled programming to bring you a Channel 4 exclusive interview with Detective Holt of the Harper Pass Police Department. Kasey, are you there?"

"I'm here, Tom. That's right. Kasey Norton coming to you live with Channel 4 News. I have with me here, Detective

Holt, of the Harper Pass Police. He's agreed to share the latest with us on the Margo Combs missing persons investigation and… on the murder of John Watson."

"Suspected murder," the detective corrects.

The cellphone slides from Angela's hand and hits the carpet. She straightens from her reclined position on the couch. Her hand fumbles on the coffee table for the remote, but her eyes remain locked on the television. She raises the volume.

"Okay, so, suspected murder. Why don't we start there? What leads the Harper Pass Police to believe John Watson was murdered?"

"Well, to be honest, we initially attributed his death to a bear attack. But after careful examination, we've determined that the wounds sustained by John Watson are inconsistent with a bear attack."

"And do you have any suspects?"

"We have some leads we're following, yes."

"So, you're saying you don't have any suspects? That there's a killer on the loose right here in Harper Pass?"

"No, that's *not* what I said. *I said* we're following some leads. We may have some potential persons of interest."

"So, suspects?"

"Potentially. Yes."

"Maybe our viewers can help. Do you have a description of the assailants?"

A flash of color washes through the detective's cheeks before he answers.

"At this time, we don't have a description we can share. But as I mentioned before, we do have a couple of persons of interest."

Several tiny wrinkles etch themselves on the bridge of the reporter's nose. She leans in closer with her microphone.

"So, what you're saying is that there's a killer on the loose, potentially looking for his next victim right now, and you don't have any suspects?"

The detective's eyes tighten for a moment. Shots of crimson flash on his cheeks before they dissipate as quickly as they arrived. The onset of a scowl melts away from his lips as his chest rises and falls with a deep breath. And after a moment, he answers.

"Ma'am, I don't think that's an accurate description at all. I'd say that's highly speculative. We don't want to cause any undue alarm in the community. The Harper Pass Police Office is aggressively pursuing any and all leads, and like I said, we have a couple of persons of interest at this point."

"Yeah, you mentioned that." The reporter's tone is caustic. Her eyes click wider the moment after making the curt comment, and she straightens her posture.

A faint smile emerges on the detective's lips, and he leans into the microphone. "I'd like your viewers to know that we're here to *protect* and *serve*. We'll do everything, and I mean everything, within our power to make sure this community and everyone in it is safe."

"That being said, where are you at in the investigation of the disappearance of Margo Combs? Especially in light of the killer on the loose."

"Again, with the Margo Combs investigation, we're working every lead."

Two uniformed police officers emerge from the woods behind the detective. They make a swift turn and disappear from the camera shot.

"Excuse me, Detective Holt, but how do you think it is that a severely autistic child's able to evade detection by the Harper Pass Police?"

"I can't answer that. But I assure you and your viewers we're doing everything we possibly—"

"Don't you think these two might be related? After all, wasn't John Watson murdered during the search party for Margo Combs?"

"No, we haven't been able to establish any connection between the two events."

"*What exactly* have you been able to establish?"

The door swings open. Angela sits transfixed on the television set, her mouth hinged open. She doesn't even notice Tee come inside. She can't get Brady out of her mind. *How did he know that John Watson wasn't killed by a bear?* Tee jitters, coming through the doorway, but Angela still hasn't registered he's in the room.

"Angela! What in the world? You *tryin'* to burn this place down?"

The oven in the kitchen continues its unacknowledged beeping plea. Alarming for several minutes, the smell of scorched cheese permeates the house.

"Oh Shit! The pizza!" Angela leaps from the couch and runs into the kitchen.

CHAPTER 41
Visitation Hour

Robby's mom arrived home from work around nine o'clock and long ago passed out in her typical spot on the living room recliner. Her loud snoring provides unconscious testimony to her exhaustion.

Robby hammers away on the controller of his PlayStation from the confines of his room. Ever since the death of his father, getting lost in video games provides a temporary escape for Robby. In those hours of respite, Robby's mind buoys an eyelash above the dark troubles awaiting him beneath the surface, taking him to a place where his anxieties seem to melt away. But it's not working tonight.

The encounter with the creature that mimicked his dad earlier in the day has awoken the pain deep within him. From that reopened wound, images of his father bubble up. He's standing over his father's open casket, eyes locked on his lifeless face. It's visitation hour at the funeral home, and it's packed with people engaged in meaningless small talk. The hands of distant relatives, his dad's friends and colleagues pat him on the shoulder and back. They tell him ridiculous things like, *it's going to be okay, it'll get easier* and *he'll always be looking down on you.* The normal well-intentioned platitudes absent any real meaning.

But their voices seem a million miles away. Robby barely even notices they're there. He's trapped inside his own mind, shackled in the moment. He can't help but think how his father looks unnatural, not at all like he remembers him, spruced up in makeup to camouflage the massive trauma his father experienced in his final moments. But Robby can see through the artifice, see where the lines of makeup meet the edges of the stitched-up lacerations on his face and neck. It's an image he can't dispel from his mind, one that percolates to the forefront of his memories of his father. And that pains him. His father was a good man and a great dad, yet all his thoughts drag him to the image of him lying in that casket. Not to the good times they shared.

"Shit!" The character Robby's controlling in his shooter game succumbs to an ambush.

As the game's continuation screen appears on the TV and the number ticks down from thirty, a faint, grainy silhouette emerges embedded in the graphics. *How can this be? Played this game a thousand times. What the hell is this?* The outline appears to show a girl with long hair, head cast down. Robby leans in closer to the television trying to make it out as the number ticks down. *27... 26... 25... 24.* The grainy image gradually moves into the foreground. The number stops ticking at 22. He taps the reset button on the controller, but the console doesn't respond, and the game freezes.

When Robby lifts his eyes from his controller, his whole body flinches. The image appears in crisp focus in the foreground. Her long strands of hair collect on the floral pattern nightgown she's wearing. A bevy of ringlet curls shrouds the little girl's face, concealing her identity. She stands motionless. Robby's frenetic fingers fiddle with the buttons on the controller, but nothing happens. The game won't reset.

His heart jumps as the image on screen lifts her head and meets his eyes. It's Margo. A grin snakes across her lips sending a shudder through Robby's body.

"You should've gone with your dad, Robby. He was going to take you home. He wants to take you home."

"You're not real!"

"I'm real. You *know* I'm real." Her demented voice crackles as a blue swirl flashes through her eyes.

Robby's body hardens, his legs petrified stumps. Every impulse in his mind screams run, but his muscles ignore the signals. Margo extends one of her hands until her fingertips reach the extreme foreground of the TV. Robby's breathing accelerates to shallow, frantic tugs for air. Her fingertips pass through the television screen and jut out a couple of inches into his room.

"You're not real. Get out! You're not real!" His screams drench the room.

"All of their fruit will wither on the vine." Margo's voice booms, her wicked smile deepening as her whole hand and wrist emerge from the TV.

Robby dives for the game console and hits the power switch, the low whine of the disk decelerating flitting into his ears. Margo still looms on the TV in the foreground of the solid blue screen. Her arm emerges from the face of the TV above him, encased in a soft blue, phosphorescent glow. He lunges for the power switch on the TV as Margo extends her arm farther outside of the screen toward his own. Robby hits the power a moment before Margo's hand reaches his. The television blips from the loss of power and she's gone, leaving only the black, reflective surface of the TV behind.

Tears rain from Robby's eyes. He sits, legs crisscrossed, with his head hanging over his lap. The words Brady spoke to him leak into his mind. *I already know you're marked. Could it be? Could that really be true? Why? What have I really ever done to anyone*? But a name bobs to the surface of his consciousness. *Sammy*. As he reigns in his breathing, he lifts his head. The TV remains idle-black. He expels a deep breath, letting the tension leave his shoulders. In the reflection of the TV, his room looks quiet behind him. He sees his bed, his dresser, and as his eyes keep moving, he catches a glimpse of the reflection of an adult standing near his doorway.

"Mom, I'm okay." Robby climbs to his feet. "I just..." He begins as he turns around.

Robby's mouth hangs open mid-sentence. His eyes balloon. His father looms in his doorway, purged of the warm face Robby remembers. His lips snarl, exposing a glint of teeth, and his nose crinkles as he sharpens his razor gaze on Robby.

"You should've listened, Robby. Listened when I told you to come home with me." The man takes a couple of deliberate steps forward.

Robby scrambles to his feet. He takes several retreating steps until his back thumps against his bedroom wall. His eyes dart in every direction. *Nowhere to go.*

"This could've been so easy. You could've just gone to where you belonged." His dad continues his slow advance.

Robby eyes the paintball rifle on his dresser counter, measuring the distance to it. But his path to it intersects with the thing approaching.

"Now it's going to be hard. *Painful*. You'll feel the pain I felt when—"

Robby darts for the dresser. The creature cuts off his advance. Robby screams as it grabs his shoulder, and its boney fingers dig deep into his flesh. The creature's menacing face morphs from his dad's snarling face to a skeletal woman. Black, stringy hair falls around its eyes, which deeply recess into its cavernous face. It throws its other clawed hand into the air and slingshots it forward in a violent motion, ripping through the soft flesh of his belly and plunging deep inside his body.

Robby's eyes shoot open. He's screaming and tearing away at his bedsheets, trying to get the creature off him. As his eyes adjust to the darkness, he realizes the crushing pressure in his belly and abdomen is gone, the pain on his shoulder also dissipated. Moisture saturates his body. *Blood?* His hand frantically searches out his bedside lamp and flicks it on. Sweat covers the entirety of his body, but there's no blood and no wounds. Only fear.

CHAPTER 42
Blind Spot

Tee and I skid to a stop at the bottom of Slippery Hill, and Devin grinds his skateboard into the pavement. Robby's waiting for us there, dark puffy circles haloing his eyes. His shoulders slump, his body resembling a melting candle as if he wears the weight of some invisible force hell-bent on scrunching him to the earth. He stares straight ahead, face peaked, hollow eyes still and blank as death.

"Man, what happened to you, Robby?" Tee's verbal joust doesn't jostle a smile from Robby.

Robby's solemn eyes meet Tee's. "Long night."

I tent my brows at Robby. "Something happen?"

"No. Just a dream. *Nothing*...really." Robby's stoic delivery contradicts his words. I'm leery to press it further.

Devin surveys Robby with lingering eyes. "You sure, man? You look like hell."

"Look, I'm fine. We need to get on with this."

"Come on, man." Tee locks eyes with Robby. "We already followed that dumbbell yesterday."

"Two hours ain't enough to know."

"It's long enough to know he's not smart as a fart."

"Look, we follow him for a couple more hours. We need to be sure. Then we head to Wadlow's house like we planned."

I shake my head at Robby.

"We're just playing with fire."

"No, man, Robby's right. We need to know if it's not him. Then we can scratch him off the list."

"Dev, you saw it yesterday. The guy's a moron." Tee tosses his hands in the air with his words.

I can sense Robby's growing irritation. We all agreed to the plan the night before, but following Sammy in the shadowy cover of dusk posed little danger of him spotting us. Five minutes of Sammy picking and flicking his own boogers highlighted our reconnaissance mission and fed our doubt, leading us all to believe Sammy's limited mental capacity precluded his involvement. And now, with the bright illumination of the summer morning uncloaking our cover, Tee and I both have reservations.

"Dammit! We're doing it!"

Tee flinches at Robby's forceful tone.

"Dude, chill."

"No, *you* chill, Tee. *We* had a plan. *You* agreed to the plan. Brooks, *you* agreed to the plan. Now quit wasting time and let's go."

Tee shrugs his shoulders and shakes his head. "All right, man. You're right."

Robby's sharpened eyes cut to me.

"Okay." My response falls out, wrapped in a breathy sigh.

Without saying a word, Robby's on his bike and pedaling. We all follow him. We know where he's going—Chandler Trace. Whether trying to or not, he's setting us on a collision course with Sammy Needles.

We find Sammy in a matter of minutes milling about on Chandler Trace. We rush our bikes off the roadway and stash them in the woods, crouching behind some foliage. Sammy rifles through the mailboxes of his neighbors.

"Stupid po' bitches." Sammy lets a pile of mail rain through his fingers.

He swings his casted arm and strikes the aluminum mailbox, denting it before yelping in pain. Tee sniggers and shakes his head.

"What a dipshit!"

I hoist a small grin at Tee. "I know, right? What's wrong with him?"

Devin's giggling eyes meet ours. "Maybe it's the pile of shit in his head he's using for his brain."

"True!" Tee snickers and gives Devin a fist bump.

"Focus guys. He could be this thing."

"I'm pretty sure he ain't, Robby." Tee's grin grows wider. "The guy's got the IQ of a dishwasher."

"You're givin' him way too much cred', brah. Those things got computer chips now."

"It *could* be him. Who else got a reason to come after us? Huh?"

Robby's question induces the desired effect. I retreat into thought. *Sammy. He's the only one that wants to hurt us. Makes sense. But he ain't that smart.* I shake my head. *How? How could he be this thing?*

Something seems to grab Sammy's attention, and he takes a few steps forward. His posture changes like he's greeting a familiar friend.

Devin draws his head back and furrows his brows. "What's he doing?"

"I don't know." I shake my head. "*Weird*. It's like he's talkin' to somebody."

"Yeah, 'cept there ain't nobody there," adds Tee.

"Maybe dude's schitzo'," Devin theorizes.

Sammy converses with thin air. He nods his head several times at various moments in acknowledgement of something. A grin sneaks across his face. He gives a final deliberate head nod and does an about-face from the curb. He crosses the street at a deliberate angle. He grabs the handle of a large trash can set out by the curb, dragging it until it blocks the entire adjacent sidewalk. He turns, starts whistling, and strolls away.

"What the hell?" There's a momentary pause between each of Robby's words.

Tee shakes his head at Robby. "That was weird."

A car reverses in the driveway adjacent to the spot where Sammy placed the trash can. The brake lights flicker as it lumbers for the street. At the same time a young boy pedals his bike hard on the sidewalk. He steers into the grass to avoid the trash can on the sidewalk, sending him into the path of the reversing car. As he races into the driveway, the car lurches at him, but a moment before impact, he swerves into the roadway to avoid it. Tee's eyes grow big.

"Holy shit."

I lock eyes with Tee. "That was close."

Devin's eyes slowly swell. "It's like he knew!"

The boy on the bike looks back over his shoulder at his near-fatal collision. But milliseconds later, his bike collides with an oncoming pickup truck. The violent collision throws the boy from his bicycle, sending him into an airborne tumble. His body and head smash into the windshield before the powerful jolt of impact tosses him to the roadside. He smacks the pavement with a skull-cracking thud. The pickup truck screeches to a halt, its tires smoking and the stench of singed rubber filling the air.

"*Oh my god.*" The utterance falls limp from my lips as a breathless whisper.

"Jesus!" Robby screams as he runs from our hiding spot.

The boy lies motionless on the roadway in the shadow of the battered pickup truck, its damaged grill steely jaws, brandishing a row of jagged teeth. A fan belt squeals its displeasure beneath the crumpled hood, and traces of blood fleck the perimeter of two large dents on the front end. The spider-webbed windshield hides the interior cab of the truck. A man staggers out from the driver's side door of the pick-up, a trickle of blood dripping from a small gash above his eyebrow.

I whip my head in the opposite direction. Sammy ambles away. He never even looks back but continues whistling. A cold chill races through my spine as I recognize the tune. It's the same song I was singing in the shower the night Margo appeared in my bathroom. My stomach collapses. *Sammy might be this thing. Probably is this thing! Same song. No way he's whistling that. Too coincidental. Didn't even turn around to look back. All that noise. How could that be unless by design?*

"Help! Help! Get some help!" Robby wails desperate pleas from his knees beside the fallen boy.

I dash to Robby with the other boys. I gulp gravel at the sight of his body strewn on the curb, blood pouring from his ears and nose, life leaking from his complexion, turning his face funeral parlor pale.

"Get some help!" Robby cries as we peer at him.

"Oh Christ!" The man from pickup truck staggers to the injured boy.

He fumbles for his phone, dials 911, and reports the emergency before crouching by the injured boy.

"Oh Jesus, oh Jesus. What have I done? It's going to be okay, kid. You hear me? It's going to be okay. You hang in there." The man seeks the boy's hand and clasps it.

Silence ensues. The boy's labored breathing deteriorates, the rise and fall of his chest growing more rapid and subtle as time passes. Within a minute, sirens wail from the distance.

Devin taps Robby on the shoulder, and Robby climbs to his feet. Devin motions with his eyes to the woods where we stashed our bikes. Robby's eyes widen.

Devin airs a breathy whisper. "Nothing we can do."

Tee motions his eyes in the direction of the approaching siren. "Ambulance is coming."

"We'll just be in the way," I add.

Robby's eyes glisten, and his lips push into a pout. He gives a somber shake of his head. None of us want to get involved in this, answer questions about what we saw, or explain why we decided to follow Sammy in the first place. We ease from the scene to our bikes.

The kneeling driver whips his head in the direction of our retreating footsteps. "Hey. *Hey, kids*. Wait!"

But we continue our hasty retreat.

CHAPTER 43

The Promise

Around the same time the boys spy on Sammy Needles, Angela brings her car to a stop on the road beside Maduro Park. The engine sputters to a stop as she pulls the key from the ignition.

As she scans the park from her car through the rusting chain-link fence, she's reminded of why she's not fond of this place. Time and neglect took what once stood as a playground bustling with children and rendered it desolate. Stands of overgrown deciduous trees encroach from all sides, and the clearing springs tall with waist-high weed growth. The rusted out, skeletal remains of the swing set still stand in the far corner of the park. But there's no sign of Brady.

Angela takes a deep breath and exits her car. She traipses through the field to the dilapidated swing set where she agreed to meet Brady. Its corroded steel chains dangle, but the wooden swings they once held have rotted away, likening it to some type of medieval torture device. *No wonder kids in town refer to this place as Murder-O Park.*

"Angela."

"Jesus!" Angela jumps.

Brady emerges from the edge of the woods.

"Christ, Brady. You scared the shit out of me."

"Sorry, didn't want to be spotted." Brady's eyes scan the roadways.

What's he looking at? Angela's eyes drift with his. *Wants to make sure no one sees him? Shit! Remote location. No witnesses.* Angela takes a tentative step back.

"Relax." Brady shows his open palms. "It's safer here. Nothing happens here. And it's private."

"Why would we need privacy?" Angela's voice crackles.

"Angela, it's me. I'm *not* gonna hurt you. Remember the promise we made?"

"What promise?"

Brady flashes a warm smile and takes a step forward. "It's been a long time since that day. That's for sure. But I always kept it."

"Kept what?"

"You're serious? You don't remember?" The crease between Brady's eyes grows deeper.

"Quit fuckin' around, Brady. You're freakin' me out, again."

"Oh wow. You *are* serious."

"Yeah. And you better be too!" Angela takes a couple of steps forward, nostrils flaring. Her fear retreats as a fiery wave rises from deep within her. Even though she called Brady and asked him to meet her, she won't allow him to fuck with her head.

"Whoa, whoa. Ang... Calm down." Brady puts his hands up.

"Don't tell me what to do. You better start talkin' or I'm outta here!"

"Okay. No problem. It's just that... I'm surprised you don't remember is all."

"Remember *what*, Brady?"

"The *day*. The day in Grief Hollow. The day the tree fort burned down." Brady studies her eyes for a glimmer of recognition. Nothing comes.

"Yeah. What about it? Why'd you even do it, Brady?"

"You."

"Wh-at?" Angela's voice breaks apart like a disintegrating airliner.

"Because of you. I did it because of you. Because that's what you told me I should do."

Something triggers in the deep recesses of Angela's mind. The neurological dam fails all at once, and a flood of suppressed memories rolls into the forefront of Angela's mind like horrible waves. She sees herself in Grief Hollow the same day Brady and his friends arrive there with their BB guns. Though she's not sure why, she's hiding behind a tree while listening to the boys talk about tent caterpillars. Without revealing her hiding place, she manages to get Brady's attention.

The words pop into her head. There's no doubt. She said them. She said them to Brady. And with purpose. They strike a haunting chord as they chime in her mind, *if they burn, they won't return. But why did I say that? That's not something I'd say. Why did I give Brady the idea to burn the caterpillars? Jesus! I'm a murderer. I killed Misty, not Brady.* Distressed tears begin spilling from Angela's eyes. She staggers a step, a dizzying spell enveloping her mind.

"Ang...Ang...are you okay?" Brady moves in closer.

Angela quakes, the ground beneath her set to a rickety sway. Her legs become flimsy, her upper body wobbling on failing struts. Terror pulses into her high-beam eyes like an amnesia patient roused from a Pollyanna existence to discover a dark criminal past. The self-realization cripples her, suggesting she's not a good person. Not the person she thought herself.

"I...I...remember." Angela's voice trembles.

Angela grabs Brady's scarred arms with both hands. She examines them, her eyes raining tears.

"I did this to you. *Oh fuck*! I did this to you."

"Angela, listen to me. You didn't do anything to me. It wasn't you. It wasn't really your idea. It was this Thing's idea. It put it into your head. That's what it does."

"But I did. I remember telling you. I remember now. Brady, why didn't you tell? Anyone? Someone? Why didn't you tell someone?" Angela breaks off into loud sobs, tears streaming her cheeks.

Brady clasps tender hands on the silky flesh below her shoulders, anchoring her. His soft eyes swaddle hers. "I made a promise to you. After the other boys ran off. You tried to help me. It was my idea for you to leave. *I made a promise.* There was no reason to ruin your life too."

"And you kept that promise." Angela's rickety voice fractures. *He gave up everything for me.* She flings her arms around Brady's neck and hugs him tight before succumbing to hysteria.

"Of course, I did." Brady presses his body snug to hers, patting her back with gentle affection as her salty tears roll down his neck.

CHAPTER 44
Incongruities

Detective Holt eyes the paperwork on his desk, twiddling with the end of his mustache. He asked Marcy to print it for him, but now he's wavering. He hates these decisions.

On those rare Friday afternoons when Chief Barton gets nostalgic, aided by nips from the stash of whiskey in his bottom desk drawer, he bends Holt's ear for a bit about his rise from Officer to Detective to Chief. He arcs his eyebrows at Holt when the phrase *you know I'm gonna retire one day* passes his lips. The most logical successor, Holt holds his tongue during the pregnant pauses when the Chief's eyes search him for a sign of interest, and the inevitable deep sigh that follows when Holt ignores the cue. An extended silence delivers Holt's answer.

If the devil designed a perfect Hell for Holt, getting saddled with the Chief's job climbs to the top of the list. He dreads the Chief's annual tropical pilgrimage. A week of getting thrust into the leadership role in the department tests the fiber of his being. Detective Holt lacks the stomach for it, the politics and daily bullshit that come along with the role. No, he's a worker, not a leader. He likes to dig into things, unravel the puzzles that confront him in his daily job, not manage a department.

His instinct tells him to sign it, but the thought of making the pen stroke cripples him. He already told Officer Clancy to take the day off, but this carries official weight, a significant blemish on the young officer's record, assuming the Chief doesn't decide to fire him upon his return. These types of documents grow legs and follow, finding a way to limit future opportunities. The paperwork might hibernate for a season, lying dormant in a filing cabinet, but in time, and given the opportunity, it's sure to raise its ugly head and crush the young officer's aspirations.

Holt runs his fingers through his mustache. *What would the Chief want me to do? Does it even matter? I'm in so much shit already. This should be the least of my worries.* Sleepy jurisdictions like Harper Pass don't experience these types of violent crime waves. Chief Barton didn't even bother to leave the information on his whereabouts in Hawaii. He always made a point, more so at the urging of his wife, to leave his cell phone behind. *His pale gut's probably hanging out on a beach somewhere right now, kicked back, carefree and having a Mai Tai. Blissfully unaware of the shit sandwich that's engulfed Harper Pass.* Detective Holt remembers him mentioning Oahu, maybe even Maui. Hundreds of hotels must dot those two islands and with no itinerary, no possible way to narrow it down. The task of finding him borders on impossible and requires far too many man-hours to devote to making all those fruitless calls. But it's more of an excuse. Because even if he could, Holt would have strong reservations about making that phone call and interrupting the Chief's vacation. Bad career move.

Nope. Chief entrusted me to make department decisions. Damn well better do that if I want to keep my own job. He takes a deep breath and lets out a heavy sigh. Detective Holt makes a few quick pen sweeps across the paperwork, placing Officer Clancy on paid administrative leave. One thing left to do, file it with Marcy.

Officer Morrow and Officer Ivansek stroll into the station. Holt flings out his top desk drawer, shuffles the signed paperwork inside, and slams it shut. The final decision can wait. *May need Clancy's help in all this, anyway.*

Morrow approaches Holt's desk. "Holt, just got word from the hospital. The boy didn't make it." He dresses his words down with somber inflection.

"Truck creamed him pretty good," Ivansek remarks in his normal, tone-deaf fashion.

Detective Holt shakes his head, a deep-set frown emerging. Tragedy of this scale and magnitude in such a short duration has never happened in Harper Pass. *And all of it on my watch.* He sent Officers Morrow and Ivansek to respond to the 911 call of a traffic accident, not anticipating another fatality.

"How'd you write it up?"

Officer Morrow shakes his head. "It was an accident. Plain and simple. Just a freak accident."

"So, no charges then?"

"Witness saw it. There was a car backing out of a driveway. The boy swerved into the street to miss it. And—"

"Cablammo!" Ivansek interjects as he smacks his palms together, making a loud clap.

"We don't need sound effects, Ivansek," Holt scolds.

"Yeah. Sorry, cap'."

"I'm not your captain. *Dammit!* What's wrong with you, Ivansek?"

"Where do we start?" Morrow barbs sarcastically.

"Holt, nothing's wrong with—"

"It was a rhetorical fucking question!" Holt glares at Ivansek.

Detective Holt examines Ivansek's slovenly appearance. *Jesus! A serious fucking brain drain happened in this department.*

Replacing my friends, seasoned veterans, with this moron. Fucking politics! To think I might be stuck with this train wreck. Clancy had promise. Damn. Kid was pretty sharp. Not like this ogre.

As if reading the disgust in Detective Holt's thoughts, Ivansek says on cue, "Yeah. You're right. Sorry, Holt."

"Interesting thing though, Holt. Witness said they saw Sammy Needles a few minutes before the accident. Just before the crash, she comes back to her window, and Sammy's gone, but she sees four boys there at the scene. Said she thought one of them was Sandra Mitchell's boy, Tee."

"And they *weren't* there when you got to the scene?"

"No. The man driving the truck said they ran off," replies Morrow.

"Probably just a bunch of scared kids," Ivansek dismisses.

"Yeah. Probably right." Detective Holt hesitates. "But maybe they saw Sammy, too. Seems to be an awful lot of people dying when Sammy Needles is around."

Morrow lifts his brows at Holt. "Yeah…but it was an accident, Holt. Don't see no way to look at it otherwise."

"Maybe you're right. But Sammy doesn't know we think that. Might help to put his ass on the hot seat about Cam Givers and the Rogers twins. Get something out of him at least."

"You gonna make that ole boy squirm, ain't ya?" Officer Ivansek's eyes delight like a child at an ice cream parlor window.

Ivansek's commentary tends to annoy Holt, but the comment doesn't even register. Holt's mind tumbles forward. He never misses an opportunity to gain some leverage on a suspect or person of interest before an interrogation. *Might just have what I need to make Sammy sing. Looking forward to breaking that piece of shit. Watching that hard façade crumble. Unmasking that coward underneath. Finally find out what the little shit's got to do with all of this.* Holt breaks from his thoughts and lands his eyes on Morrow.

"I had Clancy order me a chemical analysis. Can you get me an update on that?"

"You got it, Holt. Oh… and the Rogers family… they keep calling. They want answers. What should we tell 'em?"

The mention of the Rogers family sledgehammers Detective Holt in the gut. A wave of nausea accompanies his strong suspicions of how it will end.

"Tell them we filed the missing persons paperwork last night, we're looking for their sons, that I personally notified the neighboring jurisdictions that they're missing and that we've added them to the NCIC."

"Holt," Marcy bellows out from the lobby, "Nancy Rogers on line one again for you."

"Tell her to hold on for just a minute."

"Guess you drew the short straw," quips Morrow.

"All right. Give me a little space. Ivansek, I want you out patrolling. I want you to call me with anything unusual, anything at all. If so much as a frog farts, you give me a call. We've got to get this shit storm under control."

"You got it, Holt." Ivansek waddles out of the station.

As Holt turns to Morrow, Officer Morrow pulls out a small notepad and pen in anticipation. He's a fastidious note taker, a habit he adopted early in his career, but that's become even more pronounced with his advancing age.

"Morrow, get me an update on that chemical analysis. Finish processing that blood from the woods last night, and send it out. Call Judge Scobie. Tell him we need a subpoena for Shane and Seth Roger's medical records. I want to know what blood type they are. After that, I need you on patrol too."

"I'm on it, Holt." Morrow finishes writing on his small notepad, turns and walks away.

Detective Holt takes a deep breath and gathers his thoughts. The excruciating conversation with Cam Givers' parents the night before leaks into his mind. Upon delivering the news, Cam's mom, Karen, devolved into a puddle of pitiful jelly. Tommy, Cam's father, tried his best to keep it together, but even he succumbed to the weight of his grief. He kept repeating, "Why? Why would someone do this to our Cam?" It wasn't the indignant reaction of outrage that Holt expected, which caught him off guard and made it so much worse.

A malignant vine-like growth flourishes inside him, its tentacles spreading, strangling his hollow stomach and pushing bile into his throat. *Jesus. What the hell can I even tell her? Her boys, Seth and Shane, they're dead. I know it. Too much blood. And Cam's story... Bodies are probably somewhere in Shiners' Gorge.* But how do you tell a parent that, shatter their hope and rip the spines from their still breathing bodies? Something horrific swallows a person delivering that type of news. It's as if God peels away the imperceptible layers, allowing a clear glimpse into the ethereal gears. Holt bore witness to it before, the soul-sucking moment their eyes glaze, the life abandoning their bodies, leaving behind an empty shell. And the empty carcasses that remain all too often crumble themselves soon after.

Got a really bad feeling. Only a matter of time before next of kin notifications on this one. Holt gulps. He bites his top lip hard with his bottom teeth in a deliberate attempt to deliver himself a healthy dose of pain, almost as a reminder to stay in the moment with these desperate people. The tang of salt and heavy metal fills his mouth. He's broken the skin. He dabs at his bloodied lip with a tissue before answering the phone.

"Detective Holt h—"

"Where are they, Detective? My boys. Where are my boys?" Nancy Rogers words come in rapid-fire.

"Mrs. Rogers...I know this is a really hard time. I know—"

"You *know*? What do *you* know? *Why* haven't you found them, Tripp?" Nancy's voice trails off into tears.

The mention of his first name melts away the formality of the moment in an instant. Having grown up in this small town, it's a common occurrence, but also a glaring reminder that these people aren't faceless, nameless victims. They're his neighbors, people he goes to church with, people he went to high school with, played on sports teams together, and sometimes, girls he swapped a little spit with in his youth.

"Nancy, I'm sorry. I really am. I can't even imagine what you're going through. We're going to do our best to find Seth and Shane."

"But they're okay...I mean, *you* think they're okay, right?"

"Nancy, I can't answer that. We just don't know enough yet."

"Oh Tripp. Pleeease." Nancy's voice devolves into a pitiful whimper.

"We filed a missing person's report for your boys. I have our people out looking for them now."

"Maybe they just got lost in the woods. You know how boys are. That's probably it, don't you think? We can just go find them in those woods."

"Nancy, *don't* go in the woods. I have my men working on this."

"But they're probably scared and—"

"I mean it! Don't go in those woods."

"Okay, but I have to do something. I can't just sit here. You need to do something, Tripp. Pleeease. Just find my boys, Tripp."

"Nancy, you have my word. I'm going to do everything possible to find Seth and Shane. But I'm going to need a little more time. Can you give me a little time?" Holt drums the ground beneath his desk with his foot. Time is precisely what he doesn't have in these investigations, and he knows it.

"Okay... but..."

"I'll call you this evening. *Promise*. If not sooner. Try to get some sleep in the meantime."

"*Sleep*? I can't sleep. How could I sleep?"

"I know, but at least try to get some rest."

"Okay. I'll try," Nancy replies, her words disingenuous. "And *you'll* call me?"

"Yes, absolutely. *I'll* call you."

"Please find them." Nancy's voice trails off into a whimper.

"I will," Detective Holt replies, the words an impulse that no sooner leave his lips than Nancy hangs up the phone. *Damn. Why'd I say that? Love to walk that back a bit. Qualify it at least. Better to tamp down her expectations. Too late now. And we'll find 'em. Probably not in the condition she's hoping for though.*

Detective Holt takes a deep breath and clamps his eyelids shut. *Dammit! Too many investigations. And like two-and-a-half cops. Not enough. This masquerading as chief chewing up all my time. Feels like I'm just playin' detective at this point. Need more time. More men. Shit. And Kirsten's deteriorating. Verge of coming unhinged.* Detective Holt's pulse quickens.

"Holt." Morrow announces himself as he approaches holding a piece of paper. "Think someone may've screwed up. This is really strange. We may want to get this run again."

"What is it?"

Officer Morrow lays the paper on Detective Holt's desk and points to a specific paragraph in the middle of the page.

"Chem' analysis. Says here that black substance that we sent in for analysis is organic. No chemicals at all."

"*Really*?" Detective Holt's wide eyes meet Morrow's.

"Yeah. But that's not the most interesting thing. What really doesn't make no sense is what they say they found. Says here they likely identified at least five different instances of unique animal cells, although they couldn't conclusively identify the different species. Like some kind of Franken-goo or something."

Detective Holt's eyes flash a glimmer. *Professor Wadlow. Right academic background. Mysterious organic substance. Gotta be involved. Same substance. Multiple crime scenes. Links him to them. At the very least someone working in concert with him. Brady Palmer even.*

"Think I need to have another discussion with Latravious Wadlow."

Officer Morrow nods. "Sounds to be right up his alley."

"And what about Judge Scobie? Did he give you any guff?"

"No. He's issuing the subpoenas now."

"Good. Why don't you make a run to get those, and then take 'em to the kids' doctor's office? I want to know their blood type, ASAP."

"Why didn't you just ask Nancy?"

"'Cause I don't want to alarm her any more than she already is. She might do something stupid."

Jesus, Morrow! Have some common sense. And stop with the questions.

"Oh. Right. That makes sense. The lab should have the blood sample we collected from the tree processed by tomorrow."

"I need to know *today*. Take the sample to the hospital and have them type it for you. Tell 'em to call me if they push back. And call me as soon as you have both results."

"You got it, Holt."

Detective Holt waits until Officer Morrow exits the police station.

"Fuck!" Holt's voice explodes into every corner of the station. Marcy winces from the lobby desk.

Goddamn serial killer! Here. In Harper Pass. These murders, disappearances. Feels linked. I need more help. Could use an army.

"Marcy!"

"Hey, Holt, what you need, hon'?"

"Call Lance. Tell him we need him to report in immediately."

"But I thought—"

"I changed my mind. We need his help." Detective Holt takes a deep breath before continuing. "Also, I want you to call Kasey Norton."

"The *news reporter*?"

"Yes. Have her meet me at 3 p.m. at the Cracked Egg. Tell her I'm ready to give her the interview."

Worth the gamble. What's reactionary mode gotten us so far? More missing persons, more bodies. Whoever's behind this isn't stupid. Ex-military? Ex-law-enforcement? Know enough to stay off the radar, that's for sure. Gives 'em an advantage.

Time to go on the offensive. If it is a serial killer, maybe a little heat from the local media will help to flush 'em out.

CHAPTER 45
Teetering on the Fulcrum of Fate

S till rattled from the incident on Chandler Trace, we gather outside of Professor Wadlow's house. We journeyed here in heavy silence, my mind filling with dark contemplations of everything I'd seen. At Wadlow's house there's no sign of Brady, and all is quiet on High Street. I check my watch, already five past noon.

"Maybe he stood us up." Tee paces back and forth, his quick steps cutting a path through Wadlow's grass. He narrows questioning eyes on Robby.

"He wouldn't do that. He'll be here."

My wary eyes meet Robby's as I mull the severity of the accident we witnessed. "You think he made it?"

"Don't know, man. Didn't look good."

Devin shakes his head. "Was like he planned that. I mean, how did Sammy know exactly where to put that trash can?"

Disturbing images of the violent collision assail my mind. The memory plays on loop, revealing one subtle gory detail after another. The suddenness of the accident didn't allot sufficient time for my mind to process the event. Details that didn't even register at the time well up from my subconscious. My abdomen clenches at the memory of a gag-inducing detail, the boy's arm bent at a ninety-degree angle midway up his forearm. I wince. The more I try to suppress it, the more it envelops me. *And then the whistling. Oh shit! The whistling.*

"Guys, that song... That song that Sammy was whistling as he walked away. It's the same one I was singing the night Margo showed up in my bathroom."

"That's some weird shit." Tee bites his bottom lip as his eyes widen.

"Maybe he is this thing. You know, the skin-walker." *Gotta be. Right?*

"I don't think so."

"*What*? You were the one who was so convinced it was him, Robby. And now? Now that we see him do some weird ass shit for the first time? *Now* you don't think it's him? *Unreal!*" Tee expels the words like compressed steam.

Devin shoots Robby a crinkle-faced gaze. "Yeah. What gives, dude?"

"It's just a feeling. It's hard to explain."

Tee scowls at Robby. "Well try!"

"Okay. So, when we were watching him before all that happened, something didn't sit right, but I can't really place it."

"What? That he's a freakin' moron? I mean, come on. He hit the mailbox with his cast. *Dumbass!*" Tee smirks.

"Wait." A sparkle collects in Robby's eyes like the build of a wave. "That's it. Exactly!"

Tee puffs a blast of air through his lips. "What's it? That he's a moron?"

"No. He hit that mailbox with his cast and yelped in pain. Seems to me, if he is this thing, then why wouldn't he just change forms and then regenerate..."

Devin's lower jaw lunges. "Oh shit! That's true!"

"I mean, why would he need to have a broken arm in the first place? And for that matter, why wouldn't he have changed forms when you hit him with the skateboard?"

"*Holy crap.* That makes total sense." *Robby's right. How didn't I think of that?*

"But it's got to be related." Tee shakes his head and frowns. "That was just too weird back there."

"Maybe," Robby concedes.

"And the talking…who the hell was he talkin' to? There what'n't nobody there," Tee baffles.

Devin nods. "That *was* weird."

A car coming to a stop on the street brings our conversation to a halt. Driven by instinct, we've gathered on the driveway near the window where Tee broke-in without realizing the irony of our action. Our new status as invited guests no longer warrants the behavior of intruders. We creep up the driveway to get a better view of the street.

"That's Angela's car," Robby pipes in surprise.

"What the hell's she doing here?" Tee spouts as he begins an indignant march.

"Tee, wait."

Tee ignores Devin and continues on. He puffs out his scrawny chest, taking determined strides, steely resolve in his eyes.

As they emerge from the car, Angela locks onto Brady with a googly-eyed gaze, an affectionate smile drawing up the corners of her lips. Brady's cheeks ripen in response to this smallest of intimacies.

Tee huffs and marches to Angela. "What? Are you guys like an *item* or something now?"

Both Brady and Angela's cheeks fill with color, their eyes running from Tee's. *Ohh… Looks like it. This won't go well.* Fires roil in Tee's eyes, a scowl warping his expression.

"*Unbelievable.*" Tee vents.

Angela takes a moment to collect herself. "Well, hey to you too, Tee."

"Don't *hey* me. *What* are you doing here?"

"I invited her," Brady trumpets, his face hardening with resolve.

"Why? This is such bullshit!"

"Tee, come on. I can help," Angela coos.

A wonky grin overtakes Robby's lips. "Hey, Angela."

"Hey, Robby." Angela flashes a pleasant smile.

"No. Unh-uh. Nooooo… This is total bullshit."

"Come on, dude. What's the big deal? Maybe she can help." Robby's starry gaze lingers on Angela.

"How can *she* help? *She* doesn't even know what's going on."

"She does now." Brady tosses the verbal grenade in Tee's direction.

"*What…the…hell? You told her? Why?*"

"Cause she needed to know. You don't want anything to happen to your sister, do ya?"

"Well, *no.* Of course not."

"Well, okay then. Now nothing will, 'cause now she knows what we're up against."

Tee frowns and his posture slumps. Angela wraps an arm around his shoulder and leans into his ear.

"Tee, I promise I won't get in your way. I know this is your thing."

Tee hoists a half-smile and wriggles out of her hug. With Angela and Tee's body language indicating an armistice, Brady leads our group to Professor Wadlow's door. He gives the door several firm, backhanded knuckle raps. The third hit nudges the door on its hinges, and it slides off the door jamb. Brady's eyes widen as the door creaks open several inches. He cranes his neck, careful to keep his body outside while peering into the opening. I contort my gaze through the gap, the steady thump of my heart quickening its pace. Tiny dust particles dance in the air, moseying in a spotlight of sunshine slicing into the darkness through the cracked door.

As Angela moves closer in behind Brady, he extends his arm and presses his palm to her stomach, impeding her progress. Brady gives the door a light push with his shoe, and it opens without any resistance.

"Professor Wadlow," Brady calls out through the opening into the silent still of the house, but no one responds.

Robby presses in closer behind Brady. "Shouldn't we go inside?"

"Something's wrong. I've been here a hundred times, and this is the first time this door hasn't been locked." Brady's eyes grow wider as they flit about the home's interior, and he finds himself in the crosshairs of Robby's narrowed eyes. "*What*? Professor's damn near OCD about it. He's chain locked me out before when I've just stepped outside to get his mail. Something's really wrong."

"Maybe he just forgot." Tee pushes a puff of air through his lips. "Dude's old."

"He doesn't forget. *Not this*."

Robby jockeys for a better view and can't get one. He crosses his arms on his chest.

"Well, we can't just stand here."

Devin's head perks up at Robby's comment. "Yeah. Maybe he fell and needs our help."

"What if it's the thing? You know. The *thing*. The skin-talker." Angela's voice quavers.

Tee erupts in laughter. "You would say that. That's all you ever do is talk, talk, talk. *Skin-talker*? Don't ya mean the skin-*walker*?"

"*Shut up, Tee*! HA. HA. Laugh it up. Yeah, yeah. The skin-walker."

Robby marches forward. "*Look*, we don't know anything yet. And, *we're not going to know anything* unless we go in there."

My heartbeat accelerates. I retreat a couple of steps.

"Maybe we should split up, some of us go inside and some of us stay out here. You know, to keep watch."

"Bock, bock, bock." Tee's face beams at me, a big grin forming as he rocks his head like a bird. With his arms bent and flapping, hands on his rib cage, he starts doing a ridiculous, exaggerated bird walk. "Bock, bock, bock."

"Chicken shit." Robby coughs the words into his hands.

"*What*?" My face radiates heat as a surge of blood washes into it. "Think it's a pretty good idea for someone to stand watch is all."

"Bet you do!" Tee hops from foot to foot, tilts his head in a sideways slant, and taps his nose into my chest several times like a pigeon collecting breadcrumbs in its beak.

Angela gives Tee a nudge on the shoulder. "Cut it out, Tee. This is serious."

"Yeah. And it *is* a good idea," Brady reprimands.

"*See.*" Angela celebrates with a gratified smile.

"Someone needs to stand watch. Angela, why don't you stay out here." Brady's words erase Angela's smile.

"What? *No.* I want to go in. Besides, I think Brooks wants to stay out here."

"No one stays alone from this point on. It's too dangerous." Brady's eyes meet Angela's. "Angela, can you please just stay out here with Brooks?" Brady delivers a wide-eyed, double bounce with his eyelids to Angela and mute-mouths *puh-lease* to her.

"*Fine.* Okay, okay. I'll stay with Brooks."

"But guys, I'm good to go in, honest."

"Pipe down, *Brook.* Leave this one to the men." Tee grins as he puffs his chest out.

"*Ha. As if.*" Angela shakes her head at Tee, dismissing his manufactured bravado. She pauses for a moment, casting a somber-eyed gaze at Brady. His jawline rigid, an intense glimmer in his eyes, he prepares to go inside. "Brady, be *careful.*"

Brady nods before leading a procession into the house while Angela and I wait outside.

CHAPTER 46
A Dark Turn

Scant sunlight filters through the cracks in the blinds. It collects on the dingy carpet by the windows and affords just enough light for the boys to avoid any obstacles. Brady scans his surroundings for irregularities as they make a quiet advance through the living room. He can find none. Angela looks on from the porch, a simmering pan of nerves, as Brady, Devin, Tee and Robby disappear around a corner.

The familiar disarray of the kitchen doesn't signal anything unusual to Brady, but Tee's lips jumble.

"*Nasty.*"

"Shhh." Brady presses his index finger to his lips.

"*What*? *Dude's nasty.* How does he live like this?" Tee points to the countertops littered with dirty dishes.

"Yeah, man. Is this normal?" Devin lifts a brow at Brady as he considers the possibility of this disarray resulting from a physical struggle, versus the obvious explanation of the solitary existence of an old man so consumed with his work that he ignores basic principles of hygiene and rudimentary civilization.

"Man, it looks like a garbage dump puked in here." Tee wears a gleeful grin.

Devin nods at him. "And it smells like it, too."

"Cut it out, Tee," Robby grumbles.

"Guys!" Brady gestures with his hands for quiet.

"What? Come on. There's no one even here." Tee shrugs and takes a couple of steps forward.

Tee's shoe strikes a glass bowl. It spins away from him and spills the sloppy, reddish-brown goop it contains onto the kitchen floor before rattling to a noisy stop. Brady freezes, eyes inflating.

Devin's eyes lock with Brady's. "What is it?" His voice travels on a hushed whisper.

"*Watson.*"

Robby tilts his head at Brady.

"Who's Watson?"

"Professor Wadlow's cat. That's his food dish." Brady's voice quakes.

"What's the big deal? It's just a cat. Matter of fact, I already met that fatty." Tee snickers with a jovial smile.

"It *is* just a cat. But something's wrong. Professor Wadlow only feeds Watson at night. That bowl should be empty." Brady's eyes dart in all directions.

Tee's cavalier demeanor melts away. In its place, a steady drip of anxiety accumulates in his stomach, spawning a wave of apprehensive gurgles. It's familiar, his body conjuring the same response as it did when they encountered Myron in Shiners' Gorge. He offers nothing further to lighten the tense atmosphere. He scans the room.

"What's that?" Tee's voice trails off.

In the corner of the room, on the edge of the door frame leading out of the kitchen, four parallel gouges in the wall stretch six inches in length. Brady traipses forward, stoops, and runs his finger the length of one of the slits. He peels back the torn wallpaper, revealing the slits cut deep into the sheet rock underneath. Devin's eyes balloon.

"Whoa, that's deep bro."

"These here before?" Robby's voice wavers as his eyes connect with Brady's.

Brady shakes his head. "No, I don't think so."

Brady leads the group through the doorway and into a dining room. They find two similar sets of slits in the walls and one set of four slits dug out of the hard wood floor.

Tee's eyes flit about the room. "Think maybe we should get out of here."

Robby smirks. "What happened to all that *leave it to the men stuff*?"

"Shut up, Robby."

A creaking floorboard silences the bickering. The boys whip their heads to the kitchen. Tee's body trembles.

"What the hell was that?"

"Angela, is that you?" Brady cranes his neck.

"Brooks? Shit ain't funny, man." Tee lobs his words in the direction of the kitchen.

No one replies to their calls. The boys huddle tight together like a murder of crows eyeing a hungry hawk. Brady motions with his eyes to the basement door. *If Professor Wadlow's here, that's where he'll be.* Professor Wadlow spends an inordinate amount of time there, where he's closest to his work and farthest away from the tangles of social interaction that lie beyond his doors. As Brady clasps the door handle, Robby files in behind Brady, and Devin follows. Tee stands his ground, shaking his head, but Brady ignores the dissuasion and eases the doorknob a half-turn.

"Come on, Tee," Robby whispers.

Brady flips the light switch at the top of the stairs. The boys make a slow and quiet descent to the basement. Tee follows in tow, trailing a couple of stairs behind. At the bottom of the staircase, Brady searches out the light switch and flips it on, but nothing happens.

"Dude turn on the light," Tee agonizes.

Brady flips the light switch a couple more times.

"They're already on. Lights must be out."

A pinch of sunlight filters through the half-window across the room, casting a mixture of light and shadow into the basement. Due to the proximity of the window to the top of the basement wall, most of the light it affords collects on the exposed, wooden-beam ceiling above. The boys hold their ground as they wait for their pupils to dilate and gradually adjust to the darkness. Something scurries in the far corner of the basement, breaking the silence. Everyone's head snaps to it in unison, but the murky darkness swallows everything.

"Something's down here. . . Let's go!" Tee's fingers claw into Robby's shoulder.

Robby clenches his jaw. "We can't go yet."

"Professor Wadlow?" Brady beckons into the darkness.

"W.T.F., man? You're going to get us killed." Tee takes a retreating step to the stairs. His jugulars throb as hot bursts of blood sizzle through them.

"Professor?" Brady doubles down, projecting his voice even louder.

"Look." Devin points across the room. Robby traces the path of Devin's extended finger. With his eyes adjusting to the dearth of light, the outlines of shadowy shapes materialize from the dark slushy mass of blackness into familiar objects with defined corners and edges. Professor Wadlow's workbench emerges from the lifting sensory fog.

As more of the details render themselves, the broken glass catches Brady's eye. Strewn glass litters the workbench and surrounding floor. Some type of pooled liquid rolls drip by drip off the edge of the workbench and collects in a dark puddle on the concrete floor underneath. Robby notices the overturned microscopes and once well-organized workspace that's disheveled. Brady hurries to it, glass crackling beneath his feet as he approaches. As he surveys the desk, he traces the origin of the dripping liquid to the cabinet above the workbench.

"No. Noooo!" Brady cries out, and he flings a cabinet door open.

As the other boys bolt over, Brady flings open the other cabinet door. Professor Wadlow never synthesized any new batches of the formula, and someone destroyed the existing stockpile. A wave of nausea wrings his stomach.

"Shit. Shit. It's gone. Ruined!" Brady's movements are frenzied.

Tee pushes his palms toward the floor. "Dude, keep it down."

A horrible groan pierces the black. Brady grabs a large shard of broken glass and grips it like a dagger. Anger pours into his eyes. Through the years, Professor Wadlow became like a second father to him. Whatever happened here, whatever this means, can't be good. He's seen enough to reason that this is a deliberate attempt to put a halt to Wadlow's work, and it's not that much of a stretch to imagine that part of that might include putting a halt to Wadlow, too. And the prospect that someone's done something to Professor Wadlow enrages him. Brady hoists his glass dagger high above his shoulder and strides forward. A throaty heave, like a large animal struggling to regurgitate its meal, pierces the musty basement air, but it doesn't deter Brady's advance.

"Dude! Don't!" Tee screams before dashing to the edge of the basement staircase. He watches Brady barrel forward, expecting something to leap from the darkness at any moment and rip Brady to shreds.

Robby grabs a glass beaker from one of the tall shelves and falls in behind Brady. Devin fumbles through his pockets and pulls out a small, keychain-sized, LED flashlight. Brady loses his footing and plummets to the concrete floor. Devin turns on the flashlight as more violent, animalistic heaving ricochets off the basement walls. The flashlight illuminates the area around Brady. Scarlet, sneaker-sized streaks disrupt a thick blood trail in the spot where Brady slipped. It's part of a longer blood trail that leads beyond him down a short hallway and smears on the face of a cinder block half wall leading into a crawlspace. As the light from the flashlight envelops him, Brady vise clamps one of his hands on the other and grimaces. The shard of glass sliced deeply into his hand during his fall, and an oil strike of hot blood wells between the spaces of his fingers, a crimson rain shower pouring from his limp fingertips. Robby places his hands underneath Brady's armpits and hoists him to his feet as the horrible heaving continues to emanate from the crawlspace a few paces in front of them.

"Let's go!" Tee screams from the third step of the staircase.

As Robby drags Brady to the staircase in loop-armed fashion, Brady wriggles free of Robby's grip and shouts, "No! Not without Wadlow!" Brady lumbers toward the crawlspace opening, careful to secure his footing first this time. "*Professor*

Wadlow!" He wails in desperation as the horrid possibilities of Professor Wadlow's undoing swirl through his head.

Devin sidesteps, clearing a path for Brady. As Brady passes, Devin swivels his body around, lighting the short, albeit bloody path in front of him. As the boys close in on the opening, a deep, menacing growl halts Robby's advance and sends Tee bounding the staircase. The soundtrack of Devin's heart flips from an up-tempo *Beatles* song to the full fury of pre-stardom *Metallica*, but after a moment of hesitation, he forces himself to move in concert with Brady. Brady stops at the half wall, eyeing the black chasm before him. The swirling darkness consumes everything. *A death trap. But can't leave. Gotta save Wadlow.*

"*Latravious!*" Brady howls into the black void as Devin surges up from behind him, shining his light into the opening of the crawlspace. The light reveals blood-soaked, bare earth in the immediate vicinity of the opening, but the small halo of light the cheap flashlight produces, gets consumed by the heavy blanket of darkness a few feet away from the entrance.

An answer returns from the depths of the crawlspace in the form of a furious snarl. Devin rests his hand on Brady's shoulder as they lean in together and strain to peer into the cavernous recesses of the crawlspace. Moments later, a rapid shuffling hooks their ears and yanks their heads to the left in unison. Devin sends cease and desist signals to his trembling hand on Brady's shoulder, but it goes unanswered. Synapses fire, but the lines remain severed. The body's natural compulsion to protect itself with the well-placed instinct of fear, honed through eons of trial and error, rules the moment, overriding the instruction sent from his mind. His body disobeys the anomalous command, sticking to the hard-wired phantom commands built into his genetic code. And in this moment, Devin's body instructs him to flee.

Another snarl, this time closer, calls out from the darkness. The trembling slips down Devin's body and settles into his foot.

"*Fuck!* What is that?" Robby looks on from a considerable distance.

Heavy animal panting moves closer, stopping a couple of feet shy of the edge of the pale, LED light halo. Brady leans farther into the crawlspace and by virtue of Devin's vise grip into Brady's shoulder, Devin and his flashlight get incidentally dragged in closer as well. The momentary extended reach of the light catches the phosphorous-yellow gleam from a set of eyes, looming on the edge of the halo of light.

"*Shi-it!*" Devin shudders as he retreats a step, and the yellow eyes dissolve into the black. As Brady strains to identify anything moving in the foggy black, the soft trickle of creeping footsteps ring out like warning shots from a few yards away. As his ears lock in and track the movement, Brady realizes that whatever's doing the slinking employs an intelligence in doing so. Where the light penetrates the deepest, it moves in a deeper arc to remain undetected. It's stalking them. A sudden surge of goosebumps prickles Robby's skin, and a shiver passes through his shoulders.

"*Go. Now.*" Robby's voice quakes.

"Latravious!" Brady shouts.

Something scuffling the earth rings out a few yards beyond the halo of light. It speeds closer. Something oblong, the approximate size of a volleyball, gray and furry, rolls a couple feet past the edge of the light halo. It does one more quarter turn and comes to a stop.

"Nooooo!" Brady screams.

The pale, blood-speckled face of Latravious Wadlow lies facing his own. Stilled, pale eyes stare at him in an aimless, forever gaze. A grizzly string of torn flesh trails away from Wadlow's head and leads into the black. Devin convulses into a dry heave. His hand clasps his mouth as his eyes follow the gory string of flesh away from Wadlow's severed head. Where the oblong string of flesh approaches the darkness, he can make out white chest hair and the remnants of an areola. His legs begin to carry him backwards, but not before he witnesses a giant, patchy-haired paw smash down from the darkness onto the string of flesh. The protruded claws needle through the flesh like ice picks through a watermelon. Its knuckle joints contract, locking onto the raw meat, and it drags Latravious Wadlow's tethered head back into the darkness of the crawlspace.

"Fuuckkkk!" Devin screams as his quieted voice returns in a thunderous, shrill boom. His legs motor beneath him, and in an instant, he passes a dismayed Robby, but not before his fingers latch onto Robby's shirt. He gives Robby a yank and pulls him into a run. The small LED light bounces once off of Robby's back before falling to the ground behind them, spinning one final twirl of light around the blood-soaked basement.

With tears streaming his face, Brady backs away from the crawlspace opening. One final approaching snarl launches Brady into a full retreat. Within a couple of seconds, he's nipping at the heels of Robby and Devin as they race through the rooms of the house upstairs.

CHAPTER 47
Change of Plans

As the five minutes or so of small talk dwindle, Angela and I exchange word-starved glances, more bored than worried at this point. Turns out that high school graduates don't share that much in common with middle schoolers once you get past the overlap of popular television shows. Out of subject material, neither one of us tries to force it, and we both take a seat on the bottom step of Professor Wadlow's porch.

We both jump to our feet as the door smashes into the wall inside the house. Tee bounds the three stairs leading from the porch to the sidewalk in one running leap.

"Runnnn!" he screams, eyes ablaze with terror.

"What happened? Where's Brady?"

"Just run!" Tee screams at Angela on his way down the driveway. He grabs his bike and runs it up the driveway. Without further hesitation, I run to the base of the driveway, grab Devin's skateboard and manage to carry it in my armpit while also pushing both remaining bikes up the hill.

"Start the car! Start the car!" Brady's voice booms out from inside the house.

The door bangs into the wall again, and this time Robby and Devin come bolting through the opening. They gather their bearings mid-jump from the porch, and as soon as their feet strike the earth, they cut left to meet me on the driveway.

As we run our bikes to the street, Brady comes roaring through the door. Angela turns the key in the ignition. Tee, Robby, Devin, and I race to Angela's car on High Street as Brady jumps in.

"Meet at the Library!" Brady shouts as we're passing. "Go! Go! Go!" Brady pounds an urgent hand on the dash.

Angela presses hard on the gas as Brady gazes at Wadlow's house, eyes glistening. The inertia slams Brady's car door shut as Angela squeals away from the curb before they zoom past us.

CHAPTER 48
Cat and Mouse

As Detective Holt turns onto High Street, a sedan whizzes past him at a high rate of speed. He whips his head around. *Chase it? Nah. Beat cop days are over. Not going back to that.* A moment later a cluster of boys on bikes and one on a skateboard roar past his car. He recognizes Brooks Raker as one of the boys. *Damn. They're hauling ass. Look scared shitless.*

As he pulls to a stop on the curb by Wadlow's house, he barks into his radio. "Ivansek. You there? Over."

"Yeah, Holt." Ivansek's voice crackles through the radio.

"Where you at? Over."

"Near Jennings Pike. Over."

Figures. Only fitting he's as far away as possible when I need him.

"Do me a favor, would ya? There's a silver sedan, if I had to guess, I'd say a late-model Toyota Corolla, that just pulled off High Street headin' back toward town. I'd like to know who's in that vehicle and what they're up to. Also, if you see Brooks Raker and his buddies, same drill. They looked a fright, and I'd like to know what spooked them. Over."

"Roger that, good buddy," Ivansek blabbers like a child mimicking a trucker.

The remark elicits a scowl from Holt. He squeezes his radio talk button, his tightening iron grip squeezing the plastic to near its breaking point. *Not over the open radio. Last thing I need. Kasey Norton prying into discord in the department.* He draws a deep breath through his nose and loosens his grip.

"Just see what you can find out, will ya?" Holt growls. "And report back."

Holt studies the property outside of Latravious Wadlow's house. The front door hangs open. Considering Wadlow's social preferences, or lack thereof, it strikes him as strange. Holt retrieves his service weapon from his holster and plucks out the cartridge. He examines the clip, satisfying himself that it's full and ready before popping it into his weapon. *No way Latravious left his door open.* After exiting his car, he slinks to the porch, gun drawn and readied. This time he minces with methodical deliberation, finding the steadiest boards on the porch, determined to make a much more unannounced visit.

Taking a deep breath, he pushes the door wider with the tip of his shoe. The weathered bolts groan on the hinges as the door retreats inside the house.

"Harper Pass Police," Detective Holt mutters, not a decibel louder than required to satisfy his legal obligation.

With those quick words, he enters the house. Gun drawn, he moves in silence on the balls of his feet through the living room and into the kitchen. The house looks the same as he remembers from his recent visit. Holt scans the kitchen. A large glob of cat food smeared on the floor contains a partial shoe print. He crouches, examining it. *That pattern. Looks a whole hell of a lot like one of 'em from Shiners' Gorge.* Holt holsters his weapon, pulls his rarely used cell phone from his jacket pocket, sets a quarter beside the print for scale, and snaps off a quick picture of the print.

As he checks the image to ensure he's captured a crisp photo, he notices a small red speck on the floor a couple of inches from the shoe print. The hundreds of crime scene photos he's viewed tell him it's blood. Lowering the phone from his eyes, he confirms his suspicion. A solitary droplet of blood specks the worn linoleum floor. Using his working but rudimentary knowledge of blood spatter forensics, he determines that the lack of elongation to the droplet seems to indicate it's from a wound sustained elsewhere. And it's fresh.

Holt studies the partial shoeprint. It's the approximate size of a child's foot. He closes his eyes for a moment, trying to visualize the shoes Sammy Needles came into the interrogation room wearing. A menacing snarl emanates from the bowels of the house and interrupts his meditation. Holt's eyelids spring open, and he swivels his head in that direction. Parallel gouges, resembling claw marks, near the doorjamb on the edge of the kitchen greet his eyes. *That's no cat. Too big. No dog either. Shit! Exotic pets? Frank Gibbs. That's what he asked about.* In one fluid motion, Holt returns his cell phone to his pocket and retrieves his service weapon from its holster.

As Holt proceeds with caution into the adjacent room, he spots more claw marks and more blood droplets. He follows the blood trail to a basement door, which hangs a couple of inches ajar on its hinges. With one quick heave, the door opens, and he's aiming his service weapon down a wooden staircase leading to a shadowy basement. An infuriated snarl greets his first step. As he looks down to secure his footing, he finds two more blood droplets on the stairs. *Should've called it into the station. Ivansek knows where I'm at. Damn! Wish it was Morrow. No turning back now. Wish Morrow was here to watch my six. Can't radio. Give up my location.*

As he descends the staircase, obscure thoughts race through his head. *A tiger? In Harper Pass? Maybe. And this measly 9mm won't do shit to stop that. Kirsten might really off herself if that happens.*

"Holt, got your sedan." Ivansek's voice blares through Holt's radio as he reaches the base of the stairs.

"Shit," Holt mutters as he frantically seeks out the volume button on his radio, lowers it, and collects it from his belt. A scuttling grabs his attention, and Holt trains his weapon and eyes in that direction, straining to see through the darkness.

"Who's in it? Over," Holt whispers into his radio, unable to resist the bait of satisfying his own curiosity versus cloaking his position with silence, but he never breaks eye line from the sound's point of origin.

"Brady Palmer. Oh, and Angela Mitchell." More noises shatter the still of the basement.

"Hold 'em there for me." Holt turns his radio off, latches it to his belt, and retrieves his Maglite.

An audible click echoes through the darkness as bright light bursts from his flashlight in the direction of the growling. The light beam illuminates a significant pool of blood on the concrete floor and streaks of blood smeared on the face of a half wall, all indicative of a traumatic event. A trail of bloody shoe prints leads away from the large pool of blood to the staircase, but the zigzag pattern doesn't match the one he photographed upstairs in the kitchen. Holt inspects the nearby wall. Thick arching patterns of heavy arterial spray show progressing stages of coagulation. *Jesus! What the hell happened here?* Holt focuses his beam on the half wall. His flashlight catches the glimmer of a pair of animal eyes trained on him. He flinches, and the eyes retreat into the darkness of the crawlspace before a testy half-growl pierces the pitch.

Holt gathers himself, summons his courage, and creeps toward the crawlspace, careful not to disturb the blood evidence on the basement floor. He trains his Maglite on the crawlspace opening with one hand, and the other death-grips his service weapon, aiming into the dark abyss beyond his light. Despite his best efforts to control it, the bobbling light beam betrays his intent and broadcasts his fear. He remembers the results of the chemical analysis and the comment Morrow made about the findings. *Like some kind of Franken-goo or something. Did Wadlow genetically engineer some kind of monster in his basement? Lose control of his own creation like a real-life Dr. Frankenstein? As plausible as anything else this week. Shit. Who knows?*

At the edge of the half wall, Holt shines his light deep into the crawlspace. The packed dirt gradually slopes to the first floor above him until it crests near the top of the far wall. Another growl echoes through the crawlspace, bouncing off the enclosed walls and cinder block columns, obscuring its exact origin. Holt chases it with his flashlight until the rays of his light collect on a cinder block wall. He begins a slow trace of the wall line with his light until he arrives at a corner of the structure. He pauses before continuing on. His light gives a glimpse of a thick and short-haired, long animal tail. After a quick scurry, the tail slips into the darkness. Frantically, Holt gives chase with the flashlight, but its evasive maneuvers keep it clear of his beam. Holt tries to corral his frazzled nerves. *Racoons take up residence in dark crawlspaces. All the time in these parts. That's probably it.* Though Harper Pass is a small town, there's enough wildlife to support two thriving critter-getter businesses. A cold shiver moves through him. *But that tail was longer. Larger and skinnier. Like a goddamn jungle cat.*

Holt strains to listen into the darkness. He lowers the volume on his sense of sight to focus all his gray matter on keening his eardrums like dialing in a tuning fork, enabling him to focus in on the smallest sounds, minute vibrations.

After a moment, he's got something. Locked in, he tracks its location in his mind like a porpoise using sonar to zero in on its prey. It slinks from his left to his right, narrowing the distance between him and it ever so gradually with each step. *Holy shit! Thing's huntin' me.*

Holt detects a pause in the movement. The sensation of eyes bearing into him from the darkness beyond presses heavy on him. His heartbeat quickens. Beads of nerve-conjured sweat roll down his neck and collect in his collar. A rapid patter of paws striking the bare earth and driving toward him grabs his attention. The swift charge takes him by surprise, and bullets begin discharging from his 9mm before he can even get his sidearm raised level. Errant bullets spray up an ascending trail of dirt geysers as they strike the earth in front of him. In the melee, his flashlight tumbles to the concrete at his feet and shatters as his freed hand locks onto his recoiling firearm to secure his aim.

A large, mangy, cat-like creature bursts into the strobe effect of his muzzle flare, its menacing claws outstretched in a murderous death lunge. Holt trains his fire on it as it descends, and small explosions of bursting flesh suggest several of his shots make it home. The hollow clicking of empty trigger pulls without the corresponding gunfire ushers in renewed darkness. A millisecond later, a large thud on the earth catapults his heart.

"Shit! Oh shit!" Holt agonizes as he searches his belt for a replacement clip. *Killed it! Come on! Tell me I killed it!*

Groans emanate from a few feet in front of him followed by the earthen scraping of something dragging itself away from the entrance of the crawlspace. As he releases his spent clip and pops the new clip into his Glock, the noise abates. A dark hush rolls into its place like a thick fog, obscuring his senses.

With his flashlight out of commission, he snatches his cell phone from his pocket and hits the home button, lighting his own face in a blueish glow. A few fumbled screen swipes later, he finds the flashlight app on his phone that he gave so much shit to Kirsten for installing. He told her at the time, *what the hell do I need this for? I already have a flashlight.* The irony of that moment doesn't escape him, and he's grateful for the light source.

With a quick tap of the app, a burst of blinding, white light ignites from his phone. Once his eyes adjust to the change in lighting, the earth in the immediate vicinity of the cinder block half wall shows drag marks leading away to the darkness from the vacated spot. Holt sucks in a deep breath and begins to swivel his body and the light.

"Holy Fuck!" Holt stammers, nearly pulling the trigger before recognizing the familiar face in his flashlight as Latravious Wadlow. Holt's mind swells with wild thoughts. *How's Latravious Wadlow unscathed by the hail of bullets that I just unleashed in his direction? Why didn't he say something during the shooting? What's he doing in the crawlspace with that thing? And why the fuck does he look so calm?*

The steady precipitation of questions accumulating in Holt's mind pushes hard on his restraint. It succumbs to the pressing weight and fractures like a late-spring snowbank. The resulting avalanche of questions comes spilling out.

"What the fuck? I almost blew your head off! What the hell are you doin' in the crawlspace? Why didn't you say something?"

"Good evening, Detective Holt." Wadlow grins.

"Don't 'good evening' me! What the hell was that thing? And why are you down here with it?"

"This is my house, Detective Holt. I should ask what *you* are doing in *my* house. Making a ruckus no less." Wadlow's face remains free of tension in spite of the gunshots.

"The front door was open." Holt studies Latravious Wadlow. *Glasses. He's not wearing his glasses.*

"And?" Latravious delivers a sideways glance.

"And there was some suspicious activity on your street. Thought you might need some assistance." Holt defends himself, but if Latravious Wadlow decides to make a big deal about this, Holt knows he stands on shaky ground with flimsy justification for his actions.

"Do you mind?" Latravious motions for Detective Holt to retreat a step.

Once Holt obliges the request, Latravious begins the laborious climb of the cinder block half wall. His feeble arm quivers under his body weight as he plants it on the top of the cinder block wall and strains to hoist his body over the wall. Holt holsters his gun as Wadlow gains his footing on the concrete basement floor.

"*What* are you keeping down here? What was that thing?"

"What thing?"

"Oh, Bullshit. Don't play stupid with me, old man. The thing I just unloaded a clip into. *That thing!* What have you done?" A maelstrom of anger churns in Holt's chest.

"You just shot my cat, Watson, Detective Holt. If that's what you're referring to."

"Unless your cat's a fully grown leopard, no, that's not what I'm referring to."

"Just a Maine Coon, Detective."

"That's not what I saw. What are you keeping down here?"

"Nothing, Detective, I assure you. Just me and my cat—or what was my cat before you decided to recklessly turn my house into your own personal shooting gallery." Wadlow raises his eyebrows at Holt. A twinge of amusement pulls up on the corners of his lips like invisible strings. *He's enjoying this! Too damn calm. Too comfortable. Planning something. Gotta be. Not good.*

"If it's just you and your cat, how do you explain all the blood?" Holt gestures to the basement floor.

"I spilled some red paint is all." Wadlow settles his keen eyes on Detective Holt, studying his every subtle movement.

"Nice try. Paint doesn't coagulate, professor. Try again." Holt's comment elicits a perturbed scowl from Latravious Wadlow. "What? Am I taking up too much of your time?"

"Think maybe it's time for you to go," Wadlow growls.

"I'm not going anywhere. We're going to get some stuff figured out, you and me. Why was Brady Palmer here?"

Latravious Wadlow's wrinkled face lights up. His eyes gleam with a youthfulness and vigor that contradict his years. It's as if the mention of Brady Palmer's name takes away twenty years in an instant.

"Brady Palmer was here, you say?" Latravious Wadlow delights as he rubs the tips of his thumbs over the undersides of his gnarled fingers. Holt's growing more uneasy as Wadlow's behavior and mannerisms continue to diverge from his personality. Professor Wadlow's always a bit aloof, but Holt's picking up on a malevolent undertone that unsettles him, a wholesale change to everything he's experienced with Wadlow in the past.

"What's your connection with the kid?"

"Oh, I have many connections, Detective Holt. Connections undeterred by the passage of time. Connections I follow relentlessly. It's only for these I still live. As unfailing as the Farmer's Almanac is the perseverance with which I do my work. You can count on that. Persistent as the coming of the changing seasons. And so too shall the winter come. Their fruit will wither on the vine of retribution." Latravious Wadlow unsheathes a slanted, toothy smile.

"Enough of the mumbo jumbo," Holt barks, nostrils flaring. "Looked into your story. You were on that visitor log dozens of times. Not a couple. What's your real connection to Brady Palmer?"

Professor Wadlow lets out a devious chuckle. "I dare say a strong one. Though the boy probably doesn't know the significance of it. But he'll come to find out soon enough. The deed will not go unreturned."

"Just what is it that you're planning? Are you planning to harm Brady Palmer? Did you have something to do with Cam Givers' death?"

"*I did not set these events in motion!*" Latravious Wadlow roars as his top lip curls, displaying an underpinning of anger. After a brief pause, the indignant outrage leaves his face. It's replaced by cold determination, that of a zealot, and he continues. "But the fruit will be plucked. Sweet and ripe with the bloat of guilt, they are. An unfortunate inheritance to be sure, but one that requires a collection. A reparation due."

"You know what? No. That's enough. I've heard enough. I think it's high time you had a psych evaluation, Mr. Wadlow." Holt shines his phone light into Wadlow's eyes.

Latravious Wadlow takes another step in Holt's direction. Driven by instinct, Holt's hand lands on his holster, leveling a silent insinuation of mistrust. Wadlow's eyes drift to the gun before he raises his sunken eyes, his thin, grayish lips parting in a gratified smile.

"So, you'd shoot an unarmed old man then?" Wadlow jests, but the inflection in his voice lacks any concern whatsoever.

"No, but I'd say you got some explaining to do. And best you do that at the station." Detective Holt makes an aggressive reach, grabs a handful of Wadlow's jacket, and tugs. Holt's eyes swell, and he's met with an exalted, toothy smile from Latravious Wadlow.

Holt relinquishes his grip and recoils in horror. It's not a jacket at all. *It's skin.*

"*What the fuck are you*?" Detective Holt mutters as he backpedals.

"I'm what's always been, and what will be. The ascension. Master of this dominion. And they'll all get repayment in full." Wadlow unleashes a maniacal grin as he rises taller, straightening the aged bend in his posture with ease.

Detective Holt snatches his weapon from his holster. "Lay on the ground! Face down! And put your hands over your head!" Adrenaline courses through his body.

Wadlow begins to crouch in compliance with the instruction given before exploding into a backward jump. Holt wheels back with surprise. A nimble Wadlow lands on the top of the cinder block half wall with the precision of a grasshopper and pauses there for a moment in a crouched position. He delivers a teeth-gnashing grin as his face begins to undulate and morph. A flash of blue swirls through his eyes, before he springboards into the cover of darkness in the crawlspace.

Holt's tightening chest heaves out of control as the color retreats from his face. A spell of dizziness deluges his head. He's stricken with a crippling concoction of anxiety and bafflement that's pumping doses of paralysis into his heavy legs. Unadulterated fear, like he hasn't felt since childhood nightmares sent him running from the boogeyman in a night terror, clutches onto him. Troubling flashes of Kirsten invade his thoughts. Troubling, because this is what you see before you die, the past, the present, the future, the ones you love, and the things left undone. Funny how you'd trade years for five minutes at a given moment.

Attacking his fear, Holt corrals his breathing and fends off the unfamiliar beginnings of an ensuing panic attack. With some semblance of his faculties restored, and against all of his instincts making a desperate tug on him in the opposite direction, he forces himself to inch forward. Gun readied and raised in his trembling hand and his cell phone light wobbling at an equal clip in the other, Holt prepares himself for what portends his end.

Without warning, a grayish-white blur rockets at him from the darkness. Two blips of orange muzzle flair flash in the darkness as he hurtles his body sideways. His shoulder careens into the base of a wall. Professor Wadlow's cat, Watson, bounds the basement staircase. As Watson disappears Holt's head hits the concrete floor, and a huge exhale presses out from his lungs. A quick inventory of his body reveals he's unscathed other than his tender shoulder. Fortunate his heart still beats in his chest; it's not shy about reminding him of its pounding presence.

CHAPTER 49
Lineage

We all congregate at the top of the steps outside of the library doors, tugging at the hot, stagnant air to catch our breath. Our faces glisten in the summer sun, cheeks ripe as harvest-time strawberries. *My parents. I wish I could tell them. Warn them about what's coming. What's lurking. But what would I say? How can I explain this? I can barely comprehend it myself. They'd surely think me crazy.* The other boys stand there with vacant eyes, their grim expressions hinting at similar disheartening journeys deep into their subconscious.

Devin finally breaches the pregnant silence. "How did we beat them here?"

Robby pauses his pacing outside the Harper Pass Library and shakes his head at Devin. "I don't know. Let's just go inside."

Tee shoves Robby on the shoulder. "We're not leaving Angela!" Robby recoils, and his face shrivels like a dried fig.

"Dude, they left us! *Remember*?"

"Yeah, they're probably just freaked out man. I mean, they had a car. They should be fine, right?" Devin reasons.

Tee rubs the nape of his neck, his head set to a slight rock and his wide eyes roaming.

Robby takes a step forward and softens his voice. "Angela's like family to me too. They'll be fine. You saw them. They passed us on High Street. So, if that thing couldn't catch up to us, it's certainly not going to catch up to her."

"But I don't like it. She's *with* Brady."

"Tee, he *is* the one who saved us in Shiners' Gorge. I know they got their history, but maybe that's the best person she could be with right now. Bet they'll be here any minute. Why don't we just go get a head start on this? Get this thing figured out." Robby motions to the library door.

Tee's resistance crumbles, and he musters a frowning nod. Robby springs into action. Within a second, we're all filing into the Harper Pass Library. The sneaker squeaks of four young boys moving into the library draws the librarian's eyes from the book she's reading. She scowls at us before returning her eyes to her book.

We move a few paces deeper into the library and huddle together. I scan my unfamiliar surroundings, this just my second time ever setting foot in the Harper Pass Library. And the bewilderment on the other boys' faces indicates they share my confusion on the logic behind the organization of this place.

Robby turns to address the group. "We need to look up the history on Shiners' Gorge, the old quarry, and Grief Hollow. Find out everything we can."

"Dude, I've never even been in this library. Where do we even start?" Tee trumpets.

The librarian lifts her eyes from her book and delivers a stern *shhh* in our direction. As the sole person in the library except for us, it's clearly for her own benefit. And her agitated glare denotes deviations from the library's normal decorum won't be tolerated.

Devin keeps a sideways eye on the librarian and whispers. "Let's just look and see what we can find. Should be organized by section."

We fan out inside the library, set to aimless wandering in the rows. Robby roams an aisle of books. He pauses, pulls out a book from one of the middle shelves, and inspects the cover to approximate his bearings. *Good idea.* I replicate the strategy in my own aisle. The book I pull features a shirtless man on the cover, striking a triumphant pose atop a shiny white horse. The man's long mane of silky hair cascades his broad shoulders and falls onto his muscled chest. Tee moves in behind me and snickers.

"So that's the kinda dudes you like, huh?"

"NO!"

A rush of heat pours into my face. Tee's face ignites into a joyous grin. I give Tee a nudge.

"Screw off, man."

"We're not going to find what we're looking for with ole Fabio here. I mean, maybe you will." Tee smirks through a chuckle.

"Ha, ha. Laugh it up. Did you find anything in your area?"

"Nope. Just a bunch of little kid's books. Dr. Seuss, stuff like that."

"Oh, so *your* reading level then?"

"*Brooks Raker.* Hot Damn, I'm proud of you!" Tee celebrates my barb like a professor whose prized student and protégé goes on to win the Nobel Prize.

After a few moments, I cast eyes in the direction of the librarian. "I think we should ask."

"For real? I like you, man, but you're crazy."

"Seriously. We're wasting time."

"All right, big man. Go get it done." Tee fans his hands forward at his wrists.

Tee falls in behind my timid approach to the desk. The librarian detects my presence and lifts her eyes, peering at me with disdain through her bifocals.

"May I help you?" The haughty words roll off her tongue and ring disingenuous.

"Me and my friends..." I clear my throat. "*My friends and I* are looking for stuff on the history of the town. You know, for a school report we're doing." The words fumble from my mouth.

"*It's summer.*" She funnels her narrowed eyes through her glasses at me. I freeze in her icy glare. Tee responds without hesitation.

"Oh, yes ma'am. It's a summer project."

"Very well." She lets out a deep sigh, no attempt to hide her annoyance. She lays her book on the desk. "Follow me," she mumbles as she waddles out from behind the counter.

"We pretty much looked in all the rows." I offer a small smile with my attempt to tamp down hostility.

"Well, it ain't in the rows. It's on microfiche. In the basement. Some books. Mostly microfiche," the librarian responds robotically, unimpressed by my superficial goodwill gesture.

The librarian leads us to the rear of the library. Robby and Devin join in the parade. We pass through a door and descend a staircase into a musty basement.

"Those cabinets there. That's the microfiche. Microfiche reader is over there. You boys know how to use microfiche?" She peers judgmentally over the rims of her glasses. I nod.

"Oh, yes ma'am."

"Good. Clean up after yourselves. No shenanigans down here. The two microfiche readers on the left don't work. Use the one on the right. *And put the microfiche back where you found them when you're done.* I don't want to have to be cleaning up after you boys. Understood?"

"Yes ma'am," we respond in unison.

With that, the librarian lumbers up the stairs, anxious to rejoin her book and rid herself of us. It takes a good deal of searching, but we find microfiche on Davis Quarry and Grief Hollow. While I prepare the microfiche, Robby skims the limited book titles in the basement. Robby pulls two very old-looking hardcover books from the shelf. He nestles into a dusty cubby while we surround the lone working microfiche reader.

After some focusing on the first slide, I pipe, "Guys, check it out."

Devin raises his brows. "Whoa, dude. That looks old."

"It is. It's from 1932. Says here, in July of 1932, twin girls, Myrtle and Thalma Davis, disappeared in Grief Hollow. They were playing there and never returned home."

"What happened?" Tee's voice crackles.

"I don't know. Just says they couldn't find 'em."

"What's the date on that?" Devin points to the top of the newspaper article on screen. "It's a newspaper, so they probably didn't know a whole bunch when they printed it. We need to find the next article."

"July 9th, 1932. Saturday, looks like."

"Got it! Sunday July 10th, 1932." Tee pulls the slide from the cabinet and hustles to hand it to me. Tee peers over my shoulder as I position the slide.

"What's it say?"

"Hold on, still looking for it. Wait. Got it."

"Read it!"

"Do you wanna do this, Tee?"

I read aloud.

"SEARCH FOR MISSING DAVIS GIRLS TURNS DIRE

"FOLLOWING THE DISAPPEARANCE OF MYRTLE AND THALMA DAVIS, GRANDDAUGHTERS OF THE LAND AND TIMBER BARON, WALTON DAVIS, A LARGE SEARCH PARTY WAS ASSEMBLED AND SENT INTO GRIEF HOLLOW ON SATURDAY, JULY 9TH, 1932. THE SEARCH WAS UNABLE TO LOCATE THE MISSING GIRLS BUT DID UNCOVER SOME FOREBODING SIGNS OF FOUL PLAY. ONE OF THALMA'S SHOES WAS RECOVERED NEAR COPPERHEAD CREEK. EYEWITNESSES SAID THAT THE SHOE WAS STAINED WITH BLOOD. A TORN AND BLOODIED SCRAP OF MYRTLE'S DRESS WAS ALSO RECOVERED FROM A NEARBY BRANCH ACCORDING TO WITNESSES.

"DURING THE DESPERATE SEARCH, MAYBIN JONES, A NEGRO VAGABOND, WAS FOUND NEAR WHERE THE GIRLS WENT MISSING. ACCORDING TO REPORTS JONES WAS BLACKOUT DRUNK AND UNRESPONSIVE AT THE FOOT OF AN OAK TREE WITH A HALF-DRANK BOTTLE OF RYE AT HIS SIDE. WITH NO MEANS TO SPEAK OF, IT'S BEING PRESUMED THAT THE BOTTLE OF RYE WAS STOLEN. AUTHORITIES HAVE CHARGED MAYBIN JONES WITH PETTY THEFT AND ALSO STRONGLY SUSPECT THAT MAYBIN JONES MAY BE INVOLVED IN THE DISAPPEARANCE OF THE TWIN GIRLS. JONES HAS BEEN BROUGHT IN FOR QUESTIONING IN CONNECTION WITH THE DISAPPEARANCE BUT HAS YET TO PROVIDE ANY MEANINGFUL ASSISTANCE ACCORDING TO AUTHORITIES.

"THE GIRLS' FATHER, ROGER DAVIS, SAID, 'IF THAT NIGGER DONE SOMETHIN' TO MY GIRLS, HE NEEDS TO HANG. IF HE AIN'T GOT NO ANSWERS, HE NEEDS TO HANG.' ROGER'S WIFE, GERTRUDE

DAVIS, WAS OVERHEARD SAYING TO THE AUTHORITIES, 'IT
AIN'T THE NEGRO. IT'S THE DAVIS CURSE. IT'S HER!'

"MRS. DAVIS IS UNDERSTANDABLY DISTRAUGHT AT THE
DISAPPEARANCE OF HER DAUGHTERS AND IS NOW BEING
CARED FOR CLOSELY BY THEIR FAMILY DOCTOR.

"That's the end guys."

Tee shakes his head and frowns. "Damn. They gonna pin it
on that dude. Them's some racist assholes!"

Devin nods. "You got that right."

After a contemplative pause, Tee asks, "What's a baron?"

"I think it's like someone who's real big in business or something.
Like Rockefeller," Robby pipes from his chair while still
engrossed in his book.

"His name's Jay-Z. Roc-A-Fella's his label, dude." Devin and
I start giggling at Tee. "*What*?"

"Sleep in history class much?" There's laughter in Robby's
voice. "Not Roc-A-Fella. Rockefeller. Rockefeller was a
super-rich big oil guy or something like that."

"So, who's this Walton Davis guy?"

Robby hops up from his cubby at Devin's question and
brings a book, *The Local Heritage of Harper Pass*. He turns it
back several pages to an image.

"Here." Robby points to a black and white picture of a stoic
man clad in an old-fashioned suit. He adorns a long, mani-
cured mustache juxtaposed against his cold, hard face. "He
was the richest, most powerful man in Harper Pass. You
know where Davis Quarry is?"

We nod except for Devin, and Robby continues. "That whole
area used to be a timber farm. *His* timber farm. And later, his

family's quarry. The Davis family owned all of Harper Pass and more."

Robby turns a few more pages in the book to a two-page spread with a family tree. He points to the elaborate family tree there titled, *The Davis Lineage*. "Look. This is where it gets really interesting. You see Maxwell Davis at the top there? Looks like he died in 1843. He was Walton Davis' grandfather."

Robby traces a line from the head patriarch, Maxwell Davis, and his finger follows a twisting path of descending branches until he stops on a name.

"That's my great grandfather, on my mom's side, Vernon Davis. I'm related to this guy." Robby gives a wide-eyed shake of his head.

"Let me see that." Tee snatches the book away.

Tee scans the multitude of names. His finger stops on a name, and his eyes grow wide. "I ain't believin' it, man. But that's my great-great-nanny."

My eyes click wide. "Wait. Are you sure?"

"I know it, man. Ida Karless. Me and Angela used to joke about her name. My mom caught me sayin' '*Ida Care-less* to be given that name.' She 'bout ripped my head off. It was her favorite grandma. Me and Angela never met her though."

Energy beams from Robby's face like a supernova. "You know what this means, right?"

"Yeah, I'm related to this baron dude's piece of shit family." Tee grumbles the words as he hands the book to me.

"No, dude! It means you and I are actually related!" Robby's eyes gleam as he gives an enthusiastic fist bump to Tee.

"Brotha from another mutha!" Tee trumpets as the fist-bumping euphoria continues.

I study the family tree for a moment.

"Guys, this list. Look at the names. It's almost all the most common last names in our town. Here's my great grandfather, Michael Raker. And here's Brady's last name and Alyssa's last name. Further down, Margo's last name, Sammy's last name, and Myron's last name. Seth and Shane. Cam. They're all here! It's like half of the town's somehow related to Maxwell Davis."

"Too bad his sorry ass didn't leave me nothin' in his will." Tee's punchline falls flat.

Robby's eyes meet mine. "In the article. What did the mom say? They're cursed, right? They thought she was crazy, but what if she wasn't?"

"Yeah. What if it's all connected?" A shiver passes through me as I consider the implication of my supposition.

"Only one way to find out. Look at more of those slides. And older too."

Tee tilts his head at Devin.

"Why older, Dev?"

"So we can compare the names against that list right there."

Robby's eyes brighten. "*Damn, man. That's smart.*"

I nod in agreement.

"What you got up next for us, N.C.B.?" Tee asks.

I pull another slide and place it in the microfiche reader. As I scan through the newspaper print, I find what I'm looking for, an article entitled, *Tragedy Strikes During Davis Timber Harvest: Six in Logging Crew Dead, Another Three Missing.* I examine the article with the other boys hovering.

"Guys, this is from 1894. It says, during a timber harvest, six workers were found brutally mutilated, and another three, they couldn't find. Looks like they thought the three missing men might have orchestrated the massacre because they determined the injuries didn't come from a logging accident. They didn't think it was an animal attack either."

Robby lifts his brows. "Sounds like what we're looking for. What are the names?"

"They were led by Dalton Davis."

"Got him right here!" Devin points to a name in the book. "He was one of Walton Davis' sons. Who else?"

I list off the names of the men they found dead that day in 1894, and Devin checks them one by one. Name by name, we find that each one appears somewhere in the Davis family tree. Even two of the three names of the missing men from that day appear on the family tree, pushing us all to the point of believing the unbelievable. *This isn't a new phenomenon. It's been happening for years. Can't be Sammy. Margo, either. The skin-walker is old.*

My tummy gurgles, nervous energy bubbling inside me. The realization that bad things far too aligned with our experiences to be cast off as coincidence date back more than a century sours the contents of my stomach. The toxic brew simmers inside me like a ticking belly bomb. And from that apprehension, I let out a long, groaning fart. The pants-rippling type that reverberates in my wooden chair like a drum.

"Oh! Damn, man." Devin recoils, taking a step away from the blast radius.

"Better check your pants." Robby grins from ear to ear.

"Guys. My stomach just gets uneasy sometimes. You know, stress and stuff?" My cheeks streak red.

"Yeah, man. Best we back up. Don't want to get sprayed by any farticles!"

Devin cocks his head at Tee. "Farticles? What the hell's a farticle, Tee?"

"Shit particles carried in the air by a fart, man. You don't want to breathe that stuff in, man. It'll mess you all up." Tee preaches his words with grinning confidence, excavating a laugh from all of us. Robby grins at him.

"You're a moron, Tee."

"What? Don't complain to me when you're all laid up in the hospital with a bad case of shitty lung."

"Yeah, yeah, Tee. But in all seriousness, we need a plan." Robby surveys the group, but no one offers anything.

"We're taking this book. It could hold more clues." Devin clutches *The Local Heritage of Harper Pass* under his arm.

"And this one too." Robby holds up the *History and Legends of Harper Pass*.

I shake my head. "We still don't know who this thing is. But it's got to be related to the Davis family. Too much coincidence for it not to be."

"But we know what hurts it. What can kill it." Robby's eyes blaze with intensity. "It was stupid to go out today without our paintball guns."

"But you saw it today. That's all we got left. Wadlow's lab is trashed."

"Good point, Tee. And besides, if we did have 'em, how many shots would we have wasted in that dark basement today?"

Robby nods.

"Dev's right. We can't fight this thing in a closed-up space. We need to draw this thing out. Get it out in the open. Then, we make the most of what we got."

"We should go to the quarry!" Tee pauses for a moment and takes a deep breath before continuing. "We know it's been there. And it's wide open there once you get past the pine forest. It'll have nowhere to hide."

I draw in my lips and nod at Tee. "In too deep to turn back now. If we don't find it, it'll be coming for us, anyway. And pick us off one by one. Better to be ready. On our terms, not its."

"So, it's settled then. Tomorrow. Dawn. We meet and head to the quarry." Robby's jawline tenses after he delivers the decree.

"And we need to get Brady and Angela on board with the plan too," Devin remarks.

"Ah, come on. Does *he* really have to go?"

Robby locks eyes with Tee. "Being that he saved my ass, yeah. And the more the better to face this thing."

CHAPTER 50
Cracks to the Incredulous Veneer

At around the same time Brooks Raker and his friends settle into the library basement, Detective Holt eases behind Officer Ivansek's patrol car, his hands still trembling from his near-death encounter at Latravious Wadlow's house. He's in uncharted territory having broken every police protocol by leaving a crime scene without securing or reporting it. *What the hell even was that back there? Jesus.* He takes a deep breath and examines himself in the rearview mirror. His face carries a new, unfamiliar pallor, but that physiological manifestation is a faithful rendering of the embroiling turmoil beneath the surface.

Holt's mind slips its moorings, pushing adrift. Every promising island of rational thought he seeks for refuge makes false promise, concealing the lie of the mirage. And once he plants a firm first step of conjecture on it, it crumbles into the churning sea. The changes to his perspective and understanding of the world since the morning border on immeasurable. He struggles to reconcile the impossibility of what he's witnessed. He displayed natural aptitude for his career because of his inherent belief system, an underlying doctrine that wielded his thinking and guided his actions like an invisible hand. He saw the world with clarity, unencumbered by the gray areas of moral ambivalence that hamstrung others. No, he saw the world with an infallible delineation between *right* and *wrong*. What is true and what is not.

But the encounter with Latravious Wadlow and the creature in his basement rails against that doctrine. He accepts that he's no longer dealing with a *who*, but a *what*—an impossibility thirty minutes prior. And this profound epiphany tears at the fabric of his identity. It's a rather odd feeling for a man who's spent a lifetime never putting any stock into the occult, having to accept that his assumptions were flawed all along. What else was he wrong about? A new math begins to supplant the calculus by which he's made a lifetime of decisions. No way to ever look at things as simplistically as before. Moving forward, he'll face an unfathomable amount of possibilities that will work like a slow poison, gradually retarding his judgment and altering his decision making forever.

As Officer Ivansek spots Holt in his rearview and gets out of his car, Detective Holt wrestles all of his internal contortions down and does his best to project a façade of normalcy. He's not ready to reveal what he's witnessed to anyone, much less Ivansek. He's somewhat surprised that Ivansek's followed his order to keep Brady and Angela waiting. And Brady Palmer, the closest living link to Latravious Wadlow, may be Holt's best chance at making some sense of this.

"Holt, you okay man? You look like shit."

"Fine," Holt rattles.

"You don't look fine." A disapproving frown from Holt spurs Ivansek to continue. "I held 'em up like what you said. Morrow's been tryin' to reach you on the radio."

"Radio had a little glitch for a minute. It's working again now, though. Thanks for holding them up. Why don't you go on and get back on patrol? I'll take it from here."

"You sure, Holt? I mean, that Brady kid's got a record and all. Maybe I should stay and back you up."

"Ivansek, just do what I say." Holt's words snap like bones.

"Okay, okay. Just didn't want you to go it alone is all," Ivansek mutters as he walks to his patrol car, gets in, and pulls away disgruntled.

Ivansek turns a corner and disappears. Brady and Angela shoot neck-craning glances at him from their car as he approaches on foot. Holt grabs the passenger door and flings it open.

"Brady, step outside."

Brady looks up with big eyes.

"We done something wrong, Detective Holt?"

"Just get out of the car."

Brady complies with the order. Angela unlatches her seatbelt and begins to get out as well.

"You stay there." Holt gestures for Angela to remain in the vehicle. "Follow me." Holt leads Brady a few paces behind the car.

In all of Brady's past interactions with Detective Holt, Brady can't remember a time Holt treated him with such coarse abruptness. *What if Detective Holt's found Wadlow? He'll surely try to pin the murder on me. It'll be hard to explain away all of my connections with Latravious Wadlow. Motive just one speculation away. My fingerprints are all over that house.* Brady Palmer glances at his wounded hand. *Oh shit! My blood, too. I'm screwed.*

"What were you doing at Latravious Wadlow's house?" The certainty of Detective Holt's tone plummets Brady's stomach.

Brady's posture slumps, and Holt's eyes land on a bit of blood on Brady's jeans. *Fuck! I'm had.* Dark memories of Longfellow flood Brady's mind, the terrible shame, the contemplating ending his life every day after a new guard, Officer Robbins, arrived. The one who took an unnatural liking to him. The terrible *things* he made him do. He cringes as the haunting hillbilly voice invades his mind. *'Come on now. That's right. Get that head to bobbin' for ole Uncle Robbins.'* Brady takes a heavy gulp, the phantom odor of Officer Robbins' rank breath filling his nostrils. *Maybe prison will be better than Longfellow Juvenile Detention Center... Bullshit. It'll be worse. Much worse. I'll take the rap. Angela will be okay. Nothing tying her to a crime.* But Brady's not ready to surrender his freedom yet.

"Professor Wadlow?"

"Don't fuck with me, Brady," Holt warns, his stern tone of voice emblematic of his seriousness. "I know that was you and Angela on High Street. Saw you fly past me."

Shit! He knows Angela was there.

"We're friends. Me and Professor Wadlow."

"So why the secrecy? And what did you do to your hand?" Holt inquires as he inspects Brady's bloodied hand.

"I cut myself."

"No shit. Where?"

"I can't remember." Brady rattles off the words.

"You know what I think? I think you cut your hand in Latravious Wadlow's house. I think your blood's in that house. And if it is, you know we're going to figure that out, don't you?" Brady's posture wilts further. "Let me see your shoe."

"*What*?" Brady tilts his head and squints his eyes at Detective Holt.

"Your shoe. Let me see the bottom of your shoe."

With his gut drowning in quicksand, Brady puts all his weight on one leg, bends his other leg at the knee, and lifts his foot into the air, exposing the bottom of his shoe. Detective Holt makes a quick mental match. It's the same zigzag pattern as the bloody shoe prints leading away from the crawlspace in Latravious Wadlow's basement. He's sure of it. And Brady's eyes balloon at the narrowing of Detective Holt's eyes.

"Angela didn't have anything to do with it," Brady blurts out.

"To do with what? What exactly?"

Brady blinks his eyes several times. *Where are the handcuffs? No Miranda rights?*

"Professor Wadlow. He's..." Brady's voice quivers, before he continues. "He's dead."

A tear slides out from the corner of Brady's eye and blazes a trail on his cheek. *I'm going to prison. Repeat offender. It'll be a quick trial. A quick sentence. I'll be behind bars before Christmas.* He looks at Angela, who's all he can ever remember wanting in his entire life, as tears well in his eyes, before he offers his wrists to Detective Holt. But instead of cuffing them, Detective Holt places his hand on Brady's back.

"Put your hands down, son. How long we known each other, Brady? Years, right? I've always been straight with you. And fair, I think." Detective Holt pauses, and Brady gives him a head nod.

"I need you to be honest with me, to level with me. I know you're a good kid in spite of what happened that day in Grief Hollow. Some folks in this town hate ya for it, I know, but I'm not one of them. These are small minded folk in these parts. You got a raw deal, son. Right now, though, I need you to explain to me what the hell's going on. 'Cause I just saw a bunch of shit back there I can't explain. You say Latravious Wadlow's dead. But I just saw him. Spoke to him. Not twenty minutes ago. And if I didn't know any better, I would say it was him. But it wasn't him. It...it was something else."

Brady's eyes swell and cloud with darkness.

"What is it, Brady? Just tell me."

Brady wonders if Holt's plea spearheads some kind of trick. But deep down, there's a level of trust—*forged in fire*—that he's built with Detective Holt through the years. It's enough to override his fears. He takes in a deep breath before he begins.

"I don't even know where to start."

"The beginning. How do you know Latravious Wadlow?"

"I know Professor Wadlow from Longfellow. He came to see me there. I didn't even know why at first, but it was nice to have someone to talk to. I found him both strange and interesting. And as time went on and the visits continued, we became friends. Then, one day, it suddenly occurred to me, and I asked him why. Funny I didn't think of it before, but I was really lonely, and it was nice to have the regular company. So, I asked him, why out of all the people did he decide to start visiting me. He didn't try to hide it. He was honest. Told me that bad things had happened in Grief Hollow over the years like the bad thing that had happened to me and Misty Owens. That bad things had been happening all over this town for some time, that he was tracking them."

"What do you mean by 'tracking them?'"

"This is going to sound crazy."

"After the week I've had, nothing sounds crazy."

"Professor was convinced that what happened to me, the missing girl, John Watson—they're all connected."

Explains why they showed up to Margo's search party.

Brady studies Detective Holt for signs of dismissing his words. He can find none. Holt's earnest eyes make invitation for him to continue.

"How are they connected, Brady?"

"I don't know. That's what we were trying to figure out before..." Brady pauses, before choking out the rest of the sentence. "Before it got to Professor Wadlow, too."

"*It?* You mean the leopard thing?"

"Yes, but it can be what it wants to be. It changes forms. Professor called it a skin-walker. Said it's in the folklore of a bunch of Native American tribes."

"This thing. What else do you know about it?"

"That's just it. Professor didn't think it was a *thing* at all. He was convinced it's a person. One tied to this area because it's only around Harper Pass that these bad things seem to be happening."

"I don't understand. How could that thing be a person?"

"It's hard to explain. But he said it had a different genetic makeup than the rest of us. A special gene. Oh crap, what'd he call it? The Infinity Gene! Yes, that's it! Some kind of weird mutation or something that allows it to change forms at will."

"And did you believe him?"

"No. At least not at first, but then I saw things. Things that can't happen without it being true."

"Like what?"

"Professor was working on a formula. One he developed. One he thought could possibly deactivate the special gene. I used it on this thing in Shiners' Gorge, and it definitely hurt it. Bad."

Detective Holt takes a moment to gather his thoughts. Yesterday, if Brady told him this same story, he would've Baker Acted him on the spot. But everything about Brady's mannerisms and delivery remain consistent with someone telling the truth. And from these non-verbal cues that Holt spent a lifetime studying in interrogation rooms, Holt deduces Brady's telling the truth, or at least believes what he's saying is true.

"I shot that thing at least three times at point blank range. I wounded it, but I didn't kill it. Can this formula really kill it?"

"I don't know, but I think so. It will stop it from being able to change and heal itself. Then it can be killed. In theory, at least. But the professor's lab is trashed and the formula's destroyed."

"You know how to make it?"

"No, only Professor knew the formulation and how to make it."

"Do you have any more of the stuff?"

"Only a little bit. Half a vial at my house. Not sure if it's enough."

"And what about Angela?" Detective Holt motions to the car. "Does she know about this?"

"Yes, she knows. And her brother, Tee, and his friends too. We were all trying to stop this thing."

"*Jesus Christ*. Am I the last person to find out about this?"

Detective Holt's radio crackles from his belt followed by Officer Morrow's voice. Holt motions Brady to hold his position for a minute and lowers the volume on his radio as he takes a few retreating steps for privacy.

"Do me a favor. Turn it to the channel we discussed." Holt flips his radio to a different frequency. "You there, Morrow?"

"Yeah. I'm here, Holt."

"What you got, Morrow?" Holt eyes Brady, who's standing there with his hands buried in the pockets of his jeans.

"I've been trying to reach you for the past hour," Morrow huffs.

"Little radio malfunction is all."

"I called your cell phone, too. Where were you?"

"Jesus, Morrow. What is this, twenty questions? I was looking into some things and forgot my cell phone in the car. There, you satisfied? Now, what did you find out?"

"No offense meant, Holt. Just worried about you is all." Morrow's voice carries a much more subservient undertone.

"Look, none taken. But Christ, you're starting to sound like Ivansek. I got Kirsten worrying about me plenty so don't need you worrying about me, too. And I'm kinda in the middle of something here, so what you got for me?"

"Betsy over in the lab at Elkins Memorial ran that blood for us. She owed me a favor anyway seeing as how I let her father cut a small road through the corner of my property."

"And?"

"And wouldn't you know it? It's your lucky day. It's AB-Negative!"

"Okay. So, I'm guessing it's my lucky day because it matches the Rogers boys' blood type?"

"Well, yeah. It's a match. But it's even better than that. Just so happens that blood type is rare. Just found in one percent of the US population. Very likely that blood is from either Shane Rogers or Seth Rogers. Or both for that matter."

"Good work, Morrow. Send in the blood for a rush DNA test. See if you can get your buddy to pull us another favor and skip the line. Also, I need you to go by the Rogers' house. Gather up the boys' toothbrushes. Make it sound as routine as possible for the sake of Nancy Rogers. We don't know anything for sure yet, and I don't want her to have to swallow a poison pill more than once. Bag 'em up and send those too. After that, get back out on the streets. I'm implementing a curfew at eight o'clock tonight."

"A curfew? You sure that's necessary?"

"Yes. I'll explain later. But I gotta go."

"Okay. I'll get on it, Holt."

Radio silence ensues. Holt looks at Brady, convinced he's telling the truth, as insane as that seems. Earlier in the morning, a serial killer seemed the inevitable culprit, and he would've staked everything on that theory. *That's a walk in the park compared to this shit!* Considering the disturbing details Brady revealed, Holt understands he's dealing with something far more sinister and much more dangerous, but he's unsure of his next move. One thing's for sure. He can't dodge that reporter forever. Kasey Norton expects him to talk. And soon. He's running out of time. If he blows her off, she'll put on a full court press, make his life miserable and his job damn near undoable. *Better think of something juicy to give her. She's expecting a healthy return for sitting on that story. The only thing worse than an ambitious reporter is a competent one. And she's both. Time to get creative.*

CHAPTER 51
Booking

D etective Holt strolls through the doors of the station, Brady Palmer in tow. Brady's donning a pair of police issue handcuffs around his wrists. Marcy lifts her eyes from her computer screen and gasps. Detective Holt wears a jubilant smile, a familiar expression around the station when he solves a case.

Brady wears a frown, his eyes grazing the floor. Marcy can tell he's not handling his perp walk well. *And why should he? The boy's fresh out of juvie, and he couldn't even keep his nose clean for a few months. God knows what he's done, but this time he's going to prison. Serves him right.*

"Need to book Brady Palmer. Suspected murder of John Watson," Holt gloats. "Oh, and also Cam Givers."

"Well, well, well. Detective Holt gets his man again." Marcy unfurls a wide smile.

"Well can't say that just yet, Marcy," Holt offers in a gleeful tone as he delivers a wink that says, *Yep, got my man.* "Boy's got a right to a trial and all."

"Sign him in here, Holt." Marcy lays the log on the table.

"I want a lawyer," Brady mutters.

"You'll get your chance, hotshot. Now, let's empty those pockets. Anything sharp in here that's going to cut me?"

Brady shakes his head no before Holt burrows his hands into Brady's pockets. He pulls out a cell phone, a wallet, and some spare change. Marcy opens a manila envelope and Holt stashes Brady's personal items there.

"Do you have any drugs or weapons on you?" Detective Holt asks in an authoritative tone.

Brady shakes his head no.

Holt stares deeply into his eyes, trying to draw out a lie. "You know we'll find them, right? Best to fess up now. Judge might have a little more leniency if I testify that you were cooperative."

"I want a lawyer."

"And I said you'll get your chance," Holt scolds.

Marcy, gripping her pen to write on the manila envelope the entire time, fails to make so much as one pen stroke. A wide-eyed Marcy fixates on the exchange, admiring the power and confidence that Holt exudes. She longs for a shot at detective one day and dreams of leaving the mundane desk work behind, but she'll pay years of dues before that happens.

"Let's get these prints and mugshots."

Marcy nods. She leads Brady to a desk and prints him. A minute later, she positions him against a photo backdrop with multiple height markings. After capturing his front facing photo and profile pictures, she leads him to Holt.

"Interrogation room open, Marcy?"

"You bet, Holt. It's all yours. But before you go, Clancy was just here twenty minutes ago getting his gun and badge. He was looking for you. Said he tried calling."

"Great. Tell Lance to get out on patrol. Tell him to find Myron Thompson. Turns out Officer Ivansek was right for once. He may've lost a lot of blood, but he's alive. Advise everyone that I suspect him to be armed and dangerous and that he's also wanted in connection with the murders of John Watson and Cam Givers."

"Right away. You got it. I'll let 'em know."

"Oh, and Marcy," Holt says as he begins to lead Brady away. "Call in the public defender for this puke."

CHAPTER 52
Extended Reading

Gathered in the basement of my house, we spent the balance of the last couple of hours decompressing from the events of the day and trading some light jokes to release tension. We managed to scarf down three frozen pizzas, which my mom served with a smile. She's beaming about my newfound fortune of friends.

"We need to call Angela, Tee." Robby tries to lock eyes with Tee, but Tee's jumpy eyes prevent it.

Devin nods agreement with Robby. "Yeah, dude. Let's catch 'em up on the plan."

"You gotta phone down here, Brooks?" The immediacy of Tee's question surprises me. Whatever resistance he harbored to Brady's presence seems to fizzle.

Robby flashes an exuberant smile. "What, Tee? No bitching and moaning?"

"Shut up, Robby!"

"Around the corner over there, Tee. On the wall by the bar." I glance up for a moment from the book I'm reading, *History and Legends of Harper Pass,* as Tee hustles to the phone. I turn the page to a grainy rendering of a woman with long black stringy hair.

Robby's eyes bounce wide at the two-page spread. His jovial demeanor recedes like an ebbing tide, and all the blood in his face retreats from the capillaries closest to the skin. For a moment, words evade him, and his lower jaw lunges.

"*Where did you get that*?" Robby finally manages to crackle out.

"It's one of the books from the library. Why? What's wrong?"

"I've seen her. The nightmare I had last night. *Oh God*. How the hell's this possible?"

Devin's eyes widen, and he scooches in closer. "Are you sure?"

"It's her, Dev. I know it. I can't forget that face."

"Who is she, Brooks?"

"Says here, Samantha Mellinger. Says her fiancé, Lawrence Davis, died in the Civil War. Ooh, this is interesting. She was a coal miner's daughter. Says his family didn't approve of their son's match with her. He was supposed to marry her when he got back. But he never did. He died in the Battle of Gettysburg. When she got the news, she was so heartbroken that she wailed tears of grief every day. Let's see..." I thumb farther down the page. "Holy crap, you guys! Grief Hollow. That's where she lived. That's how it got its name. The locals started calling it that because of her!"

"*Whoa*." Devin pushes the word on a puff of air through his lips.

"But Robby, why do you think she was in your dream?"

"How should I know, Brooks!"

"Did she say anything?"

"No. She didn't. But Margo did."

"*Margo*. Oh shit." My eyes swell. "What did she say?"

"She said that I should've gone with my dad. To Grief Hollow. She said that was where I belonged. And since I hadn't, it was going to be really painful now. It seemed so real. It scared the shit out of me, guys."

"Wow." Devin shakes his head slowly as he exhales a deep breath through his mouth. "That's some crazy shit, dude."

"And she said something else too. Something really weird. It didn't make any sense, but the way she said it was super creepy. She said all of their fruit will wither on the vine."

I tilt my head at Robby. "Wonder what it means?"

"It means we're fucked." Robby's flat words linger in the air.

"Not necessarily." Devin points to the open spread of the book. "This is what we've been looking for guys. What if Samantha Mellinger is this thing? Has been all along. This might be the clue we needed."

"Still doesn't explain what she wants." I shake my head as I consider it, but I only arrive at more questions. "Why would she do this?"

"I don't know. But did you catch her fiancés' last name? *Davis*. Another Davis." Devin taps his finger on the name. "Wonder if it's all connected to the Davis curse."

"Even if this book is true, and the Davis family didn't like her, didn't want her to marry their son, it's not like they caused their own son's death. He was killed in the war."

Tee comes around the corner, his posture wilted and his body trembling.

"Brady's been arrested!"

Robby throws his hands up. "*What*?"

I lock eyes with Tee. "Angela too?"

"No. She's fine. Really upset, but fine. Detective Holt sent her away. She's at home."

I shake my head.

"*Why*?"

"Murder. That's all Angela knew. But she thinks Wadlow because she overheard Detective Holt asking Brady about being at his house."

"That's bullshit!" Robby roars. "You know that's bullshit."

"*Dammit*." Devin jerks his head forward with his blurted curse. "Just when we were getting somewhere."

A deep frown overtakes my face.

"What are we going to do now?"

CHAPTER 53
The Cracked Egg

Detective Holt gets out of his vehicle at The Cracked Egg. He's ten minutes late, not a common occurrence for a man who manages his time with diligence. Kasey Norton's already spotted him. She makes a brisk march across the parking lot, sporting a sly smirk. She's waited for this moment for a lifetime, an opportunity to realize what seemed like lofty, unattainable fantasies. On the cusp of realizing her dream, she can barely contain the smile budding below the surface. Against the conscious instruction from her brain, a virtual tug-of-war ensues, pulling the tiny levers of her facial muscles in opposite directions to a stalemate, resulting in a contorted grin, goofy and malformed.

"You're late, Detective."

"Yep."

"*Yep*? That's it? Was starting to wonder if you were going to show at all. Had a rather salacious backup piece to run about the department if you didn't." Kasey narrows her eyes on Detective Holt, her harsh tone intimating whatever he plans to share with her today better be good.

"Well, Kasey, I'm a man of my word. I told you you'd be the one to break the story, and here I am as promised. Albeit a little late. But for good reason. You won't be disappointed." A faint smile tugs on the corner of Holt's lips.

"*Good*. And don't be pullin' any of that crap you pulled the other night. I want a great interview. Got it?"

"Got it." Detective Holt swallows his pride and suppresses the temptation to squash some of this young reporter's over-inflated sense of self-importance. A less satisfying consolation, but he can use her zeal to his advantage.

"And I mean seriously, *The Cracked Egg*? Not the greatest of backdrops." Kasey scowls as she surveys the dilapidated strip-mall parking lot. Holt gives no reply.

Kasey huffs and pivots on the stem of her high heel in the direction of the news van. Norman finishes unloading his gear and takes a clumsy stumble away from the news van. After a quick trot, he files behind Kasey, camera ready.

"Okay. So, we open with this shot here," Kasey instructs as she frames the strip-mall with her hands.

"No problem, Kase." Norman backs up a few steps, his shifty eyes inventorying Holt's demeanor. Finding the air less contentious than the last meeting, he gets to work adjusting the focus of the camera lens on Kasey.

"And Detective Holt, if you can stand right over here." She ushers Holt a few steps to his left.

"Perfect," she enthusiastically chimes as Holt moves into place. "Ready?" A quick thumbs up from Norman and she's moving into place herself, everything framed in the camera shot to her meticulous specifications.

Kasey brushes her blonde locks away from her face and does a quick once-over in her compact mirror. *Cincinnati. Here I come.* She turns to Norman and says, "Roll it."

A quick finger countdown from Norman and she's off.

"Kasey Norton here, Channel 4 News, coming to you with a follow-up exclusive interview with Harper Pass's very own Detective Holt. Folks, again, this is a Channel 4 exclusive.

You're not going to see this anywhere else. Thanks for joining us today, Detective Holt."

"Happy to do it. Thanks for having me on."

Kasey leans in with the microphone and begins. "Detective Holt, the last time we spoke we discussed the investigation into the missing child, Margo Combs, and you revealed to our broadcast audience in a Channel 4 exclusive that the Harper Pass Police Office had determined John Watson's death was a homicide, not the result of an animal attack as was initially reported. Can you give us an update on these two investigations? And also, *is there anything else* you'd like to share with our viewers today?"

"Let me start with your second question first. I do have some additional information I'd like to share with your viewers. At approximately 12:45 this afternoon, Brady Palmer was apprehended in connection with the murder of John Watson. He's being held without bail at the Harper Pass Police Office."

HOLY CRAP! Did he just say that? Yes! She manages to collect herself for a follow-up question.

"The same Brady Palmer that killed Misty Owens?"

"That was a different circumstance, I think. But yes, the same one. Next of kin notifications have already been made, so I think I can also share with your viewers that Brady Palmer's also being held in connection with another suspected homicide. Regrettably, that of a young boy, Cam Givers."

"Oh, that's terrible," Kasey feigns concern, before asking, "And how was the boy killed?"

"Out of respect for the family, and this still being an active investigation, I don't think it's appropriate to reveal that at this time."

"No problem, Detective. Do you have a motive in these murders?"

"We do, but because this is an active criminal investigation, I'm not at liberty to share what those are."

"Let me circle back if I may, Detective, to my first question. Do you have any updates on the Margo Combs missing persons investigation?"

"At this time, we still haven't been able to locate Margo Combs. However, Brady Palmer will also be questioned about her disappearance. As well as the recent disappearances of both Seth Rogers and Shane Rogers."

"Are you saying there's two more missing kids, Detective?" *I can't believe this. He's opening up like a book. Surely the network will recognize my talent. Drawing out these details he's working so hard to keep close to the vest.* She gives herself a mental pat on the back and an encouraging voice calls out from deep within her—*Keep it up, Kasey!*

"That's exactly what I'm saying. So please, if you're watching this right now and you've seen Seth or Shane Rogers, give us a call at the Harper Pass Police Office immediately. My men and I are working diligently to find them, but we could also use your help."

Just stunning. A smile climbs Kasey's lips before she re-centers her focus. "Detective Holt, do you think these new disappearances could be related to the Margo Combs disappearance or even to the murders?" *Shit. Speculative question. No way he answers. Nothing candid anyway.*

"Actually, we do have concerns that they might be related. Which brings up another good point. We're searching for an accomplice suspect in the murders of John Watson and Cam Givers, Myron Thompson. If you see this suspect, please do not approach him, as we believe he's likely armed and dangerous. Please call the Harper Pass Police Office."

Kasey takes a moment and breaks character. "Detective Holt, this is being prerecorded for the six o'clock news. We'll cut it to add pictures of the missing boys and Myron Thompson for our viewers. Really put our audience to work for you." Her eyes gleam like a used car salesperson. "You're doing great. But let's get back to it."

"Detective Holt, aren't you concerned that there's a suspected killer on the loose? What can you tell us to reassure the community that they're safe tonight?"

Detective Holt leans into the microphone to deliver a strong message.

"To Myron Thompson, if you're watching this right now, turn yourself in. We know who you are, and we're going to find you. If you turn yourself in, I personally guarantee you will be unharmed, given a chance to answer the allegations and a fair trial. Should it come to it, we will use all force necessary to protect our community."

"Detective Holt, until Myron Thompson turns himself in, as you suggest, or is captured, what are your plans to protect our community?"

"Starting tonight, 8 p.m., I'm implementing a curfew which will remain in effect until 6 a.m. tomorrow. This is to ensure the safety of the public, so please comply with this temporary inconvenience. Tomorrow, we will reevaluate the curfew and make a determination moving forward."

"You heard it here first, folks. Please obey the curfew order that begins at eight o'clock this evening. Detective Holt, I want to thank you for giving this interview and being so candid with our audience. You are truly a fine example of a public servant, and everyone in Harper Pass should be proud to have you protecting us." Kasey bastes on the praise thick as viscous paint, an outward projection of the professional glee simmering inside her.

"Thank you, Kasey, for allowing me to speak to your viewers. And I want them to know that the Harper Pass Police Office will not rest until all suspects have been apprehended and brought to justice."

"Thank you, Detective Holt. And thank you, folks, for tuning in. We'll keep you posted on this story as it develops. This is Kasey Norton, and this has been a Channel Four exclusive," Kasey concludes, even though the words *this is the best moment of my life* scream for release. She motions for Norman to cut the tape.

Detective Holt lifts a brow at her. "So that's it then?"

"I gotta say, Detective Holt, I had some serious reservations about sitting on that story. But you really are a man of your word."

"So you'll call off the tail, then?"

A flood of color rushes into Kasey's cheeks. She collects herself before speaking. "How did you know?"

"It's my job to notice things. And I've seen that beige sedan one too many times."

Her eyes drift to the pavement. "Needed an insurance policy. Sorry."

A subtle smirk gathers on the corners of Holt's lips. *Yeah, right. You hired him before we even made our deal.* "No offense taken, but you'll call him off, then?"

"Yes. I'll call off the P.I." Detective Holt nods, flashes a pleasant smile and turns to walk away. Kasey's words catch him after a few steps. "And Detective Holt." He stops and turns. "Thank you for the interview. And thank you for being so candid."

"Hard work should be rewarded. It was your story. You earned the right to break it," Detective Holt lauds.

A big smile tugs on the corners of her lips, her pride too effervescent to suppress. Detective Holt walks away, confident his appearance of candor will work to suppress Kasey's natural urge to go behind him and start digging. And no way she doesn't call off that tail. He served her everything she wanted and more on a silver platter. She'll come back to eat for sure but on his terms and not hers. With the Pavlovian seeds planted, she'll fight her own journalistic instinct for another small taste of what he's just delivered. *Why hunt when you can be fed? The conditioning is complete.*

CHAPTER 54
Harbinger

After a long, traumatic day, Robby curls into the cushy comfort of his bed. Thoughts like bullets whiz through his mind, most traveling at indecipherable speeds. They're fragmented pieces to the same puzzle, firing in opposite directions. But occasionally two pieces collide to form a coherent thought—one in particular burrows into his cortex and takes root. And from that tiniest of seedlings emerges, *can we really beat this thing?*

As he ruminates on the scenarios, he realizes the probability of failure far exceeds their chance of success. Visions of tragic endings assail his mind. He shivers off a tremor, tries to quarantine his fear, and attempts to redirect his thoughts to anything else. But the stubborn question persists. Trying to beat this thing without Brady's help diminishes their odds, but the six o'clock news confirmed this as reality. Multiple counts of murder and no bail. They're on their own.

The plan rehearses itself in his head. Despite some minor tweaks, the boys all finished in agreement. Meet at dawn. Bring the paintball guns with the ad hoc ammunition injected full of Professor Wadlow's mysterious formula. Take a huge leap of faith on that working. Make the trip to Davis Quarry and draw this thing out. Beyond that, the planning borders on speculation—more of a hope than a plan—and with each hope its corresponding fear. Hope that drawing this thing out proves to make them more powerful against it and not easier targets. Hope to get a bunch of clean shots off at this thing whilst not wasting their precious ammo. And hope that shooting this thing allows them to kill it and not enrage it. *That's a lot of hoping.*

Robby pulls the covers over himself, determined to drown his troubling thoughts in the sleepy deep. He tosses and turns in his bed, his tethered sheets trailing his movements, wrapping around him, snugging him tighter with each reposition. His eyes grow heavy, eyelids shutting tight as a coffin lid. A light, hovering sensation settles into his body, and he begins to drift. The clamoring voices inside his own head grow more distant—muted. And a moment later he slips into nothingness.

"Robby." A young girl's voice beckons from the darkness. The word passes into his mind, faintly detectable, as he shuttered most of his synapses for the evening. But from somewhere deep, an initial spark, like the first electrical impulse of a computer reboot, fires. And from that spark—cognition.

Robby's eyes shoot open and the thick, murky blackness washes into them. His fingers sprint for the knob on the bedside lamp. The audible breathing in his room sends his heart into a frantic scamper. He senses something terrible shares the heavy pitch with him. A burst of light reveals a young girl standing at the foot of his bed. Robby gasps and retreats into his headboard, drawing his legs in tight. A mess of dangling hair shrouds her face.

"We must go to her." The familiarity of the voice rattles in his skull. She raises her head as slow as a salvaged ship lifting from the seabed. It's Margo, or at least an empty shell of her, her eyes distant, trance-like. But a moment later, a faint glimmer passes through them and her gaze sharpens. In the millisecond that it takes for Robby to blink and clear his wide eyes, a new consciousness checks into Margo's vacant eyes, one that's much more deliberative, cognizant.

Wake up! Wake up! Robby pinches his forearm, and the skin blanches, before his natural color races in to fill the void. *Shit! It's real. That hurt. Doesn't feel like a dream. I can think. There's pain. But it can't be real.*

Margo steps forward, her motions contrived, robotic. Transfixed, Robby's blood swarms, panic setting in, binding his body tight. Bones cast in concrete, his eyes fasten to Margo's pale face, her eyes sunken and circled with dark rings. Her fierce, unwavering gaze cuts through him as if she's searching inside Robby's head for something, checking each little dark compartment—trying to unearth the secrets he's hidden inside.

"Tell me, Robby, why have you not gone to her?" An uncharacteristic smile slides into place on her lips, one that drips of malicious intent.

"This is a dream. It's a dream," Robby mutters.

As Margo approaches, Robby delivers a brisk slap to his cheek. The resulting sharp and sudden pain startles him. *Oh shit! It's real! It's really real! Oh my God!* Robby locks his arms around his knees, interlocked fingers turning white from the immense pressure in a futile attempt to minimize his exposure.

His rapid breathing becomes frenzied and unmeasured. Margo's smile widens.

"What do you want from me?"

"What I've always wanted. What is due." The underlying satisfaction in her voice tugs at the corners of her mouth, and her smile deepens.

"Leave me alone!" Robby screams, but Margo glides forward, undeterred.

Robby hopes his mother heard his scream, but all the times he snuck out undetected pokes holes in that ballooning hope. *She's not going to wake up. No way she wakes up. Probably thinks it's the TV show she fell asleep to. If she heard it at all. Scream again. SCREAM AGAIN!*

Despite his best efforts, he can't muster another. Hot tears glaze his flush cheeks with moisture, and his body trembles. Margo cocks her head, attentive to the sight of his tears. Her skin begins shriveling, moving in on itself, leaving cavernous spaces in her cheeks and pronouncing the curvature of the bones in her fingers. Robby's eyes are shrieking. He presses his weight against the headboard as Margo leans in.

Inches from his face, Margo's mouth opens into an unnatural, yawning gape, and from the dark reaches of her throat, slithers out a forked tongue. Robby clenches his teeth tight and winces as it unwinds. The hot tongue contacts his cheek and traces his damp tear line before a slow reel returns it into its mouth. It smacks its mouth several times, dispersing the tears for closer inspection on its palate. Its eyes pulse a gleam of recognition, and it stares at Robby with heightened interest, wearing a wicked, gratified smile as it hovers above him.

A putrid-gray hue overtakes what remains of Margo's youthful complexion, a sign of the active transformation occurring. Robby clamps his eyelids shut, unable to watch how he dies. He waits for the inevitable.

"Vernon Davis," the thing whispers into Robby's ear, but his flustered mind doesn't register the words. Instead, he recognizes a change in its voice, a full departure from Margo's. Its hot breath glances against his face. It can take his life from him at any moment. *What's it waiting for?* Robby forces his eyes open, a small sliver at first. The thing no longer resembles Margo at all. Though still changing, Robby can already detect the underpinnings of Samantha Mellinger's facial features rounding into form.

"Vernon... *Davis*," it repeats, the name registering this time as his great grandfather. Robby begins to rise from the headboard, but its strong, cold hand presses on his chest, pinning him against the hard wood. The sunray pattern carved into the wood pinches into the skin of his back.

"Just do it already!" Robby screams in a fit of agony, ready for the torment to end and to take his place with his father. A swirl of blue flashes through its eyes, and it runs the tip of its bony fingers over Robby's hairline at his temple, delicate as a mother to a newborn. He's panting, chest heaving, near hyperventilation as it rises.

"Bring your friends home, Robby. To Grief Hollow. And be reunited with your kin." It hisses as it backs away.

Robby's face turns to stone—etched horror—as it spider crawls his bedroom wall, exiting through his window and slipping into the night.

CHAPTER 55
Fork in the Road

A jittery energy wafts through the air outside Tee's house as, one by one, we arrive. In a circle of solemn faces, I contemplate my fears, forced to consider the fickle nature of my own mortality. Robby arrives last. Something seems so different about him today. He casts laggard eyes at the ground, paintball rifle draped over his slumped shoulder. Not the ordinary Robby.

"It came to me last night." Robby's voice quavers.

"*Oh shit.*" A quick flinching shiver passes through Tee's shoulders.

"It wants us to come to Grief Hollow. Wants me to bring y'all there."

"*Fuck that.*" Tee shakes his head vehemently. "We ain't doin' shit this thing wants."

"It's Samantha Mellinger. *It's her!*" Robby's eyes get misty. "It changed from Margo to her. And it wants us all. It said my great grandpa's name. *Vernon Davis.* Oh fuck! How does it know? And it crawled up my wall like a goddamn spider."

Devin places a comforting hand on Robby's shoulder. He gazes into Robby's turbulent eyes—his own eyes a steadying hand on the helm of a storm-tossed ship.

"We're going to beat this thing, Robby. It could've gotten you last night. But it didn't. It wants us to go to Grief Hollow. Together. So, we don't. We stick to the plan, try to surprise it in Davis Quarry. *Meet it on our terms.*" Devin cocks his paintball rifle as he cements his jaw.

"What if it's a trick? Knows we won't do what it says?" Tee's eyes dart around the group like a frenzied rabbit as he shuffles his feet. "What if it *really* wants us to go to Davis Quarry?"

"I don't think so, Tee. *Samantha Mellinger... Grief Hollow...* It adds up. And Davis Quarry, *it's our best shot.*" My words even surprise myself. Normally, I'd try to jump on the nearest off-ramp with Tee, but there's a nagging inevitability about this that's pressing me forward. This thing's coming for us as sure as the sun will rise tomorrow. Better to face it together than for it to pick us apart one by one, each torn asunder according to its timing like a roadside vulture deciding which parts of carrion to consume first.

A gleam of surprise passes through Devin's eyes, which in turn elicits a gloomy frown from Tee as he registers what that means. Robby's sullen demeanor diminished by Devin's unwavering confidence. My resolute conviction at a moment when the others expected me to falter. A silent recognition moves through the group like tendrils of invisible smoke from the periphery of a campfire, working its way into everything—hair, skin, every fiber of our being—unseen and all-encompassing.

We are one.

We face this thing together.

We stick to our plans.

CHAPTER 56
Collecting Needles

Robby's compass is spinning. It started spinning when we cleared the pine forest. Our progress slows to a crawl. We all clutch our paintball rifles, eyes darting side-to-side like schooling fish. Devin leads the group, slugging forward on the marble-chip, gravel road. As the trajectory of the road slopes more steeply, we measure each step, legs poised to compensate for shifting ground or the unexpected ambush. Before us, a deep, wide hole cut from the earth comes into view, road spiraling around it like a tower staircase.

We enter it like a car dropping onto a freeway, ground sloping gradually above our heads, cut with dynamite through solid rock, half-moon shaped drill holes still visible in the scarred face. The road narrows as we gradually descend— to our left, a deep, bluish-green tinted collection pond where teenagers occasionally cliff dive in a display of adolescent swagger to impress their girlfriends, their presence marked by the crushed, faded beer cans that litter the road. And to our right, a jagged rock ledge steers us ever down, winding us toward the bottom.

We pass an area where another road cuts in to adjoin ours, this one more gradually sloping away to the top of the hole. Unused by the teenage crowd, the road's overtaken by tall weeds and juvenile pine trees that jut up from the rocks, unnaturally reaching on a sideways slant towards the center of the hole, each jockeying for position, compensating for the less than optimal sunlight they receive.

"Well, well, well. Looky who we got here. If ain't ole Brooks and his band of losers." The voice echoes out from behind the cover of the trees.

As if rehearsed, we circle our perimeter, each strategically facing a possible point of attack, paintball rifles raised as a deterrent. The voice—we recognize—it's Sammy Needles. But it's unclear why he's here. Sammy saunters out from behind the trees and onto the path in front of us. Devin takes a step forward and trains his paintball rifle on Sammy's face.

"*What*? You don't wanna end up like last time, *do ya*?" Devin warns as he taps his paintball gun.

"Got me a plan for that." Bo comes charging from behind and after a brief struggle, locks Devin into a strangling, choke hold. As he coughs for air, his paintball rifle falls away from his hand and clanks to the gravel. Bo gives the paintball gun a swift kick, sending it flying over the ledge, a hushed whisper of wind rushing up against it as it falls. After a few agonizing moments, it hits the water with a tall splash, rippling the surface.

"Let him go!" Robby yells as he trains his paintball rifle on Bo, his neck veins bulging and turning turquoise.

"*Don't!*" I scream at Robby, the desperate inflection in my voice a reminder of the precious ammo he's thinking about discharging.

I take a few steps toward Sammy. *What am I doing?* My feet drag me a few steps more. My heart twitches in my chest. *Ya gotta. Only way to keep the plan intact.* Sammy's grin devolves into tumult, the seething underneath warping his facial expression.

"What do you want, *snitch bitch*? You ain't gettin' out of this, no how," Sammy growls as he leers at me.

"Sammy, you don't understand. It's coming for us. *All of us*. You and Bo, too." I let my paintball rifle slide away from my hands on its strap and take a couple of tentative steps forward with my hands raised. Tee's eyes balloon, but it's the only sensible move.

"No, you don't understand, motherfucker. You ain't gettin' out of this." Sammy pulls a switchblade from his pocket and pops it open, the sharpened steel glinting sunlight.

"Sammy, you don't want to do this." I begin to back away as my heart hammers in my chest.

Sammy swoops in to separate me from the group, knife outstretched, working me to the ledge. I back up, taking tentative steps, eyes trading glances over my shoulder and back to Sammy.

"Yeah, I do. I'm going to give your little bitch face a permanent smile. Carve you up like a pumpkin."

"*Put it down!*" Tee screams as he takes an aggressive step forward with his rifle raised, eyes gleaming like exploding stars.

"You fuckin' shoot me and I'll gut this pig!" Sammy waves the knife.

Sammy lurches forward, meandering back and forth to blunt any of my escape routes. His eyes burn, blood gushing through his engorged cheeks. I inch back toward the ledge, dwindling my comfortable distance with each retreating step. Once backed against the precipice and with no possible escape remaining, Sammy's posture emulates a fencer, knife wielding arm outstretched and strategically waving, looking for the perfect cut as he closes the distance.

"Don't do it, Sammy."

"Shut the fuck up, Bo!" Sammy snaps his head around and delivers an icy glare. "Little shit's gonna get what's comin'."

"You gonna end up at Longfellow." Bo's eyes bloom wide. He begins to loosen his grip on Devin's neck.

"Stop being such a pussy, Bo." This time Sammy never breaks eye contact with me. I raise my hands into the air.

"Sammy, please. You don't want to do—"

"Stop tellin' me what I want to do!" Sammy yells as he lunges at me with the knife outstretched.

"NOOO!" Tee screams.

I sidestep, the blade of the knife tearing through my shirt, slicing into the skin of my belly, loose rocks bounding the edge behind me, skirting the edges of the jagged cliff as they topple to the water. Spots of crimson begin to emerge on my white t-shirt. *HE CUT ME!* I contemplate jumping, but I'm not in the right spot. No way to clear the face of the cliff and the rocks below without momentum. I clasp my stinging belly. It's a flesh wound, not too deep.

"What the fuck are you doing?" Bo releases Devin from his vise grip.

Devin collapses to his knees, holding his throat and tugging hard for air. Robby and Tee slink toward Sammy. He wheels around and brandishes his knife at them, warding off their advance.

"Take another step and I'll kill the fucker."

But Sammy's twisted face divulges his intent, his nostrils flaring to the rhythm of his loud breathing. Hot blood inundates his face, turning it fire-engine red. His lips curl like a venomous snake baring its fangs. *He's going to kill me! The other boys, too.*

Sammy repositions his feet and makes another lunge at me. As I contort my body away from his blade, the gravel gives, and my footing slips. The world transforms into a spinning blur of blue above me. My rib cage smashes into the rocky earth with a thud, feet dangling from the cliff in mid-air, desperate hands clutching at the sliding rocky earth. I'm losing ground, sliding, until my hand locks onto an exposed tree root. Moaning in pain as I dangle, clinging for my life, Sammy looms above me, an intoxicated madness lurking in his eyes. But that's not all I see.

The rock wall behind him begins to fissure, separating in silence, rock moving on rock. Taking on substance as it eases away. At first a large irregular cone-shaped rock peels away from the rest of the steep rock face but doesn't fall. It stays suspended, still connected. The other boys begin backing away. The moment its eyes open, the absoluteness of its camouflage becomes apparent. Uncloaked, the symmetry of the giant head becomes discernable, resembling that of a scaly wood lizard as it takes form.

"*What the fuck*?" Bo stammers, lemur-eyed.

Robby waves his arms frantically. "Sammy, watch out. *Get outta there*!" The creature separates from the wall, revealing the entirety of its body.

My eyes glaze with terror to Sammy's delight. Two parallel lines of short, curved horns peel back from its head, its lizard legs sloughing leathery skin, striated muscles rippling as it finds its equilibrium. It hoists a barbed, plated tail high above its body. Two extra appendages near its front legs unfurl into giant, gleaming obsidian pincher claws.

"Shut up! You *ain't* gonna stop me." Sammy crouches to slice my hand and send me falling to my death.

"Sammy, don't!" I shake my head with harvest-moon eyes as it approaches. "Look behind you. It's coming."

"You're dead bitc—" The creature's tail coils around Sammy's waist like a striking bullwhip and flings him like a rag doll into the same rock face it peeled away from moments before. Sammy hits the wall with a thud before crashing to the base. Before he can even move, the creature scurries upon him.

Robby darts to me, grabs my arms and hoists me onto the road. We race to Tee, Devin, and Bo who stand statuesque, jaws dropped and owl-eyed. The creature closes one of its pincher claws around Sammy's waist and hoists him into the air. For once, no words spew from his mouth, his lips bolted silent. Its barbed tail lifts and shimmies before rocketing forward, slicing through a spot between his shoulder blade and pectoral muscle, spraying a shower of hot crimson onto the rock face.

"*Jesus!*" Bo screams, his body shaking uncontrollably.

Sammy lets out a blood-curdling scream as the barb passes through him, tearing through flesh and bone. Still impaled by the barb, tears pour from his horror-hinged eyes as he screams in agony, casted arm draped on the barb. It cocks its head at a slight angle, and its tongue lolls out from its mouth. The slimy tongue slides up Sammy's face before retreating into its mouth. It smacks its mouth a few times, the slivered pupils in its eyes tightening.

"Help," Sammy whimpers.

"*Shoot it!*" Devin's scream breaks the barren silence.

"I can't get a clean shot." The paintball gun quivers in Tee's hands.

Robby fires off a shot that explodes on the rock ledge a foot to its left. Its head spins backward on its turret-like neck, identifying the threat, before its other clawed appendage clasps around Sammy's neck and clamps shut, making a coarse crackling of bone. Sammy's eyes go blank, and his heaving chest quiets, before his head wobbles and topples off the claw, a fountain of blood gushing from its absence. His head bounces twice on the gravel road and rolls a few feet before plummeting from the ledge. The creature retracts its barb, and Sammy's limp body drops to the earth. Rivers of blood spew into the gravel from his stump neck, the torrent flow piling blood on blood, making it rise with the speed of flash flood waters around the rocks.

As it wheels around to face us, Tee sizzles off a shot that grazes its face. It lets out a deafening roar and hoists its bloody barb into the air. I take aim and shoot, striking near its right eye. It lifts its forearm, rubbing its eye, trying to expel the fluid from the paintball, but it's a clean hit and its body begins quivering, pulsing. It lets out another furious roar, and Tee fires his last shot at its open mouth, but the paintball splatters on the rock ledge behind it. Another miss.

It scurries forward in an instant, moving similar to a crocodile on land, swiveling on its vertebrate—head and barbed tail whipping in opposite directions as its hinged legs propel it forward. It fastens a claw around Devin's waist, snatching him from midstride of his retreat. I fall backward, firing my last shot, striking it in the belly. It changes direction in an instant, peeling to the rock face. It pauses for a split second, glaring at us, lets out an agitated hiss and ascends the steep rock face, carrying a screaming Devin in its claw. By the time Robby can take aim, it's gone. Disappeared over the top of the ledge. Devin's cries echo through the quarry as it speeds away, growing more distant by the millisecond.

"*Dev!*"

But after the reverberation from Robby's scream, the quarry falls silent. Tee's sobbing and I can't stop muttering *no* to myself. Bo's concussed eyes can't seem to focus, set to an aimless drift. Robby collapses to his knees on the gravel road, tears streaming his cheeks.

CHAPTER 57
Never Leave Another Member Behind

A tsunami of darkness washes into Robby's eyes, inundating everything until his face crinkles like cracked porcelain, and all that remains is a froth of rage. He climbs to his feet, breaks into a sprint, and charges Bo. He delivers an adrenaline-charged shove to Bo's chest that nearly topples him. Bo slides on the rocky terrain, his balance thrown off kilter, before regaining his footing.

"*YOU DID THIS!*" Robby screams, hands clenched in fists, ready to dismantle the giant of a boy before him.

"I'm sorry." Bo's eyes glisten, his hobbled words earnest in their delivery. He hangs his head. "I didn't think Sammy would take it this far. I never meant for this to happen. Any of it. I swear."

"What did you think was going to happen? *Huh*?" Robby steps forward, sizing up Bo, stalking him like a lion.

"Let it go." I place a calming hand on Robby's chest. His heart thumps under my fingertips, the veins in his neck pulsating and swelling hot blue.

"You're right, Robby. I'm sorry." Bo strikes a conciliatory tone as his shoulders slump.

"You think *a sorry* is going to cut it? You're just like the rest of your no-good family." Robby's eyes bulge and blooms of deep crimson flower on his cheeks.

His sharp words seem to slice to bone. Bo hangs his head.

"You right, Robby. My kin ain't no good."

"You're damn right they ain't!"

"My daddy, my brother. I seen 'em hurt so many people." Bo's head sinks deeper, and he slowly shakes it. "I ain't wantin' to be like 'em."

"You're turnin' out just like 'em." Robby venom tips his words, his tone caustic. Bo's posture wilts further.

Tee locks eyes with Robby.

"That's enough, Robby."

"He got Dev killed, man!" Robby's roar echoes through the quarry.

"We don't know that. Don't say that." I shake my head at Robby with heavy eyes. "Dev could still be alive. We could still hear him when that thing was taking him away."

"Yeah. You saw what it did to Sammy. Snapped him with that claw like it was nothing, man. It could've done the same to Dev if it wanted. *But it didn't*." Tee's point injects a glimmer of hope in Robby's eyes and leads me to an epiphany. There's a pregnant pause before I break the silence.

"It doesn't want Dev. *It wants us.* Samantha Mellinger *wants us.* It could've taken Dev in Shiners' Gorge but didn't. Dev's not from here, not related to the Davis family. *Like us.* It wants us. And it wants us to come to Grief Hollow like it told Robby. Like Margo said. That's where it's taking Dev."

Tee paces, shaking his head, his turbulent eyes adrift. He kicks up gravel dust with each step before coming to an abrupt stop.

"So, what now? What do we do now? We've got one paintball left. It's not enough, man. Not even close to enough. We got no chance. We could go to the cops, but they'd lock us all up."

"*Never... leave... another... member... behind.*" Robby's eyes gleam wild and daring.

"It's a suicide mission, man!"

"*Markland X Crew protects its own.*"

"Oh shit, Brooks. *You too?* We're gonna get killed, man! *All of us!* There's gotta be another way."

"Ain't no other way, Tee," Robby says. "*He'd do it for you.*"

Tee's lips tuck into a slow frown as he hangs his shaking head.

"I'll help." We turn our heads to Bo in unison, our lower jaws gone lax. "I know I ain't Markland X Crew and all, but I feel bad for what I done. Lemme make amends."

Tee, Robby, and I exchange wary glances, studying each other's body language. We wage silent arguments. Robby delivers a fervent headshake of *no* and clenches his fists. I present two palms, and Tee gives a head shake of *I can't believe we're about to do this*. With a decision reached, Robby slumps in acknowledgement.

"It's a bad idea," Robby mutters to Tee and I before marching to Bo. "You better not screw us over, man."

Bo gives a solemn nod. "I won't." He spits on his palm and extends it for a shake. "*Promise.*"

Robby's face sours with mild revulsion. "Nah, man. I'm good. We'll just keep it at your word."

CHAPTER 58
And Grief Hollow Will Be Its Home

I t's around lunchtime when we reach the end of Parson Street, the mood of the group jittery and foreboding. We lost some time by taking a detour to Bo's house, but we determined it advantageous after he offered. Bo carries a rifle that he filched from his father's gun cabinet under his shirt, barrel protruding several inches past his basketball shorts—making his gait resemble that of a cripple. Tee's pocket bulges with the box of ammo stashed there, and a metallic clanking sounds his steps.

We lost even more time when Robby insisted that we inform Angela of the plan. No misconceptions about asking her to join us, but if we do meet our end, at least someone remains with knowledge of what happened to us. We managed to trek through town undetected, important because we're on borrowed time—or at least we figure Devin's clock nears its final stroke.

Despite our misgivings about the mission we're about to embark on, we enter the woods without delay. *Wonder if I'll ever see mom and dad again. Chances aren't good. What will they say at my funeral? The normal things people say when young people die?*

He was taken far too soon.

Heaven must've needed another angel.

Probably. Things I've heard before. Things that fall flat of resonating with any real meaning. The things that people say to try to explain the unexplainable.

Robby clutches the paintball rifle, clinging to our last hope, a solitary paintball—a perfect shot needed to deliver it. Despite his failed attempt at the quarry, Robby's a decent marksman and without question the best of the bunch. If not selected for his marksmanship, we still surely would've selected him. If for nothing else, for his grit, his gumption, his resolute manner, and his willingness to cast aside insurmountable odds without giving it a second thought.

We make the arduous trudge through the woods. My body still aches from my huge fall at the quarry, tentacles of pain knifing through the length of my rib cage, the sting of the slit on my stomach heating up with each step and corresponding abdominal flex that pulls at the perimeter of my fresh wound. The woods to Grief Hollow pass by in a blur, time hollowed out, the memory of present and past intertwined, a seamless weave—the difference between the two indecipherable. And before any of us realize it, we've come within a couple hundred yards of our destination.

Robby raises a fist gesturing a stop, a subconscious adoption from the Silver Screen—a tactic swiped from every military movie we ever saw. Grief Hollow hides its proximity behind a thick curtain of summer foliage, but the bend in the trenched streambed tells us we're close. The eerie silence of the woods, reminiscent of the day I ventured into Grief Hollow, tugs on my nerve endings. But a cry for help breaks the silence. Devin's cry. Tee's eyes bounce wide.

"Oh shit, that's Dev."

"Tee, give me the bullets." Bo outstretches his palm.

Tee digs in his pocket, pulls out the box of ammo and hands it to Bo. While Bo loads the rifle, Robby checks the paintball gun, ensuring that our last best hope still remains ready to fire.

"Listen, we need to be quiet. Bo, you approach from that way." Robby points off to the woods on the right of Grief Hollow. "The rest of us will come at it straight ahead. Draw its attention. This thing can be anything it wants to be *so be careful*. Once we draw it out. Take the shot. Take as many shots as you can. *But make sure you don't hit Dev.*"

Tee throws up his hands. "Or us!"

"Once you've hit it, I'll take my shot. My shot should stop it from being able to change. Then... *we kill it!*" Robby's plan receives a unanimous head nod.

Bo breaks away from the group and moves on a slant, rifle readied, occasional glances at our position to check his relative proximity. Robby, Tee, and I fan out a few feet from each other and move forward in a line taking precarious steps, scanning the woods for any signs of danger. Sunlight filters through the trees above, muted by swollen summer clouds. Shadows bend through the forest, shifting direction with each subtle change in light, deceiving our shifty eyes with false movement. And after a few more steps, it comes into view. We catch our first glimpse of Grief Hollow through a tangle of twisted trees, the gnarled trunks jutting from the earth like arthritic fingers. We scamper forward, fleet-footed, to a partially fallen, uprooted tree and crouch behind it.

I peer past the log. Tannish water burbles through Copperhead Creek. The fire-scarred oak behind it shrieks for attention, its bony limbs encased in a sticky, glistening mass of white filament that fastens at multiple points to the largest branches of the tree and appears strung from multiple heights. My astonished eyes follow three massive flaps of spider webs, shaped like inverted isosceles triangles, as they stretch tight from the branches and taper to singular spots of attachment on the forest floor. A large ball of the silky web, suspended from the ground ten feet or so, undulates with life. My eyes enlarge as it wriggles.

"What the hell is that?"

"Looks like spider webs," Robby whispers.

"Oh, hell no. I hate fuckin' spiders." An animated shiver passes through Tee's body.

"No, I mean the thing hanging down."

"Help," Devin's muffled voice calls out from the hollow.

I try to ascertain where his voice originated, but the echo effect of the hollow makes it challenging. But as the web sac begins to squirm again, set in motion to a gentle rock, another of Devin's muffled cries rings out. This time I'm certain it came from the suspended web sac. I point to it frantically.

"That's him. That's Dev! He's in that thing."

"How the hell are we going to get him down?"

"We're going to have to worry about that after, Tee. First, we gotta draw this thing out. Then, Bo shoots it. Then, we take it out." Robby delivers the words with the nonchalance of reading off the instructions for assembling a bicycle.

"How do we draw it out?" There's a shiver in Tee's voice.

"We go towards it. You and me, Tee. Make a bit of noise."

Tee whips his head around to me, his eyes growing big and round like a startled doe. "*Wait, what*? Robby's the one with the gun."

"Robby can't be the one to do it. He needs a clean shot. He'll never get it if we don't go out first."

Robby nods in agreement.

"So, we're supposed to go face this thing with nothin', man? Nothing to defend ourselves?"

"Not nothin', Tee. *Bo. Bo*'s going to shoot it," Robby whispers.

"Bo? Bo...*are you serious*? I'm supposed to trust my life with that sack of shit? Who's to say he ain't run away already? Left us for dead."

"That's Dev right there." Robby points to the suspended sac with boiling eyes. "You gonna help our friend or what?"

Tee lets out a huffing sigh and kicks a bit of dirt with his foot.

"Fine, I'll do it."

Tee and I creep forward toward Copperhead Creek, careful to secure our footing on the forest debris as we descend into Grief Hollow. My stomach climbs to my throat, hollow and empty, a heaving churn. As the ground begins to level beneath our feet, I call out. "Dev."

"Brooks!"

"You okay, man?" I shout the words louder than necessary as Tee and I arrive at the opposite bank of the creek, situated less than twenty yards from Devin.

"I'm okay. But it's her! It's her! You were right. I saw her. Samantha Mellinger! It's her." The sac starts swinging more frantically.

"Where is she, Dev?"

"I don't know. I can't see. Get me out of here, Brooks."

"We're gonna get you... Oh shit!" Tee screams, as a giant spider-like creature bursts from underneath the sand on the other side of the creek. Heaps of sand slide from its grotesque body, its fangs raised like onyx daggers. Tee staggers backward, tripping on an exposed tree root and plummeting to the forest floor. I hold my ground, terror just another passenger on the adrenaline train speeding through my body, as the spider rises on its legs high in the air. It spins around on nimble, wiry-haired legs to face us. Tee backpedals from his butt, all four desperate limbs working in unison to power his retreat.

"NOW!" I scream.

A high-powered gunshot rings out and an explosion of goop from the spider's waxy abdomen crests high into the air. The spider swivels on churning legs as another gunshot rings out, this time from an even closer distance. A tall splash of water fountains from the creek where the errant bullet strikes. Robby tramples through the woods behind me, closing the distance to Copperhead Creek. An ear-deafening blast rings out. A millisecond later, one of the spider's eyes explodes as the bullet connects. It hobbles backward, gravely wounded, a low hiss coming from its gaping maw. Robby runs past me splashing into the water of Copperhead Creek as the spider's legs teeter, before giving, collapsing it to the sandy earth.

As Robby runs into position, the spider summons its strength and rises, towering high above him. He takes aim and fires, grazing a few inches above the spider's wounded eye. The paintball explodes on its exoskeleton, the green fluid flowing into its open wound. A violent shudder ripples through its body as Robby runs back across Copperhead Creek. Bo fires again, the bullet slashing through one of its legs. The spider, body undulating, begins burying itself in the sand under a furious torrent of churning legs, heaps of sand hurled high into the air. A moment later, it disappears. Bo comes running, rifle in hand.

"Oh shit! Is it dead?" Tee shouts.

"I don't know," I call back, a quivering modulation in my voice.

"Somebody get me outta here."

Bo kneels and takes aim at the top of the spindle holding the sac suspended. An echoing bang rings out in the hollow and the silky sac plummets to the earth. Robby and I rush to it, tearing at the sticky webs, pulling Devin from the silky prison, his eyes filled with joyous relief.

"It's her! It's Samantha Mellinger! I saw her!"

Tee shouts again from the distance on the other side of Copperhead Creek. "Did we kill it?"

Robby shakes his head, his voice crackling. "I don't know, man."

My wide eyes lock with Robby's.

"You hit it. Hit its eye."

"You left me. Left me in the quarry."

"*Sammy?*" Bo's brows furrow.

"That's right. You left me, Bo. What? Ain't we friends?" Sammy steps out from behind the oak tree and takes a few steps toward Bo.

"Oh, shit man! It's not dead! It's not dead!" Tee screams frantically, pointing to the reincarnation of Sammy.

"Sammy. No. We're friends." Sammy closes the distance between them.

"Get away from him, Bo! That's not Sammy!" Robby screams, but it's too late.

Sammy extends an arm and grabs Bo by the throat, lifting him from the ground, his fingers delivering a crushing amount of pressure to Bo's trachea. The rifle drops from Bo's limp hands to the earth below. Tears roll from the corners of Bo's eyes. Sammy's gray, putrid tongue extends from his mouth and stretches nearly a foot to Bo's face, where it slides up his cheek before retreating to his mouth.

"Jesus!" Tee screams.

"What do we do?" I scream. *It'll kill us all! No way to stop it!*

Sammy smacks his mouth a couple of times and utters, *"Rosaline Davis."*

Bo's confused eyes cloud with darkness, his face strained, growing ripe as a cherry threatening to burst from its skin. His chest spasms with each unsuccessful heave for air.

"Join your kinfolk!" Sammy rejoices maniacally, a horrible smile thinning his lips.

With an abrupt turn of his wrist, a sickening crackle echoes through the hollow, and Bo topples to the earth, lifeless, as Sammy releases him from his vise grip. Sammy turns to me. "And now you, Broo—"

Another crackle of gunfire rings out, striking Sammy in the chest. He stumbles backward and clutches his chest, eyes blinking in a frantic flutter on his wound. His eyes gape wide as the changes in his body begin. He erupts into a violent convulsion, body undulating, beginning a change of form— features of Sammy melting away, new features emerging. Our eyes ricochet off one another. *Who the hell else has a gun?* Detective Holt and Brady Palmer storm into the clearing of Grief Hollow.

"YES!" Tee screams, pumping his fist in celebration, exalted with our sudden change of fortunes.

"Back up boys." Detective Holt takes aim and fires again, this time striking Sammy in the leg.

The changes begin to accelerate. Within moments, no semblance of Sammy Needles remains. Samantha Mellinger is dragging herself away, her body in anguish. She stops at a rut left behind by the spider and digs into the earth with trembling hands. She reemerges clutching a jumbled pile of small bones. She cradles the brittle brown bones tight to her festering chest, her ghoulish-gray body heaving in a couple of quick sobs as she gazes upon them. Our mouths loll. Her head rises at Detective Holt's approaching footsteps. Her empty eyes fill with venom.

"Your blood is owed." She coughs the words out with a glob of black sludge. "Your murderous kin!" She spits her words like acid.

She bares yellowed teeth at us, drawing rapid, shallow breaths through them. "I curse you. I curse you all. You drowned my baby Lawrence. My infant son." She rapid heaves a couple of breaths and sniffles before her eyes sharpen and cut into us. "Curse you. Curse your family. He wasn't no bastard. He was my baby. Your kin. And you killed him. Stole him and killed him."

She resumes dragging her quivering body through the sand. She finally collapses with her baby's bones at the edge of Copperhead Creek, her shaking hand dropping into the flowing water, fish curling around her putrid skin for a nibble. She nestles the infant's skull to her putrid bosom.

Detective Holt marches to her, gun in hand, his stride accentuated with anger. Samantha Mellinger's cold black eyes lock on his, venomous hate spewing forth. She grins, parting thin gray lips, gnashing yellowed teeth.

"If they burn, they won't return, Detective." Her throaty voice trails off before her eyes glaze to dial tone. No one left on the line.

Detective Holt places the muzzle against her temple and pulls the trigger. *Boom*. Her head recoils before falling still. Copperhead Creek runs red with the blood of Samantha Mellinger, coiling over the rocks and swirling down the creek.

I run to Brady and give him a giant hug. *You've got to be kidding me. Yes! But how? I can't believe Brady found us!*

"How'd you know to find us here?"

"Angela," Brady answers with smiling eyes.

Tee comes running to us, his hands gesturing wildly with his words. "But how? How'd he kill it?"

"Professor Wadlow's formula. In the bullets. Detective Holt put it in his bullets."

Robby's brows lift. "*He knew*?"

Brady nods. "Yes, I told him everything."

Devin tilts his head at Brady. "But he arrested you."

"It was all part of the plan." Brady grins.

Tee strides up and gives Brady a huge embrace, a gigantic smile plastered across his face. Tee's grievances for Brady seem to crumble in the elation of that moment, and on that foundation of rubble, a genuine acceptance grows in its place. I join in the hug, followed by Robby and Devin.

"I thought we were dead." Tee's eyes leak tears, his smile stretching the entirety of his face.

"We were dead," I echo, and Tee starts chuckling. And before long, laughter proliferates amongst the entire group.

Samantha Mellinger's body disintegrates into a black mist that dissipates moments later, leaving behind a small pile of brown bones, most no bigger than twigs. Detective Holt holsters his gun and shakes his head.

"How the hell am I gonna explain this?"

Holt strides over to us. Eying our jubilant celebration, he clears his throat as if to say, *pay attention to me.*

We look at him, all smiles.

"Listen up, boys. You weren't here today. You know nothing about nothing. The last few days didn't happen. *Got it*?"

"Yes sir," we respond in unison.

"And Brady, I'll make sure the record's set straight. Your name cleared. My word carries a lot of weight in this town. And I just found some exculpatory evidence." Detective Holt motions with his eyes to Bo's body.

"Thank you, Detective Holt." Brady gives Holt a firm handshake.

"Now get on outta here, boys." Detective Holt shoos us with his hands.

We all give each other another lingering group hug, drawn immeasurably close. Turning, looking over Grief Hollow one last time, I feel elated to be alive. And happy we're together. We turn and walk out of the hollow together, forever bonded by our shared experience.

And no one else would ever know.

CHAPTER 59
Two Months Later

A certain sadness pervades the air of the morning. As much as Tee and Angela engaged in sibling skirmishes through the years, he hates for her to go. For a time, he longed for his rise to *king of the castle, master of this domain, a quasi-only child*. But they grew so much closer the last two months, serving as each other's trusted confidants—their parents grown suspicious of their constant whispering. And they giggled off their parents' confusion, *the truth never could be revealed about the events that brought them so much closer*, so they shared that, an enduring secret, something only they could understand. And they liked it that way.

It seemed like an eternity away, time measured in summer, long days, no school, limited responsibility. But the day has arrived, and Brady's there to see her off too. Angela's changed her plans. She's still going to college, but she's not planning to find cute fraternity boys anymore. She's found a boy here in Harper Pass, the same one that lay locked in the depths of her mind all of these years. And though they'll be separated for a time, the two plan to shorten the distance between them with phone calls and weekend trips.

Angela wraps her arms around Brady's neck, pulling him in close, kissing him deeply.

"*Gross*! Cut it out guys." Tee gives his sister a playful nudge on her shoulder, but he's unable to suppress the smile bubbling up.

Angela uncoils from Brady, fingers still interlaced with his as she pulls away, smile draped across her face, happy as she ever remembers in her life.

"Let me just get my last bag." Angela heads for the door, a skip in her walk as she returns inside the house.

Moments later, she calls out from the living room, her voice carrying outside the door.

"Tee. Hey, Tee. Come here a sec."

Tee hustles into the house. Brady stays behind, content to let Tee enjoy a moment alone with his sister to say goodbye. Angela's in front of the television when Tee makes it into the room.

"Hey, Tee." She points to the screen. "Isn't that the girl you went to school with? The one who was missing?"

"Yeah. Oh my god, yeah! That's Margo! Turn it up." A contented smile crosses his face.

Angela raises the volume on the TV, and Kasey Norton continues with her reporting.

"Folks, it's not that often I get to report on a story like this. One with such a happy ending. If you're just tuning in, we've just seen a miracle. Margo Combs has been reunited with her parents after being lost for over two months. Somehow, against all odds, this special needs child found a way to survive by herself in the wilderness. Truly a miracle."

The desk anchor cuts in as the camera pans to Jim and Linda Combs. Tears of joy stream their faces as they walk Margo to their car.

"Great reporting as always, Kasey. Channel Four is sure going to miss you and your reporting. I know most of our viewers already know this, but we're so proud of Kasey. Our very own Kasey

Norton has been called up by our affiliate in Cincinnati and will begin reporting there on Monday. We're sure going to miss her here, but we know she'll do a fine job in her new assignment."

"Thanks, Tom. I'm going to miss you guys too." Kasey blushes. "And I'll miss our Channel Four audience."

As Jim and Linda Combs help Margo into the backseat of the car, the camera pans in closer. Margo's head bobbles in the backseat. As the car begins to pull away from the curb, she turns her head, glaring out of the rear window.

As the camera focuses in closer on her face, a subtle flash of blue swirls through her eyes, and the car drives away.

Acknowledgments

There are many people I wish to thank for their contributions to this book.

First to my beautiful and supportive wife Kirsten, who never complained as I locked myself away for days in the revision process, thank you. Thank you for believing in me and for sacrificing so much for my dream.

To my mom Vicki, and my sister Nikki, I'm grateful to have you in my life, and I can't thank you enough for all your support.

To my nephew Tristan, my wonderful mother-in-law Shawn, and the many Beta readers who provided valuable feedback on this novel, thank you from the bottom of my heart. You will never know what it meant to me to have you selflessly spend your time reading my story.

To my ARC readers, I cannot thank you enough for investing your time in me and in this story.

To the countless other writers who have supported me on this journey, thank you. It means everything.

To my editor Emma T. Gitani, thank you for your valuable insights, all of your hard work, and your dedication to this book.

To Mandy Melanson, who works about as tirelessly as one human being can, and is always there to help, thank you.

To Dusty Grein, thank you for caring so much about my vision, and for creating such an amazing cover for *The Tear Collector* that captures so much about the book.

And finally, to the rest of the wonderful team at RhetAskew Publishing, who are kind, helpful and a genuine joy to work with, THANK YOU! This book wouldn't be the book it is without all of you.

- Shawn Burgess

About the Author

Shawn Burgess is a speculative fiction author, whose stories reflect his love for the unusual.

Shawn has a BA in English from the University of Florida, and focused on literature for his postgraduate studies at the University of North Florida. His travels have taken him to most parts of the country, where he often draws inspiration for his stories through meeting interesting new people and experiencing unique places. He does offer a warning to those he meets . . . if you should find yourself behaving curiously within the crosshairs of his vision, you might just end up on the pages of one of his stories.

Shawn lives in Jacksonville, Florida, with his wife and two sons. In his spare time, he enjoys travelling, attending concerts, reading, and playing golf. He typically makes year-round preparations for Halloween by building props and elaborate sets. Although he claims Jacksonville as his home, he has lived all over the southeastern United States, and many of his stories are set in towns he once called home, or in fictional places inspired by them. He says, "I enjoy building upon the natural mysteries surrounding those areas I've personally experienced."

The Tear Collector is Shawn's debut novel, but he's currently working on a sequel, as well as a stand alone Urban Fantasy novel. He is active on social media, including Twitter, Instagram and Facebook.

~ Find Shawn Online ~

ShawnBurgessAuthor.com

WWW.RHETASKEWPUBLISHING.COM